The Third Testament

A novel by Pierre Rehov

Published by Thirty Trees LLC

Florida - USA

Translated from French to English by Robert Anderson

-- PROLOGUE --

Moscow -- February 16, 1992

The fear that had plagued Alexei Soloviev since the phone call was heightened when he recognized the driver behind the wheel of the black Volga parked in front of his apartment building. Why on earth had Krasnov been sent to him?

It wouldn't be daylight for several hours, and the condensation escaping from the exhaust pipe formed a cloud in which the Volga's parking lights seemed to float. With anxiety adding to the bite of the cold, Alexei tightened the collar of his coat before opening the door. He was greeted with a curse.

--You certainly took your time!

Krasnov's head touched the ceiling of the car, and his body, wrapped in a shabby fur, resembled that of a bear. His voice was oddly high-timbered for his bulk. He barely turned his gaze to his passenger when the passenger settled into the backseat, muttering:

--I'm not used to being sent for on Sundays at 5 a.m.

The car took off and turned at the end of the sleepy street towards the ring road. Soloviev unbuttoned his coat. This was the first time that the Directorate had sent him an official car during his eight-year career in the archives of the KGB and then its successor, the FSK. Anton Artyomov, his direct superior, had only informed him of the urgent nature of his presence in Yasenevo, where the *Pervoye Glavnoye Upravlenie*, the decentralized First Directorate General, had established its headquarters. So something bad must have happened. At least as serious as the collision of the nuclear submarine Kostroma with its American rival, the USS Baton Rouge, off Murmansk five days earlier. Although incidents in the field did not concern his department.

The smell of cheap cologne barely covered the stench of cold tobacco that suffused the car. Alexei searched his pockets for a cigarette and realized that he had left his package in the kitchen, next to the wall phone.

-- Comrade ...?

Krasnov answered him with a vague nod.

-- ... Do you have a cigarette?

The furry giant pulled a nearly empty package of Pirins out of the glove compartment and, without a word, tossed them onto his lap. The quivering glow of a flame briefly lit up the back of the vehicle, revealing a network of cracks in the imitation leather of the seat.

Half an hour later, the car entered the wooded area that opened onto open land, beyond which stood the 21-story building bristling with antennas and red lights that housed the archives of the KGB, recently renamed the FSK.

Soloviev relaxed. When he had seen Krasnov driving, he had feared that he would be taken to one of the secret interrogation centers that the *kontora*[1] had set up near Moscow. It had been a highly confused murky period since Gorbachev had launched his Glasnost and Perestroika, and even more so since the referendum on the direct election of the president and the conservative coup in August, which had been crushed in a bloodbath. Soloviev considered himself to be an exemplary employee, but no one was immune to slander or arbitrary decisions.

The Volga turned right into a narrow driveway. A sign in Russian and English dissuaded stray civilians from taking a further step under penalty of prosecution. The driveway ended in front of a sentry box flanking a double gate and a barrier. On the ground, retractable posts could have prevented the intrusion of an armored vehicle.

A guard in a greatcoat and *shapka* with its edges turned down leaned over the glass of the front door. Krasnov handed him his badge. They had to wait until the guard went through various checks while a member of security slid a mirror under the Volga's chassis. This was the moment the driver chose to turn to Soloviev and ask:

-- I've always wanted to know: why do they call you Wagner?

-- Even you know about it.

-- It's part of my job to be informed.

There was pride in Krasnov's tone. Alexei smiled faintly. The driver was sometimes called in to assist in armed operations, but his level of access to information was extremely limited.

-- My father is Russian but my mother was German ...

---

[1] The office, a name given internally to the KGB.

-- I know that much. But why Wagner?, Krasnov insisted as the guard handed him back his pass.

Alexei hesitated before answering. Should he admit that, before he had been assigned to the archives, he had been part of Team Zenith, an anti-terrorist unit of the KGB which had in particular worked in Afghanistan during Operation Shtorm 333? The nickname was given to him in 1979 after a rather forceful interrogation in the suburbs of Kabul. The screams of the "subject" had carried so far that the session had to be interrupted before any information was obtained. But Alexei had noticed a record player and a stack of classical music LP's in the next room. He had placed the second movement of "Parsifal" on the console and turned the sound up to maximum. Less than twenty minutes later, he was sending his leadership a full report on the degree of infiltration of the Tajbeg Palace Guard by the Hafizullah Amin's insurgents[(2)]. His teammates, who preferred Prokofiev or Shostakovich to the German composer, had nicknamed him "Wagner" to taunt him and the nickname had become his code name.

-- Because I have a weakness for German operas, he said evasively as he returned his pack of Bulgarian cigarettes to Krasnov.

There was only one left.

The barrier and double gate opened with the faint sound of well-oiled gears.

***

Alexei Soloviev expected to find the whole team of his department in the meeting room in the second basement, but there were only four out of sixteen: Gouri, Fyodor, Nikita and Oleg.

The premises, which had been, built during the nineteen-seventies, had been modernized and the neon lighting replaced with recessed spotlights that gave the room a little high-tech edge despite the fake linoleum parquet and the massive television set with a VHS cassette player placed on a formica cabinet.

Soloviev was the last to arrive. The others had already taken their places on either side of the conference table, at the end of which was a samovar, traditionally filled with tea. But it was empty this morning, and Artyomov's expression didn't bode well. The head of the 2nd Department of the Archive Services International Section, who was fairly tall and had a slightly protruding ear, a souvenir of his past as an amateur boxer, with short-cropped brush hair

[2] In September 1979, the Afghan President Nour Mohammad Taraki was assassinated during a coup by his rival Hafizullah Amin, who wanted to pull his country away from the USSR. This event led the Soviet Union to send in the Red Army, triggering a conflict with Afghanistan that lasted until 1989 and led to the disintegration of the Soviet Union.

and a flat nose, didn't really look like an executive responsible for archives. While remaining standing, he put his hands flat on each side of his leather desk pad topped with a small stack of cardboard shirts and announced:

-- Yesterday at 11:50 p.m., we received information that we have suffered a defection at the highest level.

The five men seated around the table exchanged dismayed glances. Alexei felt a surge of helpless rage. The Soviet edifice was continuing to crumble. Artyomov continued.

-- All five of you have served under this traitor at one time or another ...

Apart from the fact that Artyomov loved to manage his situations, each one knew that the lens of a video camera was aimed at his face and that an expert in behavioral psychology was interpreting their reactions from a control room whose location few knew.

-- The worst thing about this, Artyomov continued, is that this filth has not been a part of our services for almost seven years. He has therefore bided his time and perhaps even participated from the shadows in the state of rot into which the combined action of false progressives have plunged our great nation.

Alexei began to get some idea of the defector's identity and the assumption chilled him. He had only had one superior in the archives before Artyomov, but he refused to believe it could be him ...

The following words, unfortunately confirmed his intuition.

-- Soloviev, you were the last to work under Vasily Mitrokhin ... That bastard went west with a ton of secret documents.

Artyomov's tone rose as he clarified the situation.

-- Mitrokhin occupied my position between 1972 and 1984. He retired the following year and I had the honor of succeeding him. It was he who organized and supervised the relocation of the Lubyanka archives to these new premises as well as to the annexes in Vladimir, Omsk and Saratov. Prior to this position, he had belonged to the action section and his service record was always impeccable. Needless to say, the Directorate has launched an investigation to determine his motives for his actions. But you have not been gathered here this morning in order to try to understand the motives of this *podonok*[(3)]. We must assess the extent of his damage as quickly as possible. And, first of all, find out what documents he was able to get out, and how! Here's what we know ...

He opened a file folder and summarized the report.

---

[3] In the 19th century, the word *"podonok"* referred to beggars who wandered from tavern to tavern to finish off the dregs of patrons' drinks. The word may be translated as "scrapings", "rot" or, as in this case, "traitor".

Vasily Nikitich Mitrokhin had played dead for several years before jumping at an opportunity made possible by Gorbachev's reforms. In the aftermath of the official dissolution of the Soviet Empire, he traveled to Riga, the capital of Latvia, where he tried to contact the CIA through the American Embassy. He must have been turned away, because he soon went to the British Embassy, where an MI6 agent must have debriefed him. The former head of archives and all members of his family had been exfiltrated to England the same day, during an operation whose scale revealed the significance of the defection for MI6 and therefore for the West.

Artyomov's tone became even more serious and even somewhat menacing.

-- The instructions of the Directorate are very clear. Above all else, prevent contagion. Since each of you has been close to Mitrokhin for varying periods of time, your authorization level is temporarily reduced and your access to the archives limited and controlled. Starting from the present moment, your only role is to assess the amount of confidential information that might have been diverted. Your work will be subject to debriefing on a weekly basis and everyone will go to be polygraphed immediately.

Soloviev's colleagues exchanged worried looks. Fyodor and Gouri became agitated and Oleg wanted to protest, but Artyomov slammed the palm of his hand down on the table as he opened his mouth.

-- That will be all. A guard will bring you down to the fourth basement.

Alexei got up and went along with his colleagues when his superior's voice froze him.

-- Not you, Soloviev!

Uniformed guards appeared and waited in the hallway.

-- Come back and sit down, Anton Artyomov ordered him.

He waited for the door to close before grabbing one of the cardboard boxes in front of him and slipping in front of Alexei. It contained a series of color photographs taken with a telephoto lens.

-- I assume that you do recognize this person?

Soloviev felt his heart rate accelerate but then calmed down immediately. He would have recognized the young woman from among a thousand others, if only by her flaming red hair. What was her name, now? Laureen or Maureen? Was he going to be rebuked for having had a drink at the bar of the Moskva Hotel with a junior employee of the British Consulate? He hadn't known her position when he approached her, drawn to her slender figure and the unique color of her hair. The site was usually reserved for prostitutes, often students who came to trawl for tourists during the weekend. Soloviev, who had been a hardened bachelor since his wife had left him, devoted a significant portion of his salary to these pricey meetings. The young Englishwoman had laughed at his mistake before admitting to him that she had just been transferred to Moscow and that she didn't know anything about bar customs. They had had the most trivial exchange about Moscow nightlife and parted without even trading phone numbers.

The photographs showed the redhead inside a restaurant with an unknown person, driving her car down the street leading to the British Embassy, past the entrance to the Russiya Hotel and, of course, sitting at the bar facing him.

-- Yes, of course, Alexei confessed. That's a girl from the British Consulate. I just had a drink with her two or three weeks ago.

He tried to analyze his superior's gaze in the hope that this simple answer had convinced him of his good faith, but apart from a righteous anger, which he also shared, it revealed nothing.

-- According to our information, she belongs to MI6, Artyomov said.

An icy hand slid between Alexei Soloviev's shoulder blades.

-- But I didn't know that!, he protested. Send me to the polygraph. I'm ready to take the test as many times as you want.

-- I don't doubt that for a second. Unfortunately, you were Mitrokhin's right-hand man during the two years leading up to his retirement. Put yourself in my place. When President Yeltsin ordered our documents to be made available to academic researchers on August 24, I relied on your excellent record of service before entrusting you with reorganizing the operational files, as well as those for the *special examination*. But in December, your former boss defected and made copies of tens of thousands of top secret documents available to MI6. A few weeks later, a field agent, quite by chance, overheard you having a deep conversation with an intern from the same service. You must agree that that is disquieting.

-- A coincidence, Alexei protested, shrugging his shoulders.

-- You know as well as I do that we don't believe in coincidences in our profession.

-- I thought she was a whore, said Alexei, being short of excuses.

-- And you're in luck because we know you've never seen her again.

Artyomov mechanically put the file back on the pile. He liked order and the photos had had their effect. The morals of his employees did not concern him, except when they wound up putting together a file belonging to the category of *special examinations*.

-- The Directorate wanted to end your collaboration immediately, but once again you are in luck. I convinced Comrade Dimitri Volkogonov[4] that you pose less of a threat under my observation than outside. I can assure you he was in no mood for indulgence after being woken up by special ops personnel at 2 a.m. on a Sunday morning. On the other hand, it is out of the question for you to have access to any sensitive file until a thorough investigation has been completed.

-- I understand, comrade, Alexei sighed with a heavy heart.

-- In the meantime, I have assigned you to the archives of SMERSH, and more particularly to the Biederitz file. We've been getting a lot of requests from Russian and German researchers in this area for some time.

An acid reflux went up Soloviev's throat.

SMERSH, the Russian acronym for "Death to Spies", was a Red Army intelligence service created by Stalin during World War II that ceded its functions to the MGB, the Ministry of State Security, in 1946. As for Biederitz, it was the name of the river where the ashes of Hitler and Eva Braun were thrown in April 1970.

This assignment involved him being locked up in a dusty room cluttered with old metal filing cabinets and racks, some corroded by rust, without any access to the computer system and above all without a window to the outside or even adequate ventilation. The filing was performed there by means of a set of cardboard files arranged in boxes.

He was living a nightmare.

-- Comrade ...

-- A guard will lead you to the polygraph, like your colleagues, Artyomov cut in, indicating the door with a gesture. I hope for your sake that the results turn out in your favor.

***

The lie detector confirmed Soloviev's loyalty and the investigation against him did not come to any disquieting conclusions. He should therefore have been rehabilitated and returned to his post, perhaps even with a promotion, because he was above all a dedicated employee and a good patriot who showed the same ardor, whatever the task assigned.

But he was still holding the same position six months later, despite several requests for the restoration of his privileges, the last of which had been approved by Artyomov.

So, Soloviev eventually got used to spending his days in the company of the ghosts of Hitler and Eva Braun.

[4] In charge of the archives of the KGB and the CPSU between 1991 and 1995.

He who had handled sensitive information at the highest levels, including updating the individual records of hundreds of field agents, allies and enemies, found himself filing intelligence that was half a century old. Files on the Third Reich that the reorganized KGB did not care about now.

He had therefore arranged his small space as best he could. A vase filled with artificial flowers decorated the metallic desk pushed against a gray wall amidst a jumble of documents, photographs, account books, binders, decryption machines and reports dating from the 1940's and, in many cases, seized from the Berlin bunker after the Führer's suicide.

A special section of SMERSH in 1945 had the mission finding Hitler, dead or alive. History had forgotten, or at least the Soviet intelligence services had wanted to make people forget, that the first persons to enter Hitler's secret Wolfsschanze, or Wolf's Lair, in East Prussia were women belonging to the Soviet Traffic Management section and that they had hastened to loot the wardrobes of Eva Braun and Magda Goebbels. The minutes of their trial were among the first documents Soloviev had extracted from cardboard boxes that had been corrupted or invaded by mold.

The Red Army would undoubtedly have been able to monopolize vast treasures of information if SS Brigadeführer Wilhelm Mohnke hadn't ordered his men, on May 1, 1945, to splash gasoline around Hitler's office and set it on fire, erasing thousands of items of evidence of crimes of the Third Reich. Fortunately, the Führer's secretary, Traudl Junge, had kept copies of most of the letters dictated to her and notes from the meetings she had attended.

The full report on the discovery of the charred remains of Hitler, his companion, their dogs and the entire Goebbels family, including their children, was signed by Lieutenant Alexei Panasov. In response to the message sent by Marshal Georgy Zhukov confirming the death of the Nazi dictator to Stalin, the latter replied: "Too bad we didn't take him alive."

This series of original notes and testimonies was in such a pitiful state that Soloviev had to spend entire days restoring them with the means at hand. They were now protected by perforated transparent folders and stored in recycled spiral binders.

In order to bring a little spice into these boring activities, he took a lively interest in a disinformation operation engineered by Stalin that was intended to make it appear that Hitler had survived and managed to escape. In the year following the discovery of his partly charred remains, the Soviets had flooded their media with conjectures, each one more absurd than the other, the most popular one being that the Nazi dictator had taken refuge in America and was being protected by the OSS, now renamed the CIA.

When President Truman asked Stalin at the Potsdam conference in August 1945 if Hitler were dead, he replied with an evasive "No", immediately ending the conversation. The leading American judge at the Nuremberg trials had meanwhile announced that "no one could know for sure what had become of Hitler".

It had taken the relentlessness of the head of the British counterintelligence service, Dick White, and his agent Hugh Trevor-Roper to lift the veil on that Soviet disinformation operation.

But the disinformation was still fueling dozens of conspiracy theories forty-seven years later.

The testimony of Hitler's dentist, Doctor Hugo Blaschke and his assistant, Kathe Heusermann, who had categorically identified the lower jaw of their patient, appeared in the report summarizing this operation intended to discredit Westerners while directing their intelligence services to false leads. This mandible and a portion of the skull were the only nearly intact remains found among the ashes.

Ever since then, historians from all over the world, often from prestigious universities, had been asking the Russian government for access to these famous archives. They ended up on Soloviev's desk, after being examined by the Ministry of Culture and the Ministry of Foreign Affairs.

Soloviev was able to speak English fairly well, but especially German which, thanks to his mother, had accompanied his first steps and consoled him during his childhood. Long before discovering Tolstoy, Dostoevsky, Gorky or Pushkin, he was able to recite entire passages from Goethe's works, considered Nietzsche to be the greatest philosopher of all time, and forged an understanding of the world through the works of Werner Beumelburg, Ernst Jünger, Hans Zöberlein and Hans Baumann.

It took him until he entered Moscow University to discover that the authors who had nurtured his early youth had mostly belonged to Nazi culture. As did his favorite composer, who would one day earn him his nickname.

Wagner.

It was common in Soviet Russia to despise and to hate anything connected with the Third Reich, either directly or indirectly. The Russian Motherland had lost twenty million of her children to German fire during World War II, and she was not ready to forget. The fact that his own mother had belonged to the BDM or League of German Girls, the female equivalent of the Hitlerjugend, and that his maternal grandfather had worn the uniform of the SS did not help Soloviev in his career. But this handicap was mitigated by the career of his father, a decorated officer in the Red Army who had met his future wife in Leipzig, then under Soviet occupation. "True love stories are apolitical," he liked to recall, building on the prestige of his numerous decorations.

They had had only had one son, and Alexei's mother died of sepsis after routine surgery when he was sixteen.

But *Wagner* had found in communism most of what he liked in the Nazi theories into which *Mutti* had secretly initiated him when he was a teenager.

Above all, the notion of the centralization of power and discipline. The rejection of any form of individualism. A deep contempt for the bourgeoisie. A strong taste for pageantry and armed power, accompanied by the need to feel part of something greater than yourself and an unrestrained love of the nation.

And then a good dose of anti-Semitism, which hadn't displeased his KGB instructors at the time of his recruitment.

The requests for copies from the archives were placed on Soloviev's desk every morning. They consisted of original letters, stamped by the competent services, a stapled note delimiting the level of access authorized, and the urgency of the granting of the request. Since it took almost a year for even the most unimportant request to flow through the twists and turns of the bureaucracy, nothing was ever urgent.

Except this morning.

The request came from the *Deutsches Historisches Institut*, the German Historical Institute in Cologne, and concerned the "Biederitz" file. A three-line note summed up that the researcher wanted access to documents concerning relations between Nazi Germany and Tibet. It was only two months old.

A record, and one that intrigued Alexei.

It was no secret in the basements of the *kontora* that the ashes of Hitler, his wife Eva and those of the Goebbels family had been scattered in the Biederitz River at the request of Yuri Andropov. Whence the name given to the section on files concerning the Führer and his entourage.

While searching and trying to organize the thousands of pieces stored in his premises, Alexei had discovered that this delicate operation had been carried out in 1946 by a group of KGB agents whose mission was to exhume the remains buried near Magdeburg. On April 4, 1970, they opened the graves and then transported the charred bodies to Schönebeck, some eleven kilometers away, where they were soaked in kerosene and burned in the open before being reduced to dust, gathered into containers, and dispersed in the current of the river. Thus, no one could ever go to the grave of the most evil character of the twentieth century, the man responsible for the most organized massacre of all time.

Hitler was definitely not on the agenda any longer. But the successive leaders of the Soviet Union had perpetuated the ambiguity about the real fate of the Führer that Stalin had established. Nothing was easier than contaminating information in the West with fake documents and fake news. A special section of the KGB has reveled in it for decades. Soloviev remembered with amusement the time when they had made it widely believed that John Edgar Hoover, the director of the FBI, was gay and that the CIA had been involved in the Kennedy assassination ... Not to mention the rumors that NASA's conquest of the moon and Armstrong's historic first step had been filmed in Hollywood. The dark hand of the KGB was often behind conspiracy theories intended to bring ridicule upon American society.

It was already ten a.m. by his watch. Time for tea accompanied by dry biscuits, which he swallowed quickly before taking the request from the German Institute and heading to the Biederitz section.

The archives, set up on racks, stretched for over ten meters and rose to the ceiling. In addition to the documents seized from Hitler's Bunker, there were mountains of evidence from various administrations of the Reich and an electromechanical Enigma decryption machine, model M4, the last one used by the Reich's intelligence services. Everything about the concentration and extermination camps, including thousands of photographs and films, was housed in a separate department. It was these relics of horror that researchers most often sought access to, but the United States Library of Congress and the CIA had just as many.

Vasilyev quickly found what he was looking for. Several containers stacked under a cardboard tab with the word *SHAMBHALA* written in marker.

The name of the mythical Tibetan city had been the one used as a code for the Nazi expeditions to the land of the Dalai Lamas.

The first archival box contained a few hundred black and white photographs and several dozen rolls of film, visual witnesses to the many expeditions to Tibet that the Anhenerbe[5] had undertaken. He didn't care about the second box, which contained several thick books covered in a strange script. No doubt Sanskrit. A label in German designated the archived work by the translation of its mysterious name: *"Kalachakra Tantra"*.

[5] An organization with a "cultural" function founded by Himmler, the main goal of which was to reconstruct the genealogy of the Nazis and to locate the origins of the Aryan race.

Soloviev had nothing to do with these dusty, centuries-old books, the presence of which among the documents seized from Hitler's bunker momentarily surprised him. He had never had the time to open the other containers before but, according to the note, the Institute wanted to have a copy of the reports written by the scientists in charge of the Tibetan expeditions, particularly those by the mountaineers Ernst Schäfer and Doctor Bruno Beger.

He pulled a filing box marked with a black swastika towards himself, placed it on a workboard and set about his task, aided by the obsession with order that had dominated Nazi Germany but made more difficult by the fact that some sheets were stuck to others. The KGB had shown no interest in the Nazi expeditions to Tibet, which archival officials had deliberately classified as the wild ravings of Gauleiters. Some of their follies continued to provoke the derision of students of history at Moscow universities. Nazi officials were psychopaths or drug addicts, often both at the same time, who lived in a world of their own where mysticism and the most muddled theories, such as those of the "Hollow Earth" and the "Eternal Glaciation", had been part of everyday life.

Soloviev had just spotted an *Anhenerbe* letterhead signed by Ernst Schäfer when his gaze was drawn by a cardboard folder of a different kind. Unlike the other documents, this one was marked "Führersekretärin", a reference to the Führer's secretary. In other words, it came from Hitler's secretarial pool and had nothing to do with the *Shambhala* archives.

That was strange.

He carefully put down Schäfer's report and opened the file. This contained five sheets yellowed by time. The first three were blackened with blocks of typewritten letters. The second contained numbers. An indecipherable coded language for now. As for the last ...

Alexei froze.

The document was handwritten in fine, slanting, uneven and sinewy handwriting. Frau Traudl Junge must not have had time to type it up.

It bore the date April 29, 1945, and began with these words:

"This is the most important of my wills. I donate it to posterity, just as I have donated myself to Germany ..."

The signature affixed to the bottom of the text only confirmed the identity of the author whom the archivist had already guessed.

Adolph Hitler

Alexei Soloviev read the text and the read it again, unable to believe it. Then he realized that his life had just changed forever.

-- Chapter 1 --

Banda Aceh -- Indonesia

December 24, 2004

Darwis Haikal had been riding for a few minutes when he felt the first tremor.

At first he thought his moped was failing on him. The vehicle, a 'Bajaj' from the Sixties, was not on its first legs. He stopped his engine and leaned down to check the chain of the crankset. Surprised to find it intact, he put both feet on the ground and lifted up his eyes.

At that exact moment, he was on the main street leading to the Baitur Rahman Mosque, the jewel of Banda Aceh. A ragtag crowd in search of cigarettes, coffee, hot rice or scrambled eggs, crowded around the few stalls punctuating the winding artery with their squat structures with roofs of straw and tin. The drivers of the delivery tricycles were happily ringing their bells. The blackish smoke of their exhaust pipes mingled in the sky with the translucent swirls from the traveling restaurants. The atmosphere, which was sticky, already covered the serious faces of traders and customers with a veil of perspiration, especially those of the women, however accustomed they were to the humid heat under their *hijabs* which some held with one hand, as if they feared to be uncovered by the breath of some non-existent wind. The early morning sun shone on the familiar scene with a white halo on which the dense branches of mangroves and rosewoods formed immobile shadow plays.

No one was aware of the tragedy that was brewing.

With one hand on the Bajaj's handlebars, the other in his trouser pocket, checking for his wallet, Darwis gave the rear wheel of his machine a little kick before stepping back onto the seat.

It was the sudden silence that tipped him off ...

The singing of the birds fell silent, as did the cries of animals that usually mixed in with the hubbub on the streets.

This familiar soundscape was replaced by a distant rolling of a giant drum. The strange noise suddenly grew louder until it became deafening.

Then, as if in slow motion or in the unreality of a nightmare, the nearest hut collapsed, crushing the trader who had a moment earlier been holding out a small box of oily rice by his booth, and the earth rippled while the hand of a giant tore Darwis' moped away from him.

He found himself on his knees, then stretched out along his full length as a young woman rolled over him, her dress rolled up and her veil half snatched away. A few yards away, the ground split into a large crack, the foul-smelling lips of which spread apart as they lifted.

The mangroves and palm trees that lined the narrow boulevard bent under the force of a wind blowing from all sides, then collapsed into an indescribable jumble of tangled branches and roots. A car rushing towards the harbor began to rock before pulling off the road, mowing down a small group of women and children, bouncing off the wall of a batik workshop and spinning around.

Darwis's moped ended up hitting a bamboo stroller which it knocked over, catapulting a sleeping baby onto the sidewalk. As the mother rushed forward in a desperate effort to catch her child, oil-filled barrels piled up in front of a spice merchant surged over the loose earth like the cargo of a ship torn from its chains. The first barrel hit the mother and shattered her spine before crushing her infant. The others exploded against the walls, mowing down a group of soldiers and overturning stalls, the meager contents of which spilled over the moving earth.

As the fissure widened, the stilted *panggungs* collapsed in an apocalyptic crash. The expensive single-story buildings with colonnades and balconies suffered the same fate, one falling on top of the other and crushing anything that was unfortunate enough to be within reach of their foundations.

It was eight o'clock in the morning.

Off the island of Sumatra, at a depth of thirty thousand meters, the oceanic tectonic plate had just suddenly shifted from the Andaman plate with an overlapping movement of about twenty meters over a few thousand kilometers along a south-to-northwest line. The worst was yet to come.

Darwis Haikal, curling up in a fetal position, found himself thinking that the Day of Judgment had finally arrived. The mountain that blocked the horizon to the south in the direction of Medan was splitting up, and tons of rocks would soon roll towards the city to cover all of Banda Aceh, while the angels in their hosts would select the worthy pure souls to join Muhammad and all the prophets ...

But the rumbling finally died down. The ground stopped shaking. The screams of the wounded and their terrified calls gradually replaced the deafening tumult of the earth with an equal intensity.

Darwis felt his face, which was dripping with warm fluid. Moving his fingers upwardly, he briefly felt the greasy blister of a wound. Pain made him moan. That is how he knew he was still alive. In the distance, the mountain expanded its silhouette, still intact for the present time.

Allah is not finished with us yet, Darwis thought.

Nearby, a woman with ripped clothes was stretched out in an impossible posture, her left leg bent completely forward. She moaned softly, her eyes closed and her mouth bloody. The same wailing arose everywhere. The houses and trees that had lined the avenue just a few minutes ago were nothing but gaping carcasses, rubble, broken pieces and piles of objects, crushed and then scattered by the foot of some enraged titan.

Darwis understood that his city had just suffered an earthquake of terrifying force. He stood up, overcoming an emerging dizziness, and wiped the blood off his face with the back of his sleeve. Unspeakable anguish constricted his heart at the thought of Faridah and Sambyio, whom he had left in their *panggung* without a hug or a kiss since he had left so hurriedly. His first instinct was to find his moped, get on it and to return home, praying to Allah that He had spared his family and his house. A glance at the Bajaj informed him that the machine was unusable.

Darwis then leaned over the woman in excruciating pain and examined her kneecap without a word. Allah and the spirits of the island had probably chosen to let him live for the sole reason that he was a doctor.

He had to live up to their plans.

For the next twenty minutes, Darwis gathered enough injured people together to fill the waiting room at Meuraxa Hospital, where he had finished his internship some ten years before. In a calm voice, he announced that he was a doctor and began to organize rescues. The lightly injured got up. Others, who were more numerous, mingled their howls with cries of dismay and calls for the missing.

First of all, Darwis took care of the children. In the small group mown down by the car, two were dead, two had broken legs, and a fifth was lying in a pool of mud and blood, his pelvis and entire lower body fractured. He wasn't crying, his huge eyes just scanning Darwis' face as the doctor leaned over him.

-- "Did a ghost do that?", a child asked in a dying voice.

On the island of Sumatra, ghosts were considered responsible for all human misfortunes.

-- "Don't worry," Darwis replied, not knowing what else he could say. "I'll take care of you."

Blackish smoke crept up the road, bringing a foul odor of rubber, gasoline and burned flesh. While Darwis saw with despair that any attempt to save the child would be in vain and gave up on putting a tourniquet on him, a man in his fifties quickly climbed up on the overturned vehicle with one wheel still turning.

-- Ashadu an laa ilaaha illa'Allahu ...

Standing on the tips of his toes with one index finger pointing towards the sky, the short man had frozen in the traditional posture of prophets haranguing the faithful, his hallucinated gaze behind thick glasses strangely intact while one flap of his shirt hung over his waist, revealing a lacerated shoulder.

-- Ashadu an laa ilaaha illa'Allah ... I witness there is no God but Allah ...

The ritual phrase, which allowed the believer to reach the gates of Paradise, was immediately taken up by a crowd of men and women. Darwis repeated the sacred words inside him, abandoning the little dying child in an attempt to save another. And then another.

He had nothing available to him: no bandages, no disinfectant, no morphine. The nearest hospital was more than three miles away and there was no reason to believe that it was still operating. In a hurry, he asked a woman to tear off a piece of her scarf and a soldier to run to one of the few barracks still standing and bring him all the fresh water that he could. He could have used alcohol, but it was forbidden in Banda Aceh. The more able-bodied survivors began to disperse, scurrying away to locate their families.

Darwis didn't immediately understand the panicked cries preceded by another rumbling sound ...

-- Air laut naik! Air laut naik!

The doctor finally raised his head. His astonishment made him freeze in terror. It took another fraction of a second for him to associate the howls with that liquid mass, taller than a minaret, wider than a mountain, and rushing straight at him.

-- Air laut naik! The sea is coming!

The waves rushed through the streets and alleys, sweeping away humans, animals, vehicles and objects before swallowing them up. The roar was as powerful as that of the earthquake, this time accompanied by the blast of a storm. This gigantic warm and blackish flow was moving everything that the bubbling waves had torn from the earth at lightning speed. The running people were swallowed up in mid-stride, including a man on a motorbike who thought he was escaping the breaking waves but skidded and disappeared into the liquid mass.

Darwis had never seen anything so terrifying in his life. With the same movement, he seized the child he was about to treat from off the ground and rushed off to seek refuge behind the batik workshop. The blast hit him when he had barely run a few meters. Then the sea caught up with them.

Darwis was lifted off the ground, turned over, sucked in and then swallowed up as the child was torn away from him. He began to flail desperately with his arms and legs to rise to the surface, turning around on himself in this murky and moving universe. Everything was swirling. An unidentified object hit his forehead. Branches whipped his thighs. He soon felt he was suffocating, but resisted the urge to breathe with all his might. The tree trunk reappeared, tossed like a piece of straw. Darwis grabbed it instinctively. A few drops of brackish, sulfurous water forced through the barrier of his lips. A wheel from a truck, torn along in the same vortex, struck his back. Lacerated all over his body, half asphyxiated, terrified to the point of not feeling any more pain, Darwis lost consciousness.

He didn't see the body of the child he had tried to save before it collided with his, only to then be separated from him forever. The trunk to which he had been clinging struck the wall of a small mosque housing a palm grove whose trees had survived the earthquake. The trunk slid past and wedged between the wall and a palm tree, creating a natural barrier behind which Darwis, unconscious, at last found refuge.

His head, caught between the branches of the tree, was miraculously held above the water.

The mosque was located three kilometers from the coast, slightly uphill, its gardens extending along a small drop in elevation. The fluid mass had already lost its force and the sea was retreating as it would along a pebbled beach, leaving thousands of bodies and jagged fragments in its wake.

Where there once stood a bustling city with colorful arteries, there was now a swamp punctuated by a few islands.

***

Stabbing pain brought Darwis back to his senses. His back, his neck, his cheek, his head, and all of his limbs were throbbing. He studied his posture, forcing himself to lie still. His field of vision was limited to a few branches, the top end of a wall, and the arrogant blue of the sky.

First, your neck. Move your head slowly.

Darwis noted with relief that his muscles still obeyed his commands.

The feet, the legs ...

Could it be that he was still intact? Flayed and swollen, his abdomen streaked with claw marks, but still able to move?

His happiness was immediately replaced by anguish.

As he methodically pushed aside the branches and roots in order to get free, Darwis thought about his wife and child. How could he have forgotten them, even for an instant?

Their *panggung* was a stone's throw from the harbor, in the lowest and most exposed part of the city ...

Darwis managed to free himself from the tangle of leaves. Torn between anxiety and gratitude, he addressed a small prayer to the spirit of the forests to thank him for protecting him. Then another one, much more fervent, to Allah to beg him to extend His hand over his house and to allow him to again see the two beings he valued more than his own life.

Leaning with one foot on the low wall and the other on a solid branch, he straightened up to his full height, hoping to orient himself by means of the first structures he could see and, at the same time, to calculate the distance that separated him from his home.

A hand grasped his heart.

Stretched out before him as far as the eye could see, there was a sea of mud and interlocked trees, shapeless structures and overturned vehicles and stranded boats, among which he could make out hundreds of animal carcasses and human corpses. And, scattered about like hailstones, coconuts. Coconuts everywhere.

Turning his head to the east, he could see the Baitur Rahman Mosque, whose seven black domes and multiple minarets, apparently intact, towered over the desolate landscape. An entire population had gathered on the terraces and balconies of the sacred structure.

Every now and then, Darwis could see whole blocks of dwellings with roofs sticking out of the cesspool.

He regained a semblance of hope. Faridah was an intelligent and resourceful woman. Very close to their house, overlooking the Lambajat district, a large building of recent construction housed the administrative offices of the port. She was strong enough to have withstood the disaster. Faridah and her son had no doubt sought refuge there.

Around the devastated garden, he spotted people standing up, statues of mud briefly motionless but who gradually came to life.

A new sensation took hold of him.

This fresh air. That light wind that caressed his body, crept between his legs, came up his back ...

Darwis, standing on the felled tree, was ashamed to find that he was naked.

He noticed a plastic bag and a rag hanging from the branches which he tore off in order to make a kind of loincloth and thus restore his modesty. The wave had piled tons of debris underneath his shelter, leaving behind a nearly three-meter mound, from the top of which he cautiously descended, wincing in pain with every movement.

The arm of a man protruded from the heap.

Darwis pushed aside twigs, a crate, and a few palms sopping in seawater before giving up further exploration of the dam-like structure that had formed. The man, only the top of whose head and part of his chest could be seen, had been crushed to death.

When he reached the ground, his legs sank into the cesspool with a sucking sound. His makeshift shorts immediately came off and Darwis, holding the plastic and fabric up with both hands, looked about for a piece of clothing.

He had walked barely five meters when he stumbled upon a second corpse.

The man, whose waterlogged abdomen looked as if were about to burst, was just as naked as he was. A small mustache looked like a smile above his lips. Death had frozen him in a posture of rare shamelessness. Murmuring a prayer, Darwis covered him with branches. Then he resumed his north-eastward journey, towards what he believed to be his neighborhood.

It was in vain that he tried to find his accustomed landmarks: the large football stadium, the meandering Krong Aceh River, and the Penayung Bridge. The coastal route and the fishing port of Lampulo. The Peulanggahan railway and bus station, next to the spice market. None of that existed any longer.

The most unpleasant thing of all was the stench. The stench of a sulfurous swamp, with whiffs of methane.

And then, from the distance, came a continuous roar, a foul rumbling. The earth convulsed with a draining sound.

He approached an overturned bus, emptied of its contents, its doors torn off. Every step cost him a superhuman effort, especially since his bare feet, before touching stable ground, brushed against unmentionable objects. It was then that he saw a piece of cloth hanging from the frame of a door whose glass had exploded.

Trousers!

A gift from above! *Who was he to take advantage of such generosity?*

Since the garment was too large, he used the plastic bag, torn with his teeth, to make a belt. With his hands free at last, Darwis searched about the rubble for shoes, sandals, or anything that could protect his feet. Around him lay planks, junk, concrete blocks, a stool, banana leaves, rubble, a window frame, a tire ... Everything covered in mud.

He finally found what he was looking for. Two small wicker baskets, the kind used to serve rice to guests, embedded in one another. He made thongs from electric wires. The stuffing of a gutted pillow added to the comfort. Thus equipped with makeshift snowshoes, he got out of the bus and accelerated his pace.

Life -- a little bit of life -- had resumed.

People were hurrying around.

Some injured people, lying not far from the vehicle from which they had been torn, were moaning.

A small group approached him. There were two women, three men, and a boy of nine or ten. The first woman was old and appeared to be broken in two, supported by the younger woman and one of the men. Their clothes were the color of silt. Neither woman wore a veil, but their hair, instead of floating freely, formed a kind of dripping headgear. The young boy's face was stained with blood. The faces of the men bore the same fierce, hallucinatory expression. Terrified.

The doctor in Darwis noted the abnormal posture of the old woman, who seemed to be in excruciating pain.

-- Leave her to me ..., he ordered. I'll help you lay her down.

In a few strides, he was near the group.

-- I'm a doctor.

Immediately, the young woman burst into tears. As if those simple words had opened the floodgates of an emotion that had been held back for too long. Her tears turned into sobs.

-- This is my mother. I don't know where the rest of my family is.

She was wringing her hands. She had a pretty face. Darwis quickly learned that she had been traveling on the bus with her husband, mother and two children when the wave washed over them. They found themselves thrown to the sides of the vehicle as if by a centrifuge. No window could resist it and most of the passengers were eventually forced into the maelstrom.

Her family members, except for the old woman, were nowhere to be found. The others were neighbors. Everyone was looking for a loved one ... The little boy, pale as death, seemed to be in shock. The young woman didn't know who he was, but remembered that he had been with a woman, apparently his mother, who had also disappeared.

No sooner had the old lady lain down on the leaf of a door than a long rattling sound emerged from her mouth, accompanied by a trickle of pinkish drool. Her body stiffened, then relaxed completely. She was done with suffering. But her daughter didn't have any time to express her grief.

Screams, carried by the wind, warned them long before the characteristic roar.

Air laut naik lagi! The sea is coming back!

A wall of water as high as the previous one surged forward to consume them. The young boy, electrified, uttered a long shrill cry, his head in his hands, his face turned towards the sky. He broke free from the group and rushed towards the bus.

Darwis turned on his heels and ran as fast as his legs could carry him. In a few seconds, he found himself at the foot of the trunk wedged against the wall of the mosque.

The blow hit him when he was two inches from the top. He was at the top, under shelter, when the breaking wave crashed into the mosque, sending foam up into the sky.

Darwis Haikal also escaped the third wave. And then a final faltering one, which contented itself with licking over the devastated lands.

These were moments of anguish that cannot be described. Darwis was worried about his own survival, but most of all terrified that his people were all over there, so close to the seashore, in an area where the waves must have measured as high as fifty feet.

He spent those uncertain moments reliving the happy moments that his wife, Faridah, had given him. Their wedding, almost five years ago. A magnificent ceremony that had drawn the whole neighborhood for hours of celebration, while the two of them gazed at one another, not venturing to imagine the night that awaited them. Their installation in the *panggung*, not far from their two families. Their laughter, their work together, the birth of their child. Faridah, the loving woman, but also the rebel who refused to wear the *hijab*, even after the promulgation of the new religious laws. Her deep black eyes. Her lips that tasted like fruit when she gave him a kiss when out of the sight of others ...

Darwis forced himself to hold on to this image in order to overcome his anxiety.

At 10 a.m., or two hours after the outbreak of the Apocalypse, nature finally calmed down. Levelled by the backwash, Banda Aceh was nothing more than a vast wasteland.

Darwis made up his mind to come down from his makeshift refuge.

The rice baskets kept his feet from sinking too deeply into the mire. Slowly, painfully, he resumed heading northeast, which led him back to the vicinity of the bus, the overturned carcass of which had been caught in the tangle of roots of large mangrove trees.

The young woman, her mother, and the men who accompanied them, had all disappeared. Their bodies had undoubtedly been swept hundreds of meters away.

Darwis was about to pass the bus, when he once again heard the accursed phrase repeated in shouts: *Air laut naik ... Air laut naik ...*

Terrified, he immediately turned his gaze towards the sea. Everything was calm, however. No sign of a new tidal wave.

Air laut naik ...

The words came from inside the bus, emitted by a voice that could be that of a woman or a child.

After brief hesitation, Darwis began to climb the carcass lying on its side, leaning on the drive axle with one foot. With a superhuman effort, he managed to grab hold of the step and then swing his legs like a pendulum in order to come to rest on the stationary wheel. He finally picked himself up and stepped into the passenger section, part of which was submerged in the mud. The cries were coming from the last row of seats. He had to use the armrests as points of support for his hands and knees. That is how he was able to slowly walk up to the mud-covered form who was rocking back and forth while sitting with its back against the back wall of the bus.

Air laut naik ... Air laut naik ...

-- Don't be afraid, the sea has gone!, Darwis said when he found himself within a meter of the child. You have nothing to fear now.

Under the mud, he recognized the face of the child accompanying the small group that he had met before the second wave. The latter seemed oblivious to his presence as he continued his chant and continued to rock back and forth without a glance at the doctor who had come to help him.

-- Are you hurt?, Darwis asked again. Are you hurt?

The child gave no response. There was something familiar about his frantic, steady movement, but Darwis was still too shocked to dwell on it. Somehow supporting himself between an armrest and the edge of a seat, he reached out to stroke his cheek.

The scream made him jump. Behind his mud mask, the child's face had taken on a terrified and terrifying expression, like that of the damned in Dante's descriptions. He withdrew his hand and returned to his original position, gripping the armrest of the row of seats hanging above his head.

Indifferent to Darwis's presence again, the child resumed his routine of words and gestures.

Air laut naik ... Air laut naik ...

It was then that the doctor understood. The little boy wasn't in shock as he had thought.

His experience in the field of psychological disorders was limited. Cognitive science and psychology had only been taught at a basic level at his university. In Indonesia, there were many more diseases to be treated than behavioral problems, which were undoubtedly imported from the West. Darwis only knew that one should never touch a patient who has withdrawn into himself without invitation and that such a simple attempt at interaction could trigger unending crises. As for communicating with the child in front of him, it was better to appeal to his intuition than his knowledge. He stepped back a row and said, in the most casual way he could find:

-- The sea has calmed down. It won't be coming back. I will leave now. Maybe I can find your parents along the way.

It didn't affect the boy's behavior, except for a fraction of a second, when he looked up.

-- All right, then, Darwish continued. If you don't need anything, I'll be going now.

The kid interrupted his chant to stare at Darwish. He felt his heart speed up. He had chosen medicine like a priesthood and regarded each healing as a personal victory. The child's attitude very briefly eased the anguish that was gripping him. He stepped back out of the bus, only realizing how stupid it had been to crawl between the rows when all he had to do was climb over the vehicle from the rear and to then enter through one of the openings.

He waited several seconds before seeing the child's head appear, like a little devil popping out of a box. Darwis couldn't help but smile.

-- I'm heading back towards Banda Aceh now, he said in a mock joyful tone. If I see your parents, what should I tell them?

He took a few steps, then stopped. The kid was a real little monkey. Despite his young age and mental handicap, he had managed to extricate himself from the carcass of the bus in much less time than Darwis.

-- And, first of all, what's your name?, the doctor said again.

Getting no response, he continued on his way. A hundred yards away, he stopped again to look back over his shoulder. The child followed him.

-- Adhi, the boy said in a firm voice.

Darwis nodded, satisfied. Adhi was one of the most common first names in this region of Indonesia.

With the child following on his heels, they covered the first kilometer in one go.

Emergency services were starting to organize around him. Here and there, the survivors emerged from the muddy ground in order to join the crowds of the living dead. Everyone had a reason to scrape the earth, whether in search for a child or a husband or simply from desperation, being unable to conceive that the smoking swamp in which they were wading among the mounds of debris was all that was left of a house.

The first helicopters flew over the city at around 11 a.m. Darwis and the child had reached the Kampung Lima roundabout at the end of Panglima Polim Street, a relatively untouched shopping district, but all of the shops had been gutted and their contents strewn over the sidewalks. He passed a man riding a motorbike up the street as if on a cross country trip, with a baby in a bag hanging from his back. Farther along, a group of three men had converted a table with broken legs into a stretcher on which they were carrying a teenager with a head injury.

Darwis was heartbroken that he couldn't stop to help. But it would be pointless to mention his status as a doctor. He was completely helpless. However, he swore that, if he could first find his family, that he would then make himself available to the first hospital until he was exhausted.

There was a dead cow in the middle of one street. The poor creature must have absorbed hundred of liters of seawater, its stomach was so distended.

Further on, a couple was trying to open a door jammed by rubble while a hole large enough to let them in was gaping in a side wall. Darwis greeted them silently as he walked past them while they scrambled away in shock.

The carcasses of several cars embedded in each other marked the access to Lamjabat, Darwis' own neighborhood. They got there after half an hour of silent walking. No *panggung* had withstood the cataclysm and, out of the regular line of the little houses on stilts, not even the structures remained. Everything had been washed away, down to the cement slabs on which some had been built.

A new wave of relief swept over Darwis when they finally reached the administrative buildings of the port.

As he had anticipated, dozens of people had taken refuge there. The building was almost intact. At the top, several survivors waved, trying to get the attention of a low-flying helicopter. Their cries mingled with the sound of the rotors. A man in uniform, whose features one could almost make out so close to the craft, was observing the scene with the help of binoculars while hooked up to a harness.

Darwis was walking away from the building when a woman's voice called out to him.

-- Doctor Haikal ... Thanks be to Allah, you're alive!

The neighbor, whom he knew well, hurried down the soggy steps, stammering inaudible prayers. Darwis had already cared for one of her children. She had six. He didn't dare ask her how many were with her but she reassured him upon reaching him.

-- My children and my husband left for Medan last night with the truck. I only lost my house, but they must be dead with worry ...

-- How do you know that Medan was spared?, Darwis wondered.

-- It was on the radio. Someone has a little set upstairs on the top floor. The whole coast is devastated, but not Medan and not Jakarta. They're calling it a tsunami ... Educated people always have a word to describe divine punishments, don't they?

-- You're right about that, neighbor. Thanks be to Allah for protecting your family.

She looked at him gravely and blushed. She was a small woman with a piercing gaze, quick gestures, and strong determination. She put her hand on his forearm and gasped.

-- Your wife. Faridah ... I saw it ...

-- Is she here?, Darwis asked.

To his despair, the woman shook her head and her eyes filled with tears.

-- I saw her carrying your son, when the earth calmed down. She was running in the direction of the gas station over there ... Then the sea came.

-- But they were able to take refuge there, argued Darwis. The roof is still intact. They might have ...

His neighbor's face closed in an expression of immense sadness. Her eyes spoke for her. Unable to conceive of such a monstrosity, his heart on fire, Darwis shook his head and made to walk away. The woman put her hand on his shoulder to hold him back.

-- Darwis, she said, calling him by his first name for the first time in her life. It's not worth it. I was up there. I saw them ... The sea carried them away.

The doctor fell to his knees.

The pains he had felt from the moment the moped had been torn from him merged into a torment of body and soul alike. The howl of fear, pain, and dismay that he had held back through all these ordeals erupted and ended in his vomiting.

Adhi's cries were suddenly added to his own. The child seemed to share Darwis's pain with equal force. This surprised the neighbor so much that she recoiled.

The child walked towards Darwis without ceasing to scream, a little mud statue animated by some kind of devilry. When he was close enough to the doctor, he brought his right hand up to his face and then, after a brief hesitation, placed his trembling fingers on his forehead. At the same time, he stopped screaming.

Despite his immense grief, which nothing, it seemed, could ever appease, Darwis sensed a strange sensation, a sort of rippling heat that started from his forehead and spread throughout his body. His pains began to melt away -- there was no other term to describe the way they disappeared, gradually replaced by that feeling of wellbeing that you experience upon falling asleep.

Except that he was wide awake.

When he lifted his head, amazed to feel his sufferings alleviated, little Adhi was smiling at him.

-- Chapter 2 --

Washington D.C.

Present time

Still dripping with droplets, Melany shivered as she wiped herself off. The heating in her bathroom had failed, which did not prevent her from taking her freezing morning shower. According to her father, who had initiated her into this ritual, it was the best way to keep her muscles toned, boost her blood circulation and replenish her energy.

She put down her towel and allowed herself a few moments to study herself in front of the mirror. The fatigue accumulated over the past few months and the lack of sleep were evident in the swelling of her eyelids and the small fan-shaped lines she was seeing for the first time upon staring at the corners of her eyes.

How could he find me attractive? She puzzled as she thought of Jeffrey, who was still sleeping deeply when she left the bedroom to get a cup of coffee. She was approaching thirty and had never worried about the effects that her missions might have on her looks. On the positive side, she had inherited her mischievous nose, small willful chin and freckles from her English mother, but her dark brown hair and blue eyes from her father, in a rather harmonious mix. The contours of her figure were well drawn. In recent months, she had all too frequently been seen dressed in military fatigues, loosely floating fabrics in unflattering colors, and even with a hijab over a traditional *abaya*.

Noticing some unpleasant shadows, she thought to herself that, after four months spent at the K1 base in Kirkuk in Iraqi Kurdistan, it might be time to stop by her beautician.

She frowned at her image and shrugged her shoulders.

-- *Melany?*

-- I'm in the bathroom.

Jeff, the one responsible for her most recent too-sleepless night, had finally woken up. The young woman sighed. They had just shared some intense and wonderful times, but this was the first morning that they would spend together. The magic of the night had faded, so wouldn't the somewhat insane attraction they had exerted on each other since the moment they met fade as well? Melany, like all women, loved to probe.

Once dried, she was careful to put on her least appealing bathrobe, a pale blue terrycloth robe deformed by the years and innumerable trips to the washer, and what she called her *old shrew slippers*. With her hair pulled up in a towel tied over her forehead, she walked back to the bedroom.

If he still finds me sexy with this on ...

She must have made a funny face when he raised himself on his elbow to look at her, because he burst out laughing.

-- I wonder if I will prefer you disguised as a postmenopausal housewife or when you're dressed to the nines.

-- And I should take that as a compliment?

-- You may take it as you like, but it's going to take some more effort if you're planning to push me away.

Melany sat down on the edge of the bed but at a respectable distance from Jeffrey. She then remembered one of the many qualities she already appreciated in him: his gentlemanly ways seemed innate at a time when some found it ridiculous to hold the door open for a woman, or to pull away her chair to help her sit down.

They had met at a party hosted behind her back by her friends Julie and Stephan to celebrate **her birthday at the same time as his return to D.C.** They had then made a date for dinner the next day. And it was she who had offered him a nightcap at her house when he had still barely held her hand. An initiative contrary to all her principles. But, watching her serene face, the wry little pout that never seemed to leave the corner of her lips and elegantly softened her serious side, she realized that the magic of the night had nothing to do with it ...

-- Do you know what day it is?, he asked, pulling up his pillow to lean back comfortably.

-- I'd say ... Monday. But with the jet lag, I could be wrong. Was that a trick question?

Pushing aside the sheets, Jeffrey managed to brush her thigh with the tips of his toes.

-- Aren't you asking why I asked you this question?

-- No doubt to emphasize that you should already be at your desk, when I spend my day hanging out and the rest of my week shamefully enjoying well-deserved time off?

-- On target, Mata Hari, with one small nuance left ... I just informed my department that I broke both legs and that they will have to get along without me for twenty-four hours.

-- Both legs?, Melany smiled.

-- Well, a similar excuse, maybe not so drastic, but every bit as effective ...

She didn't know what Jeffrey's position was at the INR or Bureau of Intelligence and Research, the intelligence agency of the State Department to which she also belonged, except that he was aiming at a career as a diplomat while she herself was in the analysis and action section. Whence the name *Mata Hari* ... He had, like her, left Harvard a few years earlier before tackling a career at the State Department. They would probably never have met without that evening, since the departments of the same agency were so isolated from each other. She suspected her friends Julie and Stephan of having set a trap for her by inviting Jeffrey to her birthday party.

-- You shouldn't have done that, she grimaced.

He put on a sulking pout that she found really cute. Especially since he immediately added:

-- I know a truly charming little Cuban restaurant in Georgetown. We could spend the early afternoon at the Reynolds Museum and then stroll around the marina ... or at least something like that. But I fully understand that you are tired and prefer to be alone today. Pardon me my silly little initiatives ...

He pulled himself completely out of the sheets and made to stand up, but Melany stopped him with a gesture.

-- On the contrary, it's a cool plan. It is true that I had something else planned ...

-- But ...?

-- Now that you've made such a stupid move, I would hesitate to let you down.

The smile he immediately displayed was like a reward. Jeffrey had a frank look and a naive pout. A carefully groomed shadow of a beard added a touch of manly neglect to rather fine features on a dark skin that regular stays in the mountains and at the seashore had helped to tan. He sported a good build and lanky muscles that allowed him to wear suits as naturally as jeans or tracksuits.

She had no idea where their relationship would go. But we don't ask ourselves that kind of question after two evenings spent together, only one of which was alone.

-- In that case, I'm good enough to tackle the day very slowly, he concluded with a gleam in his eyes that spoke volumes about his intentions.

She laughed and moved closer to him, loosening the towel that tied her hair. After all, since he was here and had decided to stay, why waste his time in a Cuban restaurant or in a museum? The vibration of her cell phone, lying on the bedside table, interrupted her. A cloud of concern slipped surreptitiously into Jeffrey's gaze and she was tempted to ignore the interruption. But she knew the number that had just appeared only too well ...

She grabbed the cell phone, apologizing with a lip-smacking kiss.

Jeffrey took the opportunity to go to the bathroom. When he returned, she was still sitting on the edge of the bed pensively, the phone resting on her bare legs protruding from the robe. Finding her like that, he nodded and picked up his clothes from the floor.

-- You have to go in?, he asked simply.

-- I'm sorry. It's apparently urgent.

-- I can drop you off, if you like.

Melany was reluctant to accept his offer. Her code for sentimental relationships ruled out being accompanied to work after a first night spent together. This was probably a little bit ridiculous, but it is necessary to set boundaries. The little that she could see of the sky through the cracks in the curtains led to her decision. The weather was terrible. No hope of finding a taxi in this weather.

-- And you, what are you going to do?

-- Don't worry. I know someone who will be more than happy to see me when they've been expecting to do all my work for me.

Melany intentionally let her robe slip.

-- You know, I don't think they will keep me all day. If you're willing to meet me later ...

-- That can be negotiated!, Jeffrey replied before striding over to her and hugging her.

A gust of rain carrying rain slapped violently against the windows.

***

The emblem of the INR, an eagle holding arrows in its left talon and an olive branch in its right under the inscription "E Pluribus Unum", was the only decoration in the room of modest dimensions, sparingly furnished but with large windows.

At the time of her recruitment, Melany had been informed that the INR was the *"Intelligence Agency of the Poor."*

-- Forget all the spy movies you've ever seen, her senior instructor had recommended. With us, the James Bond gadgets are at best a four-color pen and access to an older generation computer terminal.

Unlike the prestigious CIA, the Bureau of Intelligence and Research, acronym INR, had a modest budget and a number of employees ranging from 300 to 500 -- fifty times fewer than the CIA --, only a quarter of whom were assigned to the ground.

After her period of instruction, Melany had encountered the greatest difficulty in securing the only position that matched her abilities. Having graduated from Harvard with a major in International Relations, she also spoke several languages, due to the numerous transfers of her father, who was a military attaché to various embassies in Europe and the Middle East.

Her obsession throughout all her studies had been to be done with pushing paper. Her only failure, which still haunted her, was to fail the series of psychological tests that would have allowed her to enter the CIA. Langley's recruiting section had viewed her as too emotionally fragile and perhaps too unstable in her emotional states. In disappointment, therefore, she fell back on the INR.

Still, she was happy to join the State Department's intelligence service.

Her first posting, to Turkey, was a sort of deflowering that allowed her to assess the populist mechanisms influencing the shift from a democratic system to a form of dictatorship. Her task had been to report regularly on human rights violations by the government. Arbitrary imprisonments, dismissals without cause, false accusations, torture ... The regular purges had wiped out the lives of hundreds of thousands of opponents of the regime. Some of the reports on the arrests of journalists and NGO officials were dozens of pages in length. She was at full capacity when she was finally transferred to Kurdistan, in the middle of a conflict zone.

Those weeks spent near Kirkuk in the company of old veterans, barely disguised CIA agents, helicopter pilots as reckless as they were bon vivants, as well as talkative and music-loving radio operators responsible for regulating the ballet involved in the transportation of arms to the Kurdish fighters, had reconciled her to her position. She had lived intensely for three months.

Her main role was to conduct interrogations of members of the Islamic State captured by the American army and its allies in order to draw up a general assessment that analysts would review before it was transmitted to diplomatic corps in the Middle East and to the United Nations.

It soon turned out that, after overcoming their initial reservations, she was doing just as well with the combatants as with the female members of their families. Her work was minutely analyzed by psychologists and other profilers up the chain of command who regularly sent her lists of questions. This had never stopped her from adding her little grain of salt and sending back reports that were frequently more in-depth than her superiors had required.

She had been patient for nearly ten minutes, with her too-watery and insufficiently sweet coffee that an intern had offered her, when they finally joined her.

-- Ms. Carson, thank you for being here. Sorry to have made you wait!

Melany had only expected to see the director of the *Department of Terrorism, Narcotics and Crime Analysis* she was attached to, and perhaps one of his assistants. But he was accompanied by two complete strangers, whom she immediately identified as belonging to outside agencies.

Their impeccable suits and ties tied too tightly to shirts without a wrinkle betrayed their positions better than any uniforms could ever done. Walter Garroni, Melany's boss, quickly made the introductions.

-- So this is Melany Carson, the author of the report I shared with you and one of the most talented of our young recruits. Melany, this is Dick Gardner, FBI Special Agent, and Robert Franckel, who has a job in Langley similar to mine here.

Melany appreciated the compliment -- sincere, she hoped -- that her boss had just given her.

-- Very honored, but quite puzzled, she conceded, shaking the hands that were extended to her.

Garroni took his place opposite Melany, flanked by the special agent and the CIA executive.

-- I'll sum it up quickly, Garroni said, taking the time to paint a portrait of a model employee and field analyst.

-- ... Which leads us to this report, he concluded at the end of his presentation.

-- I got to know your father a little bit, Franckel said, as Melany continued to show signs of her impatience. He was attached to our embassy in Cairo towards the end of the nineties, if I am not mistaken?

-- That's right, Melany confirmed. Just before being transferred to Berlin.

-- It was there that you learned to speak Arabic?

-- My father insisted that I take language courses in every country he worked in.

The executive from Langley darted an inquiring look at her that pierced her right through. Garroni thought it appropriate to add:

-- Ms. Carson is blessed with an amazing memory. She speaks several Arabic dialects fluently, in addition to Classical Arabic, Russian, German and, more recently, the Kurmanji dialect of Kurdish.

-- I only have a few of the basics, Melany pointed out modestly. Enough to haggle in the souk but not enough to hold a philosophical conversation.

-- Enough in this case ... Dick Gardner grimaced. I don't think that our Kurdish allies are very keen on phenomenology or deconstruction.

Melany hated preconceptions and restrained her annoyance.

-- On the contrary. Over the course of the century that they have been promised independence and have been abandoned as soon as they were no longer needed, the Kurds have developed a deep distaste for blather about the meaning of existence and the afterlife. My stay with them allowed me to appreciate their conception of the intangible and their keen sense of poetry. They are far from being a savage people.

-- I see that you've been taken in by their somewhat biased version of their story, Franckel observed in a grave tone in which Melany caught a hint of disapproval.

-- My role is not to let myself be seduced, but to collect facts that help my superiors to draw conclusions, she retorted with just the right amount of insolence to make Garroni smile.

-- If we could return to this report?, the man resumed. Melany, our intention isn't to spoil your well-deserved rest with an interminable meeting ...

-- Thank you, sir.

-- ... most particularly since we would like to be able to count on you in the days to come.

An icy hand gripped the young woman's heart.

-- You mean that my vacation is already over?

-- You can refuse, of course. *Legally,* nothing forces you to accept a new assignment so quickly.

Garroni's allusion to legality made his message quite clear. She could not be forced to give up her vacation while she was still suffering from jet lag, but there were many more considerations in her job than just labor rights. Unless, of course, she doesn't care about her further career.

She glanced at her watch.

-- So I've had two hours rest after 14 weeks in the field ... But as my father would say, I will have plenty of time to enjoy it when I'm dead. What's this all about?

-- I'm with you there, Garroni said appreciatively. What struck us in your report and what justifies this somewhat informal meeting is a term that repeatedly appears in your reports. *Abi Alnasr.* I would like your verbal confirmation that these words were spoken by several subjects.

Melany wrinkled her brow, recalling that she herself had tried to figure it out but unfortunately could not gather any further information. The mystery was emphasized in her report.

-- *Abi Alnasr* and *Abu Alnasr* ... They used both formulations.

Garroni nodded.

-- According to your reports, Ibrahim al-Zaouahiri was the first to use this expression ...

-- Followed by Hamza Al-Moujahid and Anwar Ibn Dimzuri. Yes, indeed.

The three men, who belonged to the Islamic State, had been captured by Kurdish fighters and transferred to the Kirkuk base under American command. Melany had spent enough time in their cells, protected by the watchful eyes of a Marine, to know their relatives' names over the course of three generations. However, the two words, thrown out defiantly, remained a mystery.

-- So you do confirm, then, that the same expression was used by these three subjects?

-- Without any hesitation, sir.

-- In what context, precisely?

-- It involved knowing their personal plans, in case they were released under a prisoner exchange deal. All three saw their imprisonment as temporary episodes and claimed that *Abu Alnasr* would release them.

-- Good ... Garroni turned to Franckel. Bob, I'll let you continue.

The CIA man, who had been scrutinizing Melany, leaned forward as if he wanted to exchange some confidential information. But it was with a loud voice that he continued, however.

-- *Abu Alnasr:* The translation is *"Father of Victory"* -- He took a paper covered with notes from his pocket, unfolded it and continued -- You wrote: "The subject did not seem affected when I informed him that the Caliphate had lost control of three of the most important Syrian and Iraqi cities since the beginning of his captivity and that its main leaders had died in the bombardments. When I insisted on their defeat, which I described as a real stampede in order to try to obtain further information on the relations between small, affiliated groups and their means of communication, he replied: "Thanks be to Allah, *Abi Alnasr* is back. You soon won't be able to do anything against us. Thanks be to Allah, you will end up accepting the only true faith."

None of the three subjects wanted to tell you anything more and, despite your perseverance, some threats within the limits of your authorization levels, and the promise to improve their lot in jail, that's all you ever got.

-- Since you are fluent in Russian and German, Dick Gardner intervened: How do you translate *Abi* or *Abu Alnasr* into these two languages?

-- *Der Siegesvater* and *Otets Pobedy*, Melany replied without any hesitation or trace of an accent.

-- And how do you explain that we find these words in several reports from teams monitoring neo-Nazi movements in Russia, in Germany, and on American soil?

Silence followed this exchange, time for Melany to digest the information.

-- I don't have the foggiest idea, sir.

-- *The Father of Victory*, Garroni said, weighing every word. In Arabic, I can understand that. "Abi" and "Abu" are honorary terms often used in the Near East to respectfully refer to a male person. The notion of victory is very vague in Eastern cultures, which often place as much importance on utterances as on facts ... But the phrase has been picked up with variations by several neo-Nazi groups in Alabama, Georgia, Pennsylvania, and other states. One of our agents based in Indonesia also alluded to this in a recent report, quite similar to yours. We came to the conclusion that this could be a unifying figure with the aim or function of strengthening the *de facto* alliance between nostalgic Third Reich devotees and certain radical Islamist movements.

Franckel in turn insisted:

-- How and why do we find this expression in the mouths of Daesh members in Kirkuk, and among former members of the terrorist organization GAM in Indonesia?

Melany now understood the reason for the presence of the two men. The CIA was prohibited from exercising its functions on American soil, while the FBI could only intervene abroad with the special permission and consent of local authorities. The INR sometimes served as a liaison between the two units because it had a role of centralizing intelligence. It was the only agency to warn the government against the invasion of Iraq by dissociating itself from the CIA on this file. She was surprised, however, to find such great efficiency. It was rare for sparse data to be assembled so quickly. The director seemed to read her mind as he clarified immediately.

-- After decades of calm, great upheavals has recently been observed in far-right movements, both at home and in Russia and across Europe. The CIA, the FBI and the INR therefore consider this information to be of the greatest importance.

-- But I thought that the extreme right was isolated, reduced, and no longer presented any danger, Melany said in surprise.

Dick Gardner took an electronic cigarette from inside his jacket pocket, weighed it for a moment, then put it back in the same place.

-- Many websites attract people nostalgic for Nazism and crazy people of all types. The largest, Stormfront, is a forum that now has nearly 200,000 members. Veterans of the American Nazi Party, members of the Ku Klux Klan, anti-Semites and white supremacists of all kinds, and more and more Salafists. Extremists become dangerous when they gain the ability to mutate in order to bond with one another ...

He appeared to hesitate, took out the small cylinder again, and this time brought it up to his lips. A scent of apples and autumn leaves emanated from it as he inhaled with obvious pleasure under Garroni's disapproving glance. He went on.

... On a purely ideological level, there is no longer much difference between the various groups of the extreme right, the extreme left, and the Jihadists. The racism embedded in their beliefs is different in its nature, but their goals are almost all the same. As long as they were disorganized and reduced to a handful of initiates, we didn't have to worry too much. But these movements have recently tended to feed off the convulsions shaking Islam. The violence of Daesh, Al-Qaida, and other more disciplined terrorist organizations like Hezbollah fascinates those on the right and excites the other extreme. Our agents have found keffiyehs and black flags on the premises of Nazi artifact collecting associations. In Russia, Stalinist devotees recently raised funds to support the defense of a handful of skinheads who had joined a Chechen terrorist cell and were preparing to carry out an attack on the Basilica in Red Square on Orthodox New Year's Day. There is no longer a clear line between the various ultra-violent rebel groups, even though they all officially hate each other. The fear of our experts is that they will find a common leader who will smooth out their rivalries.

-- *The Father of Victory?,* Melany shot back.

-- One of our assumptions, before Walter gave us your report, was that this could be the codename for an operation in the course of preparation. We are now certain that something is brewing, something that might bring the survivors of a dislocated caliphate and those nostalgic for the Reich and Stalinism together.

-- It seems to go against nature to me, Melany observed.

-- Not necessarily. During the 1930's, the Nazis managed to convince Arab and Muslim countries that they would free them from French and British colonialism. After World War II, the KGB fomented popular uprisings from the Maghreb to Turkey. This would not be the first time for pagans, atheistic communists and ultrareligious people to come to an understanding. All three ideologies promote totalitarianism. If the *Father of Victory* is a code name for a new leader, then we need to know his identity, his origins, the region he lives in and his plans ...

-- Whence our intention to infiltrate one of their groups here on American soil, said Dick Gardner.

The three men turned their gazes to Melany and watched her, until she understood their intentions. She felt herself sinking into her shell.

-- So you thought of me ...?

-- The CIA has no domestic jurisdiction, and the FBI has no legal right to intervene without a certain threat or until a crime has been reported. The target we are thinking of will be less wary of a young woman who speaks fluent German than of a man. They've been burned recently.

-- But the INR doesn't have the right to investigate inside the United States either!

-- Except that the INR won't officially intervene, Garroni explained.

-- It's that ... I've never done it before, Melany protested, trying to hide her nervousness.

-- You speak German and Russian fluently. You understand Arabic perfectly. Physically, you are of the Aryan type, and we can accentuate that even further. Your service record is impeccable, despite your young age, and you have received comprehensive training. You are perfect for this role.

Dick Gardner insisted.

-- It's not about sending you to infiltrate Daesh or Al-Qaeda deep in Syria, but relatively quiet small groups in the heart of the United States, and for a very short time. And the cavalry will be sent in to rescue you at the slightest sign of danger. But the risk is minimal.

-- And besides, damn it, he couldn't have lied ..., the CIA man snapped.

-- If you mean my dad ... I'm not sure he would appreciate knowing that I ...

-- I was thinking more of your mother, Franckel interrupted. Maureen O'Neil was one of MI6's most promising undercover agents before meeting your father while they were both stationed in Moscow. I also knew her when I was starting out. The KGB suffered from an epidemic of defections under Gorbachev, and our services were working hand in hand to separate the wheat from the chaff. Too bad Major Carson convinced his young wife to resign. The Western intelligence services had lost a top-rate recruit then.

-- It's not so much my dad ... Melany corrected in a dreamy voice.

-- Is that so? What happened?

-- I came into the world and my mother was not resigned to letting me grow up in the hands of a nanny.

-- Which is entirely honorable, Franckel conceded. But many regretted it. This would be your opportunity to take up the torch.

-- Assuming that I say yes, what precisely would my mission be?

Melany wasn't yet sure whether she would agree. There were so many new issues in her own life. But Walter Garroni's face broke into a broad smile. He stood up to clap her shoulder in a warm, fatherly gesture.

-- Do you have anything important you're doing this afternoon?

***

She had loads of important things to do.

For example, calling Jeffrey, making an appointment with him at her place, spending a good part of the afternoon in his company, then rushing to her beautician, giving herself a princess treatment, and maybe getting a massage before taking a mud bath.

Then, dinner by candlelight in a French or Italian restaurant. Calling her mother, whom she still had the greatest difficulty in reaching, since she couldn't keep still after her divorce. Inviting her to lunch if she was in D.C. Also trying to reach her father, who was stationed somewhere in Southeast Asia -- in Bali, if she remembered correctly. Obviously, getting ready to spend a second night of drunkenness, without thinking of anything else and especially not about terrorists, Nazis, Communists, and the intelligence services ...

But all of her plans had vanished in less time than it takes to arrange sheets, read a menu, or indulge in the expert hands of a beautician ...

She had agreed, in order to do a little to make up for the damage her birth had done to the intelligence agencies of the Western world. A bit out of challenge. But above all, for ideals. This mission would enable her to fight the despicable ideologies that she hated.

It was also an opportunity to be pounced on.

For several days, she would no longer be solely subservient to the INR, but to the FBI and the CIA as well. Once her infiltration was over and the meaning of the mysterious phrase was unveiled, perhaps Franckel could pull some strings and allow her to take the entrance exam again at his prestigious agency, this time successfully.

What had Jeff called her that morning? *Mata Hari*? She smiled at that.

The mirror in her bedroom she glanced at for a moment gave her a very different image from that of the morning. No sooner had she agreed than the agency handed her over to a disguise specialist, a barber, and a tattoo artist. Her dark brown hair, her eyebrows, and even her pubic hair were recolored, an operation that made her a true blonde whose original shade no expert could ever have guessed.

-- Are you sure that it's really necessary down there, too?, she asked the young woman in charge of lightening up her intimate parts.

-- Just a precaution, she replied evasively.

-- A precaution against what?

-- No need to worry. Our teams pay attention to detail. That's all.

The result was guaranteed to last at least two weeks, the maximum time allotted to her mission. She didn't really like her "squared haircut with volume" that made her look romantic and far too wise, but the most disturbing -- and the most painful -- things were those two tattoos: a black swastika circled in red on her left shoulder and an Iron Cross, symbol of the Wehrmacht and sign of recognition among the neo-Nazis, above her navel. The tattoo artist, who knew his business, had added the words *Wer Will -- Der Kann (He Who Wills -- Can)* in two parts separated by the cross. The horror of it!

Melany had almost refused to let herself be marked that way, but the specialist in charge of her preparation had reassured her that these abominations would not last. The CIA had developed a short-lived ink that disappeared without leaving a mark in a matter of days.

Now she had to get used to her new temporary identity. Since her mission would be short-term, she had been able to keep her first name, which now preceded *Hoffmann*, a family name quite common in Germany, on her new driver's license and social security card. She had been born in Berlin, emigrated with her parents in 2001, and lived in Lancaster, a town in Pennsylvania she had never set foot in ...

-- *Fräulein* Melany Hoffmann ... she repeated, wincing. More Aryan than that and you die. She remembered reading "The Devil's Elixirs" by Ernst Hoffmann, a romantic author whose work had given rise to "fantastic realism", a literary genre particularly admired in Nazi currents. His tales often turned out badly. She hoped she wasn't seeing a premonition here.

A small, familiar figure appeared in the doorway. She smiled and called out:

-- *Moutchi?*

Her neighbor's cat must have slipped out the kitchen window, which she always left open. He had sensed her presence and come to seek the caresses that she generously bestowed upon him when he visited her. With a leap, he found himself on the bathroom tiles before rubbing against her leg, purring. She dropped to the floor and spent long minutes scratching behind his ears while letting her thoughts slip away.

With a heavy heart, she would have to call Jeffrey to inform him that their plans had collapsed. Her mission had to be kept secret and, although she would have plenty of free time while waiting for the tattoos to heal, she had no desire to offer her lover the sight of a swastika and an Iron Cross placed on her skin. She imagined what Jeff would look like when he uncovered her naked body.

-- But what is this horror here?

-- Just a little whim I allowed myself by telling myself that you might like it. Don't you think it's pretty?

Since it was quite difficult to accept a one-on-one dinner without ending their evening in a more intimate way, she would have to find a reason to not see him again.

-- So you're leaving for Kurdistan already?

-- Tomorrow, yes. But I have very little time left to prepare. And then, to be honest, I'm on the verge of exhaustion. I'm going to collapse if I don't get at least twelve hours of sleep before catching the plane. See you when I get back?

She had sensed that Jeff was disappointed, but he had tried to put on a good face and had contented himself with the vague promise of a call every now and then.

-- Yeah, that's it, when you get back ... Too bad, I had so many plans to fill up your week off.

-- It was all going a bit fast, don't you think?

-- You mean between us? We may not have the same ways of thinking. Why postpone until tomorrow the pleasures we can afford today? But you're right. Above all, let's not go too fast. The paper pusher just has to wait for the backpacker to return.

-- I promise you won't regret it.

She had almost melted. Tell him everything! Demand that he rush over to her house right away. She was dying to surrender into his arms once again, and it was with a voice trembling from frustration that she ended the conversation before hanging up.

Damned tattoos!

Moutchi was tired of being petted. He headed off for the kitchen where she followed him in order to rummage through the cupboards for a little treat to offer him. The fridge was empty except for a bottle of milk, a container of yogurt, and a few beers. In desperation, she put a bowl of cornflakes on the floor, which he sniffed before giving her a dismissive look, turning on his heel, and running off where he had come from.

A little saddened, she went to the bedroom and threw herself onto the messy bed to rub the skin of her stomach and shoulder with CeraVe for Scars, a cream to use immediately after being tattooed.

She still had to familiarize herself with the thick file on the neo-Nazi groups flourishing in Pennsylvania entrusted to her by Dick Gardner.

But first of all, she had to call her mother, whom she had already tried to contact three times since returning from Kurdistan. Maureen O'Neil's silence and absences were frequent enough that Melany, although disappointed, did not get alarmed when she got her answering machine once again.

-- Okay, mom, this is my second message to you. It would be nice if you checked in on your old machine from time to time, even if you are abroad. And then, damn it, turn on your cell phone. We are living in the twenty-first century, you know! Everything is fine on my end. I will be hard to reach for a week or two. I hope to see you when you get back ... from wherever you are. Kisses!

The file prepared by the FBI contained a thick pile of photographs, some statistics and a summary of the various investigations that had been carried out on neo-Nazi movements in the United States. There was even a museum dedicated to Hitler's glory in the small town of Pennsylvania where her mission was to unfold.

Since the arrival of the Ku Klux Klan a century earlier, Odyssey had been one of the small towns where extreme white supremacism continued to proliferate. In 2011, it hosted the World Aryan Congress, a gathering of neo-Nazis, skinheads and Klan members. The police arrested a few, the most violent, but released them after a night in police custody. The only charges against them were the destruction of posters calling for the prevention of the assembly, a state of intoxication on public streets for some, and threats against a government that they claimed to have fallen into the hands of *"Niggers"*, *"Ragheads"* and *"Kikes"*. The judge, called upon to decide the amount of their bond, disregarded the racial insults.

The confidential file also indicated that an FBI infiltration operation had made it possible, six months earlier, to arrest members of an Aryan Nation action cell on more serious grounds. Illegal weapons, including assault rifles and boxes of undeclared grenades, had been found amid bags of grain and fertilizer on the farm owned by local leader Derek Mitchell. He and his own son had been released on bail and were awaiting trial. Both were at risk of 1 and 5 years in prison.

While awaiting the sentence, Mitchell quietly continued his activities. Most particularly, the maintenance of a fairly sober website, which had in the past called for racial discrimination but was now content to sell various Nazi objects and symbols. He was also the owner and curator of a 'museum' dedicated to Hitler's memory, a log construction that wouldn't have looked like much without its exhibits.

Derek Mitchell was her target. The strategy put in place had been communicated to her verbally by Bob Franckel in person.

Melany couldn't help but find the facts disgusting. How was it possible to tolerate not only the existence, but the actions of such small groups, in the name of freedom of expression?

Jet lag and fatigue caught up with her while she was reading. She fell into the documents like a lead weight and sank into a restless sleep of nightmares.

Men in brown shirts marching along the Potomac River between the Lincoln Memorial and the Washington Monument. The officer at the head of the procession held up the banner of victory: a Nazi swastika cut from the skin of a woman. Jeff walked behind, dressed in military fatigues similar to those worn by the ISIS fighters interviewed in Kirkuk. She called out to him: "Where are you going like that? And what are you doing with these people?" "To Indonesia," Jeff replied. "Meet me in Jakarta".

Melany woke up sweating and trembling in all her limbs. Her first instinct was to make sure that the skin on her shoulder was still intact. The touch of her fingers made her grimace.

It was still noticeable, even though the redness around the swastika was starting to fade. She brushed herself with CeraVe again in the middle of the night.

-- Chapter 3 --

Pennsylvania

Present time

The road sign that greeted visitors to the west side of Odyssey, a small town in Potter County in the northern part of the state, was quaint and charming: it featured the silhouette of a horse-drawn cart to remind passing drivers that they were in Amish country and that they were using the same road as them.

It had snowed abundantly the previous week and large white patches dotted with brown spots and pierced with tufts of soft-colored grass continued to melt on either side of the highway that cut through the fields as far as the eye could see.

The house holding the Hitler Museum was two hundred yards away. Although she had already seen it in the series of photographs collected by the FBI, Melany found it difficult to believe her eyes. The small, stocky building overlooked the main street from an embankment. Its sloping roof was bristling with Nazi flags adjoining star-spangled banners and Confederate battle flags. A gigantic portrait of the Führer filled the facade.

Melany felt as if her heart was about to explode in her chest as she parked the Mercedes made available to her for the duration of the operation in the museum parking lot. She opened her door window to let in the freezing air, closed her eyes, and forced herself to breathe as slowly as possible until she regained her composure.

In a few moments, she was going to meet Derek Mitchell in his stronghold and the image she had retained of him did nothing to reassure her.

She finally made up her mind to remove herself from her car and to walk up the few steps leading to the entrance to the museum shop. On the steps, swastikas carved from logs were placed on display stands, next to a turnstile offering postcards dating from the era of the Third Reich -- certified as authentic -- for a dollar and, for a few cents more, key rings bearing the emblem of the SS, the seal of the Wehrmacht, or a portrait of Hitler.

If the activities of the neo-Nazis had been limited to fetishism, it would have been less vile. There were many sick people who collected photos of Charles Manson, press articles about the carnage committed by Ted Bundy or the letters of Gary Ridgway, nicknamed the Green River killer, who was sentenced to death for having tortured and murdered more than seventy young women. Fascination with horror and abomination knows no bounds in some disturbed brains ...

Melany pushed open the door, triggering a three-tone doorbell.

-- We're closed!

The head of a man appeared in a recess between the cash register and a chewing gum dispenser with an American flag on the counter. He straightened up completely and grabbed a rag to wipe his hands. She recognized Derek Mitchell.

-- Sorry ... she said in a voice she wanted to be as neutral as possible. I took more time on the road than I thought.

-- That's your problem, little lady. We close at 5 p.m.

-- But the door was open ...

-- So what? Can't you read? But you are white, however. Our schedules are posted on the sign hanging at the entrance.

Melany blamed herself for not paying attention. She forced herself to remain unperturbed.

-- I sent a message to your site three days ago, and someone told me I could drop by whenever I wanted.

-- During working hours ... And now, if you will close the door behind you on your way out.

-- But I've come all the way from Lancaster ... I didn't expect such traffic jams.

-- Little lady, when you are civilized, you make allowances for error. There are already enough men who don't give a damn about discipline and manners.

Mitchell was much taller than he had looked in the FBI photos. With a square chin, gray hair cropped like a GI, his face marked by a brush mustache under a tiny nose, he had the build of a farmer accustomed to the harshness of farm chores. The rolled-up sleeves of his checkerboard-pattern woolen shirt revealed highly muscular forearms with hands as broad as paddles. An amused smirk floated in his pale blue eyes. Melany figured he was testing her.

She straightened her chest and took on a pinched expression.

-- You think the way you treat your guests is courteous and polite? If I disturb you so much after driving 236 miles just to take a look at the rare pieces in your collection, I can turn back. No problem.

She scowled around the overstocked room that smelled of dust and sawdust and turned on her heel. It was a decisive moment. If he dismissed her out of hand, she would have a hard time resuming her mission.

-- Wait ...

Melany froze.

-- I may have been a little bit rude. But I don't like to be interrupted when I'm fixing something.

She faced him again, without changing her offended expression.

-- I should accept that as an excuse?

He shrugged as he continued to wipe his hands.

-- It's this goddamn heating. If I don't fix it, it will go out overnight and valuables might be damaged. And then, well, you don't quite have the typical profile of an Aryan art collector.

Melany instantly cursed Gardner and his boss at INS. Nice design of the camouflage if it was transparent from the very start!

-- It's not about a collection, but about respect for history, she replied dryly. Not the little story that the government and the media want us to swallow but, as my father Herr Hoffmann would say, the one with an "H" so large that no collaborator of the Jews could swallow it.

The surprised and delighted expression spreading over Derek's face comforted her that she had hit the nail on the head.

-- Does Herr Hoffmann live in Pennsylvania too?

Melany shook her head.

-- My parents returned to live in Berlin. But I haven't come this far just to talk about them. You indicate on your site that you have several working *Luger Mauser P08 Parabellum,* including one that belonged to an *SS Obersturmführer,* as well as uniforms and other items that you can only mention by private message. I don't see anything in this room that looks like anything like that.

Mitchell's smile widened, this time with a slight air of complicity that Melany didn't find unwelcome. Curiosity about Nazi artifacts from a young woman of German descent was the best cover the CIA and FBI had found before they sent her to look him over. She suddenly realized that those in charge of her mission knew exactly what they were doing by choosing her. A pretty young blonde who looked innocent and classy was less likely to arouse suspicion in Derek and those around him than an older agent too perfect to be true.

Once she sympathized with the curator of this horror museum, it would be up to her to invent a way to fit in with the community for a while. She hadn't come up with a strategy yet. If she failed on first contact, she was instructed to not take any chances. *That way, I would have had my stomach and shoulder tattooed for nothing.*

-- Give me two minutes, time enough to screw the heat control knob back on, and I'll show you around, Derek said.

-- Take your own sweet time, Melany retorted drily. I would hate to interfere with you any further when you're tinkering.

Derek Mitchell hesitated to reply, but only shook his head briefly before disappearing under the counter again. He sprang back up less than a minute later and joined her in the middle of the room.

-- There you have several original posters from the time of the Anschluss, he said, pointing to a crowded corner. Do you know what the Anschluss was?

-- Do you really want to insult me?

Mitchell stopped within a pace of Melany. He was two heads taller than she was and was three times her size. He scratched his mustache mechanically as he slowly eyed her, eyelids narrowed.

-- You know what? You and I started off on the wrong foot. But I think you're the type I like. Did you tell me your father's name is Hoffmann? And you -- what should I call you?

She held out her left hand to show she wasn't wearing a wedding ring ...

-- Melany Hoffmann.

-- Derek Mitchell. I'm the curator of this museum dedicated to the memory of the Führer. God bless America for giving us the freedom to pay homage to him.

-- Your museum still looks more like a store to me, Melany pointed out, pointing to the prices on the labels that adorned most of the items.

She knew about another, bigger room, but the less she seemed to know, the less reason Derek would have to be suspicious.

-- You have to live, the latter smiled, revealing two rows of bright white teeth. They also sell souvenirs at the MOMA in New York.

-- Key chains and posters. But I doubt their store carries original Calders.

-- Let me guide you to the main room. I normally charge $5 for entry. But since we're closed, it will be free for you.

Melany followed Mitchell to the narrow staircase leading to the second floor, thinking proudly that she had won the first round. At the top of the steps hung a golden sign engraved with Gothic letters: "Adolph Hitler Museum -- Silence and respect -- Appropriate dress required -- Food and drink prohibited".

-- You're not allowed to take pictures, Mitchell grumbled, pushing open the door and stepping aside to let her in. Normally, I confiscate people's cellphones, but since there's just the two of us ...

The look he wrapped her in as she walked past him made Melany shudder. This man was like a mountain. If he pounced on her, it would be impossible to fight him off. She reassured herself that he would not try to abuse a pure Aryan with a German name. Unpleasant as these kinds of individuals were, they prided themselves on a certain sense of honor for their own kind. Besides, Derek already had criminal proceedings pending. If she pressed charges against him, he risked spending several years behind bars.

Her attention shifted to the room, which was noticeably larger than the shop on the lower level and dimly at for the moment. She took a step forward, bumped into a figure and let out a little cry. Derek laughed and flipped on a light switch.

The museum dedicated to Hitler's memory was revealed to Melany.

First of all, there was the life-sized reproduction of the Führer in formal military uniform that she had just bumped into. It had been placed near the entrance, giving the impression of welcoming visitors. The dictator watched her with inquisitive eyes made of marbles with blue interiors, as if reproaching her for rousing him from his lethargy. Behind him stood several glass display cases containing the insignias of various military units arranged by rank of importance. The famous Luger Parabellum pistols that Melany had said she was interested in were arranged on shelves. Propaganda posters dating from various periods of the Reich adorned the walls. The one closest to Melany showed a sepia-colored Hitler against the background of a parade of German forces and proclaimed: "Ein Kampf um Deutschland", or "A Struggle for Germany". Uniforms of SS officers and Gestapo agents dressed half a dozen window mannequins, including one without a head, which made it all the more frightening. In the middle of the room, a large square table surmounted by a wooden pyramid covered with felt offered visitors a view of a whole series of labeled trinkets, among which were regulation daggers, a canteen that had once belonged to a Luftwaffe lieutenant, cigarettes lighters emblazoned with Nazi symbols, belt buckles, a wooden snuff box engraved with swastikas, a red lantern stamped with a golden swastika and, above all, two first editions of Mein Kampf, one in English and the other in German.

Melany walked slowly past the artifacts, restraining both her astonishment and a vague feeling of nausea. Most of the objects on display were originals, brought from where she had no idea and into this museum built in a forgotten hole in northern Pennsylvania. The report that she had heard read to her hadn't contained any details about the contents of this room. It was, however, more than an exhibition staged by amateurs mired in diseased dogmas. The museum was proof of the existence of an old and solid organization.

Mitchell must have read her mind as he stood beside her and pointed to the German edition of Mein Kampf.

-- This book is our very best item. It was followed by many others during the 1930's and 1940's. Most were imported by my father. This is what makes our museum so interesting. There's nothing here that you could ever find on eBay.

-- It is remarkable, Melany murmured, pretending to examine some daggers. I had no idea that such a collection might exist.

-- But you still haven't seen everything yet.

Mitchell led her into a nook of the room cluttered with three display cases, each one displaying its contents of texts in German.

-- Here you have the very first copy of the two wills of the Führer. Unfortunately, the originals stayed with the Soviets ...

-- The Russians, Melany corrected. The Soviet Union disappeared before I was born.

-- Do you really believe that? Once a communist, always a communist. Note that those these bastards fortunately kept most of Germany under their rule for fifty years. Contrary to popular belief, the Soviets had a much deeper understanding of Nazi doctrine than our so-called democracies will ever have. Which side of Berlin were you born in?

-- In the Mitte District, Melany replied, recalling that the avenue of Unter den Linden that was its heart began on the east side of the Brandenburg Gate. Do you know my hometown?

-- No, unfortunately. But you can be Catholic without ever setting foot in Rome.

-- That's perfectly true.

With her face almost pressed to the glass protecting Hitler's wills, Melany translated aloud the opening lines of the longer of the texts.

"More than thirty years have passed since I made my modest contribution as a volunteer in the First World War which was imposed on the Reich in 1914.

Over the course of these three decades, I have only been influenced by love for and loyalty to my people in all my thoughts, actions and life. They gave me the strength to make the most difficult decisions that mortal man has ever faced."

-- Your German sounds excellent to me, Derek complimented her. Unfortunately, I can't say the same for mine.

-- What force in those words!, she said, pretending to be ecstatic.

-- As you can see, there are two documents. His political will, in which he repudiates Hermann Göring by accusing him of high treason and replaces him with Admiral Dönitz, expels Himmler from the party and appoints Karl Hanke and Paul Giesler as the heads of the police forces, and appoints Goebbels, Bormann and Seyss-Inquart to the highest offices of the State. Right next to it, there is his personal and philosophical testament and the certificate for his marriage to Eva Braun. Does all of this mean anything to you?

-- Historians agree that Hitler was certain until the last minute that Germany would recover, with or without him.

-- That's where they go wrong, Mitchell said with an enigmatic expression. The Führer was certain that Germany would recover and that Nazism would set out again to conquer the world ... but only with him.

-- But he killed himself ...

-- He ended one thing, because no one other than him had the right to take his life. But day always follows night ...

Looking at him surreptitiously, Melany noticed that Mitchell had taken on the look of a dreamer. He seemed to want to add a sentence, but held something back. It was better not to insist at this point. She noted, however, that this might be an important reflection and vowed to return to it when the opportunity came up.

The other two windows displayed food coupons, blueprints for a Volkswagen from 1943, diplomas and a passport issued in 1936 to an elderly lady, whose name had been partially erased.

-- This is truly extraordinary. But how did you manage to get your hands on all these objects?

Mitchell responded with such pride that she congratulated herself on having struck his nerve.

-- It's a long story. It begins with my father, who joined the Allied forces in 1944 and found himself stationed with other GI's in the Munich area shortly before the Russians took Berlin. Most soldiers collected souvenirs every time they took a prisoner or killed a German. Daggers, helmets, pistols, badges ... The artifacts lost their value as the American troops advanced. There were so many of them. A shirt button marked with SS runes was worth half a dollar after the early battles. A few months before the German surrender, it could barely be exchanged for 2 cigarettes. But my dad understood that all of these items would be worth their weight in gold in the long run. It was at this time that rumors spread about the atrocities committed by the Russian military against the Germans. Hitler was right to regard the Slavs as subhuman, no better than Jews. How many unfortunate women had been raped by these savages, how many fighters for the Reich were tortured and massacred, how much looting took place, encouraged by Stalin's propaganda? The US General Staff then banned the collection of souvenirs. Possession of a German watch could get you up to two months in prison. But my father, and two of his friends, had already organized a whole network that allowed them to ship their harvest to the United States.

-- Your father fought against the Germans?, Melany asked, showing a surprised look.

-- Who had any choice? It was war. Your nationality defined your camp, not your political opinions. Besides, if he hadn't come to know the Germans so well, he might not have given birth to our family tradition. His network was sufficiently well organized to also allow some officials of the Third Reich to escape. But that's another story ...

At this point in their meeting, Melany felt that she couldn't get much more out of Mitchell without arousing his suspicion. She looked at her watch and showed a look of boredom.

-- Damned traffic jams. I hadn't expected to get to Odyssey so late in the day. I was hoping to go on my way to Buffalo and spend the night in the hotel room I reserved. But I don't like driving in the dark. Do you know a good place to recommend to me?

Derek seemed to think it over.

-- There's a Comfort Inn on the highway road at the exit from town, on the north side. But that's really on the low end.

-- What makes you think I wouldn't be satisfied with that?

-- Your outfit, your bag, the watch you just looked at, Derek snorted.

-- My outfit ...?

The specialists who had organized Melany's infiltration had also taken care of her wardrobe. Warm, elegant, but discreet clothes. The eight-button mastic-colored Hugo Boss Otrenchy coat reminded those who wanted to hear that the famous couturier's brand had adorned Nazi uniforms. This was concealing a finely made sweater and a sensible skirt with a Van Laack label. Melany unbuttoned her coat as if Mitchell's thoughts had made her realize that she was no longer outside in the cold.

-- ... Who do you take me for, Mr. Mitchell?, she growled, flaunting an expression of contained fury as best she could. One of those degenerate negresses or a Brooklyn Jew who thinks they're activists by showing off in ripped jeans? I have German blood in my veins and my parents taught me that elegance is a form of respect. Your hotel will suit me very well, as long as it gives me anything a little better than a cot.

The lust in the giant's eyes that had followed her every move as she undid her coat made her regret the gesture for a moment. But he immediately recovered and nodded approvingly.

-- You're an amazing person, Fräulein Hoffmann.

-- You may call me Melany.

-- In that case, Melany, you might be able to answer my question ...

He paused to look at her, as he had done earlier on the floor below.

-- ... I don't see you as an authentic collector. What exactly did you come here for?

There was no threat in his voice, and Melany had suspected he might ask just such a question. It was nonetheless a delicate moment that she had to negotiate with the greatest finesse. She had imagined Mitchell as a rather frustrated farmer, although his information sheet conceded him an intelligence far superior to that of his clique. She was discovering a man who was even more dangerous because he knew his stuff and knew how to demonstrate his intelligence. The excuses she had made so far to justify her presence could not satisfy him for long.

Abruptly and without any sign of femininity, she lifted her sweater to show off her tattoo.

-- You know as well as I do that our country is infested with pacifists and globalists. The Jewish gangrene has spread everywhere and, even though most niggers hate them, they will always support each other against us. My family has done quite well in finance and has been safely sheltered for over a generation. Before moving back to Germany, my father approached various movements similar to yours, with the intention of making some donations. I was to spend the night in Buffalo to meet an old cousin there, before going on to Canada, where I was to meet members of the Western Guard. You happened to be on my way. Does that explanation suit you?

She pulled down the front of her sweater and waited for his reaction. Mitchell found it difficult to hide the greed that the young woman's words had just stirred up in him.

-- You're planning to make a donation to the Western Guard?

-- It all depends on what projects and infrastructure they have.

-- In my opinion, you're going to be disappointed, Mitchell sneered.

The Canadian equivalent of the American Nazi Party was a tiny organization for which the Aryan Nation had the greatest contempt. The allocation of funds to similar groups on the basis of Melany's personal judgment formed the heart of the strategy developed by Franckel and Gardner. Who can resist the promise of a donation?

-- I just want to be convinced of the merits of other causes, the young woman said.

Derek seemed to think it over.

-- There is only one cause but there are various ways of serving it. But how about discussing it longer over dinner? My wife isn't a bad cook and I'd be happy to show you some other items I have on hand, including one that might surprise you ... In the meantime, I can call the Comfort Inn and ask them to reserve the best room for you ... Without a cot, and that's a promise.

-- Chapter 4 --

Lorrie Mitchell was a plump little woman with a serious look but full of life. The wounds of time were written in wrinkles on her forehead and around her eyes, adding character to her face, which was framed in light brown hair studded with silver streaks. She had the hoarse voice of longtime smokers and wore a complicated network of tattoos on her arms ranging from the simplest, the double SS rune, to the more complex, a reproduction of the "Welcome" sign hanging at the entrance of the camp 'Auschwitz / Birkenau: "Arbeit macht frei" ... *Work makes you free.* She greeted Melany with almost subservient kindness, looking over her shoulder at Derek before shaking her hand.

-- So, you are the young lady from Lancaster that my husband has been telling me about ever since he got home from work? Please don't mind the mess. I worked all day and only had time to do a little bit of cleaning.

-- Thank you, you're very kind. It still bothers me to disturb you.

-- Not at all, Derek roared from the back of the living room. Hurry up and shut that door before we all freeze.

A young man appeared behind Lorrie Mitchell as she moved away from Melany to welcome her into her home. Apart from his eyes, which were the same brown as his mother's, he looked like Derek, whose height and build he had inherited, but not his weight. His face was pockmarked with acne scars and, and unlike his father, his hair was fairly long. He hurried up to help Melany take off her coat.

-- Welcome here, ma'am. My dad told us you are staying in Odyssey for the night. Hope you're set up comfortably.

He spoke in a monotonous tone and seemed to be pathologically shy. Melany wondered if he hadn't memorized his welcome phrase.

-- You can just call me Melany. I'm sure there's not a big age difference between us. No "ma'am" between us.

The young man blushed and stared at the tips of his shoes before stammering:

-- Me, I'm Mark and ... uh ... this is my little brother, Matthew.

A boy about ten years old rushed over to Melany and, without waiting for permission, stood on his tiptoes to kiss her cheek. He had long hair like his brother, Derek's blue eyes, and a somewhat plump figure that he would certainly have to watch out for later. From what Melany could tell, the boy had been born when Lorrie was over forty. His birth, rather late in their married life, must have come as a surprise to the Mitchells.

Melany had expected to find a nightmarish interior, but the wood-paneled living room was furnished soberly, even tastefully. A log fire crackled vigorously on the hearth of the central fireplace, giving off a good smell of pine. Two brown velvet sofas set with studs faced each other on either side of a coffee table carved from an oak log, on which a bronze sculpture of a Confederate cavalryman stood. Derek was sitting there with his feet on the table in front of a television screen on which baseball teams silently faced off. Hanging near the stairs in front of the entrance, a boar's head seemed to be watching for the arrival of newcomers. A few realistic paintings completed the decoration of the same wall, including a reproduction of a painting by Mort Kunstler depicting General Lee on horseback surrounded by his staff.

The room opened to the outside through large windows hung with heavy fringed curtains. At this hour, it was lit by a chandelier in the shape of a wagon wheel hanging from the ceiling by chains. The atmosphere was laden with various scents that were just as pleasant, ranging from dry wood to humus, including the heavy scents of home cooking.

Melany had to admit that the Mitchells were friendly, since the whole small family, except Derek, flocked around to make her feel comfortable. Lorrie came over to set down a tray with five glasses and a bottle of Southern Comfort, a whiskey with Irish roots distilled in New Orleans.

-- At our place, it's time for a little pick-me-up with the family, Derek announced. But maybe you prefer to drink something else?

-- Not at all, thank you: this suits me just fine.

Melany was surprised to see little Matthew getting his drink refilled, just like all the Mitchells. The father reached out with a toast in a gesture not unlike a Nazi salute. Everyone followed suit, including Melany.

-- Sieg Heil, he said, watching Melany, immediately imitated by his wife and children.

-- Sieg Heil, Melany said in a crisp voice before gulping down the drink.

The syrupy drink was strong and smooth, with a peachy aftertaste. She was careful not to say that, as far as she knew, no true Nazi would ever have executed a *Sieg Heil* with a drink in hand, but the most important thing was that the word *Sieg* had just been spoken. All that remained to complete her mission was to associate "Father" with the German translation of "Victory" and to understand the meaning of the phrase. However, a doubt suddenly seized her: was it really possible that she would succeed so easily where other agents more experienced than her had failed? The Mitchells might not have been the best target, and there was no indication that they had the ability to enlighten her.

A pleasant warmth radiated from her stomach and rekindled her optimism. After all, she was on the spot, Derek had believed her story and everything was going perfectly so far.

They chatted without a specific theme for about twenty minutes, with the Mitchells showing an insatiable curiosity about her present life and her past. Melany never thought she would have to answer so many questions or be scrutinized with such intensity. She almost committed the epic blunder of mentioning Harvard after Mark shyly asked her if she had graduated from college. The prestigious university had a poor reputation among nationalist extremists, who saw it as a nest of leftists dedicated to destroying the moral values that they associated with their ideology.

Barely catching herself in time, she vaguely mentioned studies in history at the University of Pittsburgh, where she had supposedly dropped out after one year. A good Nazi sympathizer like herself could not put up with the campus vibe or the student mentality for very long. Since Mark had brought up the subject, she tried to find out more about him and turned her questions on him.

-- And you -- have you studied anywhere?

The young man looked up at his father before answering.

-- I stopped after high school. My parents needed me on the farm too much.

-- And at the museum, no doubt?

-- Yes, of course, also at the museum.

-- Do you work there often?

-- No, I mostly take care of the animals.

Melany thought she saw a spark of suspicion light up in Derek's eyes and held herself back from asking any more questions. The conversation resumed its course and he showed nothing more than a distant interest in her love life when she confessed that she had not yet met the perfect mate, nor even really looked for one. Mark, on the other hand, seemed to be fascinated. Melany smiled to herself, wondering if he had a bit of a crush on her. Derek gave the signal to sit down to eat and the whole family got up at the same time.

The dining room was mostly decorated with hunting trophies. A most unpleasant sight for anyone like Melany, who loved animals. How could she swallow anything with the stuffed head of a bear above her head watching her with dead eyes? Lorrie sensed her uneasiness.

-- You don't like hunting, Melany?

-- Whatever the sport, you have to have practiced it to appreciate it, the young woman said evasively.

-- Your father never hunted animals?, Derek asked in surprise. Or anyone in your family?

-- To be honest, it's not really a family tradition. Still, I do have cousins in Montana who pride themselves on having once killed a grizzly bear ...

-- That so? Derek suddenly looked entranced. What are your cousins named?

Melany immediately sensed the danger and blamed herself terribly. What need did she have to invent this story about her cousins? She herself had never set foot in Montana and knew Kurdistan much better than that state. The Mitchells were certainly subscribers to hunting magazines that would no doubt have covered the taking of a grizzly bear. She didn't even know if this animal existed in the environment of her so-called cousins.

-- To tell the truth, I never really did believe them, she smiled. In my opinion, their grizzly bear was more of a weasel, otherwise they would have rushed to send us the picture.

The Mitchells laughed heartily and Melany sighed to herself.

-- You see the bear's head above you?, Derek asked again. It was my father who killed it. But take note -- it was an old-fashioned hunt, without a sniper rifle, not like the wimps do today. He found himself alone with the beast, after three days and three nights of stalking it in the heart of Alaska. The recoil he took before killing it would probably have taken his shoulder and left arm off if the cold hadn't cauterized his wound by the time he reached the nearest hospital to get stitched up ...

His gaze became dreamy.

-- ... Me, that's one critter I would like to take down myself one day. A tiger, a panther, a mountain lion ...

-- There are no tigers or panthers in the United States, except for in zoos, Mark pointed out, gazing down at his plate.

Melany once again noted the nervousness of the Mitchells' oldest son. Derek wasn't the type to put up with contradiction, especially in front of a guest. The latter replied with kindness, however:

-- That's why I'll treat myself to a trip to Africa, or maybe India, one day before I die.

-- Yeah, but there ain't no animals there that you want to hunt, scoffed Lorrie, coming back from the kitchen carrying the first courses.

Derek laughed, a wicked glint in his eyes. Without being charming, his rough features and well-trimmed mustache gave him a virile look from another era. His face was an open book and no one would have dared to upset him when he displayed that expression.

A delicious aroma arose from the corn buns and meatloaf that had just been placed on the table. Despite her tension, Melany discovered a sharp appetite, encouraged by the enticing smells. Too bad about the bear head above her. The animal had long been dead, and failing to honor this succulent dinner would not bring it back to life. She hoped to be served immediately, but Derek crossed his hands above his plate and closed his eyes.

The family was about to say grace.

-- Who wants to begin?, the father asked.

-- It all depends, Lorrie said, glancing over to Melany's side. Our guest hasn't been initiated into our rituals.

Derek lifted his head from his plate to examine the young woman.

-- Not to pry into your life, but what faith were you raised up in?

-- That's not prying, she replied flatly to give herself time to think ...

According to the FBI sheet, the Mitchells were former Protestant converts to Odinism, a new form of paganism that was now spreading rapidly. Like many residents of Odyssey and the surrounding area, they associated Christ with the resurrection of the Viking god Odin, whom some also recycled in German pronunciation, or Wotan.

Hitler had evidently have been a follower of this form of polytheism, which placed warrior virtues among its highest values.

Melany was careful not to admit that, without being a complete atheist, she considered herself to be an agnostic and had never set foot in a temple or a church since her parents' divorce. They themselves, when they lived together, laughingly claimed that they were Sunday believers and only went to church out of habit or for the sake of appearances. It would have been a delicate matter for a career officer belonging to the world of diplomacy to admit a lack of faith.

-- ... I'm an Evangelical Lutheran, of course, she finally added.

-- Perfect!, Derek agreed. So, I'll let you say grace.

Oh, fuck me!, Melany thought, having no idea what words to say. She stammered hastily:

-- Thank you for the honor, but we were never very conformist in my family. We prefer prayers that come from the heart to those that are from set rituals.

-- Just like us, Lorrie smiled, taking her left hand as Mark sat to her right, intertwining with his fingers. Matthew and Derek followed suit and the five formed a circle.

-- Go ahead, don't be embarrassed. My husband will conclude the prayer, as he always does.

Melany had no choice. She closed her eyes and intoned:

-- Lord, thank you for your kindness and for allowing me to meet such warm hosts.

Bless them and bless the meal that will follow ...

She felt sheepish, and not at all at home. The slight euphoria instilled by the alcohol had subsided. She paused as she searched for words, and Derek took the opportunity to take over.

-- And may Odin, from the heights of Valhalla, protect our guest and allow her to perform her task. Odin, enlighten her heart without testing her faith. Put her on the path of truth and help her in her choices. May her generosity not be in vain.

The reference to donations from Herr Hoffmann, Melany's alleged father, was obvious. But the prayer wasn't over yet. Derek lowered his tone in respect and his voice grew more subtle as he changed register.

-- Lord Odin, aid our generation in its just fight so that our children no longer have to suffer from corruption and decadence. By your power, bless our master thinker, Adolph Hitler. May his projects see the light of day, in accordance with the destiny you have traced for us.

-- *"Dann sei es"*, or "So be it", whispered all the members of the Mitchell family in German.

Derek opened his eyes wide and focused on Melany.

-- You're not too surprised?

Her throat was mostly tight and she had lost all appetite, but tried hard to answer casually.

-- I didn't know you were Odinists. This is also the first time that I've heard "Amen" replaced by its German translation.

-- *Amen* comes from Hebrew, Lorrie explained. Which just goes to show how much the Jews have polluted our culture.

-- The Führer was the first to denounce Roman Christianity as an extension of Jewish subversion, Derek added as his wife sliced up the meatloaf. He allowed us to understand that Christ was not God, but an Aryan and therefore an incarnation of Odin or Wotan. He also knew that Catholic priests were no better than rabbis. Breeds driven only by power and greed ... Would you like a beer, Melany?

She agreed and Derek ordered his oldest son to bring a pack of Coors back from the refrigerator. Matthew, who had been silent until then, now took the opportunity to ask Melany how Lancaster was, whether there were any movie theaters there, and if she went to them often? She didn't have time to wonder about the question when Derek glared furiously at his son.

-- Not very often, unfortunately. Why, aren't there any theaters in this area?

-- The closest theater is in Lakeview, Lorrie explained as Mark put the beers on the table. That's 35 miles from here. That means an hour and a half round trip, and the expense of ten dollars a head, just to see some Hollywood-made drivel that will be free on TV six months later.

-- I'd like to go, my friends all go, the young boy scowled.

Melany thought for a few moments before making a suggestion.

-- I'm not expected in Buffalo until late afternoon. If you know a movie you would like to see and your parents agree, then I could go with you to the first screening tomorrow, right after lunch.

-- Oh, yeah, I'd love that!, the young boy answered excitedly.

-- And I've told you to shut up when we have guests, Derek thundered suddenly, his face flushed.

A heavy silence fell over the table. Melany noticed Lorrie's cautious glance and Mark's increased nervousness. Not knowing what attitude to adopt, she cut herself a small portion of cornbread.

-- Forgive me, it was just to thank you for your welcome. I really didn't want to interfere ...

Derek regained his composure as quickly as he had lost it.

-- It's me who should apologize ... he growled, chewing on a first bite of meatloaf. It's generous of you, but we prefer to keep children away from all the subversions tolerated by the government. And then, in my family, we're not allowed to speak at the table until we've said grace.

Lorrie nodded darkly. Apart from the paramount questions of their family life, she didn't always seem to agree with her husband, but she knew how to look good in front of guests. Melany changed the subject.

-- Your grace? Well, now I'm just curious. Where are your religious ceremonies held in your community?

Derek's expression changed completely. He seemed eager to answer this kind of questions.

-- There are several churches in Odyssey. The Amish have theirs, a very respectable place that they invite us to from time to time. There's also the Episcopal church and that of the Primitive Baptists, not to mention the church of the Zion Christians, but that one caught fire last summer; people are still wondering how ...

He cleared his throat and gave a hoarse laugh, looking at his wife and eldest son as if seeking their agreement.

-- And then, of course, there is ours. It's not exactly a church, but a place of contemplation fully ready to welcome the divine message ...

-- Odin's, or what other one?, Melany said, trying to stay as neutral as possible.

The look Lorrie gave him told her not to go down that path.

-- Is there some irony in your question?, Derek asked with his face closed before gulping down another gigantic bite of meatloaf.

-- Melany's just curious, his wife interjected. Which is quite understandable. I don't think there are many Odinists in Lancaster.

-- None, as far as I know. You're the first ones I've ever met. And to be honest, I do find it fascinating.

Melany's reply relaxed Derek, who seemed to think it over and suddenly asked:

-- How about staying in Odyssey one more day?

-- I'm not sure I can, although I find your town really lovely ...

-- We meet in the late afternoon, just before dusk, once a week, on Saturdays. In other words, tomorrow. If you can handle one more night in your small hotel, you are more than welcome.

Melany took her time answering. Especially not to give the impression that she was hoping for just such an invitation. She finally agreed with the shy smile of someone who had just received an unexpected token of acceptance.

-- So it's settled, then: tomorrow evening, you are our guest.

The meal continued without anything disturbing the warm family atmosphere. After dessert -- a homemade *Afpfelstrudel* made from fruit from the orchard -- Melany offered to help her clear the table, but Lorrie flatly refused.

-- I promised to show you some interesting items, Derek Mitchell blurted out as Matthew walked back to his room and Mark went to help his mother in the kitchen. Would you still like that?

***

Part of the barn was used to store sheaves while awaiting threshing, as well as oats, wheat and hay for the animals. The Mitchells owned a dozen cows whose milk they sold. Melany remembered that it was there, among the bags stored there, that the FBI had discovered the weapons that led to the arrest of Derek and his eldest son. She wondered how great Mark's complicity was. The young man looked more terrified of his father than a fanatic Nazi and far too shy and fearful to be plotting anything. Nevertheless, he belonged to this dangerous community which advocated a hateful mixture of Gothic beliefs and open hatred.

Melany was suddenly ashamed of the tattoos that stained her body and had an irresistible urge to scratch them off. That impulse brought back distant memories, which she probed nostalgically.

Her parents' Jewish neighbors during the time they were living in Berlin had introduced her to some of their ceremonies and had more than once invited her to spend Shabbat with their family. The Goldmanns were cheerful and friendly people, infectiously optimistic despite the tragedies suffered by their relatives. Out of the previous generation, only the paternal grandfather had survived the death camps. He spoke little but Melany had learned that his first wife, his two parents, his five children, and three of his cousins had all perished at Sobibor. He had since rebuilt a family, but on some occasions, he would go whole evenings without saying a word, staring into the void, compulsively scratching his left forearm through the sleeve of his shirt.

Melany silently asked forgiveness from old Mr. Goldmann, who must be long dead. *But it's for a good cause,* she added, smiling at the blurry image of the tormented face she had just conjured up.

After walking through the barn, Derek pushed open a door that opened into a small office space.

-- The government wanted to put a hold on me not too long ago, he sneered, pointing to a chair. Apparently those bastards can't read the Second Amendment[(6)] to the Constitution. They had a warrant so I couldn't stop them from searching the barn, but I didn't take a step back from them. I have nothing to hide, not me. I'm not a politician. The boxes of grenades they

[6] The Second Amendment guarantees Americans the right to self-defense and therefore to own weapons.

seized were from World War II. Collectibles, I told them! They didn't want to know anything.

On the wall hung a poster reproducing the entrance to Auschwitz / Birkenau with its famous slogan grimly hanging above the gate: *Arbeit macht frei.* In front of it stood an Adolph Hitler, in uniform.

-- Do you know where that photograph comes from?, Mitchell continued. From Jakarta, in Indonesia. A friend brought it back from a visit he made last year. The painting was on display in a very popular museum. He couldn't believe it. Me neither. Just imagine: more than two hundred million Muslims spread out over a thousand islands who have never seen a Jew in their life, and yet they hate them! Isn't that proof that this infernal creature carries evil and that it must be gotten rid of at all cost?

-- As if there were need for proof, Melany sighed, just as puzzled as she was uncomfortable. This sudden connection with Islam in Derek's office echoed the words of the Daesh terrorists.

-- You want me to tell you a secret?, Derek asked. The Islamists are the real fighters today. They just lack the discipline and technology of a true civilization. But they will get there, trust me. Al-Qaida and Daesh, those were just the first stirrings ...

He paused once more and Melany felt that he wished he could say more. Something was holding him back. The words in Derek's mouth expressed more than a hypothesis or a fantasy. But his anger at the table had taught her that he shouldn't be rushed. She just contented herself with observing:

-- Nazism and Islamism ... Are you sure that such an alliance is even possible?

-- There can be no bad alliance against such a treacherous enemy, which creeps in everywhere and destroys all morals for its own benefit. Hitler wanted Stalin's skin, but that didn't prevent him from signing the German-Soviet pact. He hated Lenin just as much, but he would quote him. He wrote that you have to rally some useful idiots for any cause. Well, there they are. All that remains is to recruit the right ones from among their billion and a half believers.

Prior to being entrusted with the missions that had taken her to Turkey and Kurdistan, Melany had undergone comprehensive counterterrorism training that included a theoretical approach to Salafism and the Shiite hegemony promoted by Iran.

Her boss, as well as Franckel and Gardner, were right to worry about the eventual arrival of a leader capable of uniting the worst extremes. It was still necessary to know which movements were likely to join together.

-- I'll confess something to you, Mr. Mitchell. You do surprise me. Before getting to know you, I had a number of preconceptions. Most of all, I didn't expect to meet someone so cultured in ...

-- ... in a God-forsaken place like Odyssey? Is that why you were going to waste your time on the other side of the border? Seriously, if your dad gave you that idea, then he really doesn't know who you might be dealing with.

-- That's why he entrusted me with the task of investigating various organizations.

Mitchell opened a drawer in the glass-topped desk he was sitting behind and pulled out a packet of Marlboros that he handed to Melany. She shook her head. He lit a cigarette from which he greedily drew a first puff.

-- You're right. Very bad for the lungs. My wife stopped when they found she had fucking cancer.

-- Really? I'm sorry to hear that.

He replied with an evasive shrug.

-- A year of chemo, but we had good insurance. She's in remission now, so don't bother making a big deal out of it. How about getting to the heart of the matter? Your father commissioned you to distribute donations to organizations like ours. How much money might that be?

Melany was once again in a minefield.

-- Before I tell you that, Mr. Mitchell, you did promise to show me things that might surprise me. I can't see anything in this room ...

A predatory smile spread over Derek's face. The office lighting cast a shadow from his mustache over his upper lip and accentuated the angularity of his features as well as his menace. Melany shivered slightly.

-- Giving, giving, he sneered. Either way, that was my intention ... Here, you'll see.

He took a key out of the pocket of his heavy denim pants and opened a second drawer from which he pulled out a framed photograph. It showed Hitler sitting down in a Tyrolean hat, leaning against the railing of the Berghof, his Alpine retreat, his eyes lost in the distance.

-- It's an original, Derek commented proudly. Look especially at the signature at the bottom right of the photo.

Melany wondered once more where Derek's father had been able to unearth such treasures. She leaned down and deciphered the photographer's fairly readable handwriting.

-- Heinrich Hoffmann, she read in a low voice.

-- Hitler's personal photographer, Derek pointed out. Was he a member of your family?

A terrible coincidence and mistake on the part of the FBI and CIA, which should have been able to inform her that her cover name associated her with a Nazi official so close to the Führer. How could she have known? Her knowledge in this area was limited to common knowledge, plus a few details useful for her mission. She thought as quickly as she could.

-- It's not really that much of a coincidence, she said as casually as possible. There are tens of thousands of Hoffmanns in Germany and undoubtedly hundreds in the United States. My father vaguely told me about a Heinrich when I was younger, a very distant relative he said, but I really can't remember any more than that.

Mitchell must have been satisfied with his answer, for he nodded before putting the frame back in the drawer and pulling out another, noticeably larger one.

-- And here is the highlight of my collection. I believe that this is the only evidence we have of a certain form of thought from the Führer. It's quite rare that I show it, because not everyone is quite ready to receive this message yet. Some might take it the wrong way and turn away from the cause.

The canvas depicted a blonde Madonna and Baby Jesus, in a bucolic setting furnished with daisies against the backdrop of a wheat field. It was a well-known work by Hitler, dated 1913, when he was still dreaming of entering the Academy of Fine Arts in Vienna and becoming an architect. His admission to that prestigious Vienna school would have changed the face of the world, but he failed the entrance exam.

Melany was familiar with this painting, which had been seized by the US military and had been part of the national heritage ever since. She was about to ask Derek how he could claim to own the original of such a famous work when her gaze was caught by the child's face.

This other Christ produced by Hitler did not have the features of a baby, nor the pretty blue eyes that she remembered from visiting the World War II Museum in Natick, Massachusetts. Instead of eyes, the Führer had painted black slitted marbles with a cat's yellow iris. From the head rose two small bumps which, as they grew out, turned into horns. The child's lips were curled up in a wicked, vicious and terrifying smirk.

-- Hitler often had nightmares, Derek explained while stroking the frame mechanically. He is said to have painted dozens of portraits similar to this one and apocalyptic scenes that he was quick to destroy when he began his political career. In his youth, he belonged to various occult groups. A passion that many historians dispute. But a few, and not the least of them, claim that he was initiated into certain forms of magic.

-- What makes you think this painting isn't a fake?, Melany in fascination.

-- Nothing, Derek admitted. Except that my father was certain of its value. And on that point, I have never doubted him ...

Upon fixing on the terrifying gaze of the child, Melany felt a nasty shiver pass through her. If the work was authentic, it was premonitory and presaged the fantasies of a sick brain that would soon burn with fever. Derek interrupted his thoughts to show his main preoccupation.

-- Well, then, your donation: How much might that be?

Melany made up a number and told him. Derek Mitchell nodded thoughtfully and put the frame away.

***

The room was quite large for a hotel of this class. Melany had had the choice between a view of the parking lot or a window overlooking a factory and she had preferred the row of cars to the pollution fumes. Once the door was closed and the "Do Not Disturb" sign was hanging from the handle, she took off her boots and threw herself on the bed where she spent several minutes lying down doing nothing other than looking at the sprinkler system embedded in the ceiling.

Once her heartbeat calmed and her breathing came back to normal, she straightened up and began to take off her clothes. It was past ten and she had felt enough emotions for a first day. She only regretted not having had the opportunity to spend some time alone with little Matthew. So much can be learned from the mouth of a child ...

She took a quick shower and smeared some of the soothing cream on her tattoos before returning to the bedroom and turning her cell back on.

It was a new device, artificially aged, whose memory contained numbers and addresses in Germany, as well as those of an imaginary family. A work tool designed to prevent any compromising mishaps.

Melany hadn't expected to receive any messages, so she was surprised and delighted to find a word of encouragement from Garroni, from an unidentified number, listed as *Vater*, or 'Father" in German.

Upon taking possession of the room, she had only put her suitcases on the luggage rack before refreshing herself and fixing her makeup. The supple midnight blue Delsey contained winter pants, shoes and sweaters. The clothes rack housed a few dresses, including one of refined elegance by Betty Barclay that she had never worn before.

Since she had gained the opportunity to stay at Odyssey for at least one more night, it would be better to hang her dresses in the closet and organize herself a bit.

She undid the zipper of the clothes carrier and was immediately on her guard. The Betty Barclay dress, which she was sure she had put away last, was not at the top, but instead a woolen turtleneck sheath that should have been at the bottom.

Melany closed her eyes and tried to remember precisely how she had packed her bags. She reviewed her every move again, reconstructed her logic, and had no further doubts.

Someone had slipped into her room and searched it from top to bottom. Amateur work.

-- Chapter 5 --

Region of Aceh -- Indonesia

Eleven and a half weeks earlier.

The sunny days were exceptional during the rainy season, but the sky had been barely overcast since this morning, nature seemed to be celebrating and everyone in the village wore on their faces the joyful smiles of believers convinced that they had been blessed.

There was talk of having a small ceremony in the evening and of perhaps sacrificing a goat and some chickens. Some men had gone in search of a sago palm to prepare for the feast. The flour obtained from it was used to bake bread, and its leaves added flavor to any dish. The village chief had gazed at the sky for a long time before nodding his approval, which had elicited cries of joy from the emissaries of the small neighboring communities who had come to consult him. The Islam practiced in this region of the island, despite its purity, which would have satisfied even the most devout believers, still accommodated local superstitions and much older traditions. The sages claimed that thanking the One God with devotion for His blessings did not prevent them from practicing some rituals to ward off ghosts and other evil beings.

As he climbed the front steps of his *panggung*, Darwis was reassured to find Adhi, who was rocking back and forth sitting with his legs in the air, as he often did. The boy had become a young man. He stopped moving when he saw his adoptive father and smiled at him as he greeted him with a warm "*ayah*"[(7)]. Darwis smiled back at him. The child had grown up so fast that he sometimes wondered where the years had gone.

---

[7] Papa, in Indonesian.

-- There's going to be a festival tonight, he said. Are you happy about that?

Adhi nodded emphatically before shutting himself into his silence and resuming his swaying.

Darwis turned to greet a neighbor who never failed to say a few kind words to him as she passed the *panggung*. For months she had stubbornly brought him eggs and fruit to thank him for saving her daughter from a bad fever. Most of the villagers paid him that way when they couldn't do otherwise. But Darwis didn't need much to feel blessed, even though his faith had been shattered by the disappearance of his family in the cataclysm that left as much bruising in the land of Aceh as in the hearts of its inhabitants.

Allah had taken from him two beings more precious than his own life and entrusted him with the life of this boy in exchange. Ever since then, the survivor had tried in vain to understand the designs of the Creator of the Universe who had inflicted this ordeal on him. But he was a doctor, had chosen this path out of passion and pure humanity, and the little orphan he had taken in was unable to cope on his own. As for entrusting him to one of the few institutions in the region capable of taking care of him, Darwis knew that, due to their lack of funds, they resembled prisons at best, and places of death at worst.

The sun was already low in the sky but continued to cast its rays through a scattering of clouds of shaded colors ranging from pale pink to bright purple. Darwis had finished his day. Tired but happy that it had passed without any noticeable drama, he allowed himself a few moments to sit down not far from his adopted son.

Tangse was a large village lost in the middle of the forest halfway between the two sea coasts of Sumatra. Darwis had chosen to settle there after the tsunami had stripped him of all his possessions. When he left Banda Aceh, three-quarters of which had been destroyed by the cataclysm, he had hoped to forget and perhaps one day heal from his wounds. Adhi's presence by his side had made it more difficult for him to face the superstitions of the locals. The Sumatran people drew little distinction between emotional turmoil, madness, and demonic possession. But in Tangse, they needed a doctor, and the villagers quickly got used to Darwis and Adhi's presence, even if they avoided getting too close to the latter.

With the help of an Australian NGO, Darwis had founded a small clinic, which had always been full since its opening. No three days ever went by without his having to set a fracture, treat a bite, or stop the onset of gangrene. The six hundred inhabitants of Tangse were hunters or peasants, and injuries outnumbered illnesses.

With the exception of two families who were known for their malice and who had nicknamed Adhi *haram zadah* (bastard child), he was referred to as *anak pungut* (foster child) and, among those closest to Doctor Haikal, the few who had secretly benefited from his healing powers had given him the adjective *ajaib*, which means "magic" in Indonesian.

Because Adhi had *the* gift. He was an authentic *dukun,* a *tabib* who had come to earth by divine grace to heal, alleviate pain and suffering. Unfortunately, in such a primitive environment, it was better not to disclose the abnormal faculties of the child, now locked up in an adult body.

Darwis was especially worried that word of his gift would reach the ears of Imam Tuanku Nan Rao of the Baitul Taqwa Mosque. He was a fanatic who advocated a return to the most rigorous form of Islam and never forgot in his sermons to point the finger at the superstitions that filled the hearts of most of the inhabitants of Tangse. He and Tuanku had never gotten along. He had even threatened him with a fatwa if Darwis persisted in opening his clinic on Fridays, a day devoted to prayer and not to the care of the flesh, which was putrid by the will of Allah. Darwis had had to yield.

It had taken the unexpected intervention of the police, who were investigating a completely different matter, to prevent the stoning in the public square of a young woman who had been accused of witchcraft and adultery. Her only mistake had been to offer a herbal concoction she knew about in order to relieve the headaches of a male neighbor who had recently lost his wife. The young woman, even though she was single, had to be evacuated to Medan, the nearest town, and Tuanku had not been angry. As soon as the police left, he attacked the widower and had him beaten with bamboo. Evil tongues whispered that he had had his sights set on the young woman, but no one dared say it out loud.

Darwis had no difficulty imagining what would become of Adhi and himself if the Imam heard that his adopted son had, through the simple contact of his hands, alleviated pain, straightened scoliosis, speeded the healing of wounds, and reduced edemas.

However, there were times when he took the risk of revealing Adhi's special talent, since he had no other choice. The clinic had few medicines, and no modern equipment except an old X-ray machine, and Darwis had to wait several weeks at times to receive the antibiotics and painkillers he had ordered from Jakarta.

When he had been living in the village for barely a year, the youngest child of a couple he knew had fallen into a pond swarming with leeches. The parents, who were appallingly poor even for the region, had waited too long to bring the child to the clinic. The bites had become infected and the purulence was on the verge of sepsis, since Darwis didn't have enough antibiotics. He had almost given up, sick at heart, when Adhi, whom he believed to have remained in the *panggung*, appeared, silent as usual, his eyes riveted on the shivering body of the young child.

In desperation, the doctor asked the neighbors who had gathered around the bed to go outside and, left alone with the parents, asked them if they could keep a secret.

-- I might have a way to save your child. Nothing is certain, but it is necessary to try. Except, if I reveal it, I will put myself and my son in danger.

-- Do whatever you can, Doctor, the mother pleaded.

-- Can you swear, on what is most sacred to you, that you will never reveal to anyone what is going to happen now?

-- May Shaytan come out of Hell and come and tear me and all my family members from the earth if we ever reveal anything to anyone. Swearing on the Qur'an, your secret will be buried with us in the grave, Doctor Haikal. But save him.

-- A life for a life. I will risk mine for your child.

Darwis made a sign to Adhi, who didn't need words to understand, and he approached the prostrate child. For nearly an hour, he ran his hands over the affected parts, skimming over them without ever touching them. After twenty minutes, the fever subsided. By the end of the session, Adhi had practically lost consciousness. But the dark, smelly stains lining the wounds had begun to recede. The little child, although he had undoubtedly been doomed, recovered in less than twenty-four hours and the grateful parents had kept it a secret to this day. It was a miracle. The miracle of the *magic child*.

Nevertheless, they asked Darwis to help them again a few months later, when a cousin almost bled to death after a miscarriage. And then another time, when a hunter in their area had returned from the land of the Flower Men with his body pierced with poisoned arrows. But this time, Adhi had refused to intervene and the hunter died poisoned by the strychnine that the tribe knew how to extract from a shrub. At that time, Darwis hadn't understood why. Insisting on it with Adhi would have been pointless. And besides, healing was never a certainty.

Darwis had thus helped some nearby families, but always in the greatest secrecy. People he trusted, people he knew he could count on to be discreet. He never charged his patients when the *magic child* intervened. It was an additional guarantee of silence for him in a land where superstition took precedence over everything else. One does not betray a man who gives health, whereas some might have had fewer scruples about revealing his secret if they had had to pay for it.

Few were the refusals of Adhi, who seemed to feel the relief of an inner pain when he made use of his gifts. After two incidents similar to the first, Darwis had come to the conclusion that he did not like healing hunters.

The doctor had never really managed to communicate with him. There were no books on the condition translated into his language, and his rather rudimentary knowledge of English would not have enabled him to understand such complicated texts. He had nevertheless admitted that Adhi was in pain, locked inside himself as in a prison of flesh, without many ways to express himself.

If the boy understood the gist of what his adoptive father was trying to tell him, he hardly ever answered. His gaze, when not empty of emotion, expressed a pain so deep that it seemed to overflow his soul. The slightest unexpected incident set off a crisis that could last a long time. He then had to stay by his side and repeat the words of comfort, always the same ones, over and over again, until he regained his serenity.

So, Darwis would regularly invent new ailments for himself and allow Adhi to heal him. And when the latter, realizing that his foster father was pretending to be in pain, refused to deal with him with a stubborn nod, Darwis set off in search of a sick or injured animal. Many stray goats, dogs and cats had been saved without their owners knowing about it. These were Adhi's rare happy moments.

Just before sunset, the women piled logs in the central village square and lit large fires. Nature had been particularly lenient this year, allowing crops to be irrigated sparingly, preventing the overflowing of the surrounding rivers and allowing days of respite like today. In order to give thanks for these blessings, the schoolchildren had memorized a poem by Raden Mas Noto Soeroto praising the Most High, which they were to recite that same evening.

In Tangse, many preferred these spontaneous parties, organized in the middle of small houses with red roofs scattered among the mangroves, to evenings spent in front of communal television screens. That was the case with Darwis, who was very happy to accompany Adhi. The young man was particularly calm and peaceful when he heard music, with a preference for soft melodies and certain chants from the sacred sphere.

As night fell, the villagers flocked to the large lights that had been arranged around the wood fires. Those festive scents that accompanied the great moments of the community were in the air. The aroma of grilled carp on the embers. Chickens cut up and marinated in a brew of aromatic herbs and *kaloupilé* peppers, *soto à la mode de Médan*, not to mention the *pempek* that added its hint of vinegar to the scent of mangoes marinated in chives. Each participant brought what they were able to offer and share.

Darwis, for his part, had brought the haunch of a kid that a patient from a nearby village had given him the day before. Rama Raja, the butcher, thanked him warmly before grabbing it and placing it on the big grill where the fat of several animals was already crackling.

-- You're going to eat well tonight, the doctor said to his adopted son.

Darwis had not remarried, although he had been introduced to just about every single woman and widow in the area. He was not a very good cook, and it was usually a neighbor who cooked their dinner. That was a great help, except that she had a heavy hand with the spices. The doctor had never managed to make her understand that he and Adhi probably had a more sensitive palate than she did. Sometimes it was impossible for them to swallow more than three bites.

The village chief, Joko Mawardi, planted himself in front of the small assembly to begin his speech, which would lead, as usual, to a sermon.

-- My friends, my brothers, he began, we have just sacrificed, like every day, to the ritual of *al-Maghrib*[8] and here we are gathered to celebrate together ...

He paused suddenly to look in the direction of the entrance to the village, an open area amidst mangroves and mangroves. The people of Tangse and the few visitors from the surrounding area were mostly sitting on their heels in the Indonesian way and staring at him as they waited for the rest. Some turned around, including Darwis.

He froze as he recognized Imam Tuanku Nan Rao striding forward, accompanied by a group of strangers. Next to Tuanku, a tall man dressed in black was supporting another by the waist to help him walk. A dozen individuals armed with Kalashnikovs and machetes served as their escort, as well as two foreigners dressed in European clothes, their pants stained with mud up to their mid-calves.

-- Clear the way!, cried Beugla Tuanku upon getting close to the assembly. Let us pass, hurry up.

The presence of the Imam at a ceremony he would have described as pagan was already exceptional. That he was accompanied by such a group necessarily

[8] One of the five daily Muslim prayers recited in response to the call of the Muezzin.

made his presence dangerous. Darwis expected the worst. His fears turned to terror when Tuanku called out his name.

-- Is Haikal among you?

A worried whisper ran through the villagers. The more distant ones, who had remained in the shadows, moved furtively away. The imam was not liked by everyone, but he did wield authority over the majority of them. Everyone dreaded his rages. Since the second mosque was further away, it was in Baitul Taqwa that most assembled in on Fridays.

Darwis stood up and walked over to the group, recovering his medical instincts.

-- That's me. What's going on?

Tuanku stepped aside to let the man in black, who was still supporting his companion, reach him. Darwis had seen his face somewhere before, but couldn't quite put a name on him. His features, which were European-appearing except for his slanted eyes and full black beard, were not easily forgotten. He was wearing a black headband on his forehead and a *kukri*, the traditional Indonesian knife, on his belt. The strangers were tall, but he was still several inches taller.

-- Are you the doctor? This man is injured, he needs help immediately.

He spoke in a loud voice, tinged with an indefinable accent, which carried a long way. In a flash of memory, Darwis recognized him.

It was Habib Saragih, the legendary leader of the new GAM.

-- This way, Darwis invited him, heading in the direction of the clinic, followed by Adhi.

***

The man lying on the treatment table was gasping from pain. He had been in pain from the two gunshot wounds, one in his shoulder blade and the second in the fat of his thigh, for several hours now. Saragih had helped the doctor lay him down, his feet slightly raised so that his brain could get as much blood as possible. One of the projectiles had narrowly missed his femoral artery but had come out of the muscle, leaving two neat holes that would be easy to disinfect and cauterize. The bullet that had lodged in his shoulder bone was more of a problem. Darwis was not at all equipped for such an intervention. He told Saragih this.

-- He's lost a lot of blood and I don't have the necessary instruments to extract them. He should be taken to Medan hospital.

-- Out of the question, replied the giant with the black band.

-- His life is in danger, Darwis insisted.

-- Yours, too, if you don't do what is necessary to save him.

The doctor shuddered and his hand began to shake. Coming from someone else's mouth, he would have taken the threat as a bit of harsh language. That was common in the Aceh region. But Saragih and his men, who were waiting in the room reserved for patients along with the two strangers, were preceded by a reputation as ruthless guerrillas. It was unusual, and all the more strange, that their bloody journey led them to Tangse.

-- I'll try everything, Darwis promised in a voice as firm as he could. But I won't be responsible for anything if the bleeding gets worse. First, it is necessary to soothe the pain.

Saragih nodded, and Darwis grabbed a syringe and filled it with morphine.

The GAM, or *Gerakan Aceh Merdeka,* was an independence movement that had arisen under the Dutch occupation just before World War One. Surviving years of struggle against colonization, the organization had evolved into fundamentalism and had been calling for Aceh's separation from the government in Jakarta for the past two decades. Their plan was to impose the strictest form of Muslim law, or sharia, such as enforced in Iran or Saudi Arabia.

Dissolved on several occasions, the GAM had been able to rise from its ashes each time, officially ceasing to exist in 2005 following a peace agreement negotiated with the government. Aceh had then gained partial autonomy and many rules emanating from sharia were enforced there. Women and minorities suffered terribly, but terrorist attacks targeting the army and the civilian population had declined in number, suggesting that the GAM had changed its ways.

That was without taking Saragih's real intentions into account ...

In reality, partial autonomy was not enough for his fighters, and the separatist organization had once again gone underground under his leadership. It was rumored that they had received considerable financial aid, which the Jakarta government preferred to deny. They appeared and disappeared as they pleased among the population of the island. The jungle was their refuge. And if their recourse to violence had been rare, it was, in the opinion of some, the reflection of a new strategy which, in the long term, would prove to be dangerous.

Habib Saragih was between twenty-five and thirty years old. No one knew where he had been born or who his parents were. There was a legend that he had killed them with his own hands when he was a teenager. He had then supposedly taken refuge in the jungle, where he survived for years among tigers and orangutans before recruiting his current fighters one by one and resuscitating the GAM.

Some claimed he was a ghost, spat out from the bowels of hell. In the hierarchy of terrifying entities, the ghost held first place in Sumatra. He was not known to have a wife or companion. He did not have any children. His men had given him the title of "Sheikh", like Bin Laden, and said that he was his Indonesian counterpart.

Whether a legend or a formidable man living up to his reputation, he was now in the clinic, alongside Darwis and Adhi.

The injured man's features relaxed as soon as the doctor injected him with the morphine. Darwis then proceeded to clean his lesions and sew up the wounds on his thigh before injecting him with an antibiotic. It took him about twenty minutes. With the heat adding to his nervous tension, he was sweating profusely and was forced to wipe his forehead regularly.

-- Help me put him on his side and hold him tight, he asked Saragih forcefully.

He wasn't the kind of man to take orders, even from a doctor, but the wounded man had been drained of blood and Darwis had no time to put on gloves. With a sudden gesture, the sheikh swiveled the chest of his companion, who let out a cry.

-- Slowly! Now make sure he can't move his shoulder anymore: this is a delicate moment.

Darwis commanded the wounded man's attention:

-- This might still be painful, despite the morphine. Do you want a piece of wood or a piece of rag to bite into?

-- He doesn't need it!, Saragih said. Do your job, and be quick about it.

The doctor grabbed a scalpel from the instrument tray and began to make an angled incision into the injured man's shoulder in order to access the bullet more easily. He barely moaned when the blade made its way through the network of nerves, which were particularly dense in this part of the body. The projectile, crushed against the bone, came into view. It had lodged in a protrusion of the scalene muscle, dangerously close to the scapular artery. The man had been twice lucky, escaping a fatal hemorrhage by a millimeter. But Darwis had had enough experience to know that this kind of extraction was dangerous, bordering on the impossible. He sighed and let the bloodied instrument fall back into the tray.

-- I really can't do anything more! He should be put under general anesthesia and the bleeding stopped during the extraction. The artery might rupture if I try under these conditions.

-- And what would happen then?

-- This man would bleed to death in less than a minute. It would be immediate death.

Saragih seemed to think it over, not releasing his companion's shoulder. After a moment, he nodded to one of the men standing guard outside the treatment room. The latter moved closer to the operating table and abruptly planted the barrel of his weapon between the doctor's ribs. Darwis let out a shout of surprise.

-- Now listen to me very carefully, Saragih said sweetly. You're going do whatever you can to get that bullet out. If it is Allah's will that Banyu should become a martyr, who are we to oppose it? Only you and your son will follow him, and I cannot guarantee that the seven gates of heaven will open up for you. Do you want to live? Then do your work and pray for its success. Now hurry up!

-- I ... I can't operate on him with a weapon resting on my stomach, Darwis stammered.

The sheikh nodded and his henchman took a step back.

Darwis could hardly breathe and his heart was beating far too fast. He had the greatest difficulty controlling his hands. If he tore the bullet out a little too quickly, the artery would open, spurting out blood until the injured man was completely emptied. The result would be the same if he made a twisting movement one millimeter wrong. There wasn't even a one-in-a-hundred chance that he would complete the operation without killing his patient. The extraction forceps trembled between his fingers as he approached the wound held open by a retractor.

It was then that Adhi joined him.

Until that moment, the young man had remained standing, frozen against the edge of the operating table, silent as usual. With a wave of his hand, he indicated to Darwis that he wanted to take care of the injured man. He told him to stay away.

-- What's going on?, Saragih growled.

The doctor obviously had to make a decision. He really didn't have a choice. On the one hand, there was a great risk of exposing the young man, but on the other hand he was almost certain to be executed if he couldn't save his patient. The wounded man began to moan again. The effect of the morphine was already starting to wear off. He pulled the clamp away from the man's shoulder in order to let Adhi extend his hands.

And, once again, the miracle happened.

In a few seconds, the trickle of blood dried up. The injured man immediately relaxed, showing that he was no longer in pain. Darwis firmly grasped the tip of the flattened projectile that had become embedded in the bone. He made a slight movement of his wrist to disengage it completely. The piece of metal gave way. All he had to do was extract it, praying to Allah to not damage the artery. The bullet slipped out without difficulty. With a sigh of relief, he dropped it into the instrument tray. Barely a few drops of blood flowed from the wound. He just had to disinfect it and sew it up.

When he was done, Saragih peered at him with disturbing intensity.

-- There, Darwis said blankly. Allah, in His mercy, has decided to give your friend life.

-- Above all, you are going to explain to me what has just happened, the Sheikh grimaced.

-- Nothing, really. We were just lucky, that's all.

-- Lucky, or did you invoke Shaytan?

The tension had eased, but Darwis could no longer bear the vice that gripped his chest. He suddenly let his anger explode.

-- What, Shaytan? I am a doctor and you asked me to perform surgery. I did everything you told me to and saved this wounded man. What do you expect from me now?

A predatory smile spread over Saragih's thick lips.

-- I still don't understand what you and the mute boy did, but I do believe that you can be useful for us. Pack up your instruments and put all your drugs in a bag. You will be coming with us.

-- I am responsible for the inhabitants of this village, Darwis protested. Who will take care of them if I abandon them?

-- Don't worry, it's for a good cause. Allah will provide.

At that moment, one of the two strangers entered the treatment room and said something that Darwis did not understand. Noting his expression, he was probably urging the sheikh to not linger any longer. The doctor recognized this language he had already heard in the mouths of members of an NGO involved in the reconstruction of Banda Aceh.

It was German.

-- Chapter 6 --

Pennsylvania

Present time

Derek Mitchell had invited her to leave her car in front of his house and offered to drive her to the place of the ceremony which, despite her reluctance, she finally accepted. Lorrie, for her part, had come along, accompanied by her two children. Mitchell had referred to a "temple," so Melany was surprised to find that the Odinist meeting place was a triangular-shaped field, with a simple small building used to store cultic objects.

The plot was surrounded by high fences but, despite the evenly planted trees, the place looked more like a baseball stadium than a pagan sanctuary.

The snow, cleared away with large shovels, only persisted in the form of small mounds. Gas braziers gave as much heat as possible to the edges of an altar erected near the point of the triangle, towards which a few dozen of them converged. Melany instinctively counted them. She counted sixty-seven faithful, among whom were a few old people and a dozen children.

Behind the altar, an inverted cross had been hung from a tree to remind followers that they rejected Christianity but not necessarily Christ, whose recycled image had been adapted to their myths.

A statue of Odin and Freyja, the principal deities of the pagan cult, dominated the ceremonial altar, on which many offerings, including a large bowl of mead, a bowl of fruit, some cakes and jewelry had been placed. The whole was bounded by multicolored candles and two square hammers, symbols of the omnipotence of Thor, the God of Thunder and War.

The women were dressed in long red medieval dresses with braided belts. The men wore tunics of wool and cotton of a raw beige color. The priest, who awaited the faithful in front of the altar, a smile of welcome crossing his weathered face, was dressed in a vestment edged with gold thread. The object he held in his hand looked like a scepter.

Melany felt as if she had stepped centuries back in time.

-- We call this ceremony a *blót*, Derek, wearing the same garb, explained to her. In the language of the Vikings, it meant "sacrifice".

-- And what are you going to sacrifice?

-- Maybe you?, he joked before adding: "Don't worry, you're not in a horror movie. It's been centuries since we Odinists have practiced human sacrifice. We are not those Jews who mix the blood of Christian children at their Passover dinners.

The young woman could hardly believe that this accusation of ritual crime, one of the most abhorrent and unfounded myths of anti-Semitism, was still gaining converts.

-- That's reassuring, she said.

Derek gave her a more cynical smile than a flirtatious one and walked away.

There was hardly anything to see in Potter County, except for the vast surrounding forests and the few small lakes that were the joy of fishermen in spring and summer. With nothing better to do, Melany had spent part of the day playing tourist. One way to make things look good if she were being watched.

The center of Odyssey had been reduced to a police station, a fire station, a diner decorated in pastel colors reminiscent of the nineteen sixties, a general store, and a post office that employed no more than two people. Tidy little houses lined the streets behind gardens still covered with snow and open pedestrian paths. Nothing in this landscape, which was so typical of provincial towns where boredom was rife, suggested that it was home to a community of neo-Nazis.

She had had plenty of time to make a few calls, including one to her mother who, once again, hadn't answered, as well as to Jeffrey at the unidentified number. He was also not available and, disappointed, she had left a short message saying that she was anxious to return to Washington and that she hoped to see him after her return from Kurdistan.

A half-truth that she wasn't exactly proud of.

I wonder if you were made for this job, old lady?, she had asked herself before going to bed, still shaken by the thought that someone had visited her room and rummaged through her belongings.

And then she remembered that her mother had been conducting similar operations for MI6 before her birth had ended her career and she fell asleep with the idea, eager to one day be able to tell her about this.

Lorrie, who had crept past her without her noticing, snatched her from her thoughts.

-- You should get closer to the altar, she suggested.

-- Are you sure? I'm not part of your community, after all.

-- Oh, but you are. You're our guest.

-- What will happen exactly?

-- We're going to call upon the gods to grant mercy to us in our present incarnation.

-- Your ... present ...? I hadn't known that Odinists believed in reincarnation, Melany said in astonishment.

-- There are a lot of things you don't know about us, but it's up to you to learn. Immortality is at the heart of our beliefs.

-- Immortality, or reincarnation?

Lorrie gave him the patient smile of a devotee full of tolerance for unbelievers.

-- One doesn't go without the other. It's all about the soul, not the vessel that contains it. How could we fulfill our destiny of being divine if we only had one short and sometimes miserable life?

Melany pretended to nod at the depth of her words, wondering if the term "miserable" had any special meaning in her mouth regarding her own existence.

Derek had joined a small group of men he was talking with animatedly. Most of the participants had come as couples, some were holding hands, and the children were running through their ranks without anyone paying attention to them.

She caught sight of Matthew, who noticed her in turn and came to place a quick kiss on her cheek before finding a group his own age. Mark, his older brother, stood a little bit apart and greeted her from a distance without daring to come close. Despite the distance, Melany had the impression that he blushed when he noticed her. This all had a side that was both folksy and good-natured. It took a real stretch of the imagination to tie this innocent little gathering with the loathsome ideology that its members associated with it.

Derek returned with a middle-aged man, quite short in stature and bald as the back of a hand. He made the introductions and Melany immediately hated his shifty gaze and the bitter frown that twisted his lips. Tattoos were visible outside his tunic and covered his neck down to his ears. He squeezed her hand weakly and the young woman felt as though she were touching a mollusk.

-- Todd is also a tattoo artist, Derek announced. I told him about the beautiful drawing you showed me yesterday. Hope you don't blame me.

An alarm rang in Melany's head.

-- Not at all, she replied, trying not to frown.

-- If it's not asking too much of you, he'd like to see what someone who's more talented than he is has done sometime. Professionals are often jealous of each other. Isn't that right, Todd? Derek chuckled, patting him on the shoulder.

-- This really isn't the place ..., Melany protested.

-- Of course, of course. I didn't even think about it. Maybe later. If you would like to come along with us after the ceremony.

-- You really don't have to, Lorrie said upon noticing the embarrassed look on her face.

-- How long have you had it? Todd asked in a voice as unpleasant as the way he shook hands.

-- I don't exactly recall anymore ... three or four years.

-- An Iron Cross on the belly of a pretty woman is quite rare.

-- Thank you for the compliment. My grandfather was in the Wehrmacht. He died when I was a teenager and I wanted to pay tribute to him.

-- And where did you have it done?

-- Not far from where I live. In Lancaster.

Melany once again cursed Franckel and Gardner for not anticipating that she might have to answer these kinds of questions. He wouldn't fail to ask for the name of the tattoo parlor. But Todd nodded, showing no further interest, and walked away.

-- It's about to begin, Lorrie announced enthusiastically.

Night was about to fall and someone handed out candles, while two worshipers lit the ones on the altar. The braziers gave off enough heat, despite the icy breath that crept in among the participants. With flickering lights in their hands, the white figures of the men formed a semicircle facing the priest, while the women arranged themselves in a beautiful red secondary group. Their faces were smiling, and those of the children so innocent it was heartbreaking.

At a sign from the priest, the voices mingled to sing a sacred hymn:

Sacred gods of our ancestors
We greet you from the bottom of our hearts
Heil to the new dawn
Heil to the new beginning
Heil to the new awakening
To the standing men who reject
Slavery and servility
Heil to the Savior who will come
Heil to victory and to whoever leads us there!

In perfect unity, the participants stretched out their right arms and shouted:

Sieg Heil!

Melany shivered and was seized by an urge to cry. This affront to millions of innocent victims seemed like a nightmare, but it was just the gruesome reality of mundane fellowship in a small town in Pennsylvania. The men in white, the women in red, and even the children were joyful. They all vied to scream the loudest.

Sieg Heil!

She suddenly realized that Derek had turned his head and was watching her. So, on the verge of nausea, she closed her eyes and stretched out her right arm.

Sieg Heil!

Her lips moved, but no sound came out.

Laughter and whispering followed the greeting and the song. A somewhat elderly man appeared, accompanied by a teenage boy who was pulling a fawn at the end of a rope. The little animal must have sensed that a disastrous fate was in store for it, because it moaned and reared. It was a pretty little animal, dressed in a sparse brown coat with white spots. Any child would have associated it with Bambi. The priest greeted the newcomers by spreading his arms away from his body, his open hands pointing down.

Melany protested:

-- They're not going to do that ...

She paused, irritated at having allowed herself to speak out loud. Lorrie, standing next to her, gave her a worried look.

-- We forgot that you don't like hunting.

-- But this isn't about hunting ...

-- No. It's better. The gods appreciate the offerings. They will give back to us a hundredfold.

Melany couldn't contain herself.

-- The law prohibits the killing of young animals.

-- Speak softer, Lorrie urged on as she saw stares turning to them.

The young woman took it upon herself to contain herself. With death in her soul, she just watched the age-defying scene unfolding a few feet away from her.

Images came back to her of much larger-scale animal slaughter that she had seen in the Middle East. Men always seemed to rejoice when they behaved like barbarians in the name of some god or simple profit.

Here it was a fawn, there it was thousands of lambs and sheep and goats. Elsewhere, poachers murdered magnificent and rare animals to steal their horns, tusks, fins or blubber. Whatever the reason, it always ended in carnage and the animals, which did not ask for much, were the objects of bacchanalias and ended up as trophies.

The newcomers helped the priest clear the altar in order to place the offering on it. The terrified eyes of the fawn revealed its awareness of a fate that it shouldn't have known. Its coat quivered and it suddenly lifted its tail to defecate. The men in the first circle roared with laughter. It was as if they were at a party. The women behind them were more restrained. One of them came out of the row to go and clean the altar briefly. The priest turned to his flock.

-- How many virtues are linked to our faith?, he asked in a voice that carried far.

-- There are nine of them, the assembly answered with one voice.

-- What are these nine virtues?

The men in a semicircle raised their candles to declare.

-- Courage -- Truth -- Honor -- Loyalty -- Discipline -- Hospitality -- Independence -- Zeal -- Perseverance.

-- What are the nine obligations?, the priest asked.

An equal number of women took a step forward and the men gave way to them.

-- To be sincere and faithful in love and to be devoted to the faithful friend.

-- To never make a false oath.

-- To never treat the humble and the weak harshly.

-- To remember the respect due to old age.

-- To not leave evil without remedy.

-- To rescue the isolated.

-- To not respond to the delusions of a drunken man.

-- To provide care to the dead, wherever they may have perished.

-- To comply with the decrees of legitimate authorities.

And to wallow in hatred by adopting Nazi ideology? Melany rebelled internally. But her thought was interrupted by a new *Sieg Heil.*

-- May He who brings us this victory prosper and reveal Himself, trumpeted the priest.

-- *Sieg Heil!*

-- Odin, Freyja, Thor, protectors of our ancestors, rulers of the ground on which we advance our steps, accept this offering whose flesh we will share in Your honor. Stretch Your mighty arms over the head of the Savior. Hasten the advent of the *Father of Victory!*

-- *Dann sei es! So be it*, all the faithful thundered.

The thrill that ran through Melany was no longer just linked to the barbaric act she was rebelling against. The priest had finally spoken the words that had prompted her mission. For a split second, she forgot about the unfortunate little animal whose head the priest was holding after putting a knife back in the hand of the teenager in charge of the sacrifice.

The songs resumed in a foreign language with Nordic intonations, the meaning of which Melany did not understand. The young man raised the blade at the doe fawn, whose wails sounded like those of a newborn baby. *It's not an animal but innocence itself that these people are sacrificing*, Melany thought. The blade fell. Blood spurted out. The fawn struggled harder.

-- Start again!, the priest said, because the first blow had evidently not been fatal.

The knife carried by the teenager's too-frail hand slashed the air and missed its mark once again, nicking the coat near the ear without delivering the fatal blow that would have shortened the animal's suffering. The fawn reared up, so shaken by convulsions that it almost fell off the altar. Its severed vein let out a geyser of blood, pulsing with the beat of its weakening heart. The priest didn't have time to step aside. His vestments were stained with blood from shoulder to hip as the boy immolating the animal raised his arm a third time.

It was no longer a ceremony, but a slaughter. Melany would have given a lot to be able to intervene, but what could she do but hold back the tears and pray that they be finished as soon as possible? A murmur began to pass through the assembly of the faithful.

-- The gods are not going to be happy, Lorrie observed as if to herself.

-- The animal must not suffer, it's against our principles, continued a woman next to her.

The teenager had injured the fawn once again and it was now struggling but still clinging to life. It was then that Derek walked up to the altar. Arriving within reach of the priest, he raised his tunic, revealing a belt and a holster from which he extracted a handgun. A moment later, he pointed the gun at the fawn's head.

-- Step aside, he told the teenager.

And he fired.

The blast echoed through the night, like the shock of Thor's hammer carrying out his verdict. The fawn froze after a final jerk. Derek turned to the audience and raised his arms as if celebrating a victory.

-- *Heil Odin!*, men, women and children cried with thunderous applause.

Some food and drinks were then distributed. Participants gathered in small groups in a spirit of celebration, including the children who did not seem to have been affected by the barbaric scene they had just witnessed. The ceremony ended quickly, without Melany having the opportunity to meet or speak to anyone other than Todd.

It seemed to her that the Mitchells had taken special care of that.

-- Chapter 7 --

Melany found herself trapped in the front seat of the GMC pickup between Mark and his father, who was driving. The switchbacks in the heart of a forest area seemed to go endlessly on but might be a bit short if she wanted to get real information before leaving them.

-- So, what did you think about our little ceremony?, Derek asked as he turned the ignition key. He had put a parka on over his tunic and thus looked twice as massive.

-- I didn't expect to see this, the young woman said evasively.

The GMC moved along with other vehicles, whose headlights tore through the darkness in all directions. Derek looked at her briefly, a mysterious smile at the corner of his lips.

-- Not too shaken up? You should have eaten or at least drunk something.

-- Thank you. It was very pleasant, but it's going to be all right.

-- Mark, grab the flask of scotch from the glove compartment and offer our guest a drink.

The Mitchells' eldest son did so despite Melany's protests, and Melany had to pretend to take a sip to keep from offending her hosts. She wanted to return the flask, but Mark motioned for her to keep it. The interior of the vehicle smelled of plastic, sweat and disinfectant. A rifle was set in the gun rack between the window and the back seat. Neither of them was wearing seat belts and the warning light kept flashing on the dashboard.

Lorrie followed them in her own car, accompanied by Matthew and Todd the tattoo artist, who was seated in the passenger's seat. She greeted them by flashing her headlights and passed them in the middle of a turn. Derek saluted her with a honk.

Melany was feeling nauseous and was in a hurry to run over to her hotel and get under the shower. Everything seemed dirty to her and nothing seemed to be able to appease the disgust that this family inspired in her right now. The warmth of their hospitality and the near normalcy of their daily life further fueled her revulsion. Evil is so disturbing when it dresses itself in soothing banality.

Yet she was beginning to wonder whether the *Father of Victory* was not just a vague symbol, a rallying cry. It could be an expression to be put on the same level as the fetishes revered by the Odinists and the Nazi ceremonial that had become part of their folklore. It might perhaps be a coincidence that the terrorists interviewed in Kurdistan and Indonesia used similar words. The Mitchells, the priest and the faithful who had gathered in front of this junk altar might perhaps believe that a Messiah sent by Odin or by Thor would lead them to some kind of victory. And why not help them rebuild the Third Reich while they were at it? All that would then be extremely foolish.

In the dim light of the cabin, Derek's face reflected the luminous dials of the dashboard. He looked focused on the road or lost in some dark thoughts. She had to take it upon herself to restart the conversation.

-- I was touched by the devotion you all showed. There was a lot of emotion. And I appreciated that you put an end to the suffering of that poor animal.

-- It was nothing, Derek said, grabbing the flask, which she had rested on the seat next to her, in order to take a long sip. He wiped his mouth with the back of his sleeve and belched softly. Are you all sensitive like that, in big cities?

There was more than a bit of sarcasm in his voice but he continued in a more neutral tone:

-- You have to understand that this was an initiation ceremony. Young people are not trained until after they're confirmed. This usually goes pretty well. In two minutes, it's all over. The animal hardly feels anything and the Gods are happy. Otherwise ... well, *bang!*

With his fingers shaped like a pistol, he aimed at the road in front of him.

Melany doubled down on herself in order to forget the unease that the mere presence of Derek behind the wheel provoked. She asked:

-- Who was the boy in charge of ... uh ...

-- Of sacrificing the animal? A neighbor's kid. At fourteen, he still acts like a little girl. We all agreed to honor his parents and give him a chance but, just between us, he will remain a fucking weakling.

Derek raised his right hand, flipping his hand around to mimic the softness of the blows the front boy awkwardly landed against the fawn's throat.

-- Pardon my language, huh, he added, without really apologizing.

-- Derek, Melany said. May I ask you a more personal question?

-- Go ahead.

-- You, your wife ... how did you become Odinists?

The headlights of the pickup lit a large branch which, yielding to the weight of the snow, had collapsed across the road. Derek dodged it with a sudden thrust of the steering wheel that sent his passengers flying. Mark banged his head against the glass and groaned. His father paid him no attention.

-- You have to believe in something, don't you? Who could have created the stars, the men and all the things that surround us? My family was Protestant, but my father grew up discovering Hitler's theories. At first, it was just a curiosity related to his activities. His life changed when he read Mein Kampf. The Führer planned to abolish Christianity. A religion for the weak, according to him. And he was right. In our house, we don't turn our left cheek when we're slapped on the right ...

He patted the bulge protruding from the left side of his tunic.

-- ... we solve the problem in the best of all possible ways.

Mark squirmed, giving the impression of expressing quiet disagreement. Closed in on himself, the young man had his eyes riveted on the road. Sensing that Melany was watching him, he briefly turned his face to her. His terrified expression surprised her as much as it worried her. But Derek wasn't finished.

-- The Jews found the trick to world domination by hijacking the words of an Aryan who had come to earth to kick their ass. And they have proliferated for 2000 years while trying to make us believe that they are being massacred. Mind you, they have played it well. Proof that they have demon brains. But the Führer clearly saw through their games. He started the job, but it will be up to us to finish it.

-- Until victory?, Melany asked.

-- Yep. Sieg Heil!

-- And how do you plan to achieve that? There are so few of us ...

-- With your dough, maybe, Derek sneered. And with your daddy's.

Melany felt a growing unease. Derek could laugh at her, but he wouldn't risk mocking her as long as he hoped to get her donation. She blamed the alcohol for his disrespect. He had already drunk a lot during the ceremony.

-- Assuming I issue a report in favor of your group, what guarantees us that it will be put to good use?

-- My little lady, if what you've seen between yesterday and today doesn't convince you of our devotion to the cause, then ...

-- It's not a question of devotion, but rather one of effectiveness. You don't change the world with songs.

Melany hoped to push Mitchell to his limits, but he just chuckled once again. At full speed, the truck hit the end of a branch, which slammed against the windshield like a whiplash. She went for broke.

-- You drank a toast to the *Father of Victory*. I've never heard that expression before. Would you care to explain it to me?

Derek seemed to stiffen. He narrowed his eyelids and his lips curled up in an evil smile.

-- The *Father of Victory*, he breathed. Is that all?

Melany's heart leaped up in her chest.

-- I beg your pardon?

-- That's what you asked me, wasn't it?

-- I heard your priest say these words, they just called out to me.

-- Called out how?

Mark suddenly hit his leg against Melany's. The movement was so furtive that she wondered whether it was a warning or just a reflex due to the uncomfortable position to which the young man, like her, had been forced into.

-- Nothing in particular. Just curiosity.

-- We'll be there in five minutes, Derek said simply.

He was silent until they arrived, leaving Melany torn between frustration and anxiety. Her car was parked in front of the Mitchell house and she was getting ready to get out of the pickup, but Derek continued to drive towards the barn.

-- You ... you still have something to show me?

-- Not really ..., Derek growled.

The headlights of the pickup swept over the figure of Todd, also in a parka, who was standing in front of the entrance to the barn, his cell phone clapped against his ear. He hung up when he saw them. Derek stopped the vehicle a few feet away from him, jumped to the ground, and reached out to Melany to invite her to step down.

-- You know, I'd rather go back to my hotel now, the young woman tried. We could meet again tomorrow morning to finish this discussion ...

Derek's fingers closed around her wrist with such force that she whimpered.

-- You're hurting me ...

-- Come on, a valiant Nazi won't hurt from so little, Derek retorted, pulling her violently out of the pickup.

Melany caught herself just before reaching the door and managed to put both feet on the ground without losing her balance. Derek immobilized her by twisting her arm behind his back. She tried to escape his grip, but her fingers caught in a vice.

-- Derek, what's the matter with you?

-- Don't struggle like that, my beautiful Aryan, it's just our turn to ask you a few questions.

Mark got out on the other side of the vehicle and went to slide the barn door open while Todd got closer to Melany. He grabbed her by the hair and pressed his face to hers. His breath reeked of alcohol.

-- So, you got some pretty tattoos in Lancaster? My friend Derek is no expert, he wouldn't be able to draw an egg without it looking like a truck wheel ... Isn't that true, Derek? For me, on the other hand, stylized swastikas are kind of my specialty. So you're going to show me all this, and maybe even the rest.

-- I don't understand what you want, Melany protested.

-- Oh, don't worry, it won't take you long to figure it out.

He let go of her hair and Derek pushed her towards the barn. Mark turned on the lights before closing the sliding door and Todd rolled a barrel over the dirt floor. Mark helped him straighten it up and Derek forced Melany to sit on it.

-- No need to tie her up, he grimaced. She's not going to get very far if she gets up. Isn't that true, my dear?

Melany's heart was pounding so hard she felt it was ready to leap out of her chest. Now was not the time to panic. She held back her tears and tried to concentrate on her breathing by clearing her mind, as she had been taught during her weeks of instruction.

-- I have no intention of leaving, she retorted in a voice so calm it seemed foreign to her. Not before understanding what this masquerade is supposed to be. If you think you're going to force me to give you a donation, you really don't know my father.

The slap hit her with such force that she almost fell off the barrel. Melany straightened herself up, her cheek stinging, and shot a glare of anger at Derek.

-- Does Lorrie know what's going on in your barn right now?

-- Leave my wife out of this if you don't want to get one from the other side, Derek growled. And start by opening your coat up to show us what you're hiding underneath.

Melany was dressed in the Ugo Boss Otrenchy she had worn the night before. With trembling fingers, she began to undo the first of the eight buttons. Not fast enough for Todd's taste, who grabbed her lapel and tugged on the turtleneck sweater she had on underneath.

-- What did you think?, Melany said with difficulty. That I was wearing a wire?

-- Lift up your sweater!, Derek order.

The young woman did so, revealing the Iron Cross framed by the words *Wer Will -- Der Kann* that she had had tattooed on her stomach. Todd walked over to examine it closely.

-- You have another one?

-- Yes, on my shoulder.

-- Show us.

-- But ... I can't roll up my sleeves.

-- You've got to be kidding us!, Derek growled. Take off your coat and your sweater. Unless you'd rather have Todd take care of it.

Melany had no way of avoiding it. She stood up and dropped the Otrenchy before freeing her left arm from her sleeve, uncovering one of the branches of the swastika placed on the top of her arm.

-- I don't think she understood you, Todd mocked. Then, to Melany: You're gonna take that fucking sweater off or I'm gonna rip it right off.

He pulled up on his parka and took a pistol out of his belt and pointed it at her. Melany pulled the garment over her head, and reflexively crossed her arms over her chest.

-- That's what I thought, Todd said after looking at the swastika and the second tattoo for a long time. It wasn't one of ours who did that.

-- Really?, Melany exclaimed. And that's why you hit me and humiliate me.

She noticed that Mark, standing motionless beside Todd, had looked away and blushed. There might be an advantage to be gained from his obvious attraction to her. In a gesture of defiance, she uncrossed her arms. The cold had hardened her nipples, which protruded provocatively under the thin fabric.

-- Is that the example you want to give your son, Derek?

Mark stared at her briefly and lowered his eyes again.

-- Pretty damn good German girl, Todd sneered. Do you think she's a real blonde? Maybe we should check it out.

A network of blue veins had formed on his temples and bald head, making him look even scarier. Melany tried to keep herself from trembling.

-- You can check anything you want, but not before you explain to me why you are behaving like some ...

She didn't know what term to use and left her sentence hanging because she was faced with a simple fact: they were acting just like the Nazis they were.

-- Go ahead, tell her, Todd said to Derek.

Despite his sour expression, he looked like he was having fun.

-- We don't yet know on whose behalf you came to spy on us, but we're going to find out very soon.

-- What makes you think I'm a spy?

-- Oh, tiny little details. For example, your cousins who hunted grizzly bears or weasels in Montana. The fact that there's no Melany Hoffmann in the Lancaster directory, even among our people, and yet they're strong there. The tube of *CeraVe* that you brought with you, when you pretend you've had these tattoos for three or four years ...

-- How did you know that?, Melany protested, although she knew it only too well. Did you search my room, or what?

-- Simple precaution. The manager is a friend who refuses us nothing. And if you knew a bit more about tattoos, you would know that *CeraVe* is used to speed up healing. After several months have passed, no one uses it any longer. But that's not all. Isn't that true Todd?

He approached Melany and grazed her cheek with the barrel of his pistol.

-- The nice thing about a small community like ours is that everyone knows each other, or someone who knows someone else, if you get my meaning. Among professional tattoo artists, it's even better. Most would refuse to do the pretty designs you have on your skin, but those who do are also chatterboxes. If a stranger gets the urge to show off a little swastika on his belly or even on his butt, it always ends up coming back to us. Unfortunately for you, no tattoo artist in Lancaster remembers a pretty blonde named Melany Hoffmann.

-- And that's why ...

Melany couldn't finish her sentence. The second slap from Derek narrowly missed knocking her out. She felt her cheek swell and tears flood her face.

-- Let's make this short, Derek growled. We're not going to waste our time listening to your stories. I'll ask you a question. If I don't like your answer, I'll punch you in your nose. Then I will ask the same question again. Wrong answer, I rip your bra off and slash your breasts ... Do you understand, or should I go on explaining?

The young woman's only the recourse was to admit defeat. At least she could use her position as a threat. Derek knew he was risking a lot if he took on an official figure. She nodded and wiped her tears with the back of her hand.

-- My question, Derek said: who are you working for?

-- The government, Melany said.

Todd and Derek exchanged worried looks.

-- The FBI?

-- No. I'm an analyst agent at the INR.

-- What's that supposed to be?, Todd growled.

Derek shrugged his shoulders.

-- A kind of CIA.

-- The Bureau of Intelligence and Research reports to the State Department, Melany confirmed. I'm in regular contact with my boss and he knows exactly where I am. If I don't contact him in the next hour, expect half the cops in Pennsylvania to show up.

The bluff seemed to make the two men think. Mark, on the other hand, was so uneasy that she almost felt sorry for him. Falling for a tattoo! How naïve could she have been to have agreed to take part in such an ill-prepared operation! She tried to use the unease she had created to her advantage.

-- The INR only asks questions about the proliferation of extreme right-wing ideologies. Nothing that concerns you directly. Your community was chosen at random. If you let me go now, I give you my word that I will forget what happened in this barn. I will describe only what I've seen in my report. I didn't find anything to incriminate you.

-- What do you know about the *Father of Victory*?, Derek asked.

-- Nothing. You didn't want to answer me in the car. It's just a phrase I heard.

-- I'm certain you're lying.

-- If so, why would I ask you this question? I have no idea what it's all about. And, to be honest, I don't care a bit. That not the reason for my mission.

Derek hesitated. Melany presented him with a series of borderline problems. She insisted:

-- Okay, I lied to you about my real intentions. So what? I was just doing my job. Your museum is open to the public and your office had already been searched by the FBI. I'm leaving empty-handed, and I haven't learned anything more about your organization.

-- And to think that I invited you into my house!, Derek grumbled. I honored you with my home.

Todd stood a stone's throw from Melany, frozen in a slightly hunched posture, his arm at his side, his pistol held firmly in his hand. He had followed the exchange between Derek and the young woman with a certain calm but it was clear that he was seething on the inside. He suddenly exploded:

-- Damn it, Derek, you're not going soft on me. This bitch is working for the government! Haven't we had enough trouble with the Feds? Do you think she's going to forget that we kidnapped her and that you hit her? If she reports us, it's "Go Directly to Jail". The judge won't even give us bail.

-- What would you suggest?

The tattoo artist pointed his gun at Melany.

-- We get rid of her.

-- You heard her, her agency knows she's with us.

-- That's not a problem ...

Todd pulled a switchblade from inside his parka. He stood in front of Melany and moved the blade a few inches from her face.

-- You know what? I really like blondes with blue eyes. I would really hate to have to kill you. So, you will kindly take out your cell phone and send your boss the message that I am going to dictate to you. Can you do that for me?

She nodded. No training could have prepared her for what she was going through.

-- My bag is still in the car and my phone is in it.

-- Mark, go get it, Derek ordered as if he were talking to a dog. The Mitchell boy returned a few moments later, cell phone in hand.

-- How can you be sure that she'll send the message to the right person?, Derek asked. Who can say that they don't have a code among themselves for this kind of situation?

-- We'll know that right away. Now text something like: "There's nothing to be learned from the group I met at Odyssey, but I'm off on a new trail. Request permission to head north." If you don't get an answer in the next few minutes, you haven't sent the right message. So pray that your contact is available, and try to be convincing ...

The blade moved dangerously close to Melany's face, who instinctively closed her eyes. There was an emergency procedure to "send the cavalry in", as Gardner would have said, but Todd had been smart enough to bypass it. She was compelled to obtain a favorable response to his request, which wouldn't happen if she aroused the suspicion of her FBI contact. So she wrote the message that had been dictated to her. All she had to do was to wait, hoping that Gardner would respond within a minute.

Five minutes passed, and a cold sweat began to trickle down Melany's back, as Todd, in sheer sadism, stroked her cheeks with the flat of his blade under Derek's amused gaze. Mark, on the other hand, had turned so pale that his acne scars stood out in reddish bumps.

A brief vibration announced Gardner's response.

"What's your next objective?"

-- Write: "Ulysses," Todd ordered.

That was a town similar to Odyssey, also populated by white supremacists. Melany did so and received *"Approved, good luck!"* in return.

Todd snatched the cell phone from her hand to remove the chip and battery. She had kept the integrity of her face and preserved her eye, but the cavalry had no chance of arriving.

The two men then agreed on a plan to follow. It was agreed that Todd would pick up Melany's things from her hotel room, which she would officially leave with the manager's complicity. He would then drive her Mercedes further north to sink it in Lyman Run Lake, a deep body of water that was popular with kayakers from June to September but whose surface was currently partially frozen. If it didn't completely disappear in the mud, the car wouldn't be found until spring at the soonest. Derek and his son, meanwhile, would take care of Melany, somewhere in the depths of the forest.

Mark moved closer to his father to plead in a shaky voice:

-- Dad, do you really think this is necessary? There must be another way. She gave her word not to incriminate us.

-- Did I ask your opinion?, Derek thundered.

-- It's just that ... we've never done that before.

-- Derek, Todd interjected, I don't have any advice for your son, but if he was mine, I would know what to do ...

In front of Melany's horrified eyes, Derek grabbed his firstborn by his collar and raised the other hand high, ready to strike him.

-- Are you going to be a little girl today? Have you forgotten who you are, and who your father is? Do you know what the Führer would order me to do if he were here right now? He'd say to me, hand your gun to your son and order him to shoot that whore of a kike to see if he's really yours. Are you really mine, Mark? Your mother didn't wallow with a nigger? Well, that's exactly what I'm going to do. We're taking her for a walk, the two of us, and you'll be the one to take care of it.

He released Mark, who had tears in his eyes, picked up Melany's coat and sweater to throw them to her and grabbed her by the wrist as he had done to pull her out of the pickup truck.

-- Here, Todd sneered, we haven't checked to see if she's a real blonde.

-- Go take care of the Mercedes, Derek snapped, pushing Melany towards the barn door.

The young woman no longer even had the courage to defend herself.

***

They had driven for three quarters of an hour to reach this clearing covered with a full meter of snow on the edge of a thick forest that stretched out over hundreds of acres.

As a seasoned hunter, Derek knew his region by heart and its wooded areas down to the smallest thicket. Recovering from her initial shock, Melany had tried everything during the trip. The pleas, the appeal to his humanity, the promises she swore she would keep, the threats. Derek had remained unfazed.

She was now floating in unreality, unable to conceive that in a few minutes, an hour at most, she would be gone and that her body would be in danger of disappearing forever. Unless some scavenger dug it up. In which case, the nearby community of Ulysses would be blamed. People she had never seen, other fascists no doubt, but innocent of the crime they would be accused of. And then, for lack of evidence, the case would one day be closed.

This idea, more than her own death, because it was much less unreal, made her nauseated.

Thick clouds hid the moon and stars, so it was pitch black around the beams projected by the pick-up's headlights. Derek jumped out of the vehicle, pulled his gun from his holster, and aimed it at Melany.

-- We're gonna make a deal, you and me. You stay very good, you don't try to escape, you don't scream, and it'll all be over before you even know it. Either way, you have no way of escaping and there is no living soul within ten miles. On the other hand, if you play the heroine from some TV show and I find myself having to run after you, then we'll bury you alive and give you some air to make it last as long as possible. Understood?

The young woman got out of the pick-up, barely able to stand up straight on her legs. For a second time, she had to catch herself on the door in order to not fall down.

She had often wondered how she would react if she ever found herself in such a situation. Would she be heroic and able to maintain her dignity? Or would she, on the contrary, lose her most basic pride to throw herself to the ground and grovel before her tormenter?

For a split second, the image of those innocent people being sent to certain death that could be seen in the documentaries about Nazi atrocities crossed her mind. A superior, almost mystical form of fatalism, seemed to have taken hold of them. None had tried to flee, despite the sight of the pit already full of corpses open at their feet.

Melany now understood why. After a certain stage of anguish and despair, death suddenly appears as a relief. She just thought, sadly, that she would never see her parents or Jeff again, that she would never have children, and that for months or years everyone who loved her would jump with every ring of the phone, hoping for a miracle, their souls consumed by her disappearance.

-- Mark, grab the shovel in the back of the pickup, Derek ordered, his gun still pointed at Melany.

The light from the headlights formed a ghostly halo before which the gigantic figure of the Nazi appeared like a Chinese shadow puppet, his legs disappearing into snow up to his mid-calves. Except for the roar of the engine and Mark's footsteps, there was no sound, as if the forest had suddenly been emptied of all its inhabitants.

-- Derek, Melany pleaded again. What could I say, or do, to make you change your mind? Even though my name is not Hoffmann, my parents still have quite a bit of money ...

-- Did you get the shovel?, Derek snarled to get his son's attention.

Mark reappeared at the back of the pickup, holding the object at arm's length.

-- Dad, maybe you should listen to her.

-- Shut up!, Derek exploded.

But his son persisted.

-- If her parents really do have money, maybe we could work something out ...

-- A million dollars, Melany said hastily. My parents wouldn't hesitate to give you that amount.

Derek spat on the ground.

-- And what will I do with all that money in federal prison? We've wasted enough time. Mark, hand me the shovel and we'll be done with it.

There was something strange and quirky about the crunching of Mark's boots in the snow. Memories of happy stays in the mountains during the ski season. Melany closed her eyes, wishing she knew any prayers and suddenly in a hurry to be done with it all.

She opened them a fraction of a second later to see the shovel held in both hands by Mark fly in the direction of his father. The sharp edge hit Derek at wrist height, and Derek let go of his weapon with a cry of pain. The pistol fell within two yards of Melany.

-- You little bastard, Derek yelled, his features contorted with rage.

Against all odds, rather than rushing to retrieve his weapon, he turned on his son, who again brandished the shovel, ready to give him a second blow.

-- I just want us to let her go!, the latter shouted in a shrill voice.

It took two seconds for Melany to snap out of her stupor and regain all her reflexes. Weeks of physical training had prepared her for such a moment.

She threw herself forward and rolled over to retrieve the gun that had sunk into the snow. The Smith and Wesson MP9, which appeared to be of normal size in Derek's hand, was actually huge and heavy. She picked it up as he dodged a second blow with the shovel and rushed at his son.

-- You little piece of shit! I always knew you were just a whiner, a crybaby, a faggot.

He clenched his neck with his left hand.

The two men were the same height, but Derek easily had an advantage of forty pounds of muscle over his son. The young man tried to struggle, starved of air, his face congested. Derek abruptly let go of his grip to punch him in the face and broke his nose. Blood ran down his lips. Mark began to stagger. His father choked him again, indifferent to Melany who had stood up, pistol in hand.

-- Stop!

Derek alternated between choking and pounding on Mark's face, whose swollen eyelids swelled, cheekbones split, and lips burst. He was going to turn him into mush.

-- Derek, stop or I'll shoot!

Melany held the Smith and Wesson in both hands as she had been taught and remembered at the last minute that she had to release the safety before firing it. Derek finally realized the monumental mistake that his anger had caused him. He tried to pull the shovel out of his son's hands, but his son had a firm grip on the handle and his resistance surprised him.

Melany warned him one last time, then fired into the air. The detonation echoed through the trees like thunder, and piles of snow collapsed from the tallest branches.

But the rage had practically made Derek lose sanity.

With a punch on the shoulder, he made Mark let go. The shovel fell. The two men fought over the object that had sunk into the thick white layer of snow, but Derek quickly took it away. He straightened up and turned to Melany, the fingers of his left hand tightening on the handle. The young woman had to jump aside to avoid the fatal blow he aimed at her head. The tool slammed into the door of the pick-up, tearing off the side mirror.

Derek let out an angry howl. A blood-curdling animal cry.

The end of the shovel grazed Melany's shoulder this time, tearing a piece of cloth from her coat and gashing her skin.

The shot went off without the young woman really wanting it to. She was the first to be surprised to hear the explosion.

-- No!

The cry came out of Mark's throat, who had managed to straighten himself up and was trying to reach his father to get back at him. Derek froze, the shovel raised above his head. Then he staggered as a red flower spread across his parka at the level of his heart. Eyes wild, he tried one last time to reach Melany, but he had no strength left. The tool slipped out of his hand.

Like a mountain of flesh crumbling in slow motion, he fell to his knees in the snow.

-- Bitch of a kike!

Those were his last words before collapsing to the side.

With one eye closed tight and his face bleeding, Mark was barely recognizable. He crouched down next to Derek and touched his neck.

-- Oh, Mark, I am sorry!, Melany moaned after a long silence.

The young man looked up at her, shaking his head.

-- It's over, he said simply.

It was just a statement in his mouth. No pain, no relief in his voice. Melany moved closer in turn, the pistol still tightly held. She could hardly believe this reversal.

-- I didn't mean ... she added.

-- You had no choice, Mark admitted with a shrug that made him wince in pain.

-- Will you allow me to get closer?, Melany said. I would like to put a little snow on your face to help bring the swelling down.

-- Don't worry about me. Do what you have to do now. Here, take my cell phone ... he added, pulling the phone out of his pocket.

Melany grabbed it, and began dialing Gardner's number. She interrupted her action and asked:

-- Can I ask you a question?

-- You can ask me anything. If I can answer it ...

-- You've heard the expression: the *Father of Victory*?

-- Of course, my parents and their friends talk about it all the time.

Melany's heart leaped up.

-- What does it mean?

-- It's not a what, it's a person.

-- Oh, yeah? And who is it?

-- Adolph Hitler.

The young woman jumped. She had expected anything but that answer.

-- But he's been dead a long time. Do you mean, symbolically?

-- Not a bit. According to my father, he was a unique being with the power to return from the shadow world.

Melany shook her head. *Oh, shit! All that for a chimera.* So her mission ended with a flop and she had killed a man.

The time had come to call in the cavalry.

-- Chapter 8 --

Region of Aceh -- Indonesia

Eleven weeks earlier.

Inspector Fuad Iskandar grumbled upon discovering the state the night shift had left his office in after the soccer match was broadcast. *Worse than pigs!* His hair stood on end at the sight of ashtrays filled to the brim, papers crumpled into balls on the floor in the midst of fruit peelings, cartons of drinks overturned among his precious files, baskets overflowing with trash. The small space, fit between the staircase and the Turkish toilet, had the only television set on the whole floor. There must have been five or six of them to cause such carnage. Iskandar had never understood the pleasure his colleagues took in crowding together in front of the disturbed, barely visible image of his black and white screen. But this time, they had definitely crossed a boundary.

Angry, the inspector kicked aside two boxes still full of oily rice that prevented him from reaching his chair, into which he finally sank down.

The room with the walls cracked by earthquakes was a picture of desolation. The tiny window, set with half-rusted bars, overlooked the backyard of a building that had been under construction for years. A pile of rubble and metal structures obstructed the breathtaking view of the swampy banks of the Aceh River, the odor of which rose at nightfall to mix with the smell of urine and excrement seeping from the pipes.

Hanging from the partition wall, creaking shelves bent under the weight of a multitude of criminal files. The political prisoners, marked with a red circle, were piled up on a wicker table, one missing leg of which had been replaced by a cinder block torn from the construction site opposite the building.

They mainly concerned the resurgent GAM, which no one outside the administration dared to mention, and the *Jemaah Islamiyah* which, on the other hand, continued to be talked about too much.

More out of habit than necessity, Inspector Iskandar checked his fax machine, answering machine, and voicemail, only to find that the phone lines were down and that the computer, the only modern touch in the whole room, was no longer functioning. No matter how hard he tapped, the screen remained hopelessly blank, except for a greeting message that fluttered from corner to corner of the monitor as if to taunt him.

It was too much for the start of the day.

A few seconds later, the policeman on duty outside the front door hastily stubbed out his cigarette as he saw the inspector storm past him like a fury. Without paying him any attention, Iskandar rushed down the dark, narrow staircase that led to the underground cells. The post had belonged to the mobile brigades before it was assigned to the local police, a unit under both the central government and that in Medan.

Dug into the clay soil, the unsanitary dungeons still bore the dark mark of the tortures regularly inflicted against political prisoners, unspeakable blots staining the floor and walls, into which rings and hooks, now devoid of chains, had been inserted.

Every time he descended into these shallows, Inspector Iskandar thought he heard the screams that still seemed to pervade the place. Under his command, a team of common criminals had spent an entire week trying to clean up the traces of blood and body fluids and to erase the desperate messages carved on the walls by fingernails. In vain. The basement held memories that it refused to let go of.

Iskandar quickly surveyed the interior of the cells, in which unmoving shadows were barely discernible. Five men were sleeping in the first, sprawled out on the floor, next to a waste bucket that was about to overflow. A half-naked old man in the second one, sitting with his shoulders covered with rags, gave him a toothless smile. Iskandar moved closer to the back cell, the one reserved for criminals, where two standing men stared at him, their hands clutching the bars while the others, at least half a dozen, slept on old mattresses thrown on the floor.

The first was one-eyed, with a long slash crossing his face from his brow ridge to his chin, the lids sunken on the left side betraying the absence of an eyeball. The scar was fresh. His injury must have been recent. He wore the beard and tunic of the religiously observant. His younger companion, clad in jeans and a stained T-shirt, was in an indescribable state of filth. He was the one Iskandar chose to address.

-- Why are you here?

The prisoner spat on the ground.

-- For nothing. This is a mistake, I keep telling them.

The young man held his gaze. Iskandar understood that he was dealing with one of those fake hardliners who supposedly joined the GAM to find a pretext for their criminality.

-- Of course. You're all here by mistake. Is that why we put the sex offender sign on you? Let me guess ... She was the one who forced you?

-- By Allah, I swear ...

-- Leave Allah out of it, Iskandar snapped. He turned His face from you. You're just a miserable pig, the descendant of a breed of dogs and rats. Thieves deserve to have their hands cut off. Do you know what we should do with rapists?

A flash of malice passed through the prisoner's eyes.

-- They are the ones who provoke us and who should be punished. That bitch wasn't wearing the veil. She had turned away from Allah and I am the one who pays for her!

A second bit of sputum landed at Iskandar's feet. His one-eyed companion began to chant.

-- Let them burn in hell! They are prostitutes, people without souls. May Shaytan tear off their flesh, grill their breasts and drive stakes reddened by fire into their entrails. May larvae and vermin swarm on the sows' faces.

-- Oh, yeah? Iskandar undid the thong of the baton that hung from his belt. Did you come up with that on your own when you were reciting? Hey, you got beat up pretty good. How did that happen to you? Let me guess. You explained your way of seeing things to the nurses who wanted to treat you. What did they do with your eye? Did they throw it to the dogs?

The baton flew against the bars of the cell, narrowly missing the fingers of the one-eyed man. The noise woke up the other residents of the basement, who rushed haggardly to the gates of their cells. Their gazes tried to pierce the gloom as the toothless old man, still seated in his cell, burst into mad laughter.

Iskandar was beside himself with rage.

-- You dare to talk about religion when you are just animals. Animals hungry for pleasure. You use the sacred texts to justify your worst actions. Allah didn't create us to enslave women, but to respect them. Both of you have lost your qualities as men. Rapists, to me, are worse than murderers and pork eaters.

-- The judge might not agree with you!, snorted the young man, whose foul odor managed to overpower the worst stench of the basement. Either way, no one will come and complain. Her dad already took care of her after disowning her ...

Laughing, he traced a horizontal line on his neck with his fingertip. Iskandar was raising his baton to bang against the bars a second time when the explosion sounded from the ground floor. The walls of the basement vibrated and a cloud of dust and rubble crept into the stairwell. The prisoners thought there was an earthquake and began to scream.

-- Open the doors, let us out!

Iskandar froze. He had been a rescue worker and knew the effects of earthquakes. When the earth awoke, it made the sound of a drum roll, not the sound of a cannon shot. The explosion was likely the result of a ruptured gas line. Everything was so run down in this building.

-- Shut your mouths!, he shouted to silence the fearful voices.

He was heading for the stairs when the staccato of several automatic weapons tore through the silence that had settled in just after the explosion. Exclamations of terror and curses of all kinds echoed around him.

The inspector became aware that this was an attack and at the same time realized that he could only rely on himself if he wanted to save his life. The outpost was located far from Medan, in a particularly isolated area. He undid the strap that protected his weapon, tightened his hand on his baton and went to press himself against the wall near the doorframe delimiting the access to the ground floor.

A clamor arose from the cells. The prisoners came to understand in their turn. If there was violence, it had to be to release them.

-- Over here, over here! Come downstairs! Below! Come and free us.

Iskandar only had time to swear. The guard he had passed on entering the tunnel appeared, staggering, his head bleeding. He was followed by three men dressed in military fatigues and armed with Kalashnikovs, one of whom was pointing the barrel of his machine gun at his back. Each one wore a keffiyeh around his neck and had their faces partially hidden. They found Iskandar with his back pressed against the damp wall and one of them pointed his gun at him.

-- Drop that gun.

The inspector did so. He was a veteran policeman who had been on more than one raid, and knew from experience that it would be pointless to resist.

-- It's all right!, the masked man said.

His weapon traced a semicircle in the direction of the guard, whom he sprayed with a short burst without even looking at him. Iskandar's colleague collapsed with a cry and the clamor resumed.

-- It's the GAM, it's the GAM! Kill all those son of a bitch cops!

-- Silence!, thundered the militant who seemed to have authority over the other two.

The prisoners fell silent. He returned to Iskandar.

-- How are your cells organized?

-- I don't understand.

-- What cells are the political prisoners in?

The inspector pointed to the larger cavity that opened towards the beginning of the corridor.

-- How many do you have?

-- Yesterday there were seventeen. But the register is not up to date. I didn't count today.

-- Do you have the keys on you?

Iskandar nodded.

-- Go open it and bring them out one by one.

He obeyed. A few moments later, the basement was invaded by a motley group of haggard and staggering inmates. The youngest must have been fourteen, while the oldest was over sixty. There were sixteen of them, most of them dressed in jellabiyas studded with spots and wearing knitted skullcaps. They all had more or less full beards.

-- Which of you are ready to give your lives for Allah and the *Ummah?*, asked the masked man, referring to the community of Muslim believers.

Enthusiastic exclamations answered him. Some raised their fists, others raised their fingers in the Islamist way.

-- Go up and join the men.

Then, turning to the inspector:

-- What else do you have?

-- Common criminals.

-- Do you have thieves?

Iskandar pointed to a cell. The chief motioned to one of his men. He stood at attention between two bars and swept the inside of the cell with several bursts of gunfire. The prisoners fell into the darkness, most without even a cry.

-- Allah forbids theft and blasphemy!, he said, his finger stretched out towards an imaginary sky. And over there, what do you have there?

-- Rapists awaiting trial.

-- Go and open it up for them.

The inspector hesitated a fraction of a second too long. The butt of the Kalashnikov sank between its ribs, causing searing pain. Once again he was forced to obey. The one-eyed man stepped out first, shaken by a burst of laughter. One by one, the sex offenders appeared in the pale light of the neon lights running along the basement.

-- Are you ready to fight?, asked the leader of the militants, pointing the barrel of his gun at the group that had just formed.

They answered with an enthusiastic 'Yes'.

-- And you?, he asked Iskandar.

-- I'm a police officer. At the service of my nation and my government.

-- At least you show courage. You deserve to be able to recite the *shahada.*

The inspector, overflowing with sadness, nodded his head, having one last thought for his wife and six children and closed his eyes to recite the Muslim creed.

-- Lā ʾilāha ʾill-Allāh, wa Muammadun rasūl-Allāh.

He heard the blast, and plunged into nothingness.

***

Darwis Haikal loved the jungle. In other circumstances, there was no doubt that he would have appreciated the journey he and Adhi had been forced to participate in since leaving Tangse. This inextricable cocoon of a wet atmosphere, inhabited by thousands of indefinable cries, was one of his favorite environments.

They had been advancing for three days, with the guides in the lead pulling two donkeys whose backs were bent under the weight of baskets and bags full of weapons and provisions. The animals were less efficient, but much more discreet than elephants, the usual companions of jungle explorers on the island of Sumatra.

On the first day, the men took turns carrying the injured man lying on a makeshift stretcher. But he had recovered faster than expected, and he had been walking at the same pace as the others since the day before, supporting himself on a crutch made from bamboo.

At night, they found a waterhole and settled down on the ground around it to snatch a few hours of rest before leaving as soon as the first rays of sunlight broke through the forest canopy. They never lit a fire and had to eat their food raw, soaked in a brew of lemon and peppers. Darwis's stomach and intestines remembered this at every moment.

But it was his feet that hurt the most, sometimes to the point of making him want to scream. The day before, he had tried to negotiate a break, but had only been given five minutes to undo his shoes, burst his blisters and bandage himself up.

With the exception of Adhi, who from time to time demanded food or drink or expressed his fatigue and a man by the first name of Rama who conveyed orders to him tersely, no one had spoken to him since their departure.

Not even Habib Saragih.

The latter most often prayed while walking, sometimes gave brief orders and, in the evening, launched into long conversations in German with the two strangers. Where had he learned the language? No one knew.

At the pace they were advancing, they must have covered twenty kilometers. A record, given the thickness of the vegetation and the number of obstacles they had to overcome. It had been a long time since they had heard the calls of muezzins from the minarets, the last signs of civilization.

Devastated several times by typhoons, the area was all the more impenetrable, since thousands of uprooted trees formed natural dams in the heart of the layers of vegetation. A few trails remained, known only to members of the separatist organization. As they moved deeper into the rainforest, more men joined the small group, which had grown from a dozen to more than forty fighters.

-- How are you, Adhi? Do you like to visit the forest?

The young man turned his head towards his foster father, his features expressionless. A few meters away, nestled in the hollow of a natural bed of lianas and ferns, a half-asleep female orangutan, her baby nestled against her red fur, watched the strange procession of humans.

Despite the pain that overwhelmed him, Darwis smiled. He liked the apes, too. Those from North Sumatra belonged to an endangered species and, while several specimens still delighted a few tourists around Medan, it was rare to find them further south and along the ocean.

The track suddenly came to a waterhole formed by a torrent and a small waterfall, in the heart of a large, uneven clearing overlooking a cliff. A camp of canvas tents, which could hold a good hundred men, had already been set up there. Some men were busy around a fire. Others were carrying crates. Still others were resting, casually stretched out along the shore. They got up when they saw them. There were several foreigners among them. Blond men of impressive height in comparison with the average-sized Indonesians who bustled around them.

Saragih gave a few brief orders, and the guides relieved the donkeys of their loads of weapons. Kalashnikovs and pistols were distributed among the men, while the sheikh went up to the first tent, accompanied by the two Germans and soon joined by three other foreigners.

Rama drew Darwis' attention to a flat slab overhanging the cliff, the edge of which brushed the waterfall.

-- You two don't move until the sheikh gives you orders. Understood?

Darwis obeyed. At a nod from his adoptive father, Adhi did the same and assumed his favorite posture, feet dangling in the air, rocking back and forth chanting unintelligible words as he was used to doing.

The trail they had taken disappeared into a wall of sago palms with scaly trunks, papaya trees, nipa palms with curved leaves, and bamboos tightly entangled with yams with gigantic tubers. The canopy, which extended more than twenty meters above their heads, formed an intense green cradle around the waterhole. Multicolored birds fluttered above the waterfall, aiming at tiny iguana-headed lizards, in a magical halo recalling the of creation of the world.

-- May I ask where we are?, Darwis asked, bringing his feet closer to the waterfall.

The cold, almost icy water did him immense good. He sighed in relief.

-- Somewhere halfway down the south coast, Rama replied. Only the sheikh and the guides know our exact position.

The doctor raised a surprised eyebrow. It was the longest sentence he had heard since they had left Tangse. Rama was a short, stocky, muscular man. The fact that he was addressing him as if he were part of the group reassured Darwis, who was emboldened to ask:

-- Do you know what the sheikh intends to do with us?

Rama shrugged his shoulders to show his ignorance.

-- Do you have other wounded men for me to treat?

He answered with a sneer, then said:

-- Sometimes sick people. Often dead. Wounded people all the time.

-- And I'm the only doctor you've found?

-- We had another one. A close friend of the sheikh. But he died on a mission last month.

-- A mission?, Darwis repeated.

-- He was also a fighter, Rama suddenly said evasively and on his guard as a new group of about thirty men appeared from deep in the jungle at the other end of the camp.

Their arrival caused a stir among the tents. Most of the militants ceased their activities and those who were seated or lying down got up. Some uttered exclamations of joy, others came forward to meet them.

The sheikh appeared at the opening of his tent. He left the Germans to join the leading men and embraced the one who was evidently the leader. Half of the newcomers were dressed in military fatigues, the rest in jellabiyas, which looked more like rags.

-- Who are they?, Darwis asked in fascination.

-- Members of *Jemaah Islamiyah*, our new allies.

Rama briefly eyed the doctor.

-- And now, stop asking questions. I'll end up in trouble if I'm seen answering you too often.

Darwis nodded. Rama had always behaved decently. Better to make him an ally.

Not a minute passed before one of Saragih's men ran in their direction.

-- The sheikh wants to see both of you, he announced to Darwis.

He put on his shoes with a grimace and followed him, followed by Adhi, to the tent where Saragih had settled in, surrounded by the strangers and two members of the new group.

The floor was covered with a canvas tarp over which footstools and cushions had been thrown. A prayer rug was rolled up in one corner. An open crate that served as a support for half a dozen Kalashnikovs revealed its contents of handguns and ammunition.

-- Doctor Haikal, welcome! The sheikh greeted him with such civility that he might have thought he had been invited to a causal living room conversation.

-- Salam Alaikum, murmured Darwis.

-- Alaikum Salam, replied Saragih's new allies, as the strangers nodded at him.

-- Come and sit among us, invited the sheikh. Would you like some tea?

A metal decanter placed on a tray let out curls of steam. Saragih handed him a cup. Darwis hadn't had anything since waking up and readily agreed. While raising the cup to his lips, he quickly observed the small group that had formed around Saragih. The foreigners were oddly similar to each other. Tall, with blond or light brown hair, weathered faces, tanned skins, dressed in impeccable jungle outfits without a stain or a crease. The two members of Jemaah Islamiyah wore that fierce air that is acquired in underground combat. Their fatigues were dusty and stained with dirt, among which Darwis recognized traces of blood.

Saragih, as cordial as ever, made full introductions.

-- Our European friends belong to the organization *Grundstück und Teilung*. Do you speak German, Doctor?

Darwis replied in the negative.

-- It means "Land and Sharing". It's is an association that's helping to rebuild Aceh. But they've discovered other interests which, thanks be to Allah, are similar to ours. You must be wondering why I am bothering to tell you this? Come closer, Doctor. Leave some room for your son ... what's his name, now?

-- His name is Adhi ... Please don't touch him, Darwis added hastily seeing that one of the Germans was raising his hand towards him.

The stranger let his arm drop and said something in his own language.

-- *Gaja?*, he asked in Indonesian.

-- No, he's not crazy, the doctor protested. He's just different.

The German nodded and added a sentence for the benefit of his companions.

-- Wilfried would like to be able to study the boy, translated the man closest to him.

-- That would be difficult, Darwis said. Adhi is often on the defensive, and only I can approach him.

-- We'll be careful not to disturb him, agreed Wilfried, which was immediately translated by his companion. But our friend the sheikh is also convinced that he has certain powers. From what I understand, Adhi is endowed with a form of healing magnetism. So he might be a natural healer?

-- I don't know, Darwis confessed. Sometimes he does good things with his hands.

The Germans exchanged knowing looks.

-- He saved my brother in arms, Saragih confirmed.

Since arriving in the tent, Adhi had seemed fascinated by the case of ammunition and pistols that supported the Russian-born assault rifles: Kalaches, the weapon of all revolutions. As Saragih described the miraculous intervention that had saved his companion, he approached the object of his interest, an old Luger P08 that was still brand new. He grabbed it and twirled it around in his hands curiously.

-- Hey! The moron just grabbed a gun!, one of Saragih's men suddenly cried.

Wilfried stood up quickly while laughing.

-- *Nicht anfassen. Das ist meins!*[9].

He snatched the weapon from Adhi's hands and then turned to his companions.

[9] Don't touch that. It's mine!

-- This is a gift from Krueger to the sheikh. Fortunately, it's not loaded. Why did you leave it lying around with the other weapons?

-- Everything was transported in the same crate, the second German apologized.

Adhi froze for a few seconds. Darwis moved closer to him, ready to console him in case the incident provoked another crisis. Oddly enough, the young man had no other reaction than to cast a surprised glance at those around him. He appeared to be in the throes of an important dilemma that could be expressed abruptly by a series of unbearable screams or his withdrawal into a silence from which he would not come out for hours. None of this happened, much to Darwis's relief, who nevertheless slipped him a few soothing words.

-- So you have good control over him!, Saragih noted.

Darwis nodded vaguely. The sheikh announced, in a tone that did not invite discussion:

-- With the help of our friends here, we will provide you with a field hospital. I will allow you to choose two or three men from among my people whom you will train as medics. Does that seem possible to you?

-- I'm a doctor, not a teacher, and I don't know your men.

-- You will also have to give us the list of instruments and other portable equipment that you will need, Wilfried added, without paying attention to what he had said.

-- It might take a long time, Darwis replied, becoming increasingly perplexed.

-- Don't worry. We have almost inexhaustible funds. Ask, and we will provide.

The sheikh gave a smile accompanied by a nod of his movement.

-- We have some big plans, very big plans, he resumed. From now on, all Indonesian organizations aiming at separation from Jakarta will be united around a single power. We've been joined by *Jemaah Islamiyah*. You can't find better fighters in all of South-East Asia ...

The two activists agreed, their faces closed and their expressions dark. Darwis had to make an effort to remember that this man dressed in black, with his fine features under his well trimmed beard and his inviting smile, was above all a terrorist, a criminal who did not hesitate to massacre innocent civilians.

Saragih continued his harangue.

-- Together, we will end years of corruption, immorality and injustice. With the help of our European allies here, we are on our way to seizing power. It's just a matter of time. Do you want to join our fight, Doctor?

-- You don't give me a choice, Darwis sighed, casting a worried glance at Adhi, who was starting to rock back and forth.

-- It's not my will, but Allah's will, Saragih said again.

-- Until victory! Far beyond all of Indonesia, one of the fighters in fatigues said.

The German who served as translator stood up, imitated by his companions.

-- You have twenty-four hours to draw up this list, and one week to train your medics.

-- Chapter 9 --

Washington -- D.C.

Present time.

Despite the ice pack provided by the paramedics, the bruise on Melany's right cheekbone had spread all over her cheek. With her eyelids swollen, she told herself she looked like Hilary Swank after her first game in "Million Dollar Baby," one of her favorite Clint Eastwood films.

She could hardly imagine that barely ten days had passed since her return from Kurdistan and that her INR boss, Walter Garroni, had summoned her just a week before. This thought brought back her memories of that magical night spent with Jeff, and rekindled her sadness at not being able to see him again immediately, when he was probably just a few hundred yards from her, in another wing. from the same building.

Walter Garroni was waiting for her in his office for a debriefing although she had already answered all the questions of two special agents. He was there with Gardner, and the two men rose to greet her and to congratulate her as soon as she walked through the doorway.

-- Melany, how are you feeling?, the INR director asked with concern. The doctor who took care of you reassured me about your general health. Is there anything else we can do for you?

-- As well as possible with three stitches in my shoulder and that nasty bruise, the young woman grumbled. I'll tell you about that after a few good nights sleep.

Melany was not in the mood to be fussed over after an operation that had nearly turned out badly and from which she had not brought in much, other than the certainty that she had investigated a myth.

Hitler returned from the dead ... What could be more ridiculous?

If the neo-Nazi organizations had no other trump card to force their rapprochement with the jihadist movements, her service, the FBI and the CIA could forget about this file and devote their efforts to much more real and more present dangers.

-- You've handled yourself remarkably well, Gardner flattered her, not getting more than a shrug and a wry pout out of her. Bob Franckel was unable to join us, but he also sends his congratulations to you for such quick results ...

-- Above all, I found myself in an impossible situation, Melany retorted. Sir, do I have permission to express myself freely?

-- Of course! Please, Garroni encouraged her.

-- Forgive me, Mr. Gardner, but I'm not sure my safety was a priority when preparing for this operation.

-- What makes you say that?

-- Let's say there were a lot of gaps that Mitchell and his sidekick were able to squeeze into. I feel that I wasn't briefed enough and, since I have been forced to take a man's life to defend my own, I hope I have the right to make a few criticisms. From the moment Derek Mitchell unmasked me, I found myself totally on my own, with no back-up plan or any way to notify you. Oddly enough, the tattoos that were supposed to complement my coverage were the first things that betrayed me.

Gardner twitched. He didn't often appreciate having his methods questioned, but in this case it was an inter-agency operation in which responsibility was shared.

-- Do you really think we let you down, Ms. Carson?

-- I might not use that term, but I admit I was very scared when Todd forced me to text you. It was the end of all contact and therefore of the last-minute protection you promised me.

The still fresh images suddenly returned to haunt Melany. She could hear Todd and Derek's voices again and the memory of his distress gave her a chill. The look that Garroni and Gardner exchanged didn't escape her, however.

-- Very well, then, said the latter. Do you recall how long it took me to respond to you when you sent me this message?

-- Yes sir. Several minutes.

Melany was curious.

-- Do you know what happened between my receiving the SMS on my cell phone and the one you received in return? Of course not. What I am going to tell you should therefore reassure you in retrospect. I immediately realized that something abnormal was happening because your mission was very clear: your target remained the section of the Nazi party led by Mitchell. You had no reason to move away from Odyssey. So I called your supervisor, who acted on my hunch. If you were threatened, we had to give the illusion of falling into a trap. Weren't you surprised how short a time it took us to respond after receiving your call from Mitchell's son's cell phone?

It didn't take a quarter of an hour for the local FBI to circle Melany's exact spot as a helicopter landed in the middle of a clearing less than five hundred yards away. The *cavalry.*

-- As soon as your cell phone's GPS signal disappeared from our screens, we concluded that you were in danger. Todd was also quick to disconnect the transmitter from the Mercedes, but our unmarked cars are doubly equipped. So we were able to follow the vehicle and stop it before he went to drive it into a lake. Always saving money ...

Gardner concluded his words with a smile and Garroni followed suit.

-- All this did not prevent you from finding yourself in danger and, believe me, we deeply regret that. I would never have forgiven myself if anything had happened to you.

-- Without Mark, the Mitchells' eldest son, I wouldn't be here to appreciate your interest in me, Melany said darkly. What are you going to do with that boy?

-- After you gave your deposition, we arrested him, in his own interest. He will never be able to return to live in his community if he is suspected of having helped you. His sentence will be kept to a minimum, just to make up for it, and we will negotiate his release for good behavior after a very short time spent in a secure facility where he will not be bothered. A psychologist is taking care of him. You don't have to worry about him.

-- Thanks, Melany said, who felt she at least owed it to Mark to worry about his fate.

-- All that's left for us to do now is to get you home and wish you the best possible rest and make the most of your time off, this time for real, Garroni concluded.

-- That's all?

-- Do you have any further questions, Melany?

-- Pardon me, sir, but I really don't understand. I thought I was here for a debriefing concluding my mission. Mark told us who he thought was behind the phrase *"The Father of Victory"*, but it all didn't make much sense. The neo-Nazis practicing the Odinist cult are obviously nuts and their folklore is on the level of children's stories, but I find it hard to believe there is so much fuss around such a ridiculous concept. The return of Adolph Hitler among us. In what form? His clone, his reincarnation, his immortal soul, his descendant? Could it just be possible that Mark didn't have access to real information?

-- It is indeed possible, Gardner agreed. But that shouldn't bother you anymore. You have completed your mission and we thank you for it.

-- Do you mean ...?

-- I have good news for you, Garroni interrupted. Given the time you spent in Kurdistan, and the service you have just rendered us, I have granted you an additional week off.

-- Fifteen days of vacation? I wasn't asking so much of you.

-- You risked your life, Melany. You are young. At the very beginning of your career. Enjoy your time off. Do not hesitate to contact the agency psychologist if you have trouble sleeping or if you have signs of post-traumatic stress disorder. That will be all for today ... ah, yes, all the same, I almost forgot:

He dialed the combination of a small safe installed behind him, opened it, and pulled out a cell phone.

-- I'm returning your property to you. You no longer have a reason to hide under a false identity.

-- Am I allowed to stay blonde, since I hear it doesn't look bad on me?, Melany quipped.

One week of rest at their expense ... that was all they had found to offer her to make up for the nightmarish hours she had just endured.

-- Of course, Gardner replied, thinking she was serious.

Melany stood up to shake hands and say goodbye. But not without a last bit of impertinence.

-- Tattoos, too -- can I keep them?

***

Jeff had tried to reach her and it was a real pleasure to hear his voice in the message he had left her. He still believed she was in Kurdistan and hoped that she wouldn't get sunburned, as he had checked the regional weather and discovered that an unprecedented heat wave was affecting the region. He was also surprised that her cell phone was always off and asked for another number where he could call her, while regretting that he had not been available when she had tried to speak to him herself. Nothing but very mundane stuff, but it did her good.

There were other calls, one of which was at least as important. Her mother had finally reappeared. Melany realized that she had been worried about her and let out a little cry of joy.

She was installed in her living room, dressed in her grandmother's bathrobe, her feet resting on the coffee table in front of her television screen connected to Fox News, a bowl of cereal close at hand and in such a state of fatigue that she couldn't help but yawn every ten seconds. Her attention was fixed on the screen as the host invited viewers to join a reporter in the little town of Odyssey.

"Important blow to the neo-Nazi movements of Pennsylvania" read the scrolling headline. "Death of one of the leaders and arrest of several accomplices following an FBI operation".

The report didn't tell Melany anything except that the office had covered it up by blaming Derek's death on a settling of scores between opposing factions and that a further investigation was underway. CNN covered the same story by simply interviewing a local FBI agent she had never seen. All blah, blah, blah.

She turned off her television and called her mother. To her relief, Maureen answered on the second ring.

-- Where did you disappear to?, the latter immediately demanded.

-- It's you who should be asked that, not me!

-- Darling, seriously, I've been worried sick. I've been trying to reach you for twenty-four hours.

-- And me, for over a week ...

Melany thought deeply about it and continued.

-- ... The last time we spoke I was still in Kurdistan. At least you knew where to find me. I can't say the same about you.

-- I went on a cruise, her mother retorted, with a smile in her voice, before stopping and then adding: I've met someone.

Melany sighed. This was not the first time that Maureen had made such an announcement since she had divorced. And it certainly wouldn't be the last. This went on and on.

-- But I'm back in D.C., and I hope to see you today. What are you doing for dinner?

The young woman looked at her watch. It was only three o'clock. She had time to catch up on her lost sleep.

-- No plans, except maybe spending the evening with my mother, she replied, delighted at the idea.

***

Maureen looked amazing. With a slightly tanned complexion, with smooth, rested features and a radiant smile, she looked as if she had had the time of her life, and Melany, who was not of an envious nature, might almost have felt a hint of jealousy.

In recent years her flaming hair, the heritage of her Irish origins, had turned gray, but she refused to color it, claiming, not without reason, that her age had to be accepted and that in any case the silver threads added a touch of wisdom to her appearance. She was one of those women who dress elegantly and whose figure retains its shape despite a taste for good food. She never denied herself anything. Melany had feared the worst and felt relieved to find her in such good shape.

The converse was not true. Maureen let out a cry of horror upon seeing her.

-- My God, what's happened to you? Did you have an accident? Have you broken anything? And what's this hair color?

Their usual restaurant, Chez Billy Sud, was a reasonably chic little French bistro in the heart of Georgetown. Maureen had discovered it while her name was still Mrs. Carson and it had become one of her favorite places, especially for Dijon mussels and soft-shell crab. The maître d' always reserved the best table for her, either by the log fire in the winter or on the patio when it was open. She knew the menu by heart and was already sipping a glass of rosé wine when her daughter arrived ten minutes late.

Melany kissed her warmly and took a seat in the booth while Gerard, the maître d, slipped a menu into her hands.

-- Could I have the same? she said, pointing at Maureen's glass.

-- Excellent choice, Ms. Carson. It's a Gaillac, Domaine de Terrisses, 2016. By the glass, or by the bottle?

Gerard was a middle-aged man with a slightly bald head and a small black mustache and always in a good mood. Having emigrated to the USA decades ago, he took pleasure in forcing his French accent to stay alive, just to add a touch of local color to an atmosphere that didn't need it.

-- A bottle, of course. And then, take back your menu. Tonight, I'll just be copying everything from my mother.

-- Are you sure?, Maureen worried. I chose the escargot soup followed by beef cheek.

-- So much for our diet, Melany laughed, taking her mother's hands into hers. If you only knew how happy I am to have dinner with you.

-- And so am I. Now tell me what happened to you: You look terrible! What are those bruises on your face? You look like you went under a train.

-- You haven't seen the condition of the locomotive! Melany joked, wrinkling her nose.

-- Seriously!

The young woman took a deep breath. Her mission was over, there were no more secrets to keep, and anyway Maureen was a trustworthy person. It was enough for her to say that her disclosures were confidential in order to be sure that anything she said would remain between them. Besides, she needed some advice and still couldn't stomach being sidelined after risking her life for background information.

-- The INR asked me to do something unusual, she said at the outset.

By the time she finished telling her, the two women had each finished a glass of wine. Then the entrée came and Melany continued her story between bites. As she recalled the events of the previous days, Melany saw her mother turn pale and play more and more nervously with her drink. She barely swallowed three spoonful's of the soup, which was delicious.

-- My God! You're completely crazy for having accepted that mission. I can't believe what happened to you.

-- Oh, yeah? What would you have done in my place?

Melany immediately blamed herself for the aggressive retort. Her mother had started a promising career at MI6 and was one of the highest-rated field agents when she discovered she was pregnant. The arrival of her daughter had forced her to give up everything, to devote herself only to her and to her husband. Suddenly there was sadness in her dreamy gaze, despite the smile she continued to display.

-- Sorry ... Melany said to herself.

-- You have nothing to reproach yourself for and you did well to ask me that question. I think, unfortunately, I would have gone for it, like you did. You just can't lie, can you?

-- I'll drink to that!, Melany said raising her glass happily. But your turn now. What's all this about a cruise? And this man -- where did you meet him? What does he do, what's his name?

-- Is that all you want to know? Maureen laughed. If I don't answer, will you put me through the third degree?

It turned out that, two months earlier, she had bumped into a former MI6 colleague at an art opening near Dupont Circle. The man was divorced like her and the father of two children. He had left the British intelligence service after an honorable career and turned to financial cyber-security. His company, which had gone public, was now listed on the Nasdaq. Although the two had barely known each other in their younger days, they had found enough in common to make them want to see each other again. From romantic dinner to country weekend, a loving bond had established itself which had led her to agree to accompany him on a cruise in the Caribbean.

-- A most everyday story but God, how good it felt! Try to imagine myself lying on the deckchair on the upper deck of an ocean liner, my hair tied up in a scarf, tortoiseshell sunglasses straddling my nose. Difficult to be more out of date than that! But here's the thing. Even after a week of not being able to escape and despite my seasickness, which almost drove him crazy the first few days, we continued to get along well. He's always in a good mood. Nothing seems to irritate him. He makes me laugh. To be honest with you, he sometimes reminds me of your father ...

-- Well, then, Melany said sourly, why did you get a divorce?

Her mother sighed and took her hand again.

-- I know you've always had a hard time dealing with our separation, and I understand you. But at least your father and I parted ways like adults, remaining good friends. It's rare enough to be worth emphasizing ... Now, back to your mission. There are several details that drew my attention ...

Melany pushed back the glass she was about to raise to her lips. Fatigue and too much emotion helped her feel tipsy even though the bottle was still half full. No way to let go in the middle of such a conversation. Although she had long since retired from MI6, her mother had maintained numerous contacts with the intelligence service and her position as the wife of a military attaché had led her to sharpen her instincts far more than an ordinary woman. Her advice was always welcome and her interpretation of the facts was often very sharp. Melany focused entirely on Maureen's voice.

-- What details?

-- One, in particular. The *Father of Victory* ... I've heard that expression before, a long time ago. To tell the truth, it was during the last days of my assignment in Moscow, where I met your father. I was already pregnant with you ...

Maureen's gaze wandered off. The events she was referring to had taken place twenty-nine years ago.

Gorbachev had stunned the world with the dismantling of his Empire and his opening up to the West. Of course, anyone with even the slightest bit of information knew that he had no choice. The war in Afghanistan had brought the Soviets to their knees, the Russian economy was a disaster, and revolt was brewing everywhere. We made a hero of the last leader of the USSR and that was fair enough, but the reforms he put in place had been necessary for far too long. His *glasnost,* his *perestroika*, were just words, betraying a de facto situation that could have led to a new revolution. It was a blessed time for Western intelligence. The number of high-level defections would have been inconceivable a decade earlier. Pilots like Aleksandr Zuyev, athletes like Alexander Mogilny, Kalinikos Kreanga, scientists like Vladimir Pasechnik and Kanasian Alibekov, but above all agents of the GRU and the KGB. Stanislav Lunev single-handedly nearly ended the Cold War by revealing to the CIA the location of all KGB weapons caches on American soil. But none had brought as much information as the former head of the KGB archives, Vasily Mitrokhin, who went West with 27,000 newly made copies of documents. The problem with these defections was the same for all the intelligence services. How to know that this is a genuine betrayal and not the infiltration of a double agent? Mitrokhin got thrown out by the CIA, which didn't believe his story. So he turned to MI6. At that time, I was still in London, but the agency didn't have enough fluent Russian-speaking staff on hand. So I was sent to Moscow on a mission to approach Mitrokhin's professional entourage, including his former right-hand man, whose name I have forgotten but not his code name. Wagner.

Maureen shook her head with a smile and concentrated for a few moments on her beef cheek and took a large bite of it with a good glassful of rosé.

-- Mmmmh! Delicious. Eat, darling, it's going to get cold.

Melany imitated her mother, disappointed that she had lost all her appetite, but intrigued and eager to hear the rest of the story. His mother emitted a little conniving laugh, suddenly remembering one juicy detail.

-- My first meeting with Wagner was interesting. We knew he frequented the bar at the Moskva Hotel, a rallying point for the amateur prostitutes who abounded in those days. The Russian students could no longer even afford to buy a notebook, let alone pay for their ration tickets. For a few years, the most beautiful girls on the planet were reduced to offering their bodies for a carton of cigarettes. Normally, only passing tourists and businessmen were supposed to take advantage of this sad windfall. But KGB members often took advantage of their privileges. I had to sympathize with this Wagner and report on his opinion of his former boss's defection as soon as Russian intelligence got wind of his betrayal. So here's your mother all dressed in red, with two-inch heels, outrageously made-up and three buttons on her blouse undone to show off her charms ...

-- You must have been beautiful, Melany appreciated and decided to take a sip of rosé after all.

Gerard, seeing that she wasn't touching her plate, discreetly walked towards their booth to ask if everything was all right. The two women gently dismissed him with a nod indicating that they did not wish to be disturbed in their conversation.

-- I was *spectacular!*, Maureen laughed. That was, in any case, Wagner's opinion, who devoured me with his gaze for several long minutes before finally daring to approach me. He quickly realized that I did not belong to the category he was used to and of course was suspicious as soon as I introduced myself. A pretty woman admitting to working for the British Consulate, fluent in Russian ... I reeked of MI6. But that wasn't the problem. At my level, we were all exposed. We were banking on the willingness of the Russian secret services to reciprocate and I hoped that Wagner would be given the mission to turn me away from mine ... Unfortunately, his management reacted intelligently, and things didn't turn out that way at all ...

It was the first time that Maureen had spoken in so much detail about her years at MI6. Melany wondered where she was going with this and listened patiently. She realized that she and her mother had much more in common than she had ever wanted to recognize. If only a fierce appetite for life with a healthy dose of cynicism and a taste for complicated situations. But where did the *Father of Victory* fit in with this whole story? Maureen finally got to the heart of the matter.

-- Wagner was a true Soviet, much more attached to the system established by Lenin and Stalin than to Mother Russia. As far as I remember, his MI6 file described him as a hardline communist with fascist tendencies. He had performed violence for the KGB in Afghanistan, before being assigned to the archives under Mitrokhin. I think that his handlers didn't appreciate him getting in touch with me, even though nothing happened between us, unless there was some other mischief -- I don't have any information about that, but shortly after we met he was demoted and shunted aside. He was not the kind of individual to appreciate or to accept being treated like that ... Still, about seven or eight months after that, we met at the hotel bar, a few weeks before I resigned from MI6 to take care of my little baby ...

Maureen gave her daughter a fond smile, as if to say that she really didn't regret her decision.

-- ... I just remember it being bitterly cold, which is not unusual in Moscow. As I was walking home, the shape of a man emerged from the darkness in the hallway of my apartment building. You can't imagine the fear I had before I recognized that it was Wagner. But then, what a relief! One of two things: either he had been sent to turn me or he wanted to follow in the footsteps of his old boss. I invited him in for a drink at my place but he refused. He was worried that my apartment was full of bugs. So we remained standing at the entrance on the ground floor. Wagner believed he had important information that would in turn have enabled him to start a new life in the West. The Soviet Union no longer existed, the regime was softening, and Boris Yeltsin, a pro-Western pragmatist, had succeeded Gorbachev. For a hardline partisan, that was a lot to digest. But men are the same everywhere. He must have thought that as long as he had to endure the abominable capitalist system, he might as well do it in some style, in a country where they don't put you in jail for daring to approach a pretty girl in a bar. The unfortunate man had been transferred to the archives of the Second World War. What could he have found there as a bargaining chip for his passage to the West? You'll never guess ...

Maureen liked to make sure of her effect. She took the time to pour herself a glass of wine and finish it halfway before continuing.

-- He had in his hands a will written in Hitler's own handwriting. True, false, I don't know. Historians agree that, before he died, the Führer had summoned his secretary to dictate two documents ... Yes, the ones you saw copies of in this museum in Odyssey. This third text was his "esoteric" testament. My German was not good enough to appreciate its nuances, but Wagner said that it was in the dictator's handwriting. In summary, as far as I remember, Hitler explained that he had ordered Himmler to have metempsychosis researched in Tibet and that the Anhenerbe, the notorious center for race research run by the Reichsführer, had not only reported having proof that men reincarnate, but also the method by which souls can be found under their new identity. That's how the followers of the Dalai Lama were able to recognize their master. Wagner claimed he had two other documents, found connected to the first one, which described the method in coded form. He hadn't been able to decipher them. As a matter of conscience, I shared the information with my superiors and they did nothing but laugh at me. The only thing I clearly remember is that Hitler used the same terms for his return among the living. *"Ich werde der Vater des Sieges sein"* -- "I will be the Father of Victory". A total farce.

Melany shivered all over her body.

-- Mom, it doesn't matter if this document was true or false. After your services turned him away, Wagner had to get close to right-wing extremist organizations, or maybe Nazis in exile. In any case, the will has been circulated. Hitler didn't reincarnate, that is all hogwash, and if the laws of karma did exist, he would be fighting for his food with dung beetles on the outskirts of Auschwitz at the bottom of a garbage pit. But the risk is that some people will believe it.

-- You're right, Maureen agreed. Nothing is more dangerous than a myth.

The two women looked at each other silently, aware of the significance of the facts they had just combined..

-- Do you think Wagner is still alive?, Melany finally asked.

-- If he is, then he must be around sixty-five years old.

-- He should be lucid at that age. Unless he's taken to vodka.

-- Do you have any ideas?

-- None. But what good would it do me to have access to confidential information if I can't find a former KGB officer who decided to move to the West less than thirty years ago?

-- Melany? Seriously?

The young woman wrinkled her nose mischievously and her mother had a bad premonition.

-- Chapter 10 --

Melany woke up early after a relatively peaceful night's sleep, given what she had been through. Her shoulder was aching and she was suffering from the onset of a migraine, probably from the third glass of rosé she had finished in one go. A tablet and two strong coffees quickly ended it.

A taxi dropped her off at the State Department before the first analysts arrived. The big clock in the central hall of the building, which was reminiscent of one in a railway station, said 6:45 a.m. Garroni wouldn't be there for a good hour. The guard at the entrance nodded to her before returning her cell phone and keys, which had like her been screened by a detector.

She had a strange feeling when she sat down in front of one of the many computers in the analysts' common room. Her security level was limited, but she was convinced it would be sufficient to obtain information dating back more than twenty years. Two colleagues on the night shift were wrapping up their assignments and a mound of freshly printed papers was piling up on their desks. They had just one thing in mind, which was to get home and go to bed, and they barely paid any attention to Melany when she greeted them.

Walter Garroni would no doubt see her name in the list of employee entries, but she had a ready answer if he ever asked her about her presence at the agency. She wanted to send Mark a word of thanks, and didn't know what detention facility he had been sent to. Even if that explanation didn't work, there wasn't much that could happen to her. So she had no reason to worry.

To her relief, her passcode was still valid. The search window appeared on the screen. She entered a request for access to the CIA archives, then the code name "Wagner" and the year she was interested in. It took her less than a second to get her answer, in the form of a complete card illustrated with several photographs.

Alexei Gerhard Soloviev -- Alias: Wagner.
Date of Birth: January 19, 1942. Death: Unknown.
Parents: Dimitri Soloviev, Lieutenant Colonel in the Red Army and Magda Krueger.
German origin, born in Leipzig.
Position: KGB field agent from 1969 to 1980.
Sent to Afghanistan as a member of the Zenith unit from 1979 to 1981.
First assistant to Vasily Mitrokhin from 1982 to 1985.
Participated in the transfer of the KGB archives.
Demoted in February 1992 following the defection of Mitrokhin.
Last known domicile: 139 Borovsky Proyezd -- Solntsevo -- Moscow Oblast
Resigned from the KGB, which became the FSB, between 1995 and 1998.
Defection: Unknown.
Level of surveillance: Not applicable.

One of the photos from the sixties showed him in military uniform. The other two, more recent but blurrier, had been taken with a telephoto lens on the streets of Moscow. He was athletic-looking, appeared to be tall, had very short hair and stood slightly hunched over, in contrast to the martial demeanor he displayed in the first shot.

That was all. Melany was disappointed. Much water had flowed under the bridges on the Moskva River since 1993, but she copied down the address anyway.

-- *What for?,* she wondered, turning off the computer. *You're going to look up his phone number, give him a call and ask him if he remembers Hitler's will?*

The idea caused made her shrug her shoulders. Wasn't it enough for her to miss being buried alive in the middle of a snowy forest? Where did she get her intention to play secret agent, she whom the CIA had not even wanted?

But "Good blood can't lie," Maureen had told her with an ounce of pride. Subconsciously, Melany felt like she owed her mother something. And then, both shared the same loathing of the Nazis and any form of totalitarianism.

That such a breed could have survived into the 21st century, to the point of organizing itself into different factions and, perhaps, of finding surrogates in the jihadist movement, was beyond her comprehension. The worst thing that could happen would be for organizations like Daesh or Hezbollah to end their fratricidal conflict in order to come together under the same banner and make an alliance with the neo-Nazis.

She sighed and turned off the screen and then went back the other way. It was all political fiction and philosophical digression. Melany had no resources to carry out even the start of an investigation. The CIA, for its part, had made many errors in the past, between the false reports on the presence of weapons of mass destruction in Iraq, the failure to find the tons of deadly gas that had undoubtedly crossed the Syrian border before the American invasion and, to go back to the end of the Cold War, the foolish rejection of Vasily Mitrokhin, who had fortunately landed with MI6 but who could have given other intelligence services, less close to the United States, the benefit of the spectacular mass of archives that he had exfiltrated.

All she had to do was make the most of her two week vacation.

In order to do what? To go on a Caribbean cruise like my mother?

Immersed in her somewhat gloomy reflections, she had just put her badge on the scanner of the exit gate when a voice called out to her.

-- Melany?

She lifted her head and her heart leaped up. It was neither an illusion nor a fantasy. Emerging out of nowhere, Jeffrey stood before her, eyes rounded in surprise, elegant as usual, fingers clutching the badge he was about to scan.

What an idiot to come out through the main door instead of the side!

-- Hello, Jeff, she said in a very quiet voice.

She didn't need a mirror to know she was red right down to the roots of her hair. The guard glanced at them vaguely. It was time for the analysts to arrive and a line was starting to form in front of the detector. With a gesture, he asked Jeffrey to step aside. He did so and took Melany by the arm.

-- But, what are you doing here? I thought you were ...

-- ... in Kurdistan. I know. Would you rather we just stand here, staring at each other like faience dogs, or should I invite you to breakfast and tell you all about it?

A few minutes later they found themselves seated at a table in the Garden Café, a small hotel restaurant that was welcoming its first customers of the morning.

-- First of all, Jeffrey asked, what is that hair color? And those bruises on your face? You look terrible. You'll have to explain it all to me ...

Melany couldn't keep from laughing.

-- You sound just like my mother. Those are almost exactly the questions she asked me yesterday.

-- You will agree that I do have good reason to act like her.

-- And if I tell you I'm glad I bumped into you by chance, and I didn't dare call you, would you believe me?

She put her hand on the table and brushed Jeffrey's fingers. A sleepy waitress refilled their cups of coffee. They ordered freshly squeezed orange juice, pancakes, and an omelet for Melany.

-- So, where should I begin?, she asked.

-- From the beginning, I suppose. That call you got when we were at your place ...

Until this morning, she hadn't known what to do with Jeff. The universe of the intelligence service created habits. Never reveal anything about ongoing missions. Say as little as possible about completed operations. Keep information awaiting analysis to yourself. Avoid bringing up work-related topics, even with colleagues. And then there were those damn tattoos, which wouldn't go away for a good ten days or so. Even if it was for a good cause, she was ashamed enough to not start up again with Jeff until they were gone.

But fate had decided otherwise, and since he was there, now, in front of her, the least she could do was to offer him the explanations he deserved.

She thus revealed to him the events of the last few days, without omitting any details. Including the conversation she had had the day before with her mother and Jeffrey listened to it from beginning to end, without interrupting her once.

-- That's it, Melany concluded. Now you know everything.

Jeffrey nodded and let out a whistle.

-- As if I were expecting this!

-- I'm so sorry.

-- You don't have to apologize. I would have done the same if I were in your shoes. Except for one detail, maybe.

-- What?

-- I wouldn't have hesitated to show you my tattoos.

-- You say that because you haven't seen them yet. I assure you that they are really an eyesore.

-- Don't make me do anything more intimate.

There was happiness in his voice. In an instant, Melany felt like she was melting. She was seized with an irresistible urge to kiss him, at the risk of overturning everything on the table. Wasn't it time to exorcise all these tensions by resuming their too-brief relationship where it had left off? She restrained herself at the very last minute.

-- Their coffee is really terrible!, Jeffrey said, intertwining his fingers with Melany's.

-- I feel like you have the same idea I have.

-- Are you referring to your old espresso machine? Frankly, I've got a much better at home ...

They had barely touched their pancakes. The omelet remained intact. No sooner had the check been paid than they went out, hand in hand, looking for a taxi.

***

Jeffrey's penthouse, which was located between 23rd and 24th Street in the heart of Washington, opened onto a broad terrace blocked from the neighborhood by rows of thuja cedars and wireworts planted in pots. The luxurious apartment mixed disparate volumes in a nest designed to confer a form of intimacy to a space opened up by large bay windows. Everything was an immaculate white. From solid wood floors to designer furniture through curtains and frames displaying photographs of masters and watercolors in monochrome tones. It was an architect's apartment, designed by a man of taste. Melany had been pleasantly surprised when she arrived. The bedroom was like a cocoon.

She escaped Jeffrey's arm and crawled out of bed before asking:

-- This is ... really your place? You live all alone here?

-- Since my old dog died and my girlfriend left me to retire to an ashram after falling in love with a guru ... Yes. No one shares my life with me.

-- Are you kidding me or ...?

-- Just a little bit. It's true about the dog, not so much for the ashram.

Jeffrey crouched to take advantage of the shadow cast by Melany's body against the light.

-- How long are you going to keep that T-shirt on? I should point out that the air conditioning is set to maintain the temperature of the room at 69 degrees, winter and summer.

-- You know very well why I keep it on.

Jeffrey wasn't the type to grumble. But he did, however.

-- But your tattoos? It's not as if you're a real Nazi. I won't go so far as to say I think they're pretty, they're even downright hideous, but it's going to take a lot more than that to make you repulsive.

-- I don't agree with you. Every time I look at myself in the mirror, I feel like throwing up.

-- Just be patient. You told me yourself that the ink would be gone in a few days.

Melany shrugged and took refuge in the bathroom. The water fixture had a central basin lined with cushions that served as a bathtub, a hammam, and a shower equipped with jets.

After a few minutes, she reappeared in the bedroom wearing a hooded robe she was floating in. Jeffrey found it delicious and let her know.

-- Now you'll explain it to me, she said, letting herself fall back on the bed. You can't possibly live here on your salary at the State Department. What are you in? Prostitution or drug trafficking?

-- Both.

-- Seriously!

He took her hand to play with her fingers.

-- Alas, none of that!

-- Jeffrey?

-- I would have preferred to be guilty of trafficking. It's just part of my grandparent's legacy.

Melany bit back an admiring whistle. An apartment of this size in one of Washington's most upscale neighborhoods ... Jeffrey's grandparents must have had some means! She, who didn't give a damn about material possessions, had to admit that she was impressed. She chose to tease him.

-- Given your job as a paper pusher, I imagined you in a bachelor apartment where you were struggling to pay the rent. But now that I've found out what you live in, you'll see me more often.

-- I didn't know my Mata Hari was such a venal girl.

Melany ruffled her hair.

-- *Your* Mata Hari? And I didn't know you were an idle heir, allowed to leave your office whenever you want to have sex with a girl who only wants your money. Now that we've expressed our feelings for each other, where's the coffee you promised me? Do you have to hail a cab to get to your kitchen?

Jeffrey got out of bed naked, wrapped the towel she had dropped around her waist, and led her to the lower level that was accessible by a wide spiral staircase. In passing, he showed her his office, which had a balcony overlooking the Potomac.

-- I hope you don't take me for a show off, he apologized, showing her how the coffee machine worked. My grandparents were in manufacturing and finance. A tragedy made me their only heir.

Jeffrey's gaze darkened, briefly expressing a pain that touched Melany deeply.

-- A tragedy?

-- My parents died in a car accident. They were driving at night with my little brother when a drunk driver hit them with his truck on Arlington Road, not even two miles from their home.

-- And ... your brother? Melany guessed.

-- He lives in a facility for the disabled. The impact to his head at the time of the accident left him with only his vital functions intact. I see him from time to time. Sometimes he recognizes me ...

Melany took his hand tenderly. He gently pulled her out and gave her a sad smile that he wiped off his face as he handed her cup of coffee.

-- Do you want to drink it here or do you prefer that we go to the living room?

Seeing that Melany was still frozen, he added:

-- That was ten years ago. I've had time to recover. My grandparents died a few months later. One after the other, two weeks apart. My father was their only child. There you are: now you know the most important events of my life.

-- I'm sorry, Melany whispered.

He took her arm firmly and led her to the living room.

Melany as if she were sitting on a cloud as she took a seat on the sofa. The furniture was so comfortable that she wondered what material it was made of. To the touch, it felt like silk. The cushions fit the shape of the body perfectly. She sank into it with the pleasure of sinking into a bath. Jeffrey took a seat opposite her in a matching chair.

-- Do you remember our first morning together, when I told you that I had arranged with my office to spend the day with you?

-- I'm sorry I let you down, Melany apologized.

-- You are forgiven, but on one condition. You have to promise me you won't disappear again if I match my vacation to the two weeks you've been forced to take.

-- Why would you do that? Do you plan to take me on a cruise?

-- Let's leave these little joys to the old couples who don't know what to do so they don't get bored together.

-- That's my mother you're insulting ...

Jeffrey frowned and bit his lip.

-- Sorry, I forgot.

His gaze, tarnished by a veil of sadness a few moments earlier, had regained its sparkle. Melany expected him to follow up with a light conversation about their day ahead, their relationship, or a casual exchange. She was surprised when he announced:

-- Let's summarize what we know about the *Father of Victory*, AKA the reincarnation of Adolph Hitler ...

-- This story is unsettling, but I've let it go. What can be done if the CIA and the FBI ignore it? You told me about a little Cuban restaurant ...

-- ... The Führer has risen from the dead to impose his law on all mankind!, Jeffrey continued in the same grave tone, as if he himself believed it.

-- If it weren't so ridiculous, I would find it worrying.

Jeffrey nodded.

-- So on April 30, 1945, before committing suicide, Hitler dictated two wills to his secretary. The first one, which was philosophical, in which he expresses one last time his hatred of the Jews, whom he held responsible for all the misfortunes of humanity. The second one, political, to designate his successor. The same day, or perhaps the day before, we don't know, he writes a third testament, handwritten and esoteric this time, in which he announces that he has the proof that man is reincarnated and that he has the means to discover his next identity. Am I right so far?

Melany nodded her head in agreement.

-- In 1992, some time after the fall of the Berlin Wall, in the middle of the break-up of the Soviet bloc, a high-level KGB agent, Vasily Mitrokhin, defected and, by a happy coincidence, your mother, then an MI6 agent, was assigned to approach an archivist by the name of Wagner, who had been working under him. At the end of their meeting, Wagner finds himself relieved of his functions and relegated to the archives of the Second World War. There, he discovers the will in question and wants to use it as a bargaining chip, in his turn, to move to the West. He's a die-hard communist, a fascist to some degree, like most of them are. Disappointed at the breakup of the Soviet bloc. He contacts your mother again, but gets rebuffed by MI6 and from there we lose track of him. Twenty-seven years later, there is a rumor in neo-Nazi movements that a leader calling himself the *Father of Victory* will appear, as some sort of Messiah. But the old man in question would be nothing other than the reincarnation of Hitler. A more grotesque myth than the Reptilians, the Illuminati and the immortality of Elvis Presley. And this is where it gets interesting: not only the skinheads and other KKK freaks, plus those nostalgic for the Third Reich, but also the nastiest jihadists are all waiting for his return.

-- That's about all we know, Melany had to admit.

-- Under these conditions, let's extrapolate. Let us suppose that jihadists and Nazis are indeed joining forces around a common project. Suppose, too, that they strongly believe in Hitler's return under a new identity. Why all the fuss just now? After thirty years of silence.

-- I don't know.

-- I believe that they've found their Führer reincarnated. Wagner forwarded the documents to an organization capable of decoding them, and this band of illuminati identified Hitler's successor after successfully decrypting the documents attached to his will.

Melany bit the corners of her lips, nodding.

-- It all adds up pretty well.

-- Somewhere or other on this poor planet, a terrorist leader or a fanatic leader, a serial killer, a genocidal psychopath, has become convinced that he is the *Father of Victory*, and therefore the reincarnation of Hitler. Psychiatric asylums are full of guys who think they are Napoleon, Nero or Julius Caesar, but at least they're locked up ...

He hesitated before saying:

-- Now, if the Nazis have found their Führer, there's no reason why we can't go looking for him and identify him.

Melany took a deep breath and studied him intensely.

-- Are you serious?

-- I've never been more so.

-- And why would you do this with me?

Jeffrey wanted to give her the most honest answer possible without revealing his feelings too much. After all, they hardly knew each other yet. You don't tell a woman you've completely fallen for her after just three dates ... But it was in his nature to put passion into everything he did.

-- Would you believe me if I told you that I haven't had any serious business to take care of for a few weeks and that I was starting to get bored?

-- Hardly!

-- Good. What would you say if I explained to you that I met a fearless young woman with many other qualities, with whom I want to embark on an adventure and that I have, like her, a deep hatred for dictators and terrorists. Would that be enough for you?

There was so much naive enthusiasm and sincerity in his words that Melany felt herself melting. A few hours earlier, as she was leaving the State Department premises, she had been ready to drop everything, and now Jeff reappeared in her life and offered her the help she so desperately needed. She resisted the urge to grab him and hug and kiss him.

-- I have some questions for you, too.

-- With or without a polygraph?

Melany shrugged.

-- First, how can you take a vacation or just days off when you want?

-- I have always been a free spirit. That is not going to change now. But since you are serious about it, I am not an employee of the State Department. I have the role of an independent consultant, which allows me to manage my own schedule.

Melany's response was as long in the making as the hinted offer that he had made to her. Jeffrey waited patiently, without taking your eyes off her. He looked relieved when she said:

-- Perhaps we could draw up a list of possible candidates for the title of reincarnated Führer?

He shook his head.

-- That would take too long. You list all the leaders of terrorist organizations, add a few dictators, and you end up with the finest panoply of mass murderers on the planet, most of whom have credibility on the street and even a decisive voice at the UN. What they have in common is a ruthless hatred of individual freedoms, of democracy, of America and, of course, of Jews. Which again brings us back to Uncle Adolph. The only way to do that would be to find Wagner, if he's still alive, and decode the documents attached to the will.

Melany smiled incredulously.

-- And how do you plan to do that?

-- You have his last address. That's a good start. Start by going to Moscow.

-- You say that like we're just going to take the subway.

-- The subway in Moscow is very modern and the station under Red Square looks like an art museum. You speak Russian?

-- Fluently. But don't change the subject. We're not even sure of the authenticity of the documents. What if it's all a fake, a forgery created by Wagner to get to the West? Hitler may well have been out of his mind, but I find it hard to imagine him writing an instruction manual on how to find him in the next life while the Allies were shelling Berlin.

-- Yet he was very much into the occult, like all the Nazi officials.

Melany raised a surprised eyebrow.

-- That's a part of history that must have escaped me.

A shy ray of sunlight pierced the still low clouds, briefly flooding the living room with a pale winter light. Jeffrey reached out to cast the shadow of his fingers over Melany's chest. The grayness set in again.

-- You'd be surprised. But you just gave me an idea. Did you attend Almog Herskowitz's class when you were at Harvard?

-- He wasn't part of my curriculum.

-- He was my history professor. A specialist in pagan religions, secret societies, and the occult. He is the author of several essays on esoteric societies in Nazi Germany. I'll call him and ask him if he can see us.

-- You are joking, aren't you? Boston is four hundred miles away.

-- Do you have anything better to do?

Melany had to admit that she did not.

-- Chapter 11 --

Melany had lived or stayed in more than a dozen countries all over the world, but this was her first trip to Boston. Their route was unspectacular, as the broad, monotonous highways between Washington and Baltimore only passed through or around snow-covered cities with similar architecture. Fortunately, traffic was fairly smooth, with the exception of the immediate vicinity of built-up areas, where trucks crowded together in endless lines.

Jeffrey drove with a steady hand, his window lowered a few inches to compensate for the heat from the heater that had been pushed all the way down. He was about to laugh at his partner's reluctance, when he realized that her physical reaction was probably the result of the trauma she had suffered with Derek in that frozen forest.

By three o'clock, they had already passed Charlestown, Elkton and Brookside and were now only about thirty miles from Philadelphia. Professor Herskowitz had greeted Jeffrey's call with warmth and sympathy and agreed to meet them at his office the next afternoon. So they booked a room at the Sheraton Commander in Cambridge, which was less than ten minutes from the main buildings of Harvard. They hoped to get there before midnight.

Looking at her companion from time to time, Melany couldn't help but feel a little childish enthusiasm. Who would have thought, only two days earlier, that their relationship would start up again under such auspices? Jeff's optimism and good humor made him the ideal companion for this adventure. Even if they did not make the slightest progress in their research into the *Father of Victory*, these hours spent together on the road, followed perhaps by a return trip to Russia, would at least allow them to get to know each other and to deepen their relationship. Playing spies was still more exciting than a cruise in the Caribbean!

Thinking back to her mother's amused words, Melany frowned to suppress a smile. No, she really couldn't imagine Maureen wearing a scarf and sunglasses, lying on the deck of an ocean liner, holding hands with her new lover.

As they drove around Wilmington, a small town on the outskirts of Philadelphia, Jeffrey slowed down and stopped his car at the side of the road just before a fork in the road:

-- Do you mind if we take a little detour?

-- Not at all. But if you get tired of driving, I can replace you.

-- It's not a matter of fatigue. I just want to visit someone. It could delay our arrival in the Boston area by a good hour or two.

-- Jeff ... we have plenty of time.

He looked relieved and squeezed her hand tenderly before restarting the car and leaving the freeway. Soon, wooded landscapes alternating with large parks replaced the monotonous architecture of building blocks. Small houses with roofs and snow-covered gardens followed one another along the still wide and progressively less congested road. Despite her curiosity, Melany waited for the Jeep to slow down near a beautiful brick building, a sort of renovated English mansion with arches and patios, before asking for confirmation of what seemed obvious to her:

-- This is where your brother is, isn't it?

Jeffrey nodded silently. The guard posted at the entrance to the visitors' courtyard recognized him and immediately raised the barrier, giving him a friendly nod.

-- You really don't mind?, Jeffrey whispered.

-- Are you crazy? If I had known that his residence was on our way, I would have insisted on visiting him myself.

-- I come as often as I can. I get in my car early in the morning, and arrive in time for lunch with him ... Basically, I help him with lunch. I'm embarrassed to impose this chore on you. But since we're passing right by ...

Melany put two fingers on Jeffrey's mouth to silence him.

-- What's his name?

-- Benjamin. He was just fifteen when ...

At the time of the accident, Jeffrey's brother was sitting in the back of the vehicle with his seat belt unfastened. The frontal impact threw him clear of the bumper, which saved his life, but his head hit the front grille of the truck. The fracture resulted in ischemia. By the time help arrived, including a medical helicopter that evacuated him to emergency services, large areas of his brain had been deprived of oxygen for too long, and an intracerebral hemorrhage had exacerbated the damage. He was inoperable and his condition considered to be irreversible.

Jeffrey's voice died imperceptibly. He parked the Jeep loosely in a narrow space between a Cadillac and a Lexus. The air was freezing. Much colder and drier than in Washington. Despite the imposing presence of the buildings from another age, beautifully maintained and skillfully modernized, country fragrances floated up to the main entrance.

The Ingleside Nursing Home mainly cared for elderly patients, mostly at the end of their lives. But one of its wings was reserved for disabled patients whose condition required constant assistance and care. It was a luxurious establishment which must have cost Jeffrey a fortune. When Melany, touched by the warm atmosphere of the place, complimented him on his choice for his brother, he only replied that he had not found anything better.

A nurse in an austere outfit under a gown, whose position could only be identified by a badge, greeted them kindly and led them to Benjamin's room without ceasing to chatter for a moment.

-- It's rare to see you so late in the day, Mr. Cartright. You're being accompanied today? May I ask this young lady for her name?

-- You may ask me directly, Melany smiled before identifying herself.

-- Of course, of course, forgive my bad habits. It's Benji who's going to be happy to see you ...

-- Hillary, Jeffrey scolded her. I've told you before he always hated to be called Benji ...

-- Yes. Of course, of course ...

The corner room was large and soberly decorated in pastel tones, with the exception of the hospital bed, around which monitors and other control devices stood. The windows overlooked a park and its artificial pond on one side and the suburbs of Wilmington on the other, with a wall of skyscrapers on the horizon.

Benjamin had his back to them, being seated in front of the window overlooking the park. The room temperature was pleasant, but they had still thrown a blanket over his legs.

Melany had a small twinge in her heart when she saw him. He was the spitting image of Jeffrey as he must have been seven or eight years ago, except for his dead gaze. With his arms held by straps that held him to the armrests, his chin tilted forward and his mouth half open, he seemed to be contemplating an abyss of nothingness.

-- Hello Benjamin, Jeffrey said happily, pushing a chair to sit in front of him. It's me, your brother. You recognize me?

The young man gave a vague, almost imperceptible nod, but the expression on Jeffrey's face made Melany realize that something significant had just happened. Benjamin's range of actions was limited to a series of uncoordinated reflexes. A few rare flashes of lucidity attested to some presence, somewhere, in the windings of his damaged neurons. Jeffrey adjusted the blanket over his legs and took his hand. The young man moved his lips. Jeffrey leaned down and kissed him on the cheek. Benjamin had recognized him.

It was a good day.

***

Professor Herskowitz received them in his office, a room with wood paneling all the way up to a ceiling that seemed to defy time. The dark blue carpet was thick and soft. The furniture smelled like leather and polish. The library was overflowing with old books, some of which, protected by glass, must have been several centuries old. The professor knew Jeffrey well, not only as a former student but also as the grandson of generous donors who had helped to endow his chair. He couldn't refuse them anything.

His hair and goatee were graying, and his eyes sparkled with intelligence behind square-rimmed glasses. Herskowitz seemed to carry the weight of all human history on his shoulders. He stood stooped in his tweed jacket and velvet shirt adorned with a bow tie, making him look only a few inches shorter than he was when he was already fairly short. He invited them to sit down and called his assistant to serve them tea.

-- With or without cakes?, he asked, his finger on the intercom.

-- As you like: we don't want to abuse your hospitality, Melany replied, a little surprised.

-- Then it will be without. My wife forbids them to me, and has bribed my assistant. It seems that they're bad for my arteries, my liver, my stomach, and can cause diabetes.

-- Don't you think your wife is exaggerating?, Melany smiled.

-- You think so? But she is the family doctor. Personally, I would be unable to tell an aspirin from a mint lozenge.

-- Tell your assistant that we arrived on an empty stomach and we wouldn't mind a small plate of goodies, Melany whispered conspiratorially. Jeffrey and I will keep it a secret.

A big smile lit up the professor's face.

-- Jeffrey, I always knew you were a man of taste. Ms. Carson, will you allow me to call you Melany?

-- It would be an honor, professor.

-- Thank you. Now, tell me: you didn't come all this way just to have tea with an old man in an office as dusty as he is. Jeffrey, you mentioned Hitler and the Nazis' relationship with the occult on the phone. May I know the reasons for your sudden interest in this subject? Is one of you two working on a thesis? Tell me everything.

Melany and Jeffrey looked at each other. He nodded, inviting her to start. It was her investigation and it was best if she had an opportunity to present the case from the angle that suited her best.

In the same way that she had confided in Jeffrey, the young woman took the time to recount most of her misadventures, including her mother's confidences and the conclusions she and Jeffrey had reached. She asked Herskowitz to keep the manner of Derek's death a secret, and Herskowitz swore that he knew how to be discreet. By the time she had finished her account, the professor had swallowed all the tea cakes that his assistant -- a somewhat heavy lady with snow-white hair -- had quietly served while she spoke.

He took pains to take off his glasses and wipe them off before exclaiming:

-- Rarely in my entire career have I heard such an incredible story!

-- I hope you don't take me for a mere storyteller, Melany worried.

The professor became highly animated.

-- Quite the contrary. What is fascinating is that Hitler chose "The Father of Victory" as the title of glory for his return. He would been vengeful, all the way to the end ...

-- I don't follow you.

-- "The Father of Victory" was the nickname of George Clemenceau, to whom France owes its refusal to accept a negotiated peace with Germany in 1917. Without that 'To-the-Bitter-End-ism", the Kaiser would undoubtedly have remained in power and Germany would not have been forced to sign the Armistice of November 11, 1918, which would lead to the signing of the Treaty of Versailles. Hitler hated Clemenceau, and won power in particular through the rejection of this humiliating treaty that brought Germany to its knees.

-- So for you, then, Hitler's will wouldn't be a forgery.

-- I'm convinced of it. I can hardly imagine a KGB agent forging this kind of document in order to go to the West. He would have taken an enormous risk for not very much, since defections had become commonplace during the breakup of the Soviet bloc.

-- Finally, rational data!, Melany said appreciatively.

The professor stared at her, shaking his head.

-- You've put your finger on something extraordinary and terrifying, but I don't think rationalism is the right approach for coming to grips with all of its obscure points.

-- If this is a myth fabricated by the Führer, a growing number of extremists seem poised to join in, Jeffrey said. Our goal is to go back to the source before some guru grows a square mustache and swaps his tunic for a brown shirt in order to get himself a following!

-- Hasn't it occurred to you that Hitler might have gotten hold of hidden texts and unusual methods for reaching different states of consciousness? He had the means and the will ...

Melany frowned doubtfully.

-- Like everyone else, I know what this monster did. Nothing makes me want to explore his secret delusions.

Jeffrey gave her a look that was both sweet and mischievous.

-- And what if they weren't just delusions?

Herskowitz observed the couple for a moment before smiling and resuming.

-- Rationalists, and especially materialists, have a habit of dismissing anything they fail to explain as nonexistent. But I don't fall into that category. Hitler believed in black magic and even attempted to use some evil rituals in his early days. His relatives believed that he had psychic abilities. After the publication of a few books in the seventies about the relationship between Nazism and the occult, it became fashionable to believe that Hitler had been sent to earth by the forces of evil and that he had opened the gates of hell to let loose a horde of demons. Nonsense. But some of the strangest facts remain undisputed. His ability to hypnotize crowds, for example. We know he would go into a trance during each of his speeches and lose up to two liters of sweat by the time he stepped off the stage. His ability to survive was phenomenal. He escaped death sixteen times, including when he was a soldier in the trenches. That goes far beyond any statistical approach. His fellow combatants reported that the shells were falling around him without ever touching him or even making him shudder ...

Melany expressed annoyance.

-- Sorry, professor. You don't really believe ...

-- In black magic and charms? Of course not. As for mediumship and natural magnetism, only as much as the scientists who have seriously looked into the subject. As for reincarnation, it is the most widespread religious belief in the world. One need only look at the work of doctors who have catalogued thousands of testimonials from survivors of near-death experiences to be at least curious.

-- I've been through Ian Stevenson's work, Jeffrey said. It is true that nothing explains the memories of past lives of all the children he has studied. His critics tried to use the notion of genetic memory to counteract him, but they soon found themselves running out of arguments.

Melany had always considered herself to be a pure Cartesian. She was surprised by Jeffrey's enthusiastic intervention in a field that she didn't not consider to be serious.

-- The great tunnel, the blinding white light, the dead who come to take you by the hand ... Can you swallow that stuff?

-- I have a right to question myself. Stevenson never gave precise answers; he merely investigated all reported cases of possible reincarnation. No one could fault him for an unscientific approach, and when you read that a four-year-old boy is afraid of the water because he remembers a previous life as a fighter pilot shot down with his plane over the Pacific, gives you the pilot's name, all the details about his squadron, including some that no outsider could know -- such as the model of his still experimental plane -- it does raise some questions[(10)]. A renowned doctor like Stevenson does not spend his life fiddling with ten thousand testimonies to come to the conclusion that reincarnation does perhaps exist. He was rigorous and his methods were above reproach.

-- I like to hear you say that, agreed the professor. I am in favor of never rejecting a theory *a priori,* no matter how obscure it is ... But, let's get back to Hitler. To understand Nazism, it is not enough to survey the events of the twentieth century and judge them by the yardstick of good and evil. At the origin of National Socialist philosophy, if one may call it a philosophy, there are several currents, some of which are marked by a good dose of esotericism. These are the ones you're interested in.

The professor paused to make certain that his guests were as captivated as they should be. Their expressions encouraged him.

-- ... As for his racist obsession, the Führer's main masters of thought were Richard Wagner, Houston Stewart Chamberlain and, of course, the unavoidable Alfred Rosenberg. They shared the certainty that the purpose of man is to attain divinity and that the superior race of Aryans had to be purified in order to achieve this goal. Eugenics was the first tool used.

-- Eugenics?

-- A doctrine of Francis Galton, a cousin of Charles Darwin, who aimed at tinkering with natural selection in order to improve the human species.

---

[10] This is the authentic case of James Leininger, a child who, at the age of four, remembered in great detail his "previous life" as James Huston, an American pilot shot down by the Japanese above the Pacific Ocean in 1945.

Since man is descended from apes and before them from fish, some necessarily evolve faster than others and it would be up to the most evolved to speed up the process. That was his theory. The Nazis began by eliminating the mentally ill and homosexuals before attacking other races. Hitler hated the Jews compulsively, as is often the case in anti-Semitism, but he also had a rational reason to wipe out their existence. He did not forgive them for developing the concept that man is sacred because he is made in the image of an abstract god. Hitler considered Judeo-Christianity to be the religion of the weak, as opposed to Nordic religions, such as Odinism or Wotanism, which he intended to impose as a state religion one day.

-- That is an important point that my discussions with Mitchell helped me understand, Melany said.

-- Now, to discuss the esoteric roots of Nazism, we have to go back to the nineteenth century, to the Theosophical Society and to Madame Blavatsky, a scholar of the occult, considered to be a high level initiate, to whom we owe the fashion of oriental philosophies in the West. Unfortunately, she also developed the idea that humanity was divided into several races, one of which, the Aryans, had descended in a direct line from Atlantis. A theory that could only seduce future Nazis in their search for legitimate domination.

The phone rang. The professor picked up the receiver with an apology, ready to chide his assistant, who had been instructed to block callers. His tone instantly softened when he recognized his wife's voice. Despite the presence of his hosts, he had to detail his lunch and promise her that he wouldn't indulge in any excess.

-- Never marry a doctor!, he grumbled after he had been given the freedom to return to his visitors.

Then, as if he hadn't been interrupted:

-- At the origin of the Nazi movement lies a secret society, the *Thule-Gesellschaft* or *Thule Society*, which was founded in 1918 by Rudolf von Sebottendorf and whose symbol was none other than a swastika attached to a dagger: the Cross of Wotan. Among the members of the Thule was an occultist, Dietrich Eckart, who boasted towards the end of his life about having "made" the Führer in these terms: *"Follow Hitler. He will dance, but it was I who wrote the music. We initiated him into the secret doctrine. We opened his eyes and gave him the means to communicate with them. Don't weep for me: I will have influenced the story more than any other German."* Who is behind this "them"? Some pseudo-historians have referred to aliens, while others have just as fancifully referred to secret masters. But all agree that the Thule Society, and particularly Eckart, had a significant influence on Hitler, Himmler and Rudolph Hess, who was without a doubt the most disturbed of the three.

Herskowitz paused again to observe his counterparts. Satisfied, he continued:

-- *Die Geheimlehre*, the "Secret Doctrine" which Eckart alluded to before several witnesses on the day of his death, has two distinct meanings. The first refers to a long tradition of occult teaching, dating back to ancient Egypt and the earliest Gnostics. The second one is connected with two major works by Helena Blavatsky: "Cosmogeny" and "Anthropogenesis".

It was in "Anthropogenesis" that we find some of the foundations of Nazi racial doctrine, the professor explained. Helena Blavatsky had written down theories on evolution that were supposedly entrusted to her "by invisible beings and secret messengers" during her travels in areas of Tibet forbidden to mere mortals.

-- And yet, contrary to what some commentators have tried to make us believe, Madame Blavatsky, as everyone called her, was not a racist. On the contrary, she believed that humans, both strong and weak, should all help each other. Obviously, the Nazis took over from her theories what suited them best, as they did with Nietzsche's philosophy. Since they belonged to the Aryan race, the latter was necessarily superior and had to dominate the planet and eventually eliminate the inferior categories in order to evolve towards the ultimate destiny, divinity.

-- And reincarnation, in all this esoteric-fascist hodgepodge?, Melany interrupted, revolted by any philosophical justification of Nazism.

-- I'm coming to that. This is one of the major themes of Theosophy. Blavatsky claimed to have been initiated into Tibetan mysticism after gaining access to the authentic *Kalachakra Tantra*. This is a mythical book in several volumes, of which modified versions exist, although no one has ever found the original. This maintained that consciousness is One and Universal, that the individuality of man is immortal, that humans are unconscious of their divine nature, and that they evolve from incarnation to reincarnation until supreme enlightenment.

-- This sounds like Buddhism, Melany pointed out.

-- Blavatsky drew a lot of inspiration from that.

-- Doesn't that tell us that Hitler believed it?

-- You would be surprised, Melany, how fascinated he and those around him were with reincarnation. Hitler was certain that he had been Tiberius, the successor of Augustus and the predecessor of Caligula. Out of all historical figures, he didn't hesitate to choose one of the fiercest and bloodiest.

There was a knock on the door. Herskowitz's assistant poked her head through the opening and asked if everything was all right.

-- Will you be needing anything else, professor?

-- No, thank you, Jenny. And please don't allow any more calls to me, even if it's my wife, as long as my guests are here.

-- I only came to tell you that I was leaving.

-- Already? But what time is it?

-- Four o'clock, professor. But you do recall that I have to take care of my grandson on Wednesdays.

Herskowitz dismissed his assistant with a familiar gesture, wishing her a good afternoon before turning back to Jeffrey and Melany.

-- At least no one will bother us anymore. Where were we?

-- Hitler believed that he had been Tiberius in another life, Melany grimaced.

The professor nodded and held out an eloquent finger, in a way that reminded Jeffrey of how he captivated his audience during his lectures.

-- Hitler also took himself to be for the reincarnation of Napoleon. No, I'm not joking ... On the other hand, when his audience was composed only of uncritical admirers, he sometimes suggested that he was inhabited by the soul of the "Galilean" or the "Little Carpenter". That is what he called Jesus, to whom he refused the title of Christ because it was the Greek translation of the word "Messiah" -- a concept far too Jewish for his liking. Himmler, on the other hand, believed that he had been Henry I of Germany, nicknamed Henry the Fowler.

These little Nazis, full of complexes and often as ugly as lice, had delusions of grandeur, Melany interjected. And when I say "madness", that's an understatement!

The professor smiled knowingly and poured himself a second cup of tea. Before bringing it up to his lips, he mechanically picked up all the crumbs lying around the plate with his fingertips and wiped them all up with a discreet lick.

-- The Nazi leaders saw themselves dominating the planet through secret rituals. I will quickly pass over Wewelsburg Castle, the headquarters and place of initiation of the SS, where the most abominable ceremonies accompanied the most delusional symbols. Reichsführer Himmler didn't make any important decisions without first consulting his astrologers. Most particularly Karl Maria Wiligut, his *Rasputin*, whom he went so far as to promote to the rank of SS-Standartenführer and to appoint to an important post within the Ahnenerbe. The magus was a schizophrenic and ended his life in an asylum after being dismissed from office. Around Hitler, we might note Karl Haushofer, an authentic medium who was passionate about Japanese secret societies and who committed suicide in the Japanese fashion by committing hara-kiri after being judged guilty at Nuremberg. He had been close to Gurdjieff…

-- George Gurdjieff, the occultist?, Melany asked to show that she had some knowledge about this area.

Herskowitz nodded.

-- He is said to have instilled in Haushofer secret rituals inspired by Sufism and allowing the attainment of the state of the 'superman', the major myth of the Nazis. He would also have had in his hands the ***Kalakarma*** *Tantra*, about which he speaks extensively in his stories without, of course, revealing its secrets. Still around Hitler, you find the fraudulent magician Eric Jan Hanussen, who played to sold-out crowds at the La Scala in Berlin.

According to a 1942 OSS report, this fairground magician and genius of a fabulist, who was very close to Hitler, was suspected of having taught him how to captivate his audience with gestures and voice changes. He was in fact a Moravian Jew who posed as a Danish aristocrat.

-- Unfortunately for Hanussen, he had the unfortunate idea of using confidences, which he had doubtless received from Goebbels, to amaze his audience by predicting the fire in the Reichstag, which would be perpetrated by the SA the next day and would lead to Hitler's consolidation of power. His buddies didn't like his scheme. His body was found near a river a week later.

The list of official astrologers of the Reich was long. It included an authentic Swiss medium, Karl Ernst Krafft, initially arrested by the SS on suspicion of complicity after "seeing" and revealing an assassination attempt on Hitler's life. He would end his days in the Buchenwald concentration camp for having accurately predicted events disadvantageous to the Reich too many times.

Herskowitz quickly passed over the hazy theories that were in vogue in Nazi circles, such as that of Hanss Hörbiger, who believed that the moon was a block of ice that would crash into the earth before re-forming and whose evolution corresponded to cycles influencing civilizations. The closer the moon was to the earth, the more men belonging to the Aryan race grew, until they became giants. Or the even more absurd one about the hollow earth, in which Hitler believed so much that he devoted huge sums to try to prove its validity by sending teams of researchers, who would have been much more useful to him elsewhere, to the four corners of the planet in order to find the entrance to underground passages. There were no limits to the number of pseudo-scientific nonsensical beliefs abounding among the intellectuals who surrounded the Führer and his Gauleiters.

-- But what is most interesting about the revelations you give me is that they confirm the esoteric goals of the Nazi expeditions to Tibet. If Hitler had wanted to know about his supposed next incarnation, it is obvious that this is where he would have to look.

-- I didn't know that the Nazis had led expeditions to this area, Melany asked in fascination.

-- In order to understand this better, you have to go back to the Thule-Gesellschaft. This secret organization, founded by Rudolf von Sebottendorf in 1918, was intended to be an initiatory society bearing ancient secrets, like Freemasonry, which it nevertheless despised. Their symbol, the Wotan cross, arguably inspired the use of the Swastika, the reverse wheel of life, by Nazi Germany. Their salute was with outstretched arms, accompanied by the exclamation *"Heil und Sieg"*, which became *"Sieg Heil"* under Hitler. But I'm now getting to the essential point ... The myths of Thule and Shambhala.

Thule was the name given to the northernmost part of Europe. A mythical place for the ancient Greeks and Romans, where the god Apollo used to spend his winters. The name also referred to the legend of a population of northern Europe, the Hyperboreans. One of the avowed goals of the Thule Society was to promote the indisputable superiority of Indo-Europeans over other races. Its members were convinced that "Thule" referred to an advanced but vanished Germanic civilization of which there were traces in Hyperborea, a continent whose secrets would have been kept by "higher beings" living in underground caverns. And which the Nazis had, obviously, done everything to find.

-- In Tibet?

-- Exactly. Hence the unbelievable number of expeditions led by the Ahnenerbe at the behest of Himmler and led by two mountaineers, Ernst Schäfer and Heinrich Harrer, and an anthropologist, Bruno Beger. Besides Thule, they searched for Shambhala, the "Peaceful Place" according to Tibetan tradition, from which they were convinced that the Aryan race originated. There are two important facts to note, and which undoubtedly have a link with your discovery. First of all, when the Allies captured Berlin, they were surprised to find the bodies of many Tibetans in Nazi uniforms among the victims of the bombings. Then, and not the least, after the war Heinrich Harrer took refuge in the Himalayas where he was welcomed by the family of the current Dalai Lama, Tenzin Gyatso. Harrer was a staunch Nazi, an SS member. However, he was hired as the guardian and tutor to the Tibetan leader who is now in exile and who maintained his friendship with him until Harrer's death.

The professor continued to discuss Shambhala, which was impossible for anyone but initiates to locate on a map. The origin of the holy place goes back to the Buddha who, in order to enable King Suchandra to attain enlightenment without abandoning his royal duties, had bequeathed him a sacred text, the *Kalachakra Tantra*.

-- Himmler was obsessed with Shambhala. He apparently transmitted his fever to Hitler. But in view of your discovery, I might speculate if it was not rather the opposite. The first version of the *Kalachakra Tantra* is said to have disappeared, but I believe that it is rather jealously guarded by monks somewhere in a monastery buried in the heights of the Himalayas or the Karakoram. It is also called the *Wheel of Time*. It is one of the most important texts in the Buddhist tradition ... particularly in regard to reincarnation. Wait, I just happen to have a copy of a short essay on this legend written by one of my students ...

The professor got up to go and search a corner of his library reserved for manuscripts. He quickly found what he was looking for: a fifty-page handout titled "Kalachakra," which he placed in front of Melany.

-- Read it when you have time. I have other copies. There is a fascinating passage about the Nazis' interest in this text.

-- All of this is infinitely fascinating, Jeffrey said, who had decided to nevertheless come back to earth. But even assuming that neo-Nazi organizations have seized the will, we still remain in the realm of anecdotal evidence. I can hardly imagine an official announcement of the Führer's return. His followers would be the laughingstock of the planet.

-- Unless that's not their goal, Melany pointed out. And that's what bothers me the most. For years they kept the information a secret, but it has recently spread to groups far removed from their ideology. How to explain that Islamist terrorists suddenly share the same myth as the Nazis? Isn't that an unnatural alliance?

-- That is where you are wrong!, the professor corrected her. Many leaders in the Arab world shared Hitler's ideas during the war, if only Rashid Ali al-Gaylani in Iraq, who moved closer to the Axis and established a Nazi regime in Baghdad until Allied victory. Palestine's first Arab nationalist, Grand Mufti Hajj Amin al-Husayni, was close to Himmler and Hitler, participated in the Holocaust, and organized the Muslim Ustasha brigades in Croatia. Anwar Sadat himself, who signed the peace accords between Egypt and Israel, nevertheless confessed to having been on the side of the Nazis during World War II in order to get rid of the British. Von Sebottendorf, the founder of the

Thule Society, spent his entire youth in Istanbul. He was a follower of Sufism and an admirer of the Young Turks movement, which was responsible for the extermination of the Armenians. No doubt he influenced Hitler. According to Albert Speer, the official architect of the Reich and confidant of the Führer, he had great esteem for those he called "the Mohammedans". Their common hatred of the Jews cemented their occult alliance. At the end of the war, dozens of Nazi officials, including Alois Brunner, Eichmann's right-hand man, took refuge in Syria and Egypt, where they easily distilled their poison. Unlike Christians, Muslims do not turn the other cheek when slapped. Their warlike mentality didn't displease the Führer. Himmler, for example, kept two books on his bedside table: Mein Kampf and the Quran. What current movements, apart from the jihadists, could be so easily seduced by Nazi ideals?

The professor's conclusions were greeted with a heavy silence that Jeffrey broke after several seconds of reflection.

-- In short, the neo-Nazis have allowed themselves to be convinced of the superhuman powers of their beloved Führer, expect him to appear with a post-mortem aura of glory, and are ready to recruit an army of jihadists to help them resurrect the Third Reich. Am I wrong, or are we completely delusional?

-- The problem is that no one will take such assumptions seriously, Melany pointed out. At our level, these are just rumors and scattered facts. My boss made that clear to me ...

-- If this Soloviev is still alive, he must have kept a copy of the documents, Herskowitz suggested. And if these documents do exist, then there is a good chance that they discuss the *Kalachakra Tantra*, or at least the methods used by Tibetans to trace the supposed reincarnations of their lamas.

A glimmer of excitement passed through Jeffrey's eyes.

-- Does anyone else know these methods?

The professor shook his head apologetically.

-- Tibetan Buddhism is not my area of expertise. It would take a lifetime to really study it. Among them, the recipient of a migratory soul is called a *tulku*. In most cases, the process of recognizing a *tulku* begins by consulting a high lama and an oracle. Their meditation can last for weeks. The Tibetans in the yellow caps took more than four years to find their fourteenth and current Dalai Lama. They also based themselves on clues going back to his previous incarnation. For example, the direction of the smoke during the cremation of his body. They make use of karmic astrologers, who look for clues in the positions of the stars, allowing them to at least determine a date of birth. They would also know secret meditations reserved solely for initiates and allowing them to reach a higher state of consciousness in connection with the sacred forces of the Universe ... Once the candidates for the role of the new Lama have been identified, they decide between them through a series of tests. For example, they are presented with various objects from among which they must spontaneously find those that belonged to their predecessor. What I know about their traditions is in the public domain and won't help you very much.

-- Do you have any other ideas?, Melany asked.

-- Search through recent news items for important events that might correspond to the esoteric world. Any unsolved incident involving astrologers, seers, religious leaders or Tibetan relics might be linked to this case.

The professor ran his hand over his forehead. This conversation had exhausted him. He confessed that he often suffered from headaches in the afternoon and attributed this inconvenience to difficult digestion. Melany and Jeffrey took these explanations as a polite way of asking them to excuse him. When they got up to take their leave, he confessed that he was now going to take a nap.

-- That's the advantage of holding a chair past retirement age. I am no longer accountable to anyone. But you have awakened old memories. I will probably doze off as I reread a few lines from Hermann Rauschning. His "Conversations with Hitler" is all the more fascinating testimony, since it is disputed by Holocaust deniers. Did you know that, according to him, the Führer saw ghosts and woke up at night screaming?

-- It must have been Tiberius visiting him, Melany joked.

-- What are you going to do now?, Herskowitz asked. Are you going back to Washington?

Melany and Jeffrey looked at each other. Their next step had so far only been a hypothesis. It had now become an obligation.

-- Chapter 12 --

Jungle of Sumatra -- Indonesia

Ten weeks earlier

Although accustomed to the jungle, Cyril Marcus did not like the elephants of the Asian continent. One of the problems was that they tended to defecate when walking. Like horses, but not in the same quantities ... Those of Africa had a majestic side not shared by their cousins, with their narrow ears and stubby tusks. And with a threatening stare.

The first time he had dealt with pachyderms was in India during the making of a documentary for which he was an assistant. He had a terrifying memory of it. For some unknown reason, one of the expedition's elephants had a fit of rage and broke free of its chains during the course of a bivouac. He had trashed everything -- the tent, the food crates, the equipment -- raising a fearful trumpeting before crushing his sherpa, whom he then relentlessly trampled.

Once the animal had been slaughtered, its legs had to be scraped off with a machete to retrieve all the pieces of the unfortunate man before cremating them.

Cyril Marcus looked straight ahead, over the shoulder of his guide, to chase away the horrible memory. The silhouette of Marianne, swaying a few yards away to the rhythm of the footsteps of her own mount, was a sight pleasant enough to take his mind off things.

Between its legs, the elephant's belly emitted a gurgling sound. Two seconds later, a putrid smell was added to the multiple scents of the jungle, covering up that of humus, decaying plants and the exhalations of exotic flowers with unpronounceable names.

Cyril Marcus swore and patted his guide's arm. He grunted without even turning around. The three elephants, with Marianne's elephant in the lead, continued to waddle along the natural trail, the trunk of one touching the tail of the other.

They had been advancing like this for an hour.

Very early that the morning, a jeep loaned by *"Grundstück und Teilung"*, the NGO *"Earth and Sharing"* that they had chosen as the target of their investigation, had come to pick them up at their hotel to drop them off at the edge of the rainforest, where a special convoy awaited them.

Marianne Metzger, the producer, had insisted that they participate in this hike as soon as the director of *"Earth and Sharing"* had told her about it. It would be just the two of them, plus the guides. Cyril suspected that she had a crush on him. Marianne was rather pretty, despite her somewhat lean physique, acquired in the gyms and by dint of trekking all over the world. A face pleasing to the eye, unabashedly sensual and just as adventurous as himself.

This didn't prevent him from envying Alex, their cameraman, and Heri, their full-time translator, who had escaped the elephant ride and were now sleeping in the comfort of their hotel in Medan while he and Marianne were breaking their backs in order to keep themselves in the saddle.

The patch of jungle they had been offered to visit had supposedly been used in the past as a refuge for the GAM rebels. They were not allowed to take any cameras or recording devices, and the production translator had been excluded from the expedition. What is the use of visiting an exceptional place, Marcus thought, if you can't film it?

But Gerhard Krueger, the president of *"Earth and Sharing"* who was visiting Indonesia, had proven to be persuasive. His arguments did everything to appeal to Marianne, who was always on the lookout for sensationalism and was perhaps tired of investigating the workings of humanitarian aid and the sanitation of waterholes and rivers. A major theme for their report, but not glamorous enough for her taste.

The transfer from the jeep to the elephants had not been lacking in charm, even for Marcus, who had had to mask his concern as soon as the animals appeared. Their guides had been extremely considerate. It was difficult to imagine that these little men, silent but always smiling, had been part of an organization of extremists and that they had undoubtedly killed people.

Since a ceasefire agreement had been signed between the separatist movements and the government in Jakarta, an amnesty had allowed the militants to come out of hiding and join what was left of their families. Some of them, like their three guides, had turned to tourism.

The prisons had been opened. The mobile brigades had been dissolved. And the Aceh Liberation Organization was now part of the local landscape, along with the *warungs*[11], the Chinese market and the Grand Mosque. The members of the NGO's gladly had their photos taken with former combatants in Penayung Square, brandishing the V for victory as if they had indeed participated in a liberation.

The city that had, before the tsunami, forged a reputation for isolation and fundamentalism, had for a time taken in more foreigners than its accommodations could allow. Everything had to be rebuilt, down to the smallest infrastructure, starting with bridges, roads and the small airport, in order to allow food and medicine to arrive. But the international community, with Germany and Australia in the lead, had worked miracles. The region had increased in modernization.

This did not prevent the ultra-conservatives from imposing their harsh version of Sharia law and the GAM from recruiting and expanding its activities in dangerous ways, which the government continued to deny.

This was the central theme of the multi-part documentary Cyril Marcus was to direct for the Arte television network. It was also the first time that he had worked with Marianne.

-- *We, soon to stop, rest and drink*, his guide announced in broken English, turning to give Marcus his everlasting smile.

-- How much further is it?, the director asked.

-- We not far. We rest and drink.

-- All right, I understand. The goal of this excursion is your camp, right? How long will it take to get there?

In response, the former militant nodded yes, widening his smile. A few meters in front of them, Marianne pulled up on her hair, which was stuck to her T-shirt. The air was so saturated with moisture that sweat couldn't evaporate. Marcus was forced to scream to cover out the incessant concert of animals and insects.

-- Marianne ... Has anyone told you how long our journey will last?

The young woman turned around. She looked as thrilled as a kid on a rocking horse. Her T-shirt had attractive curves despite her thinness.

-- I've no idea. All I know is that we'll be back by this evening. How are you holding up?

-- I love it!, Cyril Marcus grimaced. But the next time we hit the jungle, it'll be the two of us, on foot.

[11] Outdoor restaurants.

-- All right, then. Have you seen the chimpanzees?

-- I think they were more like orangutans.

His guide suddenly turned to him. Not smiling at all this time.

-- No shouting in the jungle. No good shouting.

-- That so?

The director was familiar enough with tropical rainforests to be surprised. Making noise, being quiet, it made no difference. Wild animals had a stronger sense of smell than their hearing anyway. As for the reptiles, the heavy footfalls of the elephants were enough to keep them away. At night it was different. But during the day, they might as well have been accompanied by an opera aria.

-- Shouting calls evil spirits, the guide grimaced.

Marcus should have known better. By living hidden in the jungle, the former GAM militants had inevitably developed tons of superstitions. So he fell silent while waiting for the break and thought back to the events that had preceded this expedition.

So far, they had managed to box some ten hours of film, enough to put together a quarter of the program. The footage was spectacular. In the Aceh region, all you had to do was put your camera anywhere to capture sensational images. Medan was an anthill of children, veiled women, smiling men, moving by exotic means of transport, mingling with thousands of strangers.

But Marcus didn't like stories that were too elaborate. Coming from a rigorous and sectarian family, he had been brought up in a culture where Santa Claus did not manage a sled pulled by reindeer, but was chased by an ice storm only to end up with his bottom charred on the logs of a fireplace. The story of a country devastated by a cataclysm and then rebuilt thanks to international solidarity in a climate of peace at last regained, was too simple and too naive for his taste, even if the production company that had hired him asked for nothing else. He had a reputation to maintain.

What interested him was the black market. Lost cargos. The pressures from Jakarta on the local population. Food that hadn't gotten clearance and was rotting on the docks. Missing building materials. used to allocate plots of land to the privileged, to the detriment of their real owners, often orphaned children. And, more recently, the involvement of neo-Nazi movements in certain so-called humanitarian organizations. That was new. But the presence of a not inconsiderable number of martial Germans and skinheads of Russian origin was a sufficiently important phenomenon in the region to merit the attention of a journalist of his caliber.

Three days earlier, a young Indonesian from Banda Aceh had accosted him in the middle of the Chinese market in Medan. He didn't want to give his name, but promised him explosive information on the rebirth of GAM with the complicity of certain NGO's. He had refused to say whether "*Earth and Sharing*" was involved. The two men had seen each other a second time the next day on the terrace of a coffee-shop frequented by tourists. This time he had brought a document written in German, a language Marcus did not speak, but whose illustrations were eloquent: a photograph of Hitler and a swastika. Marcus had kept the paper with the intention of having it translated and had made one last meeting.

The young Indonesian was to find him that evening with several similar documents, including a compromising photograph, which he expected to hand over to him for three hundred dollars. A small fortune in this region.

He had obviously kept Marianne out of this little side investigation. No need to involve the young woman in an investigation that could be dangerous. Besides, if there were a prestigious award for the story, why share it?

The trail suddenly led to a narrow clearing with a waterhole, as is often the case. The guides pricked the flanks of their elephants until they knelt down, allowing him and Marianne to jump to the ground. The other two animals immediately adopted the same posture and Cyril, to his relief, was finally able to leave his mount. His buttocks and the inside of his thighs ached. But he forced himself to imitate the young woman's delighted look. The sweet scent of the jungle was almost suffocating. From all directions came the buzzing of insects, the song of birds and the cries of mammals.

-- We are in paradise, Marianne enthused with charming innocence.

-- I'm not sure that Adam and Eve rode around on elephants, Cyril grumbled, immediately blaming himself for this platitude.

-- Anyway, if the GAM guys were hiding around here, no wonder the regular army could never find them. Have you seen the paths we've taken? I wouldn't be able to retrace my steps by myself.

Their guides had grouped together to speak quietly among themselves, after making sure that the elephants were properly tied up. The thin rope that connected them to the trees would not have withstood a blow from a trunk, but it was a hindrance for domesticated animals. The Indonesians unhooked several bags from the saddle of the third elephant, as well as a bottle of water. The first ones contained food. The fourth bag briefly caught Cyril's attention, since they seemed to be handling it with care, but he immediately looked away to admire Marianne, who had dropped to her knees and plunged her arms into the crystal clear water.

-- Be careful!, Cyril warned. There may be leeches.

-- No, the water is too clear: look, we can see all the way to the bottom!

She called out to her guide before splashing her face.

-- Banyu, is it dangerous to touch this water?

-- Touch, OK. Not drink.

The Indonesian, who must have been barely twenty years old, jumped between the stones and creepers to join Marianne and hand her the bottle.

-- Drink this. A lot.

-- He's right, Marcus said, who let himself drop to the ground after carefully observing the rock he was sitting on. Drink as much as you can.

Marianne did so, letting a trickle of water run down her neck and T-shirt. She was suffocating in that bra and those thick jeans and boots. But she had learned her lesson before coming to Indonesia. Foreigners not wearing the veil were tolerated, even though their loose hair attracted male lust and sometimes looks of contempt. But shorts, as well as short skirts, were prohibited. Their guides, having belonged to the GAM, were even stricter on matters of religious dress.

Marianne handed the bottle to Marcus.

-- I'm going to read your mind, he said.

-- And that of your guide, Marianne retorted. I saw him sneaking a drink right before I did.

She moved closer to Marcus, intending to sit down next to him. From the thickness of the jungle there rose up foliage and cries of macaques as well as the crackling of parrots, echoed by the three-tone whistling of hornbills and Koël cuckoos.

-- There, I was sure of it, Marianne said to herself as she straightened up. Every time I drink, it makes me want to ...

Marcus made to get up.

-- Do you want me to come with you?

The young woman waddled around, scanning the forest with her eyes, looking embarrassed. The guides who had started to prepare their meal and began to cut up pieces of omelet to mix them with rice nodded their heads and the one named Banyu went to unroll a batik blanket hanging from the saddle of his elephant.

-- Come. He stays.

He pointed at Marcus. He shrugged his shoulders.

-- I hope for your sake he's not a voyeur.

-- You speak knowingly, Marianne smirked.

She followed in the footsteps of Banyu, who had thrown the blanket over his shoulder, and they both moved downstream from the waterhole to a bushy place where giant ferns formed a natural screen. Their voices, and Marianne's laughter quickly faded, then disappeared, swallowed up by the jungle.

At that moment, Marcus had a premonition. Probably because of the sudden silence of the guides who, a moment earlier, had been busy three meters away from him. Or perhaps his instinct refined by so many stays in the rainforest made him perceive a change in the tone in the orchestral carpet of the animals ...

He lifted his head just in time to catch the quick and silent movement of the two Indonesians. One of them was carrying the bag that he had noticed with curiosity a few minutes earlier. The other one threw himself at him, quick as lightning, and held both his arms behind him, pushing his spine with his knee. Marcus tried to struggle, but his posture prevented any movement.

He saw, as in a nightmare, his guide, very close to him, undo the thin strap that held the bag, open it and, in the same movement, put it around his head. Marcus was plunged into darkness. For a split second, he thought we were trying to suffocate him. Then he felt a long, cold form struggling and unfolding near his face in the darkness.

He realized it was a snake the moment the reptile sank its fangs into his neck.

Marcus screamed at the top of his lungs. Immediately, the Indonesian withdrew the bag and his companion released him. Marcus cried out harder, writhing in all directions, mad with anguish and pain.

The snake, just as terrified, rolled over on its chest, then gathered its black and white rings to slip away in a wavy line underneath the first grass, where it disappeared. A bungar, or banded krait. The most dangerous snake among the elapidae.

Cyril's neck began to swell and formed a goiter the size of a mango when Marianne, alerted by the screams, came running back.

-- Cyril? Christ, Shit, Cyril, what's the matter with you?

The two guides held him to the ground as if they wanted to save him, the first thing to do in the case of a reptile bite being to immobilize the victim in order to slow down the flow of blood. They played their comedy to perfection.

-- Snake attack. Bad bite.

Cyril could already feel the toxins from the bungar taking effect on his face muscles. The pain had gone, giving way to a state of paralysis and drowsiness. The reptile had hit the jugular, and everything would go very quickly now. He wanted to warn Marianne, to explain to her what had happened, but his throat only let out a rumbling sound. The young woman rushed for the first aid kit, prepared before their departure by the director of the NGO. She sighed when she discovered the vials of serum from Australia.

-- What, what was the snake?, she asked, on the verge of hysteria, noting that there were many kinds of anti-venom.

The guides pretended to confer, then one of them said something to Banyu, who had moved closer to Marianne.

-- A naja, the young man translated, forming circles around his eyes with his thumb and index finger. He says he saw a goggled snake.

Hearing these words, Marcus bowed down and began kicking his legs with what little strength he had left.

-- *No, it was a bungar!,* he tried to scream in vain.

But no sound came out of his lips, which had doubled in volume.

One of the guides took the syringe from Marianne's fingers and plunged the needle into Marcus's neck, injecting a highly effective serological formula against the bites of the naja, another proteroglyph of the elapidae family.

And completely ineffective against bungar neurotoxins.

***

The small hotel was not a palace, but it was the best to be found in Medan. The bedrooms were comfortable, each having either a shower or a bath. The team had been there since arriving in the region, and for Marianne, being there was a bit like coming home. Especially after what she'd just been through.

-- I don't understand ... I can't believe it ... I can see him again, he was sitting there by the waterhole ... He was joking. And when I came back I found him lying there with the guides holding his arms ...

Marianne gasped. It was the third time she had unwound her story, reliving the scene with the same fright. Sitting opposite her, in the hotel lobby, the official of the French consulate, Jérôme Fourcade, was taking notes with just the right amount of civility. Marianne held back her tears.

Shortly after the injection of the serum, Cyril Marcus had fallen into a coma. He had choked to death on the way home. There were no means of communication in this part of Aceh. The young woman had had to wait in the company of the guides for the "*Earth and Sharing*" jeep to reappear at the agreed time -- that is to say, at the end of the day. Four hours at the edge of the jungle, at a temperature at the very limit of the bearable.

The director's face and neck had doubled in size. He had become unrecognizable. A mask of pain and horror frozen in excruciating death.

The guides had waited for Marianne and Marcus' body to be taken care of by the NGO volunteers, and then they'd melted away into the jungle. On the back of an elephant, as they had come.

-- So, you saw the naja bite him?

Jérôme Fourcade readjusted his glasses. His tone was icy, with a hint of suspicion. Everything about him was gray: his hair, his skin, his shirt, and even his eyes.

-- No. Not at all. I have already explained it to the police and to Mr. Krueger, the president of "*Earth and Sharing*".

-- What does he have to do with your film crew?

-- We chose his NGO to illustrate our documentary on the reconstruction of Aceh.

Jérôme Fourcade tapped his notebook with the tip of his pen, trying to think of more questions to ask.

-- Did your guides find it?

-- They didn't find it. They were with him. From what I understand, the snake was coiled under a stone, near the waterhole. He didn't see it when he lay down. He must have made a sudden gesture. The naja bit him ... My God, it was horrible!

-- And you: where were you?

Marianne let out an annoyed sigh. Telling his story to the Indonesian police had already been an almost unbearable ordeal. The interrogation had lasted two hours. You'd think she was responsible for the death of her director. The Indonesian inspector had particularly insisted on the attitude of the guides, going over the smallest detail ten times.

She said it again, drily:

-- I've already told you. I had gone to take a pee.

Jérôme Fourcade batted his eyelashes but continued to take notes. Despite the half-dozen dusty fans installed throughout the hotel lobby, it was hotter than hell. Marianne was sweating profusely. But the consular attaché didn't have a drop of sweat on his forehead.

The worst part was that she did feel guilty. When Krueger's assistant brought up the excursion, the idea of an elephant ride in the jungle had struck her as terribly exciting. She was sure that Marcus had followed her only to be one-to-one with her. And she had to admit that his sometimes insistent glances at her figure had not left her indifferent.

-- So you were away to ... satisfy a natural need. Upon your return, you found Mr. Marcus in this condition. And you injected him with a serum. Do you remember the brand?

-- Are you kidding? No. I'm not a doctor. There were several vials. Made in Australia, I believe.

-- Do you have the death certificate?, Fourcade insisted.

Marianne took a copy out of her bag. The document contained a Polaroid photo of Marcus taken on his return to camp. The bite appeared in close up. She looked away.

-- I see here that there was no autopsy. Not even a blood test to determine the type of enzymes in the venom. However, the Indonesian authorities seemed to be keen on it.

-- That's possible. I don't know. The Indonesians let us fend for ourselves. There was no room in the town morgue. Nor in the hospital. We kept the body here in an air-conditioned room ...

The young woman's voice died. She gulped.

-- In the hotel?, The consular attaché asked in surprise.

-- In his room. Yes. I agreed to pay triple the price. The NGO lent one of its air conditioners. But repatriation is becoming urgent. When do you plan to do this?

Fourcade looked embarrassed.

-- A Banda Aceh to Toulouse flight chartered by the Red Cross is scheduled in two days. I am negotiating a place. I just need to get a coffin in time, since they refuse to carry a body in a plastic bag. We can't blame them ... Their cargo plane doesn't have a refrigerated compartment.

Marianne wondered if she were hallucinating. This icy gray fellow treated Cyril's repatriation like he was a package of meat.

-- You can't charter a means of transport yourself?

Fourcade began to put his documents and notes away in a small black cloth he had placed at his feet.

-- Miss Metzger, the French state is not responsible for this accident. You did not follow any of the recommendations posted on the consulate's website. If we help you, it's because the law requires us to do so, since your director was one of our nationals. But this will remain purely administrative assistance, and solely within the limits of our budget.

As the diplomat extended his hand to her, his lips pursed, to say goodbye, another figure entered the deserted hotel lobby. Marianne displayed a pale smile as she turned to him.

-- Mr. Krueger, I was afraid you couldn't come. May I introduce you to Mr. ...

-- Jérôme Fourcade, the attaché hastened to say, presenting his business card with the dexterity of a magician.

Gerhard Krueger was a full head taller than him. In his sixties, his brush-cut white hair was beginning to thin out; he was dressed in local fashion, with khaki-colored airy pants and a white, short-sleeved shirt.

-- A terrible story, he said, looking around, as if he were looking for someone.

-- Indeed, Fourcade agreed. We didn't need that in our dealings with the Indonesian authorities. But it wasn't for lack of warning our nationals ...

-- You can speak to me directly, Marianne said aggressively. OK, we screwed up. Cyril left his skin there, and I will probably lose my job. You don't need to add any more ...

Krueger briefly squeezed the young woman's shoulder.

-- Come on, Miss Metzger. It was a terrible accident, but no one is blaming you.

Marianne blinked her eyelids to release a tear. Every time she closed them, it was only to see the nightmarish scene in the clearing again. Marcus' screams still made her shudder.

-- It's okay. Don't worry. We have a bigger problem than my feelings. Mr. Fourcade has just informed me that the consulate does not have any logistical means to repatriate Marcus immediately.

-- In two days, perhaps, the consular attaché emphasized. As long as you find a craftsman to build a coffin within that timeframe.

-- You won't find anyone in Banda Aceh, Krueger observed. The Muslims bury their dead in a shroud in the ground and the Christian community has completely disappeared from the region.

-- And they don't know how to make a wooden box? However, a solution will have to be found.

The front desk clerk, who left his counter empty half the time, had just reappeared and was smiling affably at them, watching out for any possible requests. The fans were making a hell of a racket. A sickly cat crossed the hotel lobby with a mewing to tear your heart out. Marianne wanted to scream.

She appreciated Krueger's help and advice, although his slightly cloudy personality and martial demeanor had made her uncomfortable the first time they met. She knew that Marcus didn't like him. He said that the president of "*Earth and Sharing*" seemed to come from a Leni Riefenstahl film. The director had insisted more than once that they look for another organization. But Marianne had been stubborn.

The idea popped out of Krueger's mouth as if he had just thought of it.

-- Is there anything against him being cremated?

***

At the age of sixty-four, Gerhard Krueger was in surprisingly good shape, maintained through exercise and despite a poor diet. Every morning, during his stays in Indonesia and just like the rest of the time in his small German town, he would run at least five kilometers, pushing uphill, catching his breath before lengthening his strides, taking advantage of the flats to check his wrist tachymeter before sprinting until he lost his breath.

That didn't prevent him from smoking two packs of cigarettes a day.

This tall, white-haired man in shorts and tank top, who was training daily on the banks of a foul-smelling river, was, for the Indonesians, the subject of amusement and, despite all the respect they owed him, certainly not any model to be emulated.

Only a madman, or a foreigner, would run for the fun of it.

But tonight, when darkness had just cast its pall over the miserable quarters of Medan, transforming its imposing silhouette into an almost invisible shadow, Krueger had other worries than his physical appearance.

Of all the humanitarian organizations working in the Hacé region, this team of reporters had to choose his own to make a documentary about. So far nothing exceptional, nor very dangerous. "*Earth and Sharing*" was involved in enough aid programs to fulfill its cover function. Krueger had agreed in order to ward off any possible suspicion.

He was now pleased that he had discreetly kept an eye on the team members, including this Marcus and all the natives who had come into contact with him. One of them was a young Indonesian from Banda Hacé. The fact that he had met the director "by chance" at the Medan market, so far from home, aroused the suspicions of the trackers.

Marcus and the Indonesian had seen each other again, before the latter was abducted and taken to the rubble of an old shed to answer a few questions. Terrorized, he hadn't omitted any detail. Where did he get his information about the real purposes of "*Earth and Sharing*"? Why did he want to share it with foreigners? The interrogation had probably been a little bit too brutal, because he had not survived it.

Money had clearly been his motive. He came from an extremely poor family.

As for his source of information, it was only a network of rumors, gossip, legends, associating the blond giants sent by Allah to save the people of Aceh with the defunct GAM. The boy had gone through the rubbish bins of all the NGOs, and had found some vaguely compromising documents in those of "*Earth and Sharing*". Nothing too dangerous after all. Unless the data were exploited by a professional investigator such as Cyril Marcus.

Now deprived of its director, the rest of the team had no reason to continue its stay. Miss Metzger and her cameraman would therefore leave soon. The case was closed for now.

The narrow alley Krueger had walked along bypassed the fish market, whose watery effluent permeated the heavy, stagnant atmosphere. To the right, at the bend of a crossroads, the *kantor pos*, equivalent to a post office, difficult to spot since a prefabricated hut had replaced the old building. Opposite the market, various shops, *takas* with drawn iron shutters, barely stood out from the cement facades. In the dim light of the rare light bulbs hanging from the electric power poles, piles of rubbish poured out of crates and plastic bags piled up under wooden panels selling the wonders to be discovered in the closed stalls.

It was a moonless night.

Krueger bumped cursing against the rusty frame of an abandoned bicycle. A shaggy form escaped from it, slapping its paws on the asphalt. The animal disappeared between the loose stones of a one-story house without his being able to identify it.

His intermediary had shown him the second alley on his left, just after the post office, from the south corner of the market. An unnamed passageway, which he could only locate by following the instructions precisely. Then he had to count six houses.

Krueger found the alley and knocked on the sixth door.

A slender little man with a flat nose greeted him with bowing and scraping, like a loyal subject receiving a prince, even though the hovel was nothing like a palace.

-- *Selamat datang, silahkan masuk.*

The host gave him the polite expressions reserved for distinguished guests before leading him into a living room, pulling a chair towards him and offering him tea. The room off the entrance hall was cluttered with furniture of all sizes, immaculately clean but completely mismatched. A vertically-oriented poster of the National Monument of Indonesia, a 132-meter high tower in Merdeka Square in central Jakarta, was yellowing under a transparent plastic between a Chinese wardrobe and a double batik curtain. The furnishings smacked of foraging and patchwork repairs.

-- Wait, please!, his host invited him.

Krueger lit a cigarette. He didn't have to wait long.

A clash of cymbals preceded the first notes of a gamelan that filtered through the double curtain. This opened up to reveals three barely pubescent teenage girls, made up like Balinese dancers and dressed in ceremonial clothes.

Krueger's heart leaped up. His unbridled imagination immediately pulled him into forbidden areas. The master of the house clapped his hands. A delicate song immediately rose from the throats of the children, who moved away from each other, each taking possession of a part of the room, in which they undertook convolutions of infinite grace. The dance evoked a picture of war. Perhaps the fight of Rama and his brother Lakshmana against the odious Bâratha, for the conquest of Princess Sita?

For several minutes, the teenage girls moved about without paying the slightest attention to him, twirling the gilding of their gowns, taking turns hiding their faces behind fans, drawing volutes in the air with their outstretched or folded fingers, opening huge eyes to accompany each new contortion.

Fear, joy, suffering, abandonment, all the expressions of the human soul, were represented by exaggerated mimicry or the change of rhythm of the percussions, to which an unexercised ear gradually became accustomed, to end up enchanted.

The oldest of the dancers must have been fourteen.

Much more dazzled than he had anticipated, Krueger let himself be captivated by the magic of the fable, an allegorical living tableau whose origins date back to the beginning of Eastern civilization. Under the ceremonial clothes, he sensed the slender bodies ready to offer themselves up. Was it necessary to simulate a battle? They brushed against each other. Express a heartbreak? They brushed against each other. Where was the good, where was the bad? When the first clothes fell off, along with his completely consumed cigarette, whose incandescent tip he crushed with his heel, he saw nothing but grace and beauty. His emotions, dulled by age, remained intact at the cost of extreme measures, and he welcomed them.

In the play being performed before Krueger, the boundary between vice and virtue became as uncertain as the darkness of dawn or dusk. The roles assigned could change at any time. Each of them had the opportunity to demonstrate her strength and heroism, until the final victory, which alone defined the right.

It was the essence of the Ramayana, the most famous tale on the whole continent. A story which, for this private performance, gradually became tinged with perversion before exploring all its degrees. The fingers stopped brushing the better to touch, repeating a gesture that had to be instilled by force, if not learned in pain. The young bodies were marked by beatings and floggings, long striations that the make-up had difficulty masking.

Krueger felt himself melt. The choice was going to be difficult.

Unless you ask for all three? Did he not have all the powers and all the rights?

-- Chapter 13 --

Boston

Present time

With her back supported by the concave shape of a soft armchair and her legs resting on the coffee table in the tiny living room of their suite, Melany let herself be lulled by the classical music program that the television set diffused while she read through the fascicle Professor Herskowitz had given her.

Sitting by the window, which offered a breathtaking view of Logan Airport in the distance, Jeffrey was looking through the day's newspapers with a glass of scotch from the convenient mini-bar.

Half a page of the Washington Post was devoted to the FBI's descent on the neo-Nazi community of Odyssey. A photograph of the Hitler Museum and another of Derek Mitchell in hunting gear illustrated the article. He opened the newspaper wide to show it to Melany, but she shook her head. The mere sight of Derek's face repelled her.

-- Do you want me to summarize the essay by Herskowitz's student or will you read it later?, she asked, pulling an earpiece away from her ear.

Jeffrey put the WaPo back on the pile of newspapers provided by the hotel and grabbed the Boston Herald.

-- Not now. Unless you've found something really important ...

-- Well, yes, that's just it!

Melany was just waiting for her chance to leap at her opportunity.

-- ... Put down your papers and listen! I have come across several interesting paragraphs.

Without waiting for Jeffrey's consent, she read:

"Kalachakra"

"The event took place in southern India, in the current Andra Pradesh. In 878 B.C., the king of Shambala, Sushandra, asked Shakyamuni Buddha to help him find enlightenment without his leaving his positions as King and Warrior. The Buddha understood the importance of the stakes, since it involved a man reigning over a sacred land. He conceived for his benefit a complete initiation, gathered in several volumes, under the title of Kalachakra Tantra. One of the purposes of this initiation was to discover Shambhala, the Buddhist equivalent of the Heavenly Jerusalem.

Some people locate Shambhala in the region of Mount Kailash, the connecting point between three ancient civilizations: China, India and Tibet. Others see the mythical city somewhere on the four holy places surrounding Bodhgaya, where the Buddha found enlightenment, Mount Wutaishan in northern China, Mount Vindhaya in southern India, the Swat Valley in northern Pakistan, and Mount Kailash in southwest Tibet.

The Dalai Lamas were the successors of King Suchandra, destined to found a dynasty of a spiritual order, one visible only to initiates.

The Kalachakra Tantra would address all the themes important for the development of mankind and would provide the keys to perfect knowledge, from which Tibetan Buddhism would eventually emanate ..."

Melany looked up from the fascicle. Jeffrey had paused his readings and listening to her most attentively, his glass of scotch in his hand.

-- Now, just listen to this!

"Total war and the annihilation of humanity"

"Tibetan astrology, which is much more precise than its Western equivalent, has its source in the Kalachakra Tantra and makes it possible to reveal not only the causes of the present and the future of each man but, beyond his death, his return to earth, until the fateful year 2024 which, again according to the revelations of the Buddha, will be marked by the conflagration of the last conflict of religious origin between men.

Muslims will fight Jews and Christians. These will turn against Buddhists. The latter will free themselves from the grip of non-believers and will join the fighters of this total war, which will see the end of one era and the beginning of another.

Raudra Chakrin, the last king of Shambhala, will then take power, supported by twelve gods and as many armies. The soldiers of Shambhala, numbering ninety million, will restore peace to the planet. There will never again be war, men will live eighteen hundred years. The entire planet will be spiritual, free from its primitive religions, and this state will last twenty thousand years."

-- Basically, we have 5 years left to have fun, Melany quipped.

-- Unless you convert to Buddhism and spend your remaining time in an ashram meditating on the foolishness of mankind.

Jeffrey took a sip of the scotch, grimacing.

-- Wait, this is less fun.

Another chapter of the essay discussed the passion of the Nazis for those legends of another time, which did not go without referring to the Apocalypse or to Armageddon:

"Himmler was fascinated by reading the Bhagavad-Gîta, a much more widely known text, relating the terrestrial and celestial lives of Vishnu and his avatars. Like the gods of Greek and Roman mythology, Vishnu could take human form and become an avatar of himself. Among his most famous incarnations are Krishna, Rama, and the king of Shambhala, Raudra Chakrin.

But Savitri Devi, a famous occultist and staunch Nazi, put forward the astonishing idea that Adolph Hitler himself was an avatar of Raudra Chakrin, just like the Dalai Lama. Except that the Dalai Lama is his peaceful emanation, while Hitler was similar to Genghis Khan.

Yin and Yang. Everything is balance and equilibrium. Hitler would therefore be the last valiant warrior, destined to reign on earth after the apocalypse. In a way, this Buddhist myth joins the Judeo-Christian beliefs which have led some mystics to make the reincarnation of the Führer nothing less than the Antichrist."

And, making an effort to quote Himmler:

"Hitler was born to us out of the deepest distress, at a time when nothing was going well for the German people. He is one of those great figures to which Germanism gives birth whenever it finds itself plunged into the deepest physical, spiritual and moral misery. Goethe was one of these figures in the intellectual field, Bismarck in the political sector. The Führer is the same on all levels -- political, cultural and military. The karma of Germanism designated him to lead the struggle of the world and to save this Germanism.

Jeffrey, who rarely missed an opportunity to show his humor in its most cynical form, this time put on a worried look.

-- It's even more serious than I imagined.

-- All of this is just tales and legends.

-- Unfortunately tales and legends are often at the root of the greatest massacres. The Nazis sought by all means to attain the state of supermen and perhaps to live forever. This eccentricity caused the deaths of tens of millions of innocent people. If that dwarf with eyeglasses and the man with the mustache and flopping hair were convinced that the end of the world would be in 2024, and that the latter was the reincarnation or the avatar of a god destined to dominate what would remain of the planet, we have every chance of facing a new wave of madness seventy-four years later. I can hardly imagine the havoc that this belief could wreak if it spreads through unstable circles ... It goes far beyond a historical curiosity or a conspiracy theory.

Melany didn't waste any time thinking.

-- All the more reason to get down to business and find Soloviev ... While praying that he's still alive.

Jeffrey got up to go to the small desk, where he had opened his laptop. Melany pulled up a chair to sit next to him. Professor Herskowitz had advised them to look for any recent information that might be linked to abnormal activities in the outlandish universe of esotericism.

-- Where do we start?

-- Just input 'reincarnation'. We'll see what happens. Search the news.

She did so, and Google had over 120,000 results in an instant.

-- That doesn't help us much ...

-- So narrow down the search. Add "incident" or "event". Add a correlation with Tibet.

This time around, Google had only 2,000 results to offer, the first of which immediately caught their eyes.

Theft of the Tibetan golden urn from Yonghe Temple in Beijing.

-- The golden urn? Isn't that the object Professor Herskowitz told us about?

-- Yes. A vase that is used to decide between the candidates for the reincarnation of the Dalai Lama.

The information dated back two years and was illustrated by a photograph of an urn set with carved patterns, a true work of art covered with engraved symbols.

The article read:

"On the night of August 14 to 15, persons unknown broke into the Yonghe temple to steal one of the two legendary objects that allow us to decide between the Tulkus, or religious figures recognized as reincarnations of masters or lamas who have disappeared.

The second is still carefully preserved in the Jokhan temple in Lhasa, the legendary center of Tibetan Buddhism. Like most Buddhist temples, Yonghe had minimum security, no doubt for budgetary reasons, but also because the Chinese government attached only secondary importance to Buddhist artifacts, which are seen as ridiculous symbols of an outdated religion."

Melany quickly searched for more information about the object. Several articles in the Chinese press in the English language alluded to it.

The golden urn, and its reproduction which had just been stolen, symbolized the power of the **Qing**, the dynasty during which the Dalai Lamas arose. It was a small vase of solid gold used to confirm the identity of the chosen one. To achieve this, the monks threw sticks into the urn with "Yes" or "No" written in Sanskrit. A whole series of questions were then asked, and a child was tasked with pulling out the answers while the monks meditated and prayed. The object was donated to the 8th Dalai Lama by the Emperor Qianlong and its use was governed by decree.

-- How much should we bet that the urn wasn't stolen for its monetary value, even though it is solid gold?

Melany grabbed Jeffrey's glass and emptied it in one draft.

-- And now?

-- What if we look for astrologers?

-- In my opinion, we will find millions of them.

-- Then Karmic Astrology, perhaps?

-- That seems more precise to me. By the way, what sign are you?

-- Aries, with Aquarius rising. Which brings us together, since you are an Aquarius. But, hey ... Hitler was also an Aries.

Melany grimaced.

-- Because you're also interested in astrology? And what else? Have you been to see a psychic recently?

In response, Jeffrey pointed his finger at the screen where a series of articles had just appeared under the keyword "karmic astrology".

-- I've never seen a psychic before, he said finally, but I have a feeling that that gap will soon be filled.

According to the online archives of the Guardian and the BBC, three psychics "renowned for their ability to trace the past lives of those consulting them" had disappeared within the interval of a few weeks in 1999, seven years after Wagner's discovery of the will. The information was anecdotal but had intrigued an English journalist named Jason Pierce enough to lead an investigation at the scene of the three disappearances. One in London, the second in Madrid, the third one in Berlin. Another article, published ten years later, indicated that the body of Leslie Dunblas, alias "Juneja Rinpoche", had been found buried in the Queen's Forest and identified by a metal plate that had been screwed onto his shin after a fracture. The other two missing mediums had never been found.

-- It's insane how much you can glean from the internet!, Jeffrey pointed out with such innocence that Melany had to keep herself from bursting out with laughter.

-- Do you know how cute you are when you indulge in such deep thoughts?

-- And you, instead of laughing at me, look at the introduction to the headline to the next article instead.

Medium / spiritualist with great powers.

"Hitler's soul contacted me"

-- As if that monster actually had a soul, Melany said.

-- Click on it, you never know.

The medium in question, an American of Haitian descent living in New Orleans, was also a devotee of voodoo. One photograph showed him dressed in white, eyes rolled back, in a supposedly terrifying setting that was clearly staged. In order to contact him, you had to dial a premium-rate phone number and, for the modest sum of three hundred dollars, he would offer all kinds of anti-bewitchments with, as a bonus, his autographed photograph and a powder with beneficial virtues developed in secret by his family over the course of seven generations. Hitler visited him at night, in his dreams, to inform him of major events, such as the Florida hurricanes, the Asian tsunamis, and the outbreak of local wars. According to the medium, the Führer had changed his ways and now wanted only the greater good of humanity. For $99, the crook offered full transcripts of this vital information written by *automatic writing.*

Melany sighed and Jeffrey burst out laughing.

-- Okay, now try to link up "Hitler" and "reincarnation".

The data that emerged most often corresponded to political opinions expressed in satirical form. Most heads of state were nominated as candidates for the reincarnation of the Nazi leader by partisans of the opposing camp. All American presidents of the past two decades were entitled to it. Melany scrolled through ten pages. There was nothing to be gleaned here. She was about to leave the search engine, disappointed and annoyed, when a headline caught her attention:

Medium and specialist in regressions under hypnosis, Karl Hanussen, claims to have no connection with his namesake.

-- Hanussen -- isn't that the fraud Professor Herskowitz told us about?

Jeffrey nodded. She hurried to open the page:

"Kahla -- District of Saale-Holzland.

Erik Jan Hanussen was the pseudonym of Hermann Steinschneider, a Moravian Jew born in Vienna who, posing as a Danish aristocrat, befriended the main founding members of the Nazi Party. Very close to Himmler, he allegedly trained Adolph Hitler to perform in public and influenced several decisions of the nascent party by often fanciful predictions before being assassinated by the SA following an indiscretion. However, he had no descendants.

Karl Hanussen was supposedly born with this name, but was abandoned by his parents just after his birth and entrusted to several foster families, without any of them adopting him.

Asked about the reason for these rejections, Hanussen says that his gifts as a medium and his spontaneous way of predicting certain tragic events were too frightening for his adoptive parents every time.

In response to the question: "What is your most vivid memory as a hypnotist and magician?" the illusionist replied "The day Reinhard Heydrich's voice spoke through the mouth of a woman whom I had made regress under hypnosis, to tell me about her murder in Prague, in 1942."

Hanussen, who used to perform in public in a Berlin cabaret until 2008, now only exercises his gifts in private, in his office as a medium / hypnotist / karmic astrologer located in Kahla, a small town in the region of Thuringia, in the former East Germany. The followers of magic and sleight of hand will undoubtedly forget, during their time in entertainment, that they are in the heart of a city known above all for its large neo-Nazi population.

-- When is the article dated?, Jeffrey asked.

-- July 2010. Rather interesting. A Hanussen who practices regression by hypnosis in a city of neo-Nazis. I wonder if our friends looking for Uncle Hitler have contacted him.

-- Find out if there are any other articles about him.

Melany did so while asking:

-- Did you know that you can change your sex from one reincarnation to another?

-- Yes, that's pretty common, according to Stevenson.

The young woman rolled her eyes and shrugged. The reference to the doctor who had spent his life investigating reincarnation annoyed her more than she wanted and Jeffrey now took pleasure in referring to him.

This article published by a German tabloid was the only one about Karl Hanussen available on the internet. She stifled a yawn.

-- I feel like I've been up for three days. What time is our flight to Moscow?

Jeffrey checked the information. They were taking off in the early morning and it was already close to midnight. By mutual agreement, they decided to abandon the search for the moment.

Her head barely resting on the pillow, Melany fell into a deep sleep.

***

Since the pilot couldn't get clearance to land at Sheremetyevo International Airport because of a snowstorm, they had to fall back on Domodedovo, located to the south and much further from the center of Moscow.

Jeffrey, whose initiatives never ceased to surprise Melany, had hired a specialist agency that would provide them with a company car with a driver and allow them to receive a VIP welcome. However, the unexpected change of airports forced them to go through police and customs checks like everyone else, while the agency had to send them a new car. A black Mercedes with tinted windows awaited them in front of the terminal.

When the sedan, skillfully driven by a silent, athletic-looking driver, left the area around the airport, the road signs written in Cyrillic that lined the shoulder instilled a small wave of joy in Melany's heart. Two days earlier, she had woken up wondering what she could do with her two-week vacation, apart from scratching up some information and following from a distance the developments of a situation in which she was furious not to be more involved. And here she was near Moscow, her birthplace, which she hadn't set foot in for over fifteen years.

Soon after, they entered a patch of fog that made it barely possible to make out the taillights of other vehicles. Yet no driver seemed to find it necessary to slow down. Including their driver.

-- Are you sure you can see far enough to go so fast?, Melany worried in impeccable Russian.

-- *Da!*, the man just answered without even looking in his rearview mirror.

Very well, Melany thought to herself, observing his gruff face with its square chin and piercing little eyes. *This is a silent guy who failed his entrance exam for the secret police and failed to recycle to the B series of the Russian Mafia. Better to have that kind of guy on your own side.*

It was therefore at a cruising speed of forty-five miles per hour that they reached the first suburbs of Moscow.

The storm, which was mainly affecting the north of the city, had subsided. A thick layer of snow covered the monuments, the basilicas, certain sidewalks and the roofs of the houses. The contrast between the magnificence of the administrative and religious buildings and the simplicity, even destitution, of recent social housing, was always so striking. The difference between the Moscow of her memories and that of today lay in the mind-boggling number of cars coming from all directions, scurrying in all directions, seemingly without any rules other than those known to locals.

Jeffrey had booked a room at the Lotte Hotel, a palace located not far from the Moskva River, a few minutes from Red Square and the Bolshoi Ballet. The interior architecture seemed to have been designed for the guests of the Tsar. Dotted with black colonnades in an art-deco style, the huge reception hall opened onto a spectacular staircase covered with an empire-pink carpet with meticulous patterns and thick as a cloud. The room, of elegant luxury, opened onto the river through a large window framed by heavy drapes with the prestigious Moscow University, whose buildings evoked the very Stalinist extravagance of monuments of the Roman Empire, lying in the distance.

Melany threw herself her full length over the bed.

-- If I hadn't slept like a log as we flew over the ocean, I would be lying down and doing nothing except gazing at the paintings on the ceiling!

-- Don't overdo it, Jeffrey laughed, lying down next to her. It's not the Sistine Chapel, after all.

-- The fresco is all the more beautiful for being anonymous.

They remained silent for several minutes, studying the Rococo allegory of angels hovering above a basilica. Jeffrey stroked her a little, but with no particular intention and, if his contact with her breasts under the thickness of the sweater aroused his desire, he just enjoyed the moment without asking for more. The instant bond that had developed between them was confusing. He smiled inwardly, telling himself that their meeting was probably karmic, but was careful not to utter that reflection aloud. Melany would have had a good time making fun of him.

Both had no idea how they could get their hands on Alexei Soloviev, AKA "Wagner", if he was still alive.

Reflecting on the seriousness of their investigation, Jeffrey had to admit that they were behaving a bit like kids playing spies. But Melany had almost been killed for a few questions put to the wrong people. That simple idea terrified him in retrospect. It was not to be excluded that the mediums in question in the investigation of this English journalist had disappeared for reasons related to this case. What could the link be? Anyone who had Hitler's will in their hands and believed in his potential return would have to call in charlatans before finding a genuine medium -- that is to say, a man or woman with abnormally developed intuition. Unlike Melany, Jeffrey had no difficulty in believing that such a phenomenon could exist.

But all they had about Soloviev was an address dating back three decades. In other words, almost nothing.

With her head against Jeffrey's shoulder, Melany must have read his thoughts, for she couldn't withhold her sarcasm.

-- Do you think that our next investigation will send us in search of Father Fouettard, referring to the black-faced companion of St. Nicholas in European folklore, or on the track of the Tooth Fairy?

Jeffrey stroked her hair.

-- Our next investigation? You're being optimistic.

-- You must have contaminated me.

He thought for a moment, then said:

-- I know you struggle with esotericism. You'll have to get used to it, though. In case you haven't noticed, we're right in the middle of it.

-- I don't have a problem with it. I completely reject the idea of a parallel world, an afterlife, and all that other rubbish.

-- The important thing is not that reincarnation exists and that Hitler came to power through incantations or charms, but that an organization with resources believes in it and is spreading the myth. Remind yourself that the enemy is very real.

-- On that point, I'm with you.

-- Once we have enough material in our hands, it will be enough to publicize the matter to discredit them. Hitler will return to the river where the Russians threw his ashes, the *Kalachakra Tantra* will be stored under glass in a museum library, and the *Father of Victory* will be picked up by the comic book makers.

-- Do you think that's possible?, Melany added dreamily.

-- Of course we're going to get there ...

-- No, what I mean is, do you really think that Hitler could have been reincarnated?

Jeffrey thought about it before giving his answer.

-- I'm willing to believe anything, as long as I'm given proof. Isn't that the basic principle of Cartesianism?

-- In other words, if we manage to get our hands on this testament, and if it contains data precise enough to go back to the alleged *tulku* of the Führer, and if it turns out that he remembers his previous life in enough detail, would you be ready to be trapped by the deception?

Jeffrey took a deep breath, got up and walked into the living room, from which he returned with a bottle of mineral water in one hand and a mini-bottle of champagne in the other. He sat down on the edge of the bed.

-- I don't know about you, but this conversation is starting to make me thirsty. What time is it?

Melany looked at her watch. It was two o'clock in the morning on the American East Coast and therefore nine o'clock in Moscow. She pointed at the champagne. Jeffrey scoffed:

-- I'm turning you into an alcoholic.

-- If you tell me that you believe in reincarnation, then I'll finish off all the alcohol in the minibar.

The cork popped up to the ceiling and foam spilled over Melany's hands and skirt. She swore. Jeffrey helped her with a laugh, using a Kleenex. He sat down to continue, his eyes dreamy.

-- I know you won't agree, but I have a feeling that something remains of our consciousness when our physical shell disappears. In the nineteenth century, biologists claimed that the brain produces thought as the liver produces bile. Most current scientists reject this concept. According to Buddhists, we live in a world of illusions and it is true that our reality depends only on our five senses, if we omit intuition and imagination. Yet it is only a drop of water in the ocean of a much larger reality, the origin of which we are barely beginning to grasp.

The words were reasonable enough that Melany didn't interrupt.

-- Scientists like Niels Bohr, one of the fathers of quantum physics, were fascinated by Eastern esotericism. Einstein often used God as a reference, even though he was not religious. The physicist Wolfgang Pauli corresponded regularly with Karl Jung on the question of coincidences that both believed were messages from an unchanging elsewhere that were meant to put everyone back on the right path. Everyone, at one time or another, has wondered about the survival of a consciousness after death and concluded that, despite the immensity of their knowledge, this was an area in which they could not decide in favor of any hypothesis.

-- I thought you picked international law as your major at Harvard, Melany asked in surprise.

-- I never said anything like that. In fact, I still didn't know what to do with my life. So I gleaned from all over the place. History, philosophy. Quantum physics. Cognitive sciences. Above all, I wanted to develop a global vision of the world. A super-privileged way to find my place.

-- So go on, try to convince me.

-- You should finish your champagne first because I might bore you.

Which she did -- for the pleasure, and not for fear of being bored. On the contrary, Jeffrey was revealing a side of himself that she found exciting.

-- With modern science, we have reversed the concept that the visible parts of the world are its only reality. Quantum physics has abolished the notion of separation between matter and consciousness and introduced the notion of the participant to replace that of the observer. This late detour to the Eastern mystical vision fascinated me as much as it was able to captivate certain scholars. They have come to see the world as a web of mental and physical relationships -- that is to say, as a whole of which consciousness is an integral part and no longer a separate personal entity. From passive witnesses left to our individual destinies, we became actors as soon as Planck, Einstein, Bohr, Schrödinger, Heisenberg and other geniuses with which the twentieth century was so endowed concluded that energy, matter and time were inseparable. The fundamental question now is whether matter is the source of consciousness, or whether it is our consciousness that creates the universe. In the second case, it necessarily survives. So why not evolve from one incarnation to another? Some early Christians believed in it. The Sufis, the Hindus. The Jews, too. The list of philosophers and scientists who have become its advocates is endless. From Thomas Edison to Julian Huxley, from Lorenz by way of Nietzsche, and even Charles Lindbergh ... For my part, I have my doubts, that's obvious. But of all the theories about a possible survival of the soul after death, the one calling for reincarnation seems to me the most logical and the most defensible. As for Hitler ... I just hope he's out of the picture. There you are: you have the right to take me for a nutcase.

With that he emptied his bottle of mineral water in one gulp. Melany went to place a kiss on his lips.

-- OK, and who would you have been in your previous life?

-- I have a little fondness for Rasputin, who had a reputation for being sexually addicted. But that's mostly due to the effect you have on me when I see you lying on this bed.

Melany couldn't help but laugh. She was sinking into a world that was beyond her, but if Jeffrey was comfortable there, it was undoubtedly an asset. Herskowitz's beliefs had also stirred her somewhat. Never, ever, could she indulge in believing in anything supernatural, but since she had chosen to make this investigation her own, why not play the game to the end?

-- So I was Alexandra Feodorovna, the last Czarina, she replied in the same tone.

Jeffrey made a face at her.

-- What a pity. They tried to make it look like she was his mistress, but no matter how powerful he was, Rasputin would never have laid hands on her.

They found themselves naked, in each other's arms, not knowing who had started it.

-- Chapter 14 --

The icy wind that swirled from the Moskva River and then swept through the streets was biting. Melany felt penetrated as she walked the twenty yards that separated the hotel door from the Mercedes.

-- Thank goodness the car is already heated!, she said, dropping into the backseat immediately joined by Jeffrey as the driver got in behind the wheel.

The Russian's reaction when she gave him Soloviev's address surprised her. He turned sharply, his face serious, his eyes wide, and uttered the longest sentence they had heard him say since their arrival.

-- Borovsky Prospect? In Solntsevo? Are you sure that that is where you want to go?

Jeffrey, who didn't understand Russian, looked at Melany.

-- Yes, absolutely, the latter replied. Number 139. That's the very reason for our trip to Moscow.

The driver shook his head, looking worried, and quickly added something before grabbing his cell phone and dialing a number.

-- What did he say?, Jeffrey asked.

-- He has to call his boss before he takes us there. Wait ... He's asking him for permission to change the type of his service.

-- Very well!, Jeffrey said.

-- What does that mean?

-- Don't worry.

The driver hung up the phone and turned to them again.

-- *Da!,* he said.

-- *Da* what?

-- It's your decision.

-- But why are you so worried?

-- This is the area of the Solntsevskaya gang. The most dangerous area of Moscow. You can't walk around there in those outfits.

He looked at them with vague disgust in his eyes.

Melany's trench coat and Jeffrey's peacoat marked them as tourists as surely as a slung camera and a map.

-- You can't walk around there in those clothes!

The Mercedes still hadn't traveled a yard. The driver got out of the vehicle, opened the trunk, and returned to hand them two *shapkas* and two fur-collared coats.

-- You want me to put this on?, Melany said indignantly, sniffing the faux leather of the threadbare fur coat that had landed on her lap.

Jeffrey was already taking off his peacoat. He laughingly insisted:

-- Put this on, he knows what he's doing.

-- That's certainly reassuring ...

Melany did so, not without asking the driver for details of the gang he was referring to.

-- *Very bad!,* he replied, to show that he knew a few words of English. Very nasty.

-- Even now?

-- They're the worst criminals in all of Russia. They engage in racketeering, arms trafficking, kidnapping, trafficking in women, exporting drugs, stealing credit cards. They torture, they kill. Nobody interferes with them, they're too powerful. Even the police are terrified. *Very bad. Very bad.*

-- Okay, that's all right, the adventure goes on! -- Melany's heart was pounding -- I hope you also have some Kalashnikovs in the trunk.

-- You want one?, the driver stiffened, very serious.

-- No, that's all right. Thanks ... uh ...

Jeffrey broke off as he realized he didn't know the name of their driver.

-- Miloslav!, he said, stepping on the accelerator, quickly leaving the lavish entrance to the Lotte Hotel far behind them.

A few minutes after leaving the metropolis, the road offered a detour. Everything was white: the streets, the sky, and even the faces of passers-by. If they turned left, they would end up in Yasenevo, where the headquarters and archives of the SVR, the former KGB, were located. The landscape was a succession of groves, fields, factories whose chimneys spewed blackish smoke, and clusters of social buildings, an ugliness not unlike the worst neighborhoods of Cleveland, but with one difference. Despite the obvious misery and degradation of buildings with blackened walls stained with graffiti, the snow-covered edges of the road were crisp. The winter coat undoubtedly participated in this illusion of cleanliness.

A sign finally indicated Solntsevo. The name was tagged on the bottom with the awkward design of a double-headed eagle, topped with a royal crown.

-- Solntsevskaya!, Miloslav noted laconically, pointing to the graffiti.

-- Is that their mark?, Melany asked.

-- In part. It lacks the scepter, and the hammer and sickle are missing, but everyone understands.

The first streets were wide, clear, lined with first and alders, not at all what Melany had expected. They sank into the heart of the neighborhood. Shops sheltered in houses painted in various colors alternated with blocks of buildings with beige brick facades gangrenous from pollution, or bare cement. Many of the windows had been boarded up, sometimes with planks, other times simply bricked up. A few luxury cars parked next to genuine wrecks reflected the deep soul of this neighborhood excluded from the rest of the region where, according to Miloslav, the Solntsevskaya gang ruled like a government. No question of walking around there at night, he warned. But in broad daylight, they had a few chances of getting about without harm, as evidenced by the presence of housewives pushing shopping carts, a group of children playing in the snow that they passed, and a couple walking along holding up a little boy by his hands.

He parked the Mercedes in the shelter of a corner store with a few steps, whose windows serving as showcases displayed computers and cell phones on one side and cabbages, sausages and vodka on the other side. A sign on the door said the shop was closed until 3 p.m.

-- The yellow and brown building with balconies over there, just after the tower under construction, that is where you will be going!, Miloslav announced, rolling down his window to point out the location.

Icy air rushed into the vehicle.

"It's better if no one sees you coming in a Mercedes", he said.

Once out of the vehicle, Melany and Jeffrey pressed their shapkas over their heads before lowering the side flaps. The cold was intense, much sharper and more piercing than in central Moscow. The window of the shop gave them a satisfying reflection of two ordinary-looking and somewhat miserable Russians. The threadbare fur coat covered Melany's neck up to her chin.

There were few people in the streets and no one paid any attention to them. They arrived in front of the building pointed out by Miloslav. Up close, the leprous facade showed a poignant misery. The coating between the little balconies, some of which had been condemned, were peeling off in patches. Obscene graffiti covered the walls up to the second floor above ground. One of the panes of the front door had been replaced with plywood. Jeffrey rushed into the lobby, Melany on his heels. A scream coming from the upper floors made them tremble. Doors slammed. A woman's crying. Screams from a fight.

As they made their way to the row of mailboxes, the elevator door opened to reveal an elderly lady, bundled up in a thick woolen coat, a cap pulled down over her ears. She had the florid face and flattened nose of the Tatars, an ethnic group found more commonly in the Crimea than in the Moscow region. Melany stood in front of her to ask.

-- *Izvinite,* madame: we need some information. Have you lived here for a long time?

The woman eyed her briefly and tried to walk around her without saying a word. Then Jeffrey stood in front of her in his turn.

-- We're very sorry, Melany insisted, but we're looking for someone. An old friend.

-- *Ya ne znayu!,* "I don't know", the old lady retorted sharply in Russian, once again trying to walk away.

There was fear in his eyes. She smelled of cabbage and cold tobacco.

-- Alexei Soloviev, Melany says again. He once lived in this building. Do you know him?

-- *I don't know!,* the Russian repeated, and this time it was almost a cry.

Melany stepped to the side. This was not the place to start a scene. The old lady dragged her leg away, taking one last worried glance over her shoulder before disappearing into the street. Far away in the interior the building, the noises and howls associated with the argument resumed again.

-- Well, that's just the start, Jeffrey commented with a shrug. Can you decipher the inscriptions on the mailboxes?

There were about fifty boxes with names and numbers, but a great many were illegible. Melany scanned them quickly before giving up.

Nothing that closely resembles Soloviev, she announced, discouraged.

All they could do was to wait for other neighbors to pass by, hoping that they would be more cooperative than the babushka in the cap. It was then that Jeffrey noticed a second door by the stairs. It opened onto an interior courtyard, leading to the entrance to twin buildings hidden from the street. Gigantic garbage cans overflowed with their contents, probably accumulated over the past week or so. Everywhere the snow was frozen mud. Russian rap music pierced the windows of an upper floor, pouring out its bass notes and explosions of voices. Melany held her nose to cross the courtyard.

The mailboxes of the two buildings showed the same decrepitude as the first. With more than half of the names barely legible, it would have taken unbelievable luck to find Soloviev's name.

As they turned back to the main entrance, the face of a young man appeared behind a window on the second floor. Jeffrey immediately tried to get his attention by waving his arms. Melany called out:

-- *Pozhaluysta!* Please! Can you help us?

The window opened. The boy, who must have been in his twenties, was dressed in a simple T-shirt, but didn't seem in the least bothered by the cold. With long hair framing a gaunt face, he had dark circles that didn't correspond to his age.

-- What do you want?

-- We're looking for someone. Alexei Soloviev. He lived at this address some years ago. Does that ring a bell?

-- Soloviev?

Melany and Jeffrey had regained hope, but the young man shook his head. He was about to close the window when Jeffrey reached into his coat to pull out a twenty dollar bill. He held it up above his head and asked Melany to translate.

-- If he helps us, the money is his.

-- Do you understand what you're doing?, the young woman worried.

-- Tell him, we'll see what happens.

The figure immediately disappeared. In the upper floors, hard rock followed Russian rap. The boy, still in a T-shirt, opened the door of the apartment building. He had bare feet and jeans so dirty it was impossible to pinpoint their original color. Up close, he looked even younger, but in a disturbing state of health. A network of blue veins ran through his diaphanous skin, emphasizing the harshness of his features and his haggard gaze.

-- What's the name of the guy you're looking for?

-- Soloviev. Alexei Soloviev, Melany repeated.

-- And if I find him for you, will you give me money?

Melany translated and Jeffrey nodded.

-- Where are you two from, and why isn't he talking?, the young man asked again, who didn't even shiver from the cold.

-- We're not from here, and I'm speaking for him, Melany snapped. Do you want this money or not?

-- Wait here. I'll be back.

He disappeared into the second building as quickly as he had arrived. Melany stared at Jeffrey.

-- What are you doing? Are you trying to get killed? At least warn me in advance.

-- Calm down, Jeffrey smiled. We didn't come all this way just to go back empty-handed.

-- Well, I just want to go home alive!, Melany grumbled before adding with a moan of dread. *And shit! I was just certain of it.*

The boy in the T-shirt had just reappeared, this time escorted by three men almost as scantily dressed as himself, except that they were wearing boots, with one of them wearing a leather jacket with metal chains shining like silver. Each of them was over six feet tall, standing several inches taller than Jeffrey, and their uncovered forearms showed the same tattoo, a two-headed eagle topped with a crown. Two of the men had shaved heads, while the third one, who was wearing the jacket, had hair as long as the boy. Each positioned himself near an exit from the courtyard, thus encircling them.

Melany thought about her own tattoos, which would take several more days to fade away. At the same time, she cursed Jeffrey. Did he have to be so unperceptive as to flash dollars in the isolated courtyard of a group of buildings located in the heart of a neighborhood where the most dangerous gang in Russia ran rampant?

The man with the long hair moved closer to Jeffrey. He had a tiny goatee, meant to compensate for the disproportionalities of a face that was distinguished by surprisingly blue eyes, a wide mouth and a receding chin.

-- What do you want with Soloviev?

Hands deep in his coat pockets, Jeffrey just met his gaze, looking unmoved and almost indifferent.

-- You answer when we talk to you!, the leader of the gang insisted, taking a step closer.

-- My friend doesn't understand Russian, Melany said. We don't need anything special, just talk to him. Does he still live here?

-- Ah? Where does he come from, then, is he German?

-- *Amerikanskiy!,* one of his companions said.

-- Really? American?, said the man in the jacket. Is that why you walk around with dollars? It's nice of you to come here and hand them out to us.

His hand plunged under his jacket, only to reappear holding a military knife with a curved and serrated blade. The music upstairs stopped, plunging the courtyard into heavy silence. A rodent showed its snout at the top of a trash can, watched the scene for a moment, and fled.

-- Melany, tell him I'll give him 100 dollars if he tells us how to find Soloviev, Jeffrey said.

The young woman was short of breath.

-- Do you really want me to translate that?

-- Dollars?, the gang leader chuckled as he brought the tip of his knife to Jeffrey's coat.

That was a word he understood.

-- Tell him, Jeffrey insisted.

-- My friend has $100 for you, if you know where Alexei is, Melany sighed.

The gang members burst out laughing.

-- Do you carry around a lot of those pretty green bills?, the Russian added, placing his weapon against Jeffrey's stomach.

The barrel slipped between two buttons hidden in the fur.

-- Open this coat for me, faggot!

-- What did he say?, Jeffrey asked, unfazed.

-- He wants you to unbutton, and he said that you prefer men.

-- Oh, yeah, in such polite terms?

-- Not really. *Pidoras* means 'queer'.

-- *Da! Pidoras!,* the Russian confirmed without showing any kind of humor.

-- You can tell him that ...

-- No!, Melany cut off, as irritated by Jeffrey's nonchalance as she was terrified.

She couldn't understand her companion's calm.

Either he was completely reckless or he had a plan. She prayed for the second hypothesis. Jeffrey put his coat aside.

The gang leader broke into a vicious, nasty smile when he discovered the prize jacket, crisp jeans, and stylish sweater under the old fur. He belched.

-- Your story stinks of shit! You're going to explain to us why you are hiding your luxury faggot clothes.

-- We were loaned the furs because we weren't equipped for such cold!, Melany said indignantly, taking a step forward. We have nothing to hide and we have made you an honest offer.

The other three looked at each other and, without consulting each other, approached the couple. One of them tried to grab Melany's arm. She pulled away abruptly, which drew a sneer from him. He cocked his head over her to give her a series of grotesque grimaces while grunting.

-- Are you part of the RNU?, the Russian suddenly snapped. Are you fucking Nazis?

-- Why?, Melany asked in fascination. What does that have to do with Soloviev?

-- I'm the one asking the questions, little bitch!

-- The answer is no. We didn't come here looking for trouble. Give us the information we need, take the dollars, and let us go. You will never hear from us again.

The man who had tried to grab Melany called out to the chief, laughing.

-- Hey, Yuri, you hear that, the American is going to give us dollars. And then they'll bugger off. That's a good plan. Right?

-- Of course he's going to give us dollars, said the man named Yuri, running the tip of his knife over Jeffrey's fur. Lots of dollars. And you, the translator, you also show us what you have there.

The young man who had called in the gang laughed wildly. The two shaven-headed men grabbed Melany, each by one arm. Yuri walked over to her, his knife blade horizontal. Jeffrey stepped aside to stand between them.

-- ... Oh ..., the two men with shaved heads sneered.

-- Step aside or I'll stab you!, Yuri said simply, lifting his blade up to Jeffrey's face.

Melany hurried to undo her coat, praying that they weren't asking for more. The gang appeared to be in competition or even at war with the far-right hooligans. She had no doubt how they would react when they saw her tattoos.

-- Look at this beauty!, Yuri exclaimed. They're nosing around disguised as beggars and underneath, they're worthy of a fashion show. I'm telling you that they are from the RNU, these two bums. They're Nazi fuckers!

-- You're wrong, Melany protested. The Nazis are our enemies just as much as yours.

The gang leader shrugged and called out an order in a secret lingo that Melany didn't understand. Coded gang language. Several figures had appeared behind the windows on various floors, but none showed the slightest intention of intervening. His face close to touching that of the young woman, he put his hand between her legs and began to sniff at her like a dog.

-- I'll go first, he whispered to his gang. Then you do what you want with her.

Melany opened her mouth to cry for help, but one of the men flanking her twisted her arm viciously before gagging her with the other hand. Jeffrey was about to intervene, even if he were to leave his skin there, when an order was shouted in Russian.

-- *Stop!*

Yuri paused, surprised, and turned his head in the direction of the voice. Miloslav's imposing figure stood out in the doorway of the first building, a pistol aimed at the gang leader. With a sharp gesture, he activated the firing pin to show that he wasn't kidding.

-- Who are you?, growled the leader of the gang.

-- I'm the one asking the questions. What's your name?

-- Yuri Barsouko. A name you will remember!

Indifferent to the threat, Miloslav continued.

-- Anton Lechevsky, does that ring a bell?

A glimmer of concern passed through Yuri's eyes.

-- How do you know Anton?

-- He's a cousin of my boss, Andrei Zherdev. Last I heard, he was the head of the Solntsevskaya. Unless you've changed your head recently?

Again, the boy who had called in the gang burst out laughing. With his finger pointed at Miloslav, he slapped himself on the thighs. His cheeks had turned blue but he was still just as insensitive to the cold. One of the men with a shaved head thumped him, sending him staggering a yard away from him.

-- Do you work for Zherdev?, Yuri hissed.

-- Yes, and these two are his clients, and therefore mine. Shall we put our guns down or do I ask Zherdev to call his cousin?

Yuri hesitated, then finally let go:

-- All right, all right ...

Palms outstretched as a sign reassurance, he ordered the other two to release Melany. Jeffrey closed his coat, and brushed it off mechanically.

-- So, are we resuming our negotiations?, he asked as if nothing had happened. Melany, are you translating?

The young woman did so, but she wanted to kill him.

-- The deal still stands. One hundred dollars for any information that would allow us to find Soloviev.

-- Give them as much as needed, Jeffrey whispered.

But Yuri shook his head.

-- He's been dead a long time. I never knew him myself.

A wave of discouragement took hold of Melany. She glanced at Jeffrey, but he didn't seem too affected. All the figures from the upper floors had disappeared. Miloslav made his way to the center of the yard while putting his pistol in the holster he wore under his coat. Jeffrey asked:

-- Why did you think we were Nazis? And, first of all, the RNU -- what is that?

The driver answered for Yuri.

-- These are people nostalgic for the Third Reich. There are a few tens of thousands across Russia. They've formed a band in the area and they are at war with the Solntsevskaya.

-- Those sons of bitches forgot that their grandparents were slaughtered by the Germans, Yuri thundered before spitting on the ground.

-- Is there really nothing you can give us about Soloviev?, Melany insisted. What happened to the apartment he lived in?

Yuri looked at his companions. One nodded and the other shrugged. He finally declared:

-- Alexei Soloviev was well known in these buildings. Everyone knew he belonged to the KGB. We called him Wagner.

-- We already know that!, Melany cut in.

-- He quit. It seems that he started hanging out with the RNU guys right after he left. He died in a helicopter crash.

-- Civilian or military?, Jeffrey asked with fascination once Melany had translated.

-- We don't know a damned thing about it. The helicopter crash was a rumor that circulated around the neighborhood in the late nineties. His daughter, Roksana, inherited the apartment ...

A ray of hope rose up in Melany.

-- She still lives here?

Yuri scratched his head as he looked at Jeffrey. Then he looked at his fingers, as if something were missing.

-- I'll add a hundred dollars for him if he tells us everything he knows about her, Jeffrey said.

-- We don't know much about her. Except that she got tired of seeing our faces and took off. The daughter of a Nazi had no business being here. Maybe we told her a few times too many ...

The three Russians snickered.

Melany asked:

-- Do you have her current address?

Yuri shook his head and shrugged his shoulders.

-- We can help them find her ... intervened the man who had gagged Melany.

-- It might cost a bit more, Yuri sneered, stroking the tuft of hair that hid his receding chin.

-- A deal is a deal, Miloslav said threateningly.

-- OK! Yuri blurted out. All that is known about Roksana is that she's a nurse and that she works in a hospital.

-- Which one?

-- A state hospital. In the north or center of Moscow.

-- What else?

-- The last time we heard from her, she still wasn't married. So she had to keep her maiden name. We really know nothing more than that.

Jeffrey snatched two one hundred dollar bills from a small wad and handed them over.

-- That's half information. It merits a half payment. But, hey ...

Yuri kept his hand outstretched, his gaze still provocative, but Miloslav intervened.

-- That was the deal. Consider yourself happy to be paid at all. Now get the hell out of here.

Money changed hands. The gang disappeared.

As soon as they were settled in the Mercedes again, Melany was seized with tremors. After such a fright, she would have kissed their driver in relief, but she preferred to scold Jeffrey.

-- Do you realize what kind of a situation you almost put us in? Do you really believe that money can buy everything?

-- Everything, no. But those kinds of people, absolutely.

Melany turned to Miloslav.

-- And, first of all, how did you know you had to step in?

-- It's my job, the driver answered laconically.

-- How? Or what? Which job? I thought you were some kind of Uber ...

-- Miloslav is much more than just a driver, Jeffrey said.

-- Which means what? What is he? A bodyguard? A spook? Former KGB, too?

-- A bit of all three, Jeffrey confessed. We often use his agency when officials come to Moscow.

We, by implication, was the State Department.

-- And you couldn't tell me that earlier? I almost died of fear earlier in the yard. Now I understand why you were so relaxed. You knew he was going to step in ...

Jeffrey shook his head, a sorry expression on his face.

-- No. I didn't know. He came on his own initiative. This kind of people work on instinct.

-- *Da!*, Miloslav said from the front seat, his chest turned towards them, as if he had understood.

-- Don't you ever pull a stunt like that on me again!, Melany growled.

-- I didn't want to worry you, that's all. Now that you know, it's up to you. Do we keep Miloslav, or order a cab back to the hotel?

-- I hate you!, grumbled Melany, who above all did not like to admit defeat.

-- Me neither. More and more every day. But that's not what will help us find Wagner's daughter. Can you ask our spook driver to call his office and get all the information available on Roksana?

Once briefed, Miloslav picked up his phone and asked for help in locating, if not the address, at least the workplace of Alexei Soloviev's daughter.

They had just reached central Moscow when his agency called him back with the information.

***

The concrete-fronted block of buildings was grim as a bunker. City Hospital number 63, built in the 1970's and located at Ulitsa Durova in the north of Moscow, bore the hallmarks of the Soviet regime in its architecture.

The entrance looked like any hospital lobby on the planet, except that the emergency room line far exceeded anything seen in the West. A few rare caregivers wandered among the dozens of patients, some sitting on the floor, others stretched out on stretchers, most standing, amid the cries of pain, curses, and cries of children. The air reeked of sweat and the stench of disinfectant. The walls were a dull gray. The floor, which was covered with faux linoleum parquet, was so worn in places that it revealed large slabs of cement.

Jeffrey and Melany had traded in the old fur coats for their original clothes, and their noticeable entrance drew unfriendly glances. The young woman slipped apologetically among the patients and walked decisively towards the reception desk. The sight of these sick and injured people who seemed to be in a hurry but to whom no one was paying attention was heartbreaking. Jeffrey followed closely behind her.

The young woman planted herself with aplomb in front of the counter that accommodated several receptionists. She smiled at the couple whose turn it was and leaned over the grill to ask:

-- Sorry, just one question and I'll let you get back to work. Is Roksana Soloviev on duty today?

The receptionist in front of her, a woman in her forties with a round face framed by brown locks clumped under a nurse's cap, stared at her contemptuously before saying:

-- Have you seen our line? Take a number and wait your turn.

She was already addressing the couple Melany had snuck past. The latter insisted:

-- I'm just asking for information. Yes or no?

-- Get in line!, the receptionist snapped.

A few patients in the front rows grumbled. A man in overalls over a thick red shirt, one arm in a cast held by a splint, repeated in a loud voice:

-- Get in line!

Roksana Soloviev, Melany said, enunciating each syllable. You see, the patients are getting angry. Is it a scene that you want? You just have to answer yes or no and I will leave.

The receptionist rose slightly from her seat to observe the boisterous movement that was forming in the queue.

-- She's not here today, she finally said.

-- And when will she be here?

-- It's none of your business and if you don't leave immediately, I will call security.

-- With at least a hundred people in this room, it could turn into a riot, Melany pointed out before turning to Jeffrey. Can you give me the message?

Jeffrey pulled out of his pocket a small envelope with Roksana's name written in Cyrillic, into which they had folded a fifty dollar bill and slipped a piece of cardboard with their cell phone numbers and their hotel room number on it.

-- Hold this, and especially look inside before giving it to her. Tell her it's about her father and she needs to call us urgently. *Vklyucheno?* Understood?

The Russian saw the corner of the note discreetly protruding from the envelope. She glanced briefly at her colleagues who were all busy helping patients and grabbed hold of it.

-- And now get the hell out of here!

The man of the couple in the front of the line nudged Melany in annoyance. Jeffrey wanted to intervene but the latter stopped him with a gesture.

-- We've wasted enough of these poor people's time, she sighed.

-- *Amerikanskiy!*, the worker in the overalls rasped. American bastards walking right past us.

A muffled murmur arose from the crowd of patients. Some who were sitting on the floor with their backs pressed against the wall straightened up. The nearest ones scowled threateningly.

-- We're leaving, Melany said. Nothing's happened. Sorry!

The Russian in overalls spat at her feet as she walked around him. Looking dignified, she continued on her way, escorted by Jeffrey, to the double emergency room access doors, avoiding patients the same way as when they had arrived.

They finally got out and safely reached the vehicle behind which Miloslav was waiting.

-- And now?

-- We change at the hotel and go to dinner, Jeffrey suggested.

-- And what if she doesn't call?

-- We know where she works, so finding where she lives shouldn't be too complicated.

Jeffrey straightened the sides of his coat as if he were cold, sighed, and closed his eyes. The jet lag was starting to take its toll. Melany rested her head on his shoulder.

The next moment, she was dozing.

-- Chapter 15 --

Jungle of Sumatra, region of Aceh

Seven weeks earlier.

The man was a stranger. He could have come from Aceh, or anywhere on the island of Sumatra. He wore combat fatigues and a black scarf and, at his side, a machete that he refused to give up and which had to be taken by force before he was laid down on the operating table.

A bullet had passed through his abdomen. Another had torn off a good chunk of his thigh. He had lost so much blood that his survival was a miracle. How had he managed to hold out for two days, thrown over the back of a mule, while his comrades made a forced march through the jungle?

For a few minutes, Darwis Haikal thought he could save him. Adhi was at his side. If Allah had decided to spare this man until now, He probably wouldn't take His gracious hand away now ...

But Adhi had refused to help. No threat, no plea had changed the resolve of the "miracle child". For a reason unknown to Darwis, his adopted son selected the recipients of his gifts in accordance with criteria defined by himself alone. When he said no, nothing could make him change.

The man died as Darwis inserted the needle from a transfusion bag into his vein. The monitor's heart rate line went hopelessly flat. Attempts at resuscitation using the defibrillator were unsuccessful.

Darwis, deep with anxiety, had no other recourse than to report the fighter's death to Saragih.

The third in two days.

***

Nothing is easier for a humanitarian NGO with significant resources than obtaining the medical supplies needed to set up a field hospital.

In less than two weeks, following a list drawn up by Darwis Haikal and completed by specialists in the treatment of wounded in conflict zones, "*Earth and Sharing*" had managed to collect some four hundred kilos of medicines and portable equipment, a mobile operating theater distributed among half a dozen containers, tents with inflatable walls, several electric generators, and around thirty cots. The equipment had been transported on the back of an elephant to the headquarters of the new GAM in the middle of the jungle. Six caravans had been organized on different dates in order to not arouse suspicion. Saragih's men, working with machetes and chainsaws, had to clear an area large enough to contain the structures and then cover the whole thing with camouflage netting covered with vegetation. Three volunteer medics had then appeared, recruited from all over the island, the doctor did not know how.

The hospital had become operational under his direction forty-eight hours after the arrival of the last items.

The task, however, appalled Darwis. He was a general practitioner, not a surgeon, let alone able to operate on war-wounded. But Saragih didn't want to hear anything like that.

-- You did well the first time, thanks to your son. You just have to start over.

The first casualties arrived the day after the hospital had been set up. They belonged to Jemaah Islamiyah, now merged with GAM under the leadership of Saragih. The latter confided little in Darwis, and never concerning his strategies or actions, which meant that the doctor was completely ignorant of the operations carried out against the police stations and the official armed forces scattered around the region.

There was no longer any question of concealing Adhi's healing powers, since both Saragih and the Germans had discovered his special gift. The latter called it "healing magnetism," but Darwis had never heard of such a phenomenon. Although educated and endowed with a scientific mind, the doctor had been brought up in religion and left all inexplicable gray areas to the highest authorities. Ghosts, the evil eye, tsunamis, and the abilities of his adopted son were among them.

But Adhi had refused to participate in the recovery of the wounded since they had begun to fill the field hospital, however.

And Darwis, who now ran a field hospital that must have cost hundreds of billions of Indonesian rupees, was more distraught than ever.

An aide-de-camp from Saragih burst into the operating room while the doctor was washing his hands. A self-contained electric generator powered a pump that pumped water from the river through a network of pipes to the tap over a sink.

-- The sheikh wants to see you!

Darwis quickly wiped himself clean. Adhi had stayed in their tent. There was no point in keeping him at his side as long as he refused to help treat the wounded. From the common room came the moans and groans of two men in poor condition whom he had nevertheless managed to save. Saragih believed that a true fighter should offer his suffering up to Allah, and therefore demanded that the use of morphine be restricted.

The doctor, preceded by the aide-de-camp, found the sheikh in a second clearing, also cleared with machetes, and surrounded as usual by his German "staff". There, standing on a flat rock, he harangued an imaginary crowd, without uttering a word. The pantomime would have looked ridiculous if Saragih hadn't looked so dangerous. One of the Germans was teaching him a gesture, which consisted of slapping himself on the chest, raising his fists, pointing a finger at a virtual opponent, and appealing to a higher power by pointing to the sky and then closing his hand to seize the force and bring it back to him.

The choreography was so well orchestrated that Darwis felt chills.

Saragih did it several times before noticing the doctor's arrival. With his face closed and his eyes vague, as though still in the grip of the powers he claimed to capture, he climbed down from the rock and dismissed the Germans.

-- Send me Hamdani, he ordered the aide-de-camp.

He invited Darwis to sit down next to him. He had trimmed his beard and mustache, which gave his Eurasian features extra elegance and underlined the fever of his slanted eyes.

-- My friends are teaching me to speak to large audiences, he said in the opening remarks. That doesn't surprise you too much, does it, Doctor Haikal?

Saragih made a point of always treating the doctor with respect, even when his words contained explicit threats, buried in convolutions whose secrets he alone knew.

-- I have been past the stage of surprise since you forced me to leave my village, Darwis retorted.

The sheikh smiled. His eyes, a deep black, brightened several shades, almost to gray when he was satisfied.

-- By Allah, he whispered, as if continuing his silent harangue after finally finding his words. We are at the beginning of a war and our victory will be such that in a thousand years our enemies will crawl in terror at the mere mention of our names. Yesterday some martyrs died for the greater glory of the Most High. Today a hundred thousand of our brothers are ready to sacrifice themselves in the same way. Tomorrow they will be millions. But that's just the point.

His hand snapped on Darwis' forearm, which he dug his fingers into with all his might, raising a surprised cry from the doctor.

-- ... Speaking precisely, I find it difficult to accept the death of these martyrs, when Allah has obviously sent you and your son to help our cause. What's happened?

Saragih had therefore learned of the death of the third fighter, while Darwis had not even finished writing the notes on his failures which he was recording in a notebook.

-- I have told you many times that I am a doctor, not a surgeon. Expect more deaths as long as you refuse to admit it.

-- I well understand that, and I would agree with you, Doctor, if you were just a regular doctor. But when Allah places such gifted beings as your son at our service, and he disobeys the will of the Most High, then there is a problem that we will have to resolve quickly. Ah, here is Mr. Hamdani ...

The newcomer had magically appeared from the thick of the jungle. Small in stature, he wore round glasses and a thin mustache that outlined the edge of his upper lip like a pencil line. His very fair skin betrayed more Chinese than Malay origins, but his features were decidedly Indonesian. Darwis had seen him several times, wandering around the camp, but he was unaware of his real function.

-- Mr. Hamdani has also studied medicine, Saragih explained. When I met him, he called himself "Doctor", like you. But since then, he has acquired another term. Can you tell us what this is, Mr. Hamdani?

His interlocutor shook his head, indifferent to the sheikh's request, which left Darwis to assume that he had some influence over him.

-- They call him "the tormentor," but he doesn't like that very much, Saragih added confidentially, as the fair-skinned Asian pulled a small notebook from his pocket, which he handed to Darwis.

Several bound plastic sleeves contained reproductions of photographs yellowed by age. Postcards. The doctor shuddered at the sight of the first one ...

-- The oldest of these photos was taken in 1903, Hamdani commented in a creaking voice to make one cringe. This is a *lingchi*. If you are unfamiliar with this Mandarin term, then understand that *lingchi* was used as a punishment for the most serious crimes in China until the Revolution. The executioner was tasked with carefully cutting the culprit into pieces until death ensued. The most gifted managed to keep their victim alive by leaving only their organs intact. The rest -- the arms, legs, back and chest muscles -- were thrown into a basket. Then, the condemned was untied, in order to finally be beheaded. The foreign soldiers and diplomats stationed in Beijing who had fun buying these postcards, which were printed by the authorities for obvious purposes of deterrence, gave the practice a name. *Death by a thousand cuts.* In reality, *lingchi* means slow death ... very slow.

Hamdani paused under Saragih's amused gaze to make certain Darwis was flipping through the little notebook while listening to his presentation. The expression he deciphered on his features must have suited him, for he continued, a slight tic tugging at his lip.

-- In order to keep the condemned man alive as long as possible, the assistant administered an opium-based potion which, while slowing the heart rate, reduced the intensity of the pain, which was intolerable if not to the point of being deadly. The punishment, executed in the public square, thus retained its spectacular and deterrent aspect for as long as possible. Despite the massive dose of opium, the pain was still excruciating, almost to the limit. They started with the chest, then the biceps, then the belly fat ... It took real talent and a perfect knowledge of anatomy to practice the art of the executioner at such a high level. Few deserved the honor of being able to practice *lingchi* in the name of the Emperor, and each incision had to be accompanied by apologies and thanks. Take a look at the last photograph.

Darwis did so, already being at the verge of nausea. Human anatomy obviously held no secrets for him. But the abominations of which man was capable had always left him breathless.

The last photograph was recent, in color. The victim had been dismembered and his genitals cut off. Ropes held his trunk up. His mouth, wide open with an interminable cry, was as bloody as his torso with cauterized and smoking wounds. This was no longer a vestige of a bygone history, but proof that this tradition of torture had never been lost.

In this photo, Hamdani was holding the knife.

-- Thank you, Mr. Hamdani, you may go back, said the Sheikh before focusing his gaze on Darwis. My European friends have taught me that punishment is only a deterrent if it is truly spectacular. Our allies in the Islamic State have provided proof of this by sowing panic among our enemies with video recordings similar to these photos. But what is a slaughter, drowning in a cell or even death on a stake, when compared to this slow agony?

-- Why did you show me these horrors?, Darwis protested. You forced me to join you to treat your wounded, not to torture them.

-- Precisely so, Doctor ...!

The sheikh's voice took on a dangerous intonation. His eyes had turned black. His contorted features underscored the relentless hatred that he had a reputation for showing, apart from his refined manners.

-- ... Your first surgery, with the help of your son, happily surprised me. According to my foreign friends, his gift is rare, but they gave me examples of similar cases. Except that three dead out of five wounded in two days is a percentage that I cannot tolerate. What happened?

-- I really do not control Adhi, Darwis confessed with a heavy heart. Of the three, at least two had no chance of surviving. The wounded come to us after two to three days of walking in the jungle, and you've lost many more along the way. The one I tried to save this morning had lost so much blood that it would have been a miracle for him to survive. Adhi is a healer and I am a doctor. He is no more a magician than I am a surgeon.

-- Well, Doctor, Saragih said while getting up, that will have to change. You're going to have to talk to your son and convince him to do more ...

The sheikh bent down to gently grab a butterfly that had landed on a fern by its wings. He watched it for a moment, breathed on it like he wanted to breathe life into it, and threw it into the air, delighted to see it soar, twirl, and disappear into the jungle.

He turned abruptly.

-- The next time I summon you about this, Mr. Hamdani will not just show you pictures. Be persuasive with your son, Doctor.

-- Chapter 16 --

Moscow

Present time

For dinner, Jeffrey had chosen a restaurant tea room frequented by oligarchs, considered to be the new Russian aristocracy, and wealthy tourists. Established on the two floors of a baroque-style mansion built in the seventeenth century, the Café Pouchkine, which was divided into several themed rooms, belonged to the list of the best restaurants in Europe and largely deserved its reputation because of its interior architecture, its old-fashioned atmosphere, and the quality of its dishes.

The rich wood paneling was inspired by the splendors of Imperial Russia, in an atmosphere of a literary café where one might have expected to meet Tolstoy, Dostoyevsky, or even Chekhov and Turgenev. The furniture dated from the same period, and shelves and displays offered a unique collection of scientific and artistic objects, from a copper telescope to a planetary globe, to pendulums, mechanical clocks, baroque musical scores, harps, flutes and engravings.

-- The menu is so tempting, I don't really know what to choose, Melany sighed after scanning it up and down.

-- Just ask the maître d' what's the best and let yourself go.

They decided by mutual agreement on a typical Russian dinner from the pre-communist era, consisting of borscht, piroghis, smoked salmon, eel, sturgeon and Pozharsky cutlets, washed down with a Château Pétrus of fine vintage that had been suggested by the maître d' who spoke fluent English with a strong French accent.

-- Did you see who's sitting at the table between the library and the two telescopes?, Jeffrey remarked after the maître d' congratulated them on the excellence of their choice.

Melany turned discreetly and shook her head in ignorance.

-- I don't know.

-- Oh, those are just delegates from the United Nations human rights organization that I've met during the course of my work. Fortunately, they won't recognize me. These charming characters are going to spend a lot of taxpayers' money before taking part in further votes in favor of the dictatorships they came from. Tonight, they've traded in their traditional dress in order to go unnoticed. Always expect to meet high level officials at the best restaurants. The more their population dies of hunger, the more they gorge themselves.

-- I didn't know you had such subversive ideas, Melany quipped.

-- If realism is subversive, then yes. Truman and Churchill would turn in their graves if they knew that the worst dictatorships regularly find themselves in charge of UN committees supposed to protect individual liberty, women's rights, minority rights, or arms control. Unfortunately, it's part of my job in the State Department to maintain a cordial relationship with them. In the 1970's, the Secretary General of the United Nations, Kurt Waldheim, was a former Nazi.

-- Leave me some illusions. After all, the world is changing.

-- Go ask them if they've heard of the *"Father of Victory."* I'm sure at least four bodyguards will jump on you. But you'll get the answer in their looks ...

Melany made to get up.

-- No, stop, that was just a figure of speech!

-- Will you still allow me to go to the bathroom?

Like a perfect gentleman, Jeffrey rose to his feet as a waiter rushed to pull out the young woman's chair.

The washrooms were extravagantly luxurious, like the place itself. Authentic porcelain basins and sinks, fine gold-plated faucets, mirrors standing or recessed in the woodwork. Melany looked at herself there for a moment. Her makeup skillfully camouflaged the bruises on her face. The glow in her eyes was feverish. But she looked in better shape than when she had come back from Kurdistan.

-- Don't look at me like that, she scolded herself, grimacing. *It's true, he's very much your new guy, but he's doing a bit too much.*

She stuck out her tongue at her image and it returned her courtesy. She locked herself into the stall and squirmed to undo her underwear.

As Murphy's law demanded, her cell phone vibrated in her bag the instant she sat down on the toilet.

The number was unidentified.

-- Melany Carson!, she announced, cursing the call and restraining herself as best she could.

-- You know my father?, said a woman's voice in Russian.

Melany's fingers twitched on the cell phone.

-- Roksana?

-- I asked you a question, the nurse retorted. Who are you, and how do you know my father?

-- That's not the kind of question you can answer over the phone. The best thing would be for us to meet as soon as possible.

-- American?, Roksana asked.

The young woman admitted it.

-- In two hours, in front of your hotel. A beige Volkswagen Polo, Alexei Soloviev's daughter said before hanging up.

When Melany sat down across from Jeffrey again, the first entrees had been placed on the table. The waiter was waiting to hold the chair for her. He lifted the silver dome that retained the heat of the borscht.

-- That's it!, she announced.

-- Yes, that's something I like about good restaurants. The service is fast and efficient.

-- I'm not talking to you about the soup and the smoked fish!, Melany sighed. That was it. Roksana contacted us.

Jeffrey gave a delighted little laugh.

-- Did she call you when you were in the bathroom?

-- We have an appointment in two hours.

-- Well, then, that's great! That gives us plenty of time to enjoy dinner.

At that moment, the maître d' presented the bottle of Chateau Pétrus on a silver stand.

***

After the two hours had passed, Melany and Jeffrey waited for over twenty minutes, standing outside in the cold. Roksana was arguably not the prompt type, unless she first wanted to gain a true profile of the Americans who had contacted her. They were on the verge of giving up and heading back into the hotel lobby, even if they had to come out again if they received another call, when the Polo finally showed up.

The vehicle was in poor condition: it was missing a side light and its paintwork, more creme than beige, had lost all of its shine.

A woman in her thirties was behind the wheel. The round face with high cheekbones, slightly slanting eyes, short and straight blond hair, features tensed by apprehension. She leaned over to release the door lock, and motioned for Melany to take a seat next to her.

-- No, not him!, Soloviev's daughter said firmly when Jeffrey tried to get into the back of the vehicle.

-- But he's with me!, Melany protested.

-- I don't know either one of you. I spoke to you on the phone. Either he walks away, or you get out of my car and I'm out of here.

Melany and Jeffrey looked at each other. After a brief hesitation, he removed his fingers from the door handle and indicated that he would wait in the lobby.

-- Are you sure?, Melany asked anxiously.

-- I understand her. If I were in her place, I wouldn't trust anyone either. But I'm sure you have nothing to fear.

Roksana shifted into gear as soon as Jeffrey turned away. The little Polo jumped forward.

-- Where are you taking me?, Melany asked.

-- Nowhere. We'll just ride around while you explain to me who you are and what you want from me.

The car reached Smolenskiy Boulevard, which was beautifully lit at this time of the night and, without slowing down, turned into Ulitsa Prechistenka, which led to central Moscow. Roksana drove nervously, oblivious to speed limits, rights-of-way, or stop signs. The two women were silent for a few minutes, but then Melany attacked:

-- I don't know your father. I only know that he belonged to the KGB, that he was nicknamed Wagner, and that he left you his apartment in Solntsevo. Some years ago, he got hold of important historical documents, which he attempted to hand over to the British intelligence services in return for passage to the West. We are looking for these documents and we think you can help us.

-- My father is dead!, Roksana exclaimed.

-- I know that. And I'm sorry.

The features of the Russian woman hardened. A truck marked Pepsi Cola in Cyrillic letters forced her to slow down. She abruptly downshifted in a groan of tortured mechanics, accelerated in the same movement and overtook the heavy vehicle on the right, without taking into account the row of cars parked on the side of the road that she came dangerously close to.

-- Do you have to drive this way?, Melany protested.

Roksana evaded her protest.

-- If you think that my father's disappearance hurts me, or that I regret it, then you have been misinformed. And, first of all, who are you? Who was that man with you?

Melany replied calmly, adding that she represented a US intelligence agency, which was only half a lie. She spoke of the reasons for their investigation without going into details, not knowing which side Roksana belonged to, but encouraged by the animosity towards her father that the young woman had shown. While frustrated by Soloviev's disappearance, Melany felt a familiar excitement gradually take hold of her. Hadn't she and Jeffrey succeeded in finding the person closest to the Russian agent in record time?

-- How do you know about the existence of those documents?, Roksana asked.

-- Before I tell you more, I would like you to answer a question or two.

Soloviev's daughter braked to take advantage of a gap between two cars before changing lanes and performing a U-turn.

-- I'll take you back to your hotel.

-- Wait! We are not your enemies. We mean you no harm.

-- They all say that.

-- Who do you mean, they?

Roksana shot Melany a look in which suffering and hatred met despair.

-- How did you learn of the existence of these documents? she said, this time in an uncompromising tone.

-- Do you believe in coincidences?, Melany replied.

-- I am Russian.

She was no doubt referring to the Slavic soul, passionate and naive, quick to espouse the slightest illusion, provided it had the virtue of forgetfulness and hope. Melany continued in her more neutral voice, reserving an ounce of emotion for her conclusion.

-- In 1992, your father met an MI6 agent at a bar. Shortly after that, he was stripped of his post in the new KGB. A few months later, no doubt angered at having been shunted aside, he got in touch with the same agent to negotiate his passage to the West. In return, he offered documents he considered to be of great importance, signed by Hitler's own hand. MI6 didn't want them. I guess that the CIA also didn't. Vasiley took up his position again, in a cupboard in the KGB archives where his dignity was unravelling day by day. He ended up resigning. A few years later, he disappeared in a helicopter crash. A tragic end that could have ended our investigation. But I have a personal reason for not giving up until we have exhausted all the leads. This MI6 agent that he twice met with was my mother. She was pregnant with me at the time and didn't know it yet. She was the one who informed me of the existence of the will.

A long silence followed. Melany watched Roksana, whose gaze remained focused on the road, hoping she had managed to strike a cord with her. The Russian woman finally slowed down the vehicle.

-- I was very young at the time. My father didn't speak much. I didn't know then that he was trying to get to the West.

-- Then? So he tried again?

Roksana just shook her head, which could mean she didn't have any disclosures or just that she didn't want to talk about it.

-- So you are not a *storonnika?*

-- A *storonnika?* A supporter of what?, Melany asked in fascination.

-- You are apparently not very knowledgeable about the RNU[(12)].

-- This is the second time I've heard that name since arriving in Moscow.

-- *Storonniki* ... That's what the members of this organization are called. The *Supporters.*

-- Do you think I look like a neo-Nazi?

Roksana didn't even look at Melany.

-- The people my father met looked like everybody else. Some could have passed themselves off as Americans or Germans. That didn't prevent them from belonging to the Pamyat, a small ultra-violent nationalist group that began to experience its moment of glory when its second-in-command, Barkashov, founded the RNU with the most active and disciplined members of that group of racist criminals.

The Polo slowed down again. Roksana disengaged again and switched from fifth gear to fourth. The dial displayed a speed of about forty miles per hour, in accordance with the rules posted all along the traffic artery.

-- The RNU is not much talked about in the international press. It probably doesn't matter much any more?

-- Not important? As long as Russia was communist, the people were content with the false information the party tossed them, along with a new

[12] The RNU, or Russian National Unity Party, which was founded by Alexander Barkashov in 1990, has branches in 250 Russian towns and villages and publishes several "newsletters", including Russky Poryakov, which has more than 150,000 registered subscribers. Along with Pamyat (Memory), it is close to the far-right German NPD (National Democratic Party of Germany), the Belgian Bloed, Bodem, Eer en Trouw (Blood, Soil, Honor and Loyalty), the Serbian Nacionalni Stroj (National Machine), the KKK, and the American Aryan Nation.

pair of shoes every five years. Things changed with the disappearance of the Soviet Union. Many were shocked and ready to cling to any ideal. The most virulent Stalinists changed sides as soon as the newborn Nazi parties rang the bell of despair and pointed to those responsible for our misfortunes: the Uzbeks, the Tajiks, the Azeris, the Georgians and, of course, the Jews. Some apparatchiks wanted to revive the project of a Russia destined to dominate the world. My father was able to cleverly play out their fantasies ...

-- Because of the will?, Melany asked point-blank.

-- In part, I suppose.

-- Do you know its contents?

-- Only little bits and pieces.

-- How did you find out about it? Did your father ever tell you about it?

-- I was little, I told you. My dad looked after me on the weekends once or twice a month, when he couldn't find a way out of the drudgery. There were always members of Pamyat and then of the RNU at our house ... He spoke with them a lot. He was trying to convince them of a project that I didn't understand much about. He was dreaming of destabilizing the West in order to end the dictatorship of the financial world, and I don't know what else.

-- He discussed the will in their presence?

-- Yes. As soon as he uttered Hitler's name, his audience would be inflamed, but not necessarily in a way that would have satisfied him. Sometimes, they made fun of him. One evening, it almost turned into a fist fight. He chased them away by threatening them with his service revolver, which he had kept after his resignation. I heard them arguing and walked out of my room. When my father saw me, he yelled at me and pushed me away with all his might. I banged my head against the wall and almost lost consciousness, but it didn't move him for a moment. I had never seen him in such a state of rage. He locked me up and I wasn't allowed to go outside all weekend.

-- I'm sorry you went through that kind stuff. How old were you?

-- Ten or twelve years, I'm not really sure anymore. Every time his *friends* from Pamyat or the RNU came, he would polish off an entire bottle of vodka. When my father died, I thought I was free at last. I hoped I would never have to be around that kind of people again. That was the case for years. The RNU was gone from my life, but then the gangs arrived in the neighborhood. I woke from one nightmare, only to wake up in another. In the view of the *Solntsevskaya*, I was close to the RNU. They called me the Nazi's daughter. I had to move out.

The two women were a few blocks away from the Hotel Lotte, in a relatively busy street lined with luxury shops with illuminated windows. Roksana saw a row of parallel parking and parked the Polo.

-- If I answer your questions, will you be able to help me?

-- As far as I can.

-- The CIA has a lot of power.

-- I do not belong to the CIA, but always say I do. What is it that you need?

Roksana gave a squeaky laugh.

-- As if you haven't figured that out already. Somehow I'm my father's worthy daughter, you know.

A Russian couple walking along the sidewalk, their hands cluttered with packages, stopped in front of the Lanvin window directly in front of the Polo. The store was closed at that hour. That didn't prevent them from standing there gazing at the dressed mannequins and the multicolored balloons that brightened up the storefront encrusted in a gray marble facade. Melany sighed.

-- If you're referring to your father's attempts to cross over to the West, times have changed. As long as you have a passport, it shouldn't be too difficult to get a visa for yourself.

-- It's not a visa that I want, but a green card. I want to live in the West. I've never left Moscow other than once, to go to Saint Petersburg. If you could see where I live, you would understand. Without the ridiculous pension that my father arranged to be sent to me, I couldn't even afford that, and the apartment I inherited in Solntsevo is not salable because of the gangs infesting the neighborhood.

A red light flashed in Melany's brain.

-- The money your father sends you? What do you mean by that?

Roksana replied with a frown.

-- After his death, I was contacted by some kind of lawyer who informed me that my father had made arrangements for me. Every month, I see 12,000 rubles appear in my bank account ...

She shook her head, angry and desperate.

"I calculated that that isn't even two hundred dollars. Life in Moscow is not what it was under the Communist regime. Prices have skyrocketed. I fight regularly with my landlord to prevent rent hikes. My job as a nurse is exhausting and I earn little more than my father's post-mortem transfers. Can you help me, yes or no?

There was a pleading tone in her voice now. Melany felt compassion for the young woman. Unfortunately, there wasn't much she could do for her by herself. Her position at the INR would not even allow her to get her a visa. Jeffrey couldn't be much better off. She reluctantly confessed:

-- I wish I could answer you differently.

Roksana shrugged and gave a faint smile.

-- It was worth a try. I didn't have much to give you in return anyway.

-- Would you still be willing to tell me what you know?

-- And you, will you promise me that you'll try to intervene on my behalf, even if you're sure that you'll fail?

Melany promised. She was sincere.

-- I know hardly anything. I just heard snippets of phrases and I really can't remember them well. There was talk of Hitler, of course, and something totally absurd that puzzles me when I think back on it today. I must have misheard ...

-- Do you mean the return of the Führer to life?

Roksana suddenly turned her face to Melany, her eyes widening.

-- You know about that? So I hadn't wandered off?

-- The "Father of Victory" -- does that expression mean anything to you?

-- Vaguely, I'm not quite sure.

-- What else do you remember?

-- My father claimed to have information that would allow him to change the course of events on a planetary level. He had a plan. He just lacked access to some data. These were in code ... Wait, yes! I remember now. There were documents attached to a handwritten letter signed by Hitler. Encrypted documents. There was also a lot about money and instilling fear into the entire planet. He wanted to create alliances with neo-Nazi movements and all extremist organizations. His role model was the Baader-Meinhof gang. He raved about their operations, which he called heroic, and about how they functioned. You can see why I avoided my father's company as much as I could.

Melany shuddered. She remembered the series of attacks by the Red Army Faction, also known as the "Baader-Meinhof Gang" after its main leaders. The far-left terrorist organization had made bloody headlines from the sixties to the end of the nineties. Assassinations of political figures. Blackmail. Aircraft hijackings. Their extreme ideology, their alliance with the East German Stasi and the Palestinian factions, and their methods were reminiscent of those of Nazism, although its members claimed to belong to an entirely different camp.

-- And your mother? Did you talk to her about this? How did she react?

-- Oh, my mother ...

Roksana restarted her vehicle.

-- ... She didn't care about what he could do. As long as he paid her alimony and she could lie sprawled in front of her television, a bottle of absinthe close at hand. That's what took her away, shortly after my father's accident.

-- Roksana, Melany said after brief reflection, I promise to really do everything I can to get you a permanent visa. Just give me a little time ... I have one last question for you: The money you receive each month -- do you know where it comes from?

The Russian shook her head. The facade of the hotel appeared in front of them. She parked her vehicle again and grabbed her purse, which she had thrown in the backseat. She pulled out a bank statement which she handed to Melany.

-- I don't know much about it, but you will find information about the last transfer.

A quick glance over the document made Melany realize that the money was coming from an anonymous numbered account. She took out her cell phone and asked:

-- May I take a picture?

-- Of course. I was going to suggest it to you.

Roksana's gaze was vague. She seemed hesitant to let go of a final revelation. Which she wound up doing, stumbling over the words.

-- There's ... Maybe ... I'm really not sure. I know someone ... Well, I knew him at the time.

***

In slippers and bathrobe, Melany announced that she did not wish to face the cold and preferred to have dinner served in the bedroom. Jeffrey could find nothing to complain about that. He was exhausted himself. The information confirming the transfer Roksana received was clearly visible on Melany's cell phone screen.

-- With this information, do you think we could find the holder of the bank account from which the payments are issued?

-- Every institution has its own codes, but part of the data relates to the country in which it is located. We should be able to locate the bank easily. Then you'll have to come up with a trick to find out anything more.

-- I might have an idea for that, Melany said.

-- Do you know a good hacker?

-- No. But my mom is dating a man who founded a big cybersecurity company.

It was noon in Washington. Melany even messaged her mother via WhatsApp asking if she was close enough to her new companion to get a favor out of him. With the communications system encrypted, she had nothing to fear from a leak or possible surveillance. Anything was possible where she was.

She immediately received a message in return.

-- What kind of service?

-- Does his company handle financial cybersecurity?

-- Yes. Where are you writing me from?

-- Moscow. I'm asking you the same question.

-- Knocking around Washington. Looking for a new bedside lamp. I broke mine yesterday.

Melany expelled from her imagination one of the ways her mother and her lover could have broken the lamp. After all, maybe it had only fallen.

-- If I send you information about an anonymous account, do you think he could trace the sender of the wire transfers?

Several seconds without an answer. Suddenly the phone vibrated. At the other end of the line, Maureen's voice was strained with concern.

-- What are you doing in Moscow?

-- I'm not alone, mom. Don't worry.

-- Don't tell me you're looking for the will!

-- Yeah, and we're one step away from getting our hands on the ...

Jeffrey cut her off abruptly, raising a finger to his mouth.

-- Intercontinental lines aren't safe!, he whispered.

-- That's him?, Maureen asked. What's his name?

-- Jeffrey Cartright, Melany said, detailing the face of her companion, which she found decidedly more attractive with every passing day.

-- Tell him from me that he'd better watch out for my little girl, or he'll be hearing from me, and not in a way he will necessarily like.

-- I'll tell him, Melany laughed.

-- Send me your info and I'll see what I can do, her mother concluded before hanging up.

-- Chapter 17 --

Article from the Jakarta Post

One month earlier

More and more violent upheavals shake West Sumatra

Despite the agreements made between the Indonesian government and the GAM, the terrorist organization is suspected of being behind the attacks in Banda Aceh and Medan which have, to date, claimed more than one hundred victims.

Several trade unions have criticized the local authorities for their laxness and the government for the lack of resources to fight this scourge, and demonstrations have broken out in the main cities of West Sumatra. The police intervened to counter the demonstration at Banda Aceh, which turned into a riot, so that the police were ordered to fire live ammunition. There were seventeen dead among the civilians, including five women and two children.

Despite official denials, ten police officers were also reportedly killed.

The most worrying point was the refusal of the army to intervene. General Mahyadi Abdurrahman said he would never order his troops to shoot civilians, especially Muslims.

The coming days will be decisive in terms of the future of this region, which a popular rumor says that the GAM wants to seize in order to impose sharia *law. It is, according to many observers, a political tsunami in the making.*

Jungle of Jakarta -- Region of Aceh.

Darwis still wondered how he had managed to convince Adhi.

Was it his expression of terror displayed after the interview with Saragih that persuaded the young man of the importance of his cooperation? He had no idea. However, Adhi agreed to join his adoptive father in the operating room during the following days.

He had since then helped him to treat a dozen or so fighters.

Half of them would undoubtedly have died without the joint intervention of the two men. Darwis particularly remembered a boy of about fifteen whose body and face were covered with third degree burns and whose back was riddled with shrapnel. It had taken him nearly two hours to tear the pieces of metal from his tortured flesh. His screams as he arrived had caused a crowd to gather around him, and the small dose of morphine -- granted by Saragih -- failed to ease his pain.

But it was enough for Adhi to brush his body with both hands, with his eyes closed, for the boy to calm down. Darwis had then been able to operate and save him.

Since the camp was completely isolated from the rest of the world, the doctor had no idea what actions were being carried out under the sheikh's orders. Skirmishes, clashes, attacks? His army had grown to several hundred militants, but his plans remained secret.

Darwis was kept in the dark. He ended up getting closer to one of his medics, a former employee of the main Padang hospital who was named Kusumo. The latter sometimes managed to get him out of his troubles through his good humor and his outspokenness. Unusual qualities among the men in the camp.

Kusumo, who was the same age as Adhi, had also developed an affection for him and was now one of the few people he sometimes agreed to communicate with.

-- You have to understand it, he's all alone in there!, the medic exclaimed, tapping his forehead after one of Adhi's crises. He's all alone, and he's scared.

Kusumo never ceased to amaze him with his insights. What promise could they have given him to make him agree to join Saragih?

The answer came to him during a vigil after evening prayers, the only time of relaxation for the combatants.

-- Of all my family, I only have one sister left. The sea tore all the others away from me. Saragih's men showed me pictures they took of her ... while she was asleep, and that made me think. As long as I cooperate, nothing will happen to my sister. But don't repeat what I just told you. That would put us both in danger.

Adhi was sleeping peacefully, lying in the tent on a mattress made of burlap stuffed with rags.

In his relationship with his adopted son, the doctor had retained the almost obsessive attachment that he had for him. The young man did not know how to show his emotions, other than by crying out when he was upset.

Kusumo had summed up his condition with this wise sentence: "He's all alone, inside, and he's frightened". If that was the case, and Darwis had a hunch that the medic wasn't wrong, then how could he reach out to him, end his loneliness, and tear out his fear?

The doctor remembered the day that he had met and rescued the boy, and how the boy was able to ease his pain and sorrow a little later, in the middle of devastated Banda Aceh. Who could his parents have been?

Fifteen years later, he still often cried at night in memory of his wife and son, whose features were gradually disappearing from his memory. He had found nothing in the remains of his shattered house. Not even a photograph. The tsunami, that divine punishment that had claimed over two hundred thousand victims, had taken everything from him.

Everything but his life.

But while Darwis remained convinced that he had a mission, he now found it difficult to accept that it was to save the fighters of a terrorist organization at war against his government, and therefore against his country. In order to reach the camp, so well camouflaged in the jungle that no helicopter had ever spotted it, you had to know the special agents, whom only Saragih was entitled to appoint. Other Germans and Russians thus regularly came by to enlarge the small group already present around the "Sheikh." They now numbered around thirty, each one with his own specialty.

Despite the restriction of movement imposed on him, Darwis had come to understand that the foreigners were divided into three distinct groups. Those who trained Saragih to harangue crowds. The scientists. And the combat instructors.

Kusumo, who was much more inquisitive than he was, had informed him that these were the sheikh's general staff.

-- Ah, he's got some real plans! And even more, dreams of greatness. The Germans put it into his head that one day he would become the master of the world.

Darwis had almost burst out laughing at that.

-- For now, his empire has been reduced to a few trees in the middle of the jungle. These Europeans are even crazier than I thought.

Kusumo shook his head.

-- Just be careful. A bad seed planted in fertile soil can sprout and spread faster than a man can imagine.

The medic's philosophical flights of fancy contributed to the affection the doctor had for him.

The newcomers that day were of a completely different type. The agents had appeared first, emerging from the jungle like demons from a plant box. But the main guest, a tall white-haired man, was accompanied by two unusual men: Asians with shaved heads dressed in long orange and yellow tunics with the sides linked by a cord and wearing big sandals.

Darwis had never seen people like that before.

That was not the case with Kusumo, since the medic immediately identified them as Tibetans. Buddhists. Maybe even monks.

-- How do you know these things?, Darwis asked in fascination.

-- Haven't you ever watched National Geographic programs?

-- I've never owned a television. My parents said it was the Devil's favorite instrument for seducing the hearts of believers.

-- And you believed them?

Darwis's face broke into an amused smile.

-- Yes. Until I began my studies. But then the habit had been set. Tibetans, you say? What would they be doing here?

He would never get an answer to this question because, as soon as they arrived, the two Tibetans, along with their personal belongings, were taken to a separate clearing from which no one saw them return. Only the Germans and Saragih would visit them, and the entire camp wondered what they were surviving on, since no one was in charge of bringing them food or drink.

The clearing around the river had gradually turned into a large village, which continued to expand visibly. Since the tents and communal infrastructure were camouflaged under thick foliage, no satellite could detect them. As the population grew, new pockets of dwellings were torn out of the jungle, whose settlement and construction occupied just about everyone. For shooting and combat training, the fighters had gradually swapped their various styles of clothing for a black uniform, similar to Saragih's clothes. There were no women among them, and the sheikh had said he would not allow any as long as they were living hidden deep in the rainforest.

Darwis Haikal finished his morning chores, which consisted of checking the progress of his patients, completing the training of his medics, and filling out a journal.

He came out of the hospital and decided to wander near the waterfall for once. Because it was always being pumped for the needs of the camp, the river that fed the waterfall was diminishing and began to carry so much waste that it was beginning to be worrisome. Darwis walked upstream, happy to be able to give himself a few moments of strolling while inhaling the tropical scents, mingled with the spices that the Bataks used to spice their food.

Adhi followed him for a while, but stopped on the bank and sat down with his feet in the water in order to withdraw into himself, indifferent to the nature around him. Darwis glanced at him and, reassured by his stillness, gave himself a few moments of solitude as he plunged further into the jungle. He followed a natural path for a hundred yards that meandered through the trees to a rocky outcrop, which he climbed. All the magnificence of a valley carved into an overgrown landscape furrowed by the blue line of a river.

The world seemed to be born in this place.

Darwis was so overwhelmed by a feeling of freedom and surrender that he was intoxicated and nearly overcome.

After a few seconds of contemplation, he wanted to take the path back. But the jungle is treacherous and, believing he was heading for the camp, he stumbled into the pockets of secondary dwellings where Saragih had recently settled.

The sheikh had had a crude log hut built for himself, with a veranda and a power generator, so well camouflaged that you had to approach within twenty meters to distinguish it from the vegetation.

Darwis immediately turned back.

-- Halt!

A guard, whose presence nothing had betrayed, emerged from the foliage, the barrel of a Kalashnikov pointing at him. He was dressed in black, and his short-sleeved shirt was decorated with a small red and gold metal badge.

-- Sorry, I must have lost my way, Darwis pleaded as he got closer.

The guard recognized him.

-- What are you doing around here?

-- I wanted to get away from the camp for a little while. We're wading around in the mud over there. I just went up the river and I think I got lost while retracing my steps.

The guard didn't let go of his suspicious look. He had a poisonous look in his eyes and his lips were pursed.

-- I can't let you leave like that. I have to inform the sheikh; follow me.

-- But you know me ...

-- Rules are rules. Don't make me force you.

By this time, Darwis was close enough to the guard to make out the design engraved on his badge: a swastika. The Hindu swastika. The emblem of the Nazis. That surprised him. But he had learned in school that his country had gained independence after World War II because of the Japanese, allies of the Germans, and nothing about Saragih and his project could surprise him any longer.

He had to wait outside the house for the guard to report on his unexpected presence. He came out after a few moments and ordered him to stay within sight.

-- The sheikh is in a meeting. He'll see you when he's done.

-- You shouldn't have interrupted him for so little, Darwis objected anxiously.

The other one shrugged and turned his back to light a cigarette, shielding himself from the warm, damp wind blowing from the river.

Saragih appeared a quarter of an hour later, when the doctor had started worrying about Adhi. He was accompanied by the German who arrived at the same time as the two Tibetans.

-- Did you have any particular reason to come running around this area?

Darwis forced himself to laugh, despite his apprehension.

-- I'm not running around. I just went up the river to stretch my legs and left my son halfway along the trail. I'd better go find him or he might panic.

-- That would certainly be unsettling.

The sheikh looked him over with such intensity that Darwis shuddered. Then he relaxed suddenly.

-- But I'm neglecting my duty. Since you have come all this way, let me introduce you to our benefactor, Mr. Gerhard Krueger.

-- Is this the doctor you told me about?, asked the tall, white-haired German.

-- He and his son have been of great service to us since I had the chance to discover them, Saragih said in the same language that he used.

He turned to Darwis.

-- Come in for a minute, Doctor. You will tell us what you saw along the river and you will be able to find ... what's his name again? Adhi, in a few minutes.

The interior of the cabin was spartan and the atmosphere hot and humid. Saragih had only a work table and a raised corner in which to sleep on a foam mattress. A laptop computer with a headset and a satellite modem sat on a rough table near the bed.

-- Are you surprised to see so much comfort in the middle of the jungle?, Saragih asked ironically. It took my men a good week to build this little palace.

Despite his nervousness, or precisely because he was in fear, Darwis had a sudden inspiration.

-- What I saw on the way, others might see. Heaps of rubbish carried by the current, which reappear on the surface below the waterfall. I don't know where the river it feeds goes, but I'm sure it must reach populated areas ...

He didn't need to say anything more. Saragih understood him instantly. He spat an order and the guard appeared in the doorway immediately.

-- Take several men with you, run to the camp immediately and make certain that no more rubbish reaches the river. Have it cleaned up immediately. Recruit all possible helpers!

That was translated for Krueger and he nodded in agreement. His features seemed to be forever frozen in an extreme coldness, and the pale blue of his eyes fixed on a terrifying future. His tongue struck like a whip.

-- This kind of intolerable mistake could be costly. Take your men, Saragih!

Although he didn't speak German, Darwis understood the meaning of his command.

He didn't need to see or hear any more to know that this highly dangerous-looking man was calling the shots. Saragih was just a pawn.

-- Chapter 18 --

Moscow

Present time

Sergei Vyazminkin had lost his left arm and eye in Afghanistan. Half of his face was just a single scar, from the corner of his lips, deformed by a frozen grin, to his earlobe, part of which had also been swept away when a Stinger rocket exploded less than ten meters away from him. He felt lucky, because all of his comrades had died in the explosion. He had been awarded the Order of the Red Banner for outstanding behavior in combat. In reality, misfortune had dictated that he was assigned to an elite Spetsnaz group and sent to fight in Maravaz Pass, in Kunar province, as soon as he was forcibly inducted into the Soviet army. Six months of training and three days of war had earned him these horrible wounds and the granting of a veteran's pension that barely covered his morphine needs. He must have been between fifty and sixty, but he looked fifteen years older.

Sergei had agreed to meet them in the Church of the Nativity of the Virgin in Putinki, a majestic building dating from the seventeenth century and restored towards the end of the nineteenth. Miloslav had dropped them off nearby and they were surprised to find such a beautiful piece of architecture in a corner of the south-eastern Moscow suburbs surrounded by public housing with walls blackened by pollution. The three variegated pyramids, the peaked roof and the monumental bell tower with an octagonal roof that dominated the cornices shone in all their colors in a dirty and desolate gray universe.

When they joined him, Sergei was kneeling in prayer, his right hand on his chest, in the middle of the *kliros* or choir stall. It was four in the afternoon and they were alone. He eyed them suddenly by way of greeting or welcome.

-- Are you both Christians? I didn't see you make the sign of the cross when entering.

Melany wondered how he could have seen them, since his back had been to them. She reached out and answered in a warm tone.

-- We are Christians, of course, but not Orthodox. Thank you for agreeing to meet with us. Roksana told us you are a close friend ...

-- Close? I haven't seen her for more than three years. And him -- can't he speak?

The old soldier darted his good eye towards Jeffrey, who purposely stood a little way off, three paces behind Melany.

-- He doesn't speak Russian, she excused him. Mr. Vyazmikin, we don't want to waste your time. We would like to get right to the heart of the matter at hand. Alexei Soloviev ...

Roksana had at the last second remembered Sergei, the only one of her father's friends who seemed to have maintained some decency over the years. She thought he had joined their group more out of curiosity and boredom than out of ideology. Others respected him because of his war wounds, which allowed him to express himself freely. He never hesitated to oppose Soloviev and, when Soloviev got angry with him, all he had to do was extend his right arm, like a Hitler salute, to silence him. Not because of the salute, but because of his missing arm.

After Soloviev's death, Sergei had regularly asked about his daughter's fate. He was very fond of her. For several years, she had turned to him whenever she needed advice.

Unfortunately, his phantom pain, which was common after amputation, had increased and Sergei had a growing need for morphine, which led him to attempt a few thefts to supplement the insufficient dose granted him by the Russian medical services. He had done time in prison. Roksana had tried to visit him, but since she was not a close relative, she had been denied permission. They had lost track of each other.

Sergei was too poor to afford a cell phone. The only number Roksana had was for a veterans' shelter. She had left him several messages in the past. He had never returned her calls. But Jeffrey and Melany had been lucky. Since the beginning of winter, he had again been living among the poor being cared for by the Orthodox Church. An official with a surly voice had sent someone to tell him that some foreigners were looking for him. When they called back an hour later, he was quickly persuaded to meet with them.

A little too quickly.

-- What do you want to know about that son of a bitch?, he asked as soon as he heard Soloviev's name.

-- Roksana told us that you spent a lot of time with him once but often disagreed with him.

-- Disagreed ...? He said with a snort that ended in a coughing fit -- You might say that, pretty lady! When I learned that he had died in that chopper with the three other bastards, I went off to buy half a bottle of vodka to celebrate his demise. What do you want to know about him?

-- What interests us is the content of certain documents that he shared with the members of the group.

-- Ah, the so-called Hitler will? Is that what you've come for?

The former Soviet soldier, still wearing his army fatigues, a grimy patched-up garment, winked an eyelid. A flash of mischief lit up his eyes for a moment.

-- Two Americans in Moscow following in the footsteps of good old Soloviev and his plan to change the world ... I don't think you two are lily white and pure. Who are you working for -- the CIA or the Mossad?

Melany flinched. It had not occurred to her until now that the Israeli intelligence agency might be on the same track as they were. It wouldn't be surprising, though. The Israelis were the first to be affected by the turmoil from terrorist organizations. All the more so if neo-Nazis, or extremists in the Baader-Meinhof mold, were involved.

-- Neither one, she replied. We belong to the INR, an intelligence agency serving diplomacy, which has nothing to do with the CIA.

-- Never heard of it.

-- Want to see our ID?

-- What the hell for? That's not what interests me.

-- Mr. Vyazminkin ...

-- Call me Sergei. Everyone calls me Sergei.

-- Sergei, you now know what we came here for. So tell us. And, in our turn, how might we help you?

The Russian glanced greedily at Melany's face and body, for what he could tell from the trench coat. He lingered over her breasts, then came back to her eyes.

-- What could a poor guy like me, with just one arm, one eye and a face that scares children, want? Don't worry, I'm not going to ask you for a night of love. Still... if that were offered, I wouldn't say no. But I'm not dreaming. What's it worth to you and your mute friend, the asshole, and how much is it worth to me?

Melany quickly translated this for Jeffrey.

-- It's up to you to negotiate.

The door of the small church opened for a priest in a black cassock and a shoufeika headdress. The priest looked at Jeffrey and Melany with curiosity and smiled discreetly at Sergei, who responded by crossing himself. Melany turned towards him.

-- How much? It all depends on what you have to offer.

-- That's what I like about bourgeois capitalists, Sergei laughed. Always ready to negotiate.

-- Sergei, if you had access to the documents retrieved by Soloviev and if you did didn't agree with him, you know the danger that he represented ...

-- Yeah. He could've represented that ... But now he's dead.

-- Except that the contents of the will have been disclosed and his project seems to be moving ahead without him. Does the phrase *"Father of Victory"* mean anything to you?

-- It might ...

-- Did you have the will in your hands?

-- I once did ...

Jeffrey approached Melany and whispered to her, without taking his eyes off Sergei.

-- Tell him that he will get twenty dollars for each correct response to your questions.

-- How many did I hear?, Sergei grumbled. Fifty dollars?

-- Go for fifty, Jeffrey yielded.

The Russian stretched forth his good hand. Jeffrey dipped his into his pocket and pulled out a few bills. Melany attacked immediately.

-- How many times did you attend Soloviev's meetings?

-- That depends. Sometimes we saw each other just to talk politics and the future of our damned nation. The great Soviet Union. The paradise of equality and justice. The bastards who led us were never able to go through with their project. Twenty million died during the war, not counting the thirty or forty million Stalin killed in the Gulag and in organized famines. To achieve what? Soloviev was right about one point: the only greatness of Russia today is that half of our women sell their bodies instead of working in factories ...

Other than that?, Melany interrupted.

-- Other times we would get together to talk about his project. Some, like me, laughed and made fun of him. But others took him seriously. Can you imagine that? He wanted to bring Hitler back to earth and set out with him to conquer the world.

A laugh. A fit of coughing.

-- ... The worst thing is that he really believed in it.

-- Give us more details.

-- First of all, my fifty dollars!

A note changed hands.

-- You'll have to tell us more before we give any more, Melany threatened.

-- Okay. Fucking Americans, you deserve your reputation. You give nothing for nothing, right?

-- I return your compliment, Sergei.

-- It's all right, pretty lady. I'll tell you everything. We met once or twice a month. Vasilei, I didn't really know him and I never liked him. We had a mutual friend, Petrov. He died with him in the chopper near the border. What the hell were they going to do there? Who knows? Petrov was tough, like Vasilei. He was convinced that Stalin should have done everything to preserve the German-Soviet pact, even if it meant ceding territory to Hitler. Keeping that alliance would have allowed us to win the war against the Americans and finally impose our system on the rest of the world. Petrov had lost his father and almost all the male members of his family at Stalingrad. Except that they didn't fall to German bullets, but were mowed down by our own machine guns, which shot them in their backs to make them run faster during the attacks. As soon as he drank a little bit too much, Petrov cursed Stalin and was full of praise for Hitler. Apart from that, he was a pretty good guy. Soloviev had gotten into his head with his psychotic project.

-- Do you know the details?

-- Some of them. In those days, Soloviev was lacking too many items. Several documents were attached to the will. But the text itself was in code. There were blocks of letters that didn't mean much and then series of numbers. The first page was some raving about reincarnation. You know what that bullshit is for Buddhists and other Chinks? Hitler claimed to have found the key to his future lives, and Soloviev was determined to convince us that this was no hogwash. Considering all the crap he had to do in his life, better for him to believe that crap than in the Christian hell. Let him sleep better at night.

Sergei closed his fingers on a second fifty dollar bill.

-- Do you remember the exact contents of that page?

-- It was a long time ago. No one took Alexei very seriously when he took out his bottle of vodka and his yellow papers. Basically, Hitler would one day return in another body and the attached documents, once decrypted, would allow him to be found and restored to his power and might.

-- Blocks of letters?, Jeffrey asked in fascination after Melany translated Sergei's words for him. Ask him to be more specific.

The Russian shook his head.

-- It was all written in German. If I remember anything about the will, it's because Soloviev translated it out loud for us. As for the blocks, they were like five or six letters together separated from the others by about twenty lines.

-- Just blocks of letters, one next to the other, without any meaning or logic, Jeffrey asked.

-- Yeah. That's it. Lots of blocks on lots of lines.

-- Hitler used an Enigma machine, Jeffrey concluded.

-- How do you know that?, Melany asked in fascination.

-- The State Department had me take cryptology classes during my training. I wouldn't be able to decipher a text, but we had gone over all the methods known historically, and what Sergei is describing corresponds to the machines that the Germans developed during the war ... without knowing that the Allies had captured several and had managed to decipher the whole system. That episode was also decisive in the victory against Germany.

Without understanding a word of what he was saying, Sergei seemed to be drinking Jeffrey's words.

-- One last question: you said you knew the expression, the "Father of Victory".

Sergei nodded his head, roughly scratched his scar, and sneered.

-- Oh, yes I do. Soloviev was convinced that that was the name by which Hitler would be recognized when he returned to earth. But it had a double meaning. The return of the Führer and the means to restore his power. That was the "Father of Victory". A gift package.

-- The means to restore its power? What do you mean by that?

-- Are you ready to hear Alexei Soloviev's last delirium, may his soul rot in hell until the end of time? If we weren't in a church, I would spit on the floor in his honor.

In order to get a response, Melany grabbed a new fifty dollar bill and held it up. Sergei discovered what was left of his teeth and gave a smile that wiped out his smirk.

-- "The Father of Victory" was the German atomic bomb. The one that Hitler had supposedly succeeded in building towards the end of the war, but which he didn't have time to use because we and the Americans were at his doorstep.

Do you understand the level of insanity in this whole story?, Sergei grimaced as he pocketed the last bill.

-- Chapter 19 --

The curtains of the small suite were opened to the sparsely lit buildings of Lomonosov University, whose silhouette blocked the horizon beyond the Moskva River. Under the pale halo of spotlights, which are so rarely available for use, the river carried blocks of ice that sometimes burst against the frozen banks, splashing translucent flakes on the ropes of barges immobilized by winter. The dark, low clouds that had raced across the Moscow sky all day had coalesced into a blanket impervious to the twinkling of the stars. This scene, deformed by the plates of frost stuck to the panes of the window, was enough to make anyone shiver.

Melany came out of the bathroom wrapped in a towel, to find Jeffrey wearing nothing but his underwear, sunk in the chair, his feet on the coffee table, scribbling on the pad of paper provided by the hotel.

-- What are you doing?

-- I'm writing down all the information that we've managed to glean so far. This will allow me to take stock in my head.

-- Can I see?

She crossed the room. He handed her the pages.

Jeffrey had summarized all their information in two columns in fine, even writing. One column contained what they knew about the various neo-Nazi movements and their possible connections with the Jihadists. He had underlined "Baader-Meinhof gang model" with several lines. The second column listed details about Hitler's will. There was a big question mark next to "The Father of Victory", which pointed at two interpretations by means of two arrows.

-- You were right to underline your question marks. Every time we think we have an explanation, it just turns into a huge hole in our faces.

-- I'm not so sure about that, Jeffrey argued.

-- What are you not sure about?

-- That these are huge holes. On the contrary, I have the impression that things are clearing up a bit.

Melany sat up on the bed and put her feet on Jeffrey's legs while perching on the edge of the mattress.

-- You'll have to explain that to me.

-- This is what we know, he said, taking the notepad back from her hands. Vasilei Soloviev went from communism pure and simple to Nazism after discovering Hitler's will. According to Sergei, the first page was a kind of instruction manual that referred to encrypted documents. Although he and some of his cronies made fun of Soloviev, he didn't question the authenticity of the will. So I try to put myself in the Führer's shoes to see if he really believed that he had discovered the secrets of the Dalai Lamas. What was the name of the holy book written by the Buddha?

-- The *Kalachakra Tantra*.

-- That's it. So suppose that scientists or gurus from the Ahnenerbe had analyzed and decoded the secrets contained in this Buddhist bible written in Sanskrit. Here is our Hitler at the end of his life. He knows that he's just lost the war. In three days at most, the Red Army will have reached his bunker and he is already planning to kill himself. It only remains for him to transmit this secret so that one day some disciple will find it in the same way that the Tibetans find the soul of the Dalai Lama ...

-- His *tulku*, Melany corrected him.

-- You have a better memory than I do.

-- I know. We're in full science fiction mode, but go on.

-- I would rather opt for a gothic tale like the Golem or Frankenstein's monster, but that's not the most important thing. Let's accept the premise that Hitler firmly believes he will reincarnate some day -- he was paranoid, drugged up and hallucinating enough for that. He's not going to let his ... his *tulku* come back to earth destitute. The pages attached to the instructions ... I mean the will, therefore, contain, as Sergei told us, the means to restore his power. Power, in politics, is of two kinds. Money, lots of money. And weapons. Or, rather, a weapon. The deadliest one of all. "The Father of Victory".

-- Your reasoning holds up. Except for one little detail. The Nazis never had the atomic bomb.

-- Are you so sure of that?

-- Well, that's obvious enough.

-- Yet Einstein was convinced that the Germans were working hard to become the first nuclear power. If he hadn't convinced Roosevelt of that by sending him that now-famous letter, the Manhattan Project might never have been launched.

-- And if the Germans had succeeded in developing the bomb before the Americans, they would have won the war.

Jeffrey looked at his watch.

-- There's always a way to find out more.

He leaned over to grab the bedroom phone, changed his mind and replaced it with his cell phone. Moments later, he had contacted Almog Herskowitz's assistant. The latter was absent for the day and he had the greatest difficulty in convincing his interlocutor to give him a number where the professor could be reached. She kept Jeffrey on the line while she got permission to divulge her boss's private number. Herskowitz answered on the first ring, excitement in his voice.

-- I've been looking forward to your call, Jeffrey. It's so good of you to keep me informed.

-- I especially have a new question for you.

-- I'll gladly answer if I know the answer. But first of all, do tell me everything. Don't let an old man languish. Where are you with ... you know who?

Jeffrey offered some general information, without naming names or places. He just announced the death of the *person we were looking for*, mentioned the meeting with his daughter, and summarized their progress. The professor was drinking in all his words. Assuming that the line was being listened in on, prying parties would be left to their own devices.

-- Now tell me everything you know about the Nazi nuclear weapons program. Is there any chance, however slight, that they managed to develop the bomb in secret?

-- That's an interesting question, the professor retorted, a little bit surprised. The answer may seem complicated to you. Do you have a few minutes to spare?

As a preamble he referred to the axiom according to which no event involving men can be understood outside its historical context. He then explained that, although theorized by many scientists, including Einstein, nuclear fission was only discovered in 1938 by the German chemist Otto Hahn. As early as April 1939, a few months before the invasion of Poland, the Nazis launched a first plan for the development of atomic energy, called

Uranprojekt or *Uranverein*. The project was abandoned at the start of the war, because the German General Staff felt it would not contribute significantly to victory.

-- They had another problem, the professor commented, not without a satisfied chuckle. Most of the scientists who could have actively participated in the development of nuclear weapons were either Jews, and therefore expelled from their positions and sent to concentration camps, or were already mobilized and on the front lines.

As the result of scientific publications and symposia on the use of nuclear fission, several German scientists who had become convinced of Nazism began individual research at the Georg August University in Göttingen. But the most important individuals, Joos, Hanle and Reinhold Mannkopff, were called up in their turn, which ended their activities. It was in September 1939 that the Nazi regime launched the second Uranprojekt, under the leadership of eminent physicists, including Otto Hahn, Robert Döpel, and the famous Werner Heisenberg. However, he reportedly said that it would take many years to master nuclear power and to possibly develop an atomic bomb. History would maintain that he deliberately dragged his feet and hid some of his own findings in order to prevent Hitler from getting the bomb. But that was just guesswork.

-- Officially, Germany was in dire need of uranium, and without uranium it was impossible to continue research. An industrial company, the Auergesellschaft, happened to have stockpiles of residual uranium from which it had extracted radium. The company had the capacity to produce tons of uranium oxide. This is where historians are missing information. No one knows exactly how much uranium 235 was produced by Germany during the war. The Allies, Russians and Americans alike, found scattered stocks that they hastened to requisition one by one. As for heavy water, another element that could help in the manufacture of an atomic bomb, the Germans had to conquer Norway in April 1940 in order to acquire a technology in which that country had already become an expert. Obviously, the allies didn't let that happen and one sabotage operation followed another, slowing down the production of the coveted liquid.

-- Professor, interrupted Jeffrey, beside whom Melany seemed to be impatient. Could you skip a few steps and just summarize the situation before the end of the war for me?

-- Of course. Pardon me. I always feel like I'm teaching a class.

-- And your lessons are exciting, professor. They were some of the best times I had at Harvard.

-- You are nothing but a flattering villain, but I understand your impatience. I will therefore pass over most of the episodes, technological advances, failures, abandonments and relaunching of projects which, according to Albert Speer, architect and close advisor to Hitler, sowed hope and annoyance among supporters of German nuclear development during this short period. It should simply be noted that the project to develop the German atomic bomb was abandoned in the fall of 1942. This didn't prevent certain army corps from developing a uranium engine, the precursor of nuclear power plants, as well as a cyclotron. I would like to take this opportunity to point out that the American atomic bomb might never have seen the light of day without the help of about fifteen scientists, most of them Jewish, who had fled Germany when Hitler came to power, with Einstein, Gerhard Herzberg, Felix Bloch and Erwin Schrödinger being among the most famous. Now, to answer your question more directly, some historians, and not the least important ones, have claimed that the Nazis had, in fact, succeeded in developing an atomic bomb and even conducted tests near the Ohrdruf concentration camp in Thuringia on March 4, 1945. This hypothesis was revealed in particular by a historical essay by Rainer Karlsch, which he is said to have written on the basis of unpublished documents discovered in the KGB archives. According to these archives, several witnesses saw a flash of light of unbelievable intensity, red on the inside and yellow on the outside, which is one of the characteristics of nuclear explosions. After these publications, the German government took samples on the spot, without finding the slightest trace of old radiation. The Americans, for their part, were eager to collect or destroy anything related to the Uranverein project at the end of the war. Particularly a prototype reactor, all the heavy water available, and hundreds of uranium ingots that they hadn't known existed, since the entire stock was supposed to have been reconverted.

Herskowitz fell silent. Jeffrey took the opportunity to summarize everything he had just said to Melany. She asked:

-- Assuming that this Karlsch and other historians are not publicity-seeking storytellers, and therefore that Nazi Germany had actually succeeded in creating an atomic bomb, why didn't Hitler use it when he knew the war was lost?

-- Hitler actually never really realized, except perhaps for the last two days of his existence, that the war had been lost for the Axis. Remember that he suffered from a dozen physical and mental illnesses, and that he received up to 20 injections of various drugs every day. Assuming that they carried out this nuclear test on March 4, 1945, we are less than two months from the defeat.

The Russians and Americans are advancing with great strides on German soil. Exploding a nuclear weapon in Germany itself was out of the question. To launch it across France at England or towards Russia, they would have had to use missiles powerful enough to carry a very heavy bomb. The one dropped on Hiroshima weighed 4.4 tons, including only 64 kilos of uranium 235. It is not enough to be able to develop a nuclear bomb to be able to make use of it, even as a deterrent. Between you and me, I have the greatest doubts about this "explosion" in Thuringia in March 1945. But I don't totally reject the hypothesis that the Nazis were the first to know how to make an A-bomb, or that they hid stocks of uranium that were never found by the Allies.

-- And if that's the case, Jeffrey concluded as if he were thinking aloud, Hitler would have indicated in his will, in a coded way, the location of these stocks and plans, if not that of a bomb in the making ... in order to bequeath them to himself in some future incarnation.

At that moment, the doorbell rang.

-- Did you order anything?, Melany asked.

Jeffrey shook his head.

A woman's voice, with a heavy accent, followed the ringing.

-- Good evening. I am the housekeeper. May I make up the room?

-- Professor, thank you very much, I won't hold you any longer, Jeffrey said before saying as he approached the door. Thank you, we don't need anything.

He stepped up to take a look in the peephole. A dark-haired woman in a pantsuit was standing in the hallway, her gaze fixed on the eyehole. She was wearing a hotel employee badge. She insisted.

-- I have to check the minibar. It will only take a minute.

-- Let her in, Melany pleaded.

Jeffrey released the security. The door burst open. Two armed men rushed in. One pushed Jeffrey hard and pointed the barrel of his pistol at his chest, while the other one grabbed Melany by her arm and dragged her with him while he went around the living room and checked the bedroom. He let her go in order to take a position near the window, where he drew the curtains.

The brunette in the pantsuit entered in turn, closed the door and stood in the middle of the room between Melany and Jeffrey.

-- Ms. Carson and Mister Cartright?, she said in a tone more affirmative than questioning.

Not ten seconds had passed since the intrusion. Melany, dazed, stroked her bruised arm. Jeffrey rose in protest.

-- Who are you? And by what right do you come barging into our room this way?

The woman slowly turned to him.

-- We just have a few questions for you. Be cooperative and everything will go very well.

Her English was impeccable, but her accent was hard to place.

-- It will be difficult to answer without knowing who you are!, Melany protested.

The woman barked an order. The man who was holding Jeffrey at gunpoint strode over to him, raised his gun, and slammed its butt into his face. Blood poured from his cheekbone. He stifled a curse. Melany screamed but the woman grabbed the TV remote, brought up the Russian version of MTV, and turned up the volume.

-- This is how we're going to play, she announced, sitting down on the edge of the desk. I'll be asking you questions. If I don't like your answer, your friend gets hit and then I'll question him. If the answer isn't correct, I'll hit you, and then we'll start over. *On vklyuchen?*[13].

-- No need to pretend to be Russian, Melany said bravely.

-- You have a good sense of observation, but that isn't going to help you any. So, first question: what did you come to Moscow to do?

The woman turned her face to her accomplice. Again he raised his gun.

-- Wait!, Melany said hurriedly. You know very well why we are in Moscow. Your violence is staged and your accent is ... is Israeli!

With a gesture, the woman stopped her sidekick. The pistol resumed its position, barrel pointed at Jeffrey.

-- So we're on the same side, Melany added. In any event, we have the same enemies.

-- If that's the case, perhaps you will explain to me how you managed to get in touch with Alexei Soloviev's daughter?

Melany glanced quickly at Jeffrey, who was pressing a handkerchief to his cheekbone. The blood had stopped flowing. He encouraged her with a shrug.

-- Do I have to repeat that?, asked the Israeli.

-- You must know perfectly well who we are and what organization we belong to, Jeffrey said.

She turned to him contemptuously.

-- Yes, indeed. You're two kids who want to play at being spies, which is a bit laughable at your age. You, Mr. Cartright, work in the State Department as a dilettante. Why make an effort to pursue your career when you've received a nice inheritance? Might as well use your time and money to impress your new

[13] "Is that understood?" in Russian.

conquest. You, Ms. Carson, have been a field agent for the INR, but in my opinion you will not last long. Gathering information is not a game. So I will ask you for the last time: what the hell are you doing in Moscow and how did you track down Soloviev's daughter?

Melany sighed.

-- Why don't you stop the threats and begin at the beginning? Such as by introducing yourself, for example. May I sit down and have a glass of water?

The Israeli woman's face was furrowed with deep wrinkles, witnesses of the torments that had accumulated during a life lived without respite. Her eyes, a steel blue, expressed as much sadness as they did hardness. She handed Melany the bottle of water that was lying on the coffee table. The TV was showing a Ukrainian rap clip, featuring miniature tanks painted pink and uniformed girls with oversized breasts. The music was awful. She turned down the volume.

-- My team and I are investigating Russian neo-Nazi movements. That's all you will know about us for now. Now it's your turn. Speak!

The man who punched Jeffrey was a Middle Eastern type, while the one standing by the window had an East European appearance. Melany took a long swig and put the bottle back on the desk pad next to Jeffrey's notes.

-- The INR assigned me a mission in ultra-nationalist American circles. That investigation has led us to suspect the existence of an ultra-violent international network that might be affiliated with Islamist terrorist movements. We went back to Soloviev, and a bunch of punks at his old address told us about his daughter. From then, it wasn't too difficult to find her.

-- Why Soloviev?

-- If you are so well informed, you must probably know that my mother was an agent at MI6. In the 1980's, just before she resigned, Soloviev contacted her in the hope of exchanging unpublished documents signed by Hitler for his passage to the West. Those papers are said to be linked to the neo-Nazi network to which I was sent on a mission.

The astonishment that could be read on the Israeli woman's face surprised Melany in turn. She knew their history, but many things seemed to be missing from her file. The woman pulled herself together and the questions poured out, some routine, some trivial, some relevant. It was the good old method of destabilization used by the intelligence services. As she spoke, the Israeli woman's attention was drawn to Jeffrey's notes. She grabbed them.

Moments later, Melany saw her turn pale.

-- "The Father of Victory" and the Nazi nuclear weapon. Who put you on to such leads? That wasn't by Soloviev, since he's long dead, nor his daughter

... The Israeli refrained from explaining how the Mossad got wind of Alexei Soloviev's plans or how they had spied on Roksana. Melany had no choice but to discuss their meeting in the church with Sergei. The woman assumed a dreamy expression.

-- That's amazing ...

-- What amazes you?, Jeffrey intervened curtly. That two idiots playing at spies have learned more than you have in such a short time?

-- Have you shared this information with anyone else?, the Israeli asked evasively.

-- We may be amateurs, but we don't want to be taken for fools, Melany said curtly.

The Israeli seemed to like this. She finally gave her whole identity. Whether this was true or false didn't matter to Melany and Jeffrey as long as they moved on to a more cordial relationship. Anat Galil was part of a team of *kidonim*(14) based in Moscow. All spoke fluent Russian. The recent interconnections between Islamist organizations and neo-Nazi groups had given rise to this particular operation, which was in close collaboration with the CIA. The extreme left was in essence allied with the terrorist movements, as long as they exercised their barbarism in the name of national liberation movements. But the ultra-nationalists were now also getting into the game since they had, it seemed, unlimited funds at their disposal. This unnatural alliance had everything to worry Western intelligence agencies, but their agents had to investigate while walking on eggshells.

Anat folded up the sheet with Jeffrey's notes and put it in the pocket of her suit.

-- Now I can tell you the reason for our visit. I am carrying a message from Robert Franckel.

-- Bob Franckel ... the CIA Chief of Operations?, Melany asked in surprise.

-- His message is short, and he expects you to follow it to the letter. Should I deliver it to you as is, or should I sweeten it?

Melany shook her head. She expected the worst.

-- Stop messing around with an operation that doesn't concern you. Pack your bags and jump on the first plane to Washington! Those are his exact words. If you stay in Moscow, Franckel will make arrangements with his FSB counterpart to have you arrested before repatriating you in a month or two. And believe me, you don't want to know the color of the walls in Moscow jails.

[14] Field agents reporting to the action and elimination section of the Mossad.

-- Chapter 20 --

The all-glass dome of the Aeroflot terminal appeared through the snowflake-studded fog that was beginning to lift. Since they had awoken, Jeffrey had had a distant gaze, tense features and a closed expression. It was an expression Melany hadn't seen on him before. That of a man whom nothing generally resists and who broods in his rage in the presence of an unforeseen obstacle.

There was no direct Moscow-Washington flight and the most convenient one they could find, operated by Aeroflot, took off at 10:15 a.m. to land in New York.

The weather had deteriorated further and the snow was falling again in large flakes that the wipers of the Mercedes were struggling to clear. A distant, hazy sun shrouded the city in a grayish halo, reflecting their mood and even that of Miloslav, who was more sullen than ever.

-- I wish you a safe flight, the driver said after parking his luxury car between two limousines in front of the terminal entrance reserved for international flights.

Melany's cell phone vibrated as she put her hand on the handle of her door. She almost didn't pick it up, but recognized her mother's number.

-- You're still in Moscow?, Maureen asked in greeting.

Jeffrey gave Melany a questioning look. She whispered "my mother" and quickly replied that she was about to return to Washington.

-- I have the information you asked for, Maureen then announced.

Melany's heart raced. Her mother was up late, since it was the middle of the night on the East Coast, but she didn't dwell on that.

-- The pension that this woman receives -- what's her name again? ... Roksana Soloviev ... comes from a bank account in Lichtenstein.

What's the use of knowing that?, Melany thought to herself. Either way, their adventure ended there. Franckel had been very clear on that point. She still asked, however:

-- Did you find out who it belongs to?

-- It's is a numbered account, but Larry doesn't know how to be nice to me, so he tends to spoil me. He's put his best specialist on the case.

It was the first time Maureen had mentioned her new companion's name. She continued.

-- The account belongs to a German organization, which is itself part of a nebula that is part of a large NGO headquartered in Berlin, but with administrative offices in a small town in Thuringia in eastern Germany.

The region of Thuringia triggered a recent but vague memory. Melany agreed to herself to think about it later.

-- Do you have the name of the NGO?

-- Of course: "Grundstück und Teilung"

-- "*Earth and Sharing*"? Never heard of it.

-- They operate in the Middle East and Southeast Asia. According to Larry, they came under scrutiny by the financial section of the NSA after one of their subsidiaries was flagged for money transfers to Hamas and the PFLP. The management of "Grundstück und Teilung" immediately closed its satellite and refocused on its charitable activities in Asia, especially in Indonesia, where they seem to have a big operation.

-- Do we know the origin of their finances?

-- Not exactly, it's too delicate. It would take the collaboration of specialized hackers to find out anything more. But I can't ask Larry for more. Do you need anything else?

Melany hesitated. She found deep within herself that spark of excitement that had animated her since the first day of the mission she had set for herself. As Jeffrey watched with increased interest, she recalled the latest events, including Robert Franckel's intervention that justified their forced return.

Silence, then:

-- Are you asking me for advice?

-- As always, mom.

-- Well, I'll sum it up: You have two possibilities. One, you obey Franckel, who is not your direct boss, and you get your butt back to Washington to give your friend and yourself the soap of your life, before you're both put on a sidetrack that will delay any advances in your career by at least ten years.

-- And the second one?

-- You will take a tour of Thuringia, where the NGO is headquartered. If you succeed in revealing the existence of a dangerous conspiracy stemming from the latest delusions of the greatest criminal in the history of mankind, I believe that the CIA will not make you retake your exam to accept you into its ranks. If you fail, you will be kicked out of the INR for disobedience and face a one-year suspended sentence. It's your choice.

-- What would you do if you were in my place?

Maureen sighed heavily. Melany knew her mother's character to be a mixture of cold pragmatism and controlled passion. In emotional terms, she was a woman capable of putting long-term necessities ahead of emotional reactions. Her response showed that.

-- If you weren't my daughter, I would tell you to go headlong. But since you are my daughter, I'd rather invite you both over to dinner tonight to introduce you to Larry. Unfortunately for me, the choice is yours.

-- As well as Jeffrey's, Melany said, suddenly smiling at her companion. One last thing. Do you have the name of the city in Thuringia where the headquarters of the NGO is located?

-- It had escaped me, but now I recall: Kahla.

Melany opened her eyes wide. Kahla? That was no coincidence. That was why the region of Thuringia seemed familiar to her.

-- You promise to be careful?

-- I swear!

She hung up and stared at her companion, who was seething with impatience while waiting to hear the content of the conversation.

-- You remember that article about a fairground hypnotist specializing in past lives who lived in a small German town swarming with neo-Nazis ...

-- Yes. But I've forgotten the name of the village.

-- Kahla. In Thuringia. The region of Germany where, according to Rainer Karlsch and Herskowitz, the Nazis carried out a nuclear test in March 1945.

She didn't need to hear his answer to know that he was already wondering which airline best served that part of Germany.

***

The international airport nearest to Kahla was in Erfurt, but there were no direct flights to it from Moscow. They would have to make a stopover in Prague and wait six hours to change planes and then, once in Thuringia, drive fifty kilometers in a rental car.

As soon as they had disembarked in Prague, Jeffrey and Melany were taken to the Savoy Hotel, an establishment close to the airport, where Jeffrey preferred to book a room rather than wait in the terminal for six hours.

There, they spent their time gathering all the information available about Kahla on the internet. What they learned about its community reminded Melany of the atmosphere of Odyssey, Pennsylvania and the face of Derek Mitchell came back to haunt her again.

The small town was best known for the quality of its porcelain, which was produced in a two-century-old factory that drew its raw material, a very pure kaolin, from a nearby hill: the **Wapelsberg**. But another of its past activities had been all but erased from history. It was in this granite and limestone promontory, which was riddled with galleries, that the Third Reich had decided in 1944 to set up a factory to manufacture the Messerschmitt 262, a jet fighter aircraft, the first of its kind. It was given the name REIMAGH, an acronym created in honor of Reichsmarschall Hermann Goering, the initiator of the project.

Barely thirty planes, many of which were defective, would leave the factory before its destruction.

The REIMAGH needed abundant manpower, because Germany was losing the war on all fronts and the Reich was in a state of emergency. Several concentration camps were established nearby to house those picked from among the prisoners of war to dig the underground galleries and to set up the workshops under abominable conditions. Out of 15,000 forced laborers, 6,000 would die from exhaustion, malnutrition, mistreatment, or being buried alive as the result of collapses.

The Allied forces, mainly American, liberated the camps on April 14, 1945 but, to the misfortune of its inhabitants, Thuringia would then fall under the control of Stalin and be integrated into East Germany until the collapse of the Soviet bloc and the reunification of Germany.

The local inhabitants, some of whom had been hostile to the Nazi regime, found themselves under the yoke of another form of totalitarianism which perpetuated the atmosphere of fear and hatred from which they had just escaped. The camps had not been liberated by the glorious Red Army. Their location therefore remained without the benefit of any commemoration for a long time.

It was in this climate of denial of the duty to remember that those nostalgic for the Third Reich, now under Communist rule, transmitted their ideology to the following generations, giving birth to a large community of young neo-Nazis in the very heart of Kahla.

The National Socialist Underground, or NSU, one of many extremist organizations, was able to recruit new members and racist incidents increased from the 2000's onwards, culminating in 2013 in the burning down of the headquarters of a democratic party, followed by a "Thuringian Youth Day," an event that was reminiscent of the heyday of Hitler's youth.

The ban on the NSU by the German authorities led to the birth of an even more radical local movement, the "FN", for "Freies Netz" or *Free Network*. Every year, the *Freies Netz* celebrated Hitler's birth in a ceremony that had the main objective of terrorizing the local population and recruiting new members. The worst Russian and British extremists were warmly invited to attend, including disturbed hard rock bands advocating ultra-violence.

-- I wonder if I don't regret having changed direction, sighed Melany, dismayed by these readings. By this time, our flight would have begun its descent towards JFK, and all we would have to do is take the Red Eye(15) to collapse into a nice cozy bed in Washington.

-- Yours or mine?

-- Doesn't matter. As long as I can close my eyes without having to think about Hitler.

-- You forgot our appointment in Langley.

She took his hand and hugged him.

-- Franckel's going to look funny when he realizes he's been stood up.

-- Because you think he doesn't already know that?

It was not a certainty, but the speed with which the CIA had found their tracks in Moscow was not surprising. Since both were affiliated with a secret service, all their movements were necessarily tracked and traced. Their departure for Moscow must have triggered an alert and it was useless to try to keep a low profile from now on. After all, they were fighting for the same cause like two free electrons. Melany's mother had defined the risks and both had accepted them.

Thinking she knew enough about Kahla, Melany entered "*Earth and Sharing*" into the search engine.

Amnesty International, the International Red Cross and the Red Crescent all praised the NGO's interventions in refugee camps in the Middle East and other disadvantaged regions, particularly in Indonesia.

The spokesman for "*Earth and Sharing*" had been interviewed by the German daily *Die Welt* after the affair of funds transferred to Palestinian terrorist organizations under the guise of humanitarian aid. He denied any

[15] Early morning flight that connects New York and Washington.

involvement by the NGO, and claimed that an internal investigation had been undertaken, the findings of which would soon be published.

But it was another article from a French daily paper that had been picked up by the English press that caught Jeffrey's attention.

"Horrible death of a documentary filmmaker in the jungle of Sumatra, during a report on the NGO 'Earth and Sharing'".

The producer, Marianne Metzger, narrated her adventure, which had turned into tragedy. She was a few feet away from her cameraman when he had been bitten by a naja. She warmly praised the invaluable help of Gerhard Krueger, the president of the NGO. The documentary project was abandoned following the accident.

-- This organization smells a bit like sulfur, Jeffrey noted.

-- Could it be a good idea to contact this woman and to find out more about what happened?

They immediately found the production company that employed Marianne Metzger, but learned that she had gone to Bolivia, this time on the trail of the volunteers of Coordination Sud, a French humanitarian organization. They left their contact information with little hope of being called back.

It was time to go to the terminal. Melany glanced sadly at the bed they hadn't even undone. She suddenly felt very tired, all the more so because she didn't know in what Nazi hangout they were going to land in the middle of the night.

-- Chapter 21 --

Article from the Jakarta Post

Two weeks earlier

Indonesia heading towards chaos?

The electoral campaign for the presidential and legislative elections opens against the backdrop of renewed terrorist attacks and riots.

While several regional governments in West Sumatra are considering regulations to further restrict the rights of women and minorities, including the gay and lesbian community, attacks are increasing in Banda Aceh and Medan, where several hotels and tourist residences have been the target of bomb attacks. There have been no fatalities, but the damage has been extensive and the affected establishments were forced to close temporarily. Other attacks, including the unclaimed one in the Padang market, unfortunately claimed several victims. Leaflets were distributed that attributed these barbaric acts to the central government, which denies any involvement.

The local population, which one might think would be hostile to this climate of insecurity, seems on the contrary to approve of the slogans of the GAM, which claims its own actions "against corruption, Westernization, and the secular excesses of the government." For several months now, operations have been carried out against the army and police forces by groups trained in guerrilla warfare and with significant resources at their disposal. The leader of the new GAM, the enigmatic Habib Saragih, remains nowhere to be found, despite the size of the forces deployed to track him down. There are rumors of complicity within the army itself and increasingly frequent sabotage by military personnel, including high-ranking officers. The general denies the rumors.

Since West Sumatra is the most religiously conservative region of the country, the parties participating in the elections hope to win over a large number of voters with promises of measures to limit individual freedoms and to limit the island's access to tourism. These commitments, however, do not seem to have convinced the voters. According to a recent poll, the commitments to vote for the GAM would increase to more than fifty percent if the banned organization were allowed to participate in the elections.

Asked about the situation following demonstrations calling for "a return to a purer Islam and the institution of sharia", the current mayor of Medan, the modernist Jamal Bersendjata, worried about the possibility of a coup d'état. "Whoever takes power in the west of the island can take the whole island," he asserted. "Medan is the open door to Jakarta."

Jungle of Sumatra

Two weeks earlier

That atmosphere of calm that precedes the storm prevailed in the camp while the assemblies around Saragih and his German staff grew in number. The small army, now five thousand strong, alternated between missions and training in the heart of the jungle, where a course strewn with traps had been laid out. Rumor had it that *"it"* would be in a week to ten days, maximum. Yes, but what?

Darwis had put eighty-seven wounded back on their feet in the space of one month. The camp now resembled a large tent city crisscrossed with alleys, drainage ditches, a dump dug into a nearby clearing and a clean-up team made up of the weaker fighters, whom everyone laughed at.

Living in the heart of the jungle, two days' walk from any civilization, represented a daily challenge, which Saragih's advisers had taken into consideration and knew how to master. For his part, Darwis had organized a life as quiet as possible in the company of Adhi and Kusumo, far from the warlike fevers that moved through the camp in waves.

The incident that would upset the relative calm of a submissive existence with no possible escape occurred precisely twelve days before the "big operation".

Darwis had gone to the center of the camp with his adopted son and Kusumo in order to answer the discreet call of the muezzin and to participate in the *al-maghrib*, the prayer at sunset.

Adhi didn't understand what was going on and didn't know how to behave when he attended these large meetings where each man unfolded a rug on a corner of dry land, knelt down, and bowed towards the northwest. Darwis had given up teaching him the ritual of prayers, and the young man was allowed to stand and sway back and forth while all the others were engaged in *salat* toward Mecca.

Once the prayer was over, they returned to their tent, which they now shared with Kusumo, since the massive arrival of new fighters had forced the camp's inhabitants to reduce their resting space.

-- A week to ten days, that's all we hear, Darwis complained again, angered that he didn't know any more. The groups go off to fight, bring back the people, abandon half of them along the way, we fix them up, and we still don't know what we're taking part in.

-- In terrorist actions, may Allah help us, replied Kusumo, who had crouched down in front of their tent to roll a cigarette.

-- But for what purpose? What is this big operation that everyone's is talking about?

-- You want my opinion?

Kusumo lifted the cover of the camouflaged burner at the opening of the tent to light his cigarette and took a first puff with obvious pleasure.

-- ... Saragih believes that he can take over the country, and the Germans have trained him to do that. He sows terror, provokes people and reaps the fruits of his actions by arranging for the people of Aceh to side with him against army reprisals. That's a classic tactic.

-- And these preparations, then?

-- That's the next step in taking power. Saragih is going to try to seize Medan or Banda Aceh, put the population on his side, declare sharia for the greatest happiness of the fanatics, who are unfortunately the most numerous in our region, and to stage a coup d'état.

Sitting on a large root that formed a natural bench, Darwis nodded pensively. His passion for medicine had kept him away from political movements throughout his life. He didn't understand much about it, however, except that some men had a sick need for power in their genes that led them to behave in a hostile manner and whose actions only harmed the great majority. He had come to earth, by Allah's will, to repair what others were trying to destroy, and that paradox had often challenged him.

-- Your deductions will never fail to surprise me, he said by way of a compliment.

A pale moonbeam that had barely penetrated the canopy bathed the rainforest in a ghostly glow. As it did every evening, the relative silence of the day had given way to a concert of whistling, croaking, hooting and buzzing.

Nocturnal predators were on the prowl. Not far away, a colony of cutter ants was rebuilding a nest that a resident of a nearby tent had kicked up. A large tarantula watched them from the corner of a huge web spread between two trees where it had been lurking. A flock of small insects appeared out of nowhere and swarmed around Darwis and Kusumo who, with a habitual and mechanical gesture, began to slap themselves on the legs while continuing their conversation.

-- Everything I know I learned from the other medics, Kusumo said again. When the time comes, our hospital will be dismantled. What they will do with it next, I have no idea.

-- What concerns me most is what they will do to us.

A furtive movement between creepers and ferns drew Darwis' attention. The silhouette of an ape appeared in the dim light. Kusumo stood up to chase him away, but Darwis held him back, laughing. It was a *siamang*, one of the most peaceful and gentle of gibbons, recognizable by the length of its arms, the goiter the males had under their jaws and their pale gray faces, under a comically flattened head of hair that was reminiscent of actors in silent movies.

Upon noticing him, Adhi came out of the tent, shouting little cries of pleasure. It was rare for an ape to come so close to the camp, and they only did so when everyone was asleep. At dawn, the men discovered that they had been the victims of theft and cursed them. Let the one who hadn't put his food supplies under cover beware.

The siamang limped over towards the three men. He must have been in a fight, or perhaps he had narrowly escaped a wild animal, for blood stained his fur from his right shoulder to his elbow. He was moaning. Darwis did not have time to turn to Adhi to urge him to calm down. The young man had never been able to resist the sight of a wounded animal. He rushed towards the ape, stammering sounds imitate his language, but the animal became frightened and fled to the thickets from which he had emerged. His figure reappeared for a moment, flying from vine to vine before being swallowed up by the vegetation. Adhi froze, dumbfounded, then let out a cry and set off on its trail.

Darwis leaped to his feet, but the jungle had already closed over Adhi. He in turn plunged into the wall of plants, followed by Kusumo. But Adhi was fast, much faster than the two other men. Darwis called out to his adopted son at the top of his lungs, pushing his way through the giant leaves of aralias, lianas and ferns. Without a machete, his progress was slow. Kusumo followed a parallel path, pulling a little bit ahead of the doctor.

Heavy clouds suddenly obscured the faint crescent moon and the forest was plunged into total darkness. Darwis and Kusumo froze. If they continued in that direction, they might get lost. Anguish gripped the doctor's throat. This wasn't the first time Adhi had run off, but it was rare for him to go so far away. He would usually find him sitting by the river, or crouching near an anthill that he could spend hours watching without moving. The medic and the doctor called out his name over a dozen times, then Kusumo joined Darwis.

-- If we go any further, we won't be able to retrace our steps.

-- I can't let Adhi get lost.

Kusumo grabbed him by the arm.

-- We've moved a good two hundred meters away from the camp. Beyond that, we'll be taken for deserters and Saragih has the best trackers in Sumatra. We have to turn around and pray. Your son is in the hands of Allah, Darwis. He alone can return him to you.

The doctor freed himself, shaking his head.

-- Go back to camp. Explain what's happened. Ask for help. I'm not giving up.

Kusumo nodded. The darkness made it impossible to make out his worried frown and sad expression. He stepped aside, stumbled while swearing at a root, and took the opposite path, advancing blindly with his hands stretched out in front of him. He hadn't walked ten meters when a scream paralyzed the two men.

It was Adhi.

In response to his cry, the concert of roars, crackles, buzzes, and chirps intensified. The jungle was mocking them. Adhi was on their left, halfway to the camp. Darwis rushed in that direction, indifferent to the vines that slapped him and the thorns that scratched him. He got his feet caught in a root and fell sprawling forward. Kusumo joined him as a gap in the clouds once again allowed a pale ray of moonlight to fight the darkness. The shouting resumed, not to be interrupted anymore. Somehow, Darwis and Kusumo reached its origin.

In the middle of a space cleared by machetes, two men in black uniforms were holding Adhi, who was struggling like a devil without ceasing to shout.

-- Leave him alone!, Darwis shouted. Don't hurt him!

And then, to his adopted son:

-- Adhi, it's me. Don't worry. Everything is fine. The ape isn't in pain. He left to join his family. Calm down Adhi, they will let go of you. Calm down.

As the doctor walked towards him, the young man's screams subsided. The guards looked at each other, undecided. One of them recognized the doctor. He quickly told his comrade and they released Adhi, who immediately fell silent and took refuge in Darwis' arms.

-- And you -- who are you?, one of the guards asked sharply, pointing the barrel of his gun at Kusumo. He raised his arms reflexively, his lips fringed in a soothing smile that froze into a grin of surprise.

-- Banyu? It's you? What are you doing here?

The guard, in his turn, put on a stunned expression.

-- Kusumo? By Allah!

He burst out laughing and the two men rushed towards each other to embrace each other.

-- Darwis ... Kusumo called, excited as he took the guard by the shoulder. This is Banyu, my childhood friend. We went to school together in Padang.

The old long-lost friends kept slapping each other's backs and grabbing each other's hands, as Darwis continued to calm Adhi down.

-- Doctor Haikal is my friend and my boss, Kusumo explained to the two guards. Thank you for finding his son. He could have gotten lost in the jungle.

Darwis joined his thanks to Kusumo's. Then the small group continued in the direction of the camp. Adhi reluctantly followed them, still looking over his shoulder, hoping to catch a glimpse of the siamang.

Banyu explained that Saragih's men were going from village to village recruiting, and that the number of his followers kept growing. The elections were near and anger was brewing as unemployment was on the rise and the economies of Aceh and West Sumatra were close to collapse. He himself had lost his job as a delivery man, the only one he had been able to find despite his skills. He had therefore joined the sheikh's troops, attracted by the promise of a modest pay that would allow him to get by.

Darwis couldn't help but wince.

A few scattered, fragile and dancing glimmers, invisible from the treetops, betrayed the presence of the village camouflaged beyond the thickets.

-- I'm going back to my beat, Banyu announced. Try not to lose this boy again.

-- Wait, Kusumo said suddenly. How long have you been here?

-- I arrived last week, with the latest recruits.

The medic's face lit up.

-- So maybe you've heard about my sister, Nirmala? I haven't seen her in two months.

A mixture of embarrassment and sadness clouded the face of the guard. His expression alerted Kusumo.

-- Banyu?

-- You don't know?

-- I don't know what? Banyu, tell me! Something happened? How is my sister?

-- Listen ... it's the fault of fate.

-- What? What is the fault of fate?

Banyu swallowed painfully.

-- Nirmala was shopping when a bomb went off.

-- A bomb, but who ... how?

-- The papers say it was a suicide attack, but I can't believe that. According to Saragih's recruiters, it was a provocation by the government, in the hope of blaming the GAM. They must have planted the bomb next to a gas line. Half the stalls were blown up, and the roof of the covered market fell in ...

Kusumo grabbed his friend by his shirt collar.

-- And Nirmala, Banyu?

-- She was treated at the Padang Hospital, where you worked. But Allah had decided to call her back ... She didn't survive her wounds, Kusumo. I am sorry.

Silence followed this revelation. Darwis delicately pushed Adhi away to get closer to his friend. He trembled and shook his head in all directions, a mask of pain stuck on his features.

Everything then happened with the speed of lightning.

Kusumo grabbed Banyu's weapon, a Kalashnikov AK 47 with a curved magazine. Startled, the other one offered no resistance and the assault rifle changed hands in an instant. Despite the darkness, the second guard realized that something abnormal was occurring, but he had no time to react. Kusumo moved away from the two men in one bound, pushing past Darwis without paying attention to him and pointed the barrel of his weapon in their direction.

-- Kusumo, what's the matter with you?, Banyu yelped.

-- Sorry, the medic growled. You were my friend, but now you are one of Saragih's men. You, throw your gun away from you.

The second guard did as he was told. The Kalach landed in a nest of ferns and vanished.

-- Kusumo, calm down, Darwis tried to intervene.

-- Stay out of all this.

Sensitive to the intensity of the drama, even if he didn't understand everything, Adhi started to make little cries again. Then a phrase came out of his throat, which he kept repeating:

-- *The sea is coming. The sea is coming. The sea is coming...*

-- What?

For a fraction of a second, Kusumo let himself puzzle over Adhi's calls, but he pulled himself together. His face was bathed in tears, and his mouth contorted in an evil grin.

-- Saragih's recruiters promised me that nothing would happen to my sister if I agreed to follow them and work for them as a medic. They lied. Everything they touch is cursed.

-- *The sea is coming,* Adhi repeated, rocking back and forth. The sea is coming ... And the scene, bathed in the light of the moon, had something unreal and absurd about it.

-- But it wasn't the sheikh's fault!, Banyu pleaded.

Kusumo grew angry with his old friend.

-- Because you believed everything that Saragih's men wanted to make you swallow? That the elected government would detonate bombs in the markets in order to blame the Sheikh? I thought you were smarter than that, Banyu. But Allah has made you stupid, or mad. Now, walk ahead, we're going to visit him.

-- Kusumo ... Aren't you going to think about it? Your not going to attack Saragih.

The exhortation came from Darwis. Adhi's voice rose to a high pitch.

-- *The sea is coming. The sea is coming...*

The barrel of the Kalashnikov traced a semicircle towards Adhi's chest. Kusumo's voice was close to hysteria.

-- Darwis, shut him up!

-- I can't, you know him. He's frightened, that's why he's reacting.

-- So stay here with him.

With a wave of the weapon, Kusumo ordered the other two to move forward. Darwis hurried to Adhi's side and made the gestures that sometimes managed to calm him down. *The sea is coming. The sea is coming. The sea ... the sea ...*

Kusumo and the two guards disappeared and the young man fell silent.

The group reached the edge of the sleeping village. Men lived to the rhythm of the stars and the *adân*, dined after the twilight prayer, fell asleep after the night's prayer was over and celebrated the new day at the first light. No one saw them sneaking between the tents to the river. The surrounding thickets were crisscrossed by a multitude of guards, but the camp itself was not under any special surveillance.

-- Kusumo, Banyu pleaded, you're going to get us all killed!

-- Maybe, but not before getting Saragih's hide.

The path leading to the secondary camp, the residence of the sheikh and his staff, was bounded by black alluvial rocks whose volcanic origin recalled the proximity of Sorikmarapi, Tandikat and Talank, whose eruptions had shaken the entire area shortly after the tsunami.

The second guard, whose name Kusumo didn't know, stumbled against one of the stones and narrowly missing sprawling forward. He made up for it by grabbing a vine and cursing.

-- Stop there!

Bright spots appeared among the trees that framed the path. It took a moment for Kusumo to realize that these were the eyes of several fighters assigned to Saragih's security. Their faces were coated with black shoe polish, down to the roots of their hair. In the darkness, it was almost impossible to make out their silhouettes, which were as dark as their faces. Five barrels pointed at the medic, five more at the two guards. Banyu raised his arms to the sky and shouted:

-- Stop him! He wants to kill the sheikh. We tried to ...

The brief staccato of a machine gun covered the end of his sentence. Banyu collapsed. Kusumo turned his barrel in the direction of the thickets, but at the same moment ten Kalashnikovs spat their fire. The medic's body began a frantic dance as sprays of blood spurted from all his limbs and his chest.

He slumped down and his head struck a black rock.

His features, in death, seemed to calm down.

-- Chapter 22 --

Kahla -- Region of Thuringia -- Germany

Present time

An odor of rancid cabbage reeked on the landing with its gangrenous walls whose paint was peeling off in large patches. The elevator was awaiting repair, as noted by a sign more than a month old. They must have climbed four flights of stairs. The gold-plated sign attached to the wall announced in black letters:

"KARL HANUSSEN -- MEDIUM

Karmic Astrology -- Regression under Hypnosis

Extra-lucid clairvoyance"

Melany watched for a moment as Jeffrey, who seemed to find it amusing, shrugged his shoulders and, with a determined gesture, pressed the button to the buzzer. A bright light spread immediately in the entrance hall and a woman's voice came out of the videophone.

-- *Bitte stellen Sie sich vor*[(16)].

-- Melany Carson and Jeffrey Cartright. We have an appointment with Mr. Hanussen.

The sound of vibration preceded the opening of the door and they found themselves facing a long corridor with paneled walls bathed in subdued lighting. A woman appeared from a side opening. She was quite a character. With her purple-dyed hair pulled up in a bun, her vintage tortoiseshell-rimmed glasses, and her weighty blouse with a big bow belt, she seemed to have stepped straight out of a 1950's soap opera. Melany smiled at her. Jeffrey held out his hand. Indifferent, she announced in a dry tone:

[16] Introduce yourself, please.

-- You're early. The waiting room is at the end of the hall, on your right ...

She then disappeared into what must have been a reception office and slammed the door shut.

-- Charming ..., Jeffrey whispered.

They settled into the room indicated, which resembled the waiting room of a doctor's office in every detail, including the diplomas hung in frames and the recycled magazines piled on a coffee table. Melany mechanically grabbed the latest issue of *Der Stern* and opened it to the international news page. A feature article with photographs described the riots that had been plaguing Indonesia for several weeks. She showed the report to Jeffrey:

-- There seems to be some turmoil in the region where *"Earth and Sharing"* is operating.

-- Perhaps it's the turmoil that attracts its presence, not the other way around as you imply.

They had arrived in Kahla the day before yesterday and had found a room at the Zum Stadttor, a hotel with typical Teutonic architecture, with vaulted openings, latticework on the façade and its name spread out in Gothic letters on a gray and pink wall. The place was comfortable and the welcome warm, despite the actions of the receptionist, who was surprised by the presence of Americans in his city. They had had no trouble finding Karl Hanussen, whose name was spelled out in the pages of advertisements in local newspapers, and Melany managed to secure an appointment within twenty-four hours, despite the weeks of waiting mentioned by his assistant. Americans who have come all this way to "meet a magus of international reputation"? It was a sufficiently flattering event that Hanussen stepped in and asked her to put them into his overloaded appointment book.

-- Ms. Carson? Mr. Cartright?

The man standing in the doorway bore no resemblance to the image they had both had of him. Karl Hanussen looked like a provincial notary, quite overweight, balding and wearing a three-piece suit from which the chain of a pocket watch protruded.

-- Mr. Hanussen, how nice to meet you, Melany said, as she stepped forward to shake his hand.

-- Doctor Hanussen, the medium corrected. As you can see from the framed diplomas.

Neither had paid attention to the contents of the frames, believing that they were just part of the decor.

-- Pardon me, I didn't know.

-- You needn't apologize, Hanussen replied affably. Everyone is unaware of it. But just because I was barred from practicing medicine doesn't mean that I lost my title. Let's go inside, please. What brought you from so far?

He stepped aside to invite them to precede him with a ceremonial gesture.

His consulting room was cluttered with old and unattractive furniture, including a library loaded with old books, pseudo-scientific books, and grimoires. A brown velvet-covered couch stood in the middle of the room, separated from a matching armchair by a triangular coffee table with rounded corners. Hanussen invited them to sit down and took a seat behind a desk with a formica cover plate. It seemed as if time had stopped passing in this place.

-- So, which of you needs my services?

-- Do you speak English?, Melany asked.

-- Enough, the medium replied.

-- Perfect, that will save me from having to translate everything. My partner doesn't understand German very well.

Hanussen put on half-moon-rimmed glasses and opened a notebook to a blank page.

-- As my secretary told you, I have a busy schedule. A complete regression takes about an hour, and I will only be able to deal with one of you. So, which one?

Melany and Jeffrey exchanged glances. The day before, on the telephone, they had given no indication as to the reason for their visit, other than that it was urgent. The information network that had led them to Kahla could well have led to a dead end, but the presence there of a medium with a historical name linked to Nazi Germany and, moreover, a specialist in "past lives" exceeded the probability of mere coincidence. They had thought long and hard about how to approach him and concluded that the best way to gain his trust would be to talk about personal difficulties to be solved in an unconventional way.

-- My fiancée and I are facing an infertility problem, Jeffrey announced.

The young woman had a discreet gulp that was supposed to express all her repressed pain. She gave Hanussen a sad, hopeful look.

-- For now, it's the former doctor talking to you, the magus said after making a note in his notebook. What exams have you undergone? What treatments have you tried?

-- We've consulted with the foremost specialists in Washington and the surrounding area, Jeffrey replied in dismay. Everyone has come to the same conclusion: conventional medicine can do nothing for us.

The medium seemed to be touched. He asked in a sympathetic tone:

-- So you came to the conclusion that the problem lay not in your physical makeup, but perhaps in a non-biological inheritance?

-- What do you mean by that?

Hanussen placed his hands flat on his desk.

-- We all inherit our parents' genes, sometimes their personalities, and it is difficult to tell the difference between what is innate and what is acquired. But there is another form of inheritance that does not involve our birth parents or our immediate environment. If you have come to see me, I assume that you are familiar with the notion of karma?

-- Obviously!, Jeffrey said.

-- Regression under hypnosis makes it possible, in some cases, to go back to previous lives and to find the causes of a current illness. The mechanism is the same as that of psychoanalysis. Bringing memories of a past existence to the surface allows us to unblock the situations they cause by remaining in the unconscious. But I must inform you that my powers are limited. I am not a magician. Some people are resistant to hypnosis, and the result is not guaranteed.

-- I promise not to sue you if you should fail, Jeffrey joked.

-- Another question, the medium continued. Why consult me? Don't you have specialists in past lives and karmic astrology in America?

-- You were recommended to us by a friend, a university professor, who read an article about you. And since we were planning to visit Germany, we took this opportunity to meet you.

She observed the medium, who seemed to be delighted by her words. The lie was going well.

-- May I know the name of this professor?, he asked again.

-- His name wouldn't mean anything to you, Jeffrey replied. He's a specialist in occultism with a chair at Harvard.

-- You will thank him for me. Now, let me ask you. What do you know about reincarnation?

-- We've talked about it a lot, Melany and I. I must confess that I am the least skeptical of the two. I had to convince her that you might be our last chance and that we should give it a try.

Hanussen narrowed his eyelids, his gaze fixed on the young woman.

-- You don't believe it, because you received a purely materialistic education.

-- I had a normal education, Melany retorted.

Hanussen smiled.

-- This way of looking at the world is the legacy of the mechanistic sciences of the nineteenth century. I sense the very strong presence of a man, someone who travels a great deal. Military. A high ranking officer, no doubt. Your mother would have had a more flexible approach to spirituality if he had allowed her think for herself. But he's a bossy man, a beautiful soul deep down, but who doesn't believe in anything ...

-- My parents are divorced.

-- Pardon me. This is just intuitive information. I usually ask permission from my patients before entering into their thoughts. On the other hand, something is bothering me about what I've seen ...

-- Just open up and tell me!

-- I have the impression that you didn't come to my office for health problems. I sense ... curiosity. A search. A quest. A fight. Something confused in you ...

-- Doctor Hanussen!, Jeffrey interrupted, emphasizing his title. You just told us that you do not use your gifts without authorization!

-- That is true. But sometimes the patient's psyche is so strong that I have trouble closing the channel.

He shook his head, confused.

-- Let's leave it at that, if you don't mind ...

All affability had disappeared from his face. He made to get up.

-- Wait!, Melany said ...

-- Miss, don't try to mislead me any further. You should know that you can't fool a psychic that easily -- and I am one, even if you don't believe it.

-- Our approach has been honest, protested Jeffrey ...

Hanussen kept staring at them and his gaze was so penetrating that, for a moment, Melany thought he was undressing her. The magus continued in a voice from which all emotion had vanished.

-- I'm already going to give you some good news. You are both fertile, and I would even go so far as to recommend that you take precautions if you do not want to have a child immediately. Believe me, I am able to guess a woman's pregnancy from the first days and announce the sex of the unborn child. This is the most elementary part of clairvoyance, for those who are even a little familiar with this discipline.

-- A discipline?, Melany wondered, restraining a mocking tone.

Hanussen was on his feet, ready to take escort them out. Jeffrey said hastily:

-- You're right. That was not the real reason for our visit and we are sorry for trying to mislead you.

-- If you are journalists, I have nothing more to tell you, Hanussen growled. I don't speak to the press.

-- But there was this article ...

-- A mistake. Nosy people. That will not happen again.

-- Doctor Hanussen, take a good look at me, Jeffrey said. We don't belong to the media and our approach is personal. If your intuition is as powerful as you say it is, then you know that I am telling the truth.

The magus stared at him for a long time and seemed to relax. Melany took the opportunity to step into the breach.

-- We are here out of curiosity. My companion and I often argue over spiritual matters and he challenged me to try a regression. That's all there is to it. Sorry for lying to you but we've heard that psychics are touchy and we didn't know how to approach you.

Hanussen sat down again, obviously in the middle of a dilemma. He mechanically crossed out the first line of his notebook.

-- I don't sense anything unhealthy in you ... he finally announced. I don't believe in curiosity as a motive for your approach either, but since you blocked an hour in my schedule ... It will be one hundred and fifty euros. You can pay in dollars.

Jeffrey paid it with relief. The bills disappeared into the desk drawer. Again, the magus stared at Melany.

-- ... So, what makes you think you have only one life, and that no soul is in control of it? Just give me one or two arguments.

-- I have several, Melany said.

-- I'm listening.

-- My brain contains my thoughts, and I have no reason to believe that they will survive once it stops working. Before I was born, I was nothing. So it is into nothingness that I will return after my death. I have no memory of the lives I might have lived previously, so I don't see the point of a belief based on amnesia. As for the laws of karma, which I know little about but which I summarize, we would be punished for acts about which we have no awareness. What nonsense!

-- Karma is not a mechanism for punishment, but for the evolution of the soul. Punishment after death is an invention of religions. A way to gain control over society. Good and evil are only human concepts that change according to cultures and evolve over time. No, karma has nothing to do with any of that.

Hanussen walked around his desk to approach Melany. He closed his eyes, then put his hand on her shoulder in a theatrical gesture before opening them again and letting them glaze over.

-- You believe that you are going to die because you identify with your ego and not with your spirit. But if the brain receives the thought instead of producing it, why would the thought disappear?

-- That is where we disagree.

Hanussen displayed the smile of a wise old man used to the rejections of the incredulous.

-- Modern physics has shown that man is not separate from the world around him but is an integral part of it. To sum it up, let's argue that the universe only exists in our collective consciousness. Of course, your ego will disappear. That is what you call death. But, what is the ego? A combination of instincts, fears, jumbled thoughts, the will to survive. It's just the driver of your vehicle, which is developing in a world of illusions. But when you are in pain, Melany, who is in pain? When you are afraid, who is afraid? You don't believe in the soul, and, according to you, we are only thinking machines. You're going to tell me that fear and pain are only the result of chemical reactions in the brain. Yet I challenge you to make the most sophisticated computer, even one with artificial intelligence, feel the slightest emotion. Look at yourself in a mirror. What do you see? A shape. But who is looking at this shape? As soon as you question yourself, the real *you* appears to you. It's a compendium of intelligent emotions along with all of your memories, including the ones you think have been erased. It is this *you* who are in pain, who are happy and who love without knowing why. That which observes *you* in its half-sleep will wake up one day, like yourself in the morning after a night filled with dreams. Outside of time and matter, which are inseparable, it will activate the memory of all the lives you have ever lived. You will then know who you really are and will make a conscious decision about your next incarnation.

Hanussen paused and seemed to come back to himself.

-- You see, it's all really quite simple. And now, if you would lie down, I will try to satisfy your *curiosity*. We only have three quarters of an hour left, so let's make it quick. Mr. Cartright, would you mind waiting in the next room?

Melany hesitated for some time. Hanussen had confused her a little, but it was still all just folklore. If she had to go through this fantasy in order to keep playing the game and, perhaps, to get more from the so-called medium, then she was in no position to back down after so many lies. So she went over to the couch.

-- May I ask you to dress as lightly as possible? I will turn up the heat if you want. But you need to feel comfortable, perfectly relaxed, just like at home. You'll have a hard time with that big coat.

-- Do I have to take off my sweater, too?, Melany asked as she complied.

-- Only if you have a blouse on underneath.

Jeffrey left the office. Melany lay down on the couch, Hanussen standing in front of her, his features tensed with extreme concentration. She expected him to pull out a pendulum or a talisman of some kind, as she had seen in movies depicting this kind of situation, but he did not. His voice, calm, deep and vibrant, reached her like a wave of warmth. He asked her to relax and concentrate on her limbs, one after the other, moving up her body. Melany gradually entered a state of pleasant torpor, similar to that of a daydream in a country setting on a beautiful sunny afternoon.

Guided by Hanussen's words, she relived her meeting with Jeffrey, and it instilled a wave of happiness in her. She returned quickly to Kirkuk. Dust, screams, the roar of helicopters, gunshots in the distance. Then to Istanbul. Boredom. Reports on an intolerable situation. Confusion. The magus asked her to travel through time, keeping her memories to herself. Which she did. She returned to Harvard, walked hand in hand with her first lover, but felt a wave of sadness when she saw her parents divorce. As a little girl in Cairo, she loved the school where an eccentric teacher taught her Classical Arabic every morning. Another leap in time. Moscow. Her mother was so beautiful when she was young, and her father, Major Carson, had such presence with his military discipline. They had made a remarkable couple. When she was four years old, she had fallen from a bicycle, which left a scar on her elbow and knee.

Melany remained conscious throughout the session, if only to remember at one point a dream she had forgotten. She was dressed like a farmgirl and her father, whose face she did not recognize, was leading her to the body of a farm building resembling that of the Mitchells, with its red roof and grain silo. She didn't want to follow him, but he held her hand firmly. Cries of animals being mistreated escaped from the building. She entered it, constrained and forced, and immediately slipped in a pool of blood ...

She straightened up suddenly.

-- I ... How long have I been under hypnosis?, she asked.

Without her being aware of it, the magus had placed a large blanket across her body. He was smiling. She came out of it.

-- About forty minutes, he replied. How do you feel?

-- Like after a good nap. So this is hypnosis? I didn't go into a trance for a single moment.

-- No one asked you to. This wasn't some fairground hypnosis.

He walked back behind his desk, allowing her to reorient herself and to put on her sweater.

-- You don't have to tell me what you saw. But I am curious, though: did you feel like you were remembering a dream?

Melany nodded her head, really confused this time.

-- People imagine that regression through hypnosis will lead them to relive their past lives on some kind of movie CinemaScope screen with stereo sound. It is not like that at all. Your delocalized memory has recorded the events experienced by your soul in the area where your dreams are also stored. Hence the feeling of reliving a dream during the regression.

-- I saw a man, and I knew it was my father, but his face was unknown to me. There was a farm. Animals slaughtered under horrible conditions ...

-- Quite an injustice, wasn't it?, Hanussen conceded. Don't be surprised if something stronger and greater than yourself pushes you to fight to repair the evil that men are capable of.

A noise on the side of the window startled the magus. It was just a crow that had bumped into the glass when it landed on the ledge. The snow continued to fall and the bird shook to remove the melted flakes from its wings and then flew into the air again.

They called Jeffrey back and he immediately asked how the session had gone. Melany's absent mood disturbed him.

-- Is there anything else I can do for you, now that I have reconciled your companion to a universe she didn't even know existed?, Hanussen asked.

-- Did you really do that?

At Jeffrey's scrutinizing gaze, Melany replied with a frown. The purpose of their visit had not been for her to come to believe in reincarnation or black magic. He attempted a final maneuver:

-- We would indeed like to ask you something else. How does karmic astrology work?

Hanussen laughed.

-- It would take me a whole week to answer you. And again, I'm not sure I could do it.

-- In the broadest terms ..., Melany insisted.

He stared at the door and, for a split second, his eyes expressed a disturbing fear. Jeffrey spun around, just in time to see the door shut silently. When he came back to himself, Hanussen had regained his composure.

-- Let us start from the principle that there is no other destiny other than the one we have forged in the past, in previous lives. The universe and we form a single whole. This link allows classical astrology to define the main features of our lives in addition to the main aspects of our personalities. Just as the moon causes the tides by gravitational effect, the position of the planets influences everyone's destiny according to their place and date of birth. Karmic astrology is a bit more complex than that. Its function is to decipher the lunar nodes and retrograde planets, terms on which I have neither the desire nor the time to expand, in order to arrive at a reading of past lives and the present destiny linked to them. Have I been clear enough so far?

-- The lunar nodes?, Melany asked in fascination. Could you explain that to us?

Hanussen gestured broadly to his library.

-- More than half of the books you see are devoted to reincarnation. A good quarter of them deal with karmic astrology. How would you like me to summarize? The lunar nodes are the points in the orbit of the moon as it crosses the ecliptic, that is to say, the relative trajectory of the sun. The virtual meeting of these two points at defined moments makes it possible to draw a parallax that will serve as a tool for understanding an individual's karma.

Melany was about to admit that she didn't understand a thing, but Jeffrey stopped her with a gesture.

-- So, just as in classical astrology, you are able to draw up a chart from the positions of the planets. Can you also find dates and places of birth in the future?

The question challenged Hanussen, who thought about it deeply.

-- It's extremely complicated.

-- That could be interesting!, Melany said.

-- It is impossible to know the next incarnation of a being as long as he is still in this world.

-- And if he had died half a century or more ago, would it theoretically be possible to know who he might have been reincarnated as?

-- Is this a relative?

-- A relative or a historical figure ...

Jeffrey regretted revealing himself so much, since Hanussen froze and closed himself off abruptly.

-- I seem to have told you enough ...

-- All right, okay, we'll be leaving in a minute. But is there a mathematical rule?

-- The interval between our visits to this planet is based on sacred numbers. But I really am out of time now.

As he spoke, Hanussen scribbled a few lines in his notebook. He tore off the page, folded it in four, and handed it to Jeffrey.

-- There you go, you may look at that later. Use your date of birth with this little slide rule and you may find out when your last incarnation took place. Now, please be kind enough to leave me.

-- Doctor, Melany asked suddenly, why did you lose the right to practice medicine?

The medium's face darkened.

-- Maybe I shouldn't have let that patient find out that he had died by hanging in a past life. The shock was so bad that he choked to death. I failed to resuscitate him and was taken to court for charlatanism and aggravated professional malpractice. But that was a long time ago.

-- I am sorry for you.

Jeffrey wanted to add something, but it was Melany's turn to interrupt by taking him by the arm and leading him towards the exit. When they opened the door, Hanussen's assistant was standing behind it with an evil look.

-- Doctor Karl, she scolded, you're late, and Herr Schneider is getting impatient.

They hurried down the stairs and, since they had left the rental car near their hotel, they hailed a taxi passing in the street.

***

The snow-covered sidewalks and the classic architecture of the houses lined up along the streets gave the small town a calm and quiet appearance. In the heart of a lively neighborhood, they passed a gang of young bikers clustered in front of a bar, their machines backfiring as they stopped. Each one had the number 88 in red numbers on a white background on the back of his jacket. Melany asked the driver in surprise:

-- Who are these young people? A local gang?

The man glanced at her briefly in the rear-view mirror.

-- Why local?

-- I don't know. I know about the Hells Angels. This is the first time I've seen that acronym.

-- That's not an acronym, it's a profession of faith.

-- Oh well, that's amazing. What does it mean?

The man turned around sharply. He had a gaunt face, steel blue eyes, and cropped, jet-black hair.

-- What is surprising is the presence of tourists in Kahla. Is there nowhere else for Americans to visit in Germany?

Melany and Jeffrey remained silent until they arrived outside the hotel. The cab's meter had been turned off and the fare seemed exorbitant to them. However, this was not the time or the place to start a conflict over a few stolen euros. They contented themselves with leaving no tip. Once freed of his passengers, the driver set off again with a roaring start.

Their room had been cleaned and the bed made up during their absence. Since her experience in Odyssey, Melany had learned to be wary of hoteliers. She immediately checked that the pin discreetly between the two suitcases was still there. Its presence reassured her. No one had come to search them.

-- Do you want to know what the number 88 corresponds to?, Jeffrey said after tapping on his cell phone.

-- Another esoteric trick?

-- Not really, but much worse. The letter H is in the eighth position in the alphabet. 88 therefore corresponds to a double H.

-- OK. And that leads us to what?

-- H plus H. Heil Hitler. 88 is the rallying code of the neo-Nazis.

Melany thought for a few moments. Beneath its peaceful appearance, the small town was indeed the lair of supremacists described by the media. In the heart of Germany, whose successive governments had committed themselves to suffocating them for good, the movements were nevertheless nostalgic for an era dominated by hatred and obscurantism. Evil, like a phoenix of darkness, always rose from its own ashes again.

-- Do you want to tell me now what happened during your hypnosis session?, Jeffrey asked.

-- To tell the truth, not much. I do admit that it was relaxing. Hanussen is really quite a character, under his appearance of an innocent provincial. I was able to take stock of quite a few things in an hour. And I remembered an old dream, which has faded again. That's all.

-- So our past-life magus has failed to convince you of the reality of karma, or even send you to the time of the Crusades?

-- If I had to choose time travel, I would have chosen another era, believe me.

Their two cell phones had been ringing regularly since the day before, each time displaying "unidentified number". This happened again and Melany finally picked up the phone, annoyed but convinced that the calls were coming from Franckel.

It was Anat.

-- You're both really stubborn!, she said as soon as she heard Melany's voice.

-- I return your compliment.

-- There's a difference. I'm just doing my duty.

Melany answered sharply:

-- Doing one's duty is not just about obeying orders. Do you know Edmond Burke's saying? "For evil to triumph, it is enough for good men to do nothing". Tell Franckel that if he wants to yell at us, he can do so directly.

-- I'm not calling you for his sake, the Israeli woman said.

-- So ... why have you been trying to reach us since yesterday?, Melany guessed.

She signaled Jeffrey to come closer with the idea of moving the phone away from her ear so that he could follow the conversation. He was sitting on the bed and eagerly going over the lines that Hanussen had written on his notebook page.

-- I'm beginning to find your way of acting interesting!, Anat admitted. Your flea-hopping across Europe just might lead to something ... if no one swats you before.

-- Are you dissociating yourself from Franckel?, Melany asked.

The Israeli took on a new tone. There was a background of sadness in her voice.

-- For the CIA, this mission is nothing but routine. They don't view the neo-Nazis as a real threat. Their alliance with Islamist movements is not new and Franckel does not want any upheavals that could tip off the media. Since Iraq, political correctness has been the order of the day. But for us, it's an existential question. Nazis and Islamists have a common obsession. The extermination of our people. For reasons beyond me, it seems to you and Jeffrey are ahead of the intelligence services.

-- Don't tell me you're asking us for our help?, Melany said.

Jeffrey looked troubled by his reading and tried to get her attention. She was suddenly anxious to hang up.

-- And why not?, the Israeli replied. You have been ordered to return to Washington, but instead of obeying you are in a small German town that is home to a community of little Nazis. I take it that you've discovered something again and I need to know what it is.

It was no surprise that Anat, too, had found them so easily. The GPS connection of their laptops made it possible to track them. But she was basically right. They were sharing the same fight.

-- Assuming that we do help you, what would you give us in return?

-- My protection. This is not a game, Melany! You can't fight alone and at some point you're bound to need me.

-- Perhaps. But we don't have much more to tell you. Except that we were trying to investigate a humanitarian aid NGO ...

-- ... Most of whose operations are carried out in Indonesia?, Anat asked.

-- You know about "Earth and Sharing"?

-- I know that it operates out of the city you are in right now.

-- Have you been investigating them for long?

Silence. It became evident that Anat wouldn't be answering that question. Then:

-- I did mean it, Melany. I'll send you an SMS with a cell phone number. Use it in case of danger. But above all, you two should be careful.

-- Anat, what exactly do you expect from us?

-- Perhaps you were going to offer them the voluntary services of two idiots stupid enough to believe that this kind of NGO really has humanitarian goals? You do have the right profiles. But I haven't told you anything.

-- Thanks for the compliment, Melany grimaced.

Jeffrey called her as soon as she had hung up.

-- Come and read this!

-- Don't you want to know what Anat told me?

-- Later. This is more important.

Jeffrey had every reason to be excited. The page torn from Hanussen's notebook contained much more than what he had pretended to offer them.

He would meet them that same evening at an address outside of Kahla.

-- Chapter 23 --

Article from the Jakarta Post

Three days earlier

Banda Aceh in the hands of the GAM. Soon Medan?

After two months of clashes between radical Islamists, mostly GAM supporters, and government forces, Banda Aceh fell into the hands of Saragih's men, who is still nowhere to be found.

Across the entire region of Aceh, new riots broke out in a way that might appear spontaneous if they were not punctuated by targeted attacks, but which the regional governor is being accused of instigating.

In Medan, more than half of the members of the armed forces are said to have joined GAM as the insurgency gradually spreads throughout Sumatra.

Jakarta has declared a state of emergency and has just launched an appeal for general conscription, raising other protest movements that could ultimately shake its power.

The slogan on the streets of Banda Aceh, Medan, Padang and as far away as Palembang is "Saragih in power, our only law is sharia*". It is broadcast through thousands of leaflets and repeated calls in a loop by regional radio stations stormed and occupied by militants.*

The United Nations Security Council will meet tomorrow at the express request of China, Australia, New Zealand and Malaysia.

See our analysis on page 3.

Jungle of Sumatra

Three days earlier

The camp was in its last days and the field hospital was about to be dismantled. Darwis had spent part of the night making an inventory and putting away his equipment, helped by his two medics. Adhi, who hadn't left his side since Kusumo's disappearance, was unusually calm and even tried to help out. His adoptive father had taught him how to fold sheets, towels and blankets for storage in transport bags reserved for this purpose, and he went about his task with particular concentration, showing evident pleasure.

Although he never tolerated his confinement, the activities that Darwis had been forced to engage in since his abduction had brought him some satisfaction. He was born to heal, to save and to alleviate suffering. It didn't matter which camp his patients belonged to. But Kusumo's death, which came after so much tragedy, had marked him so deeply that he was now mechanically and soullessly occupied. The question of his future did not even manage to preoccupy him. If he hadn't yet attempted a desperate gesture, such as a suicidal escape, it was only to protect Adhi.

Once again, one of the sheikh's messengers burst into the small operating room, now emptied of its equipment, and demanded that he and Adhi follow him. This was a new habit. The commander had been summoning him regularly ever since Darwis' escapade near the river which had led him to discover the headquarters of Saragih by mistake.

With the exception of the Germans, the sheikh's immediate entourage was composed of frustrated fighters and religious fanatics, and few in the camp had the level of culture and open-mindedness of the doctor. In a way, Darwis had become his own guinea pig, representative of a missing sample.

That is how he had learned from Saragih himself that a revolution was breaking out on the national level and that Indonesia, after the failure of Daesh, would soon become the heart of the true khalifate. This time the decadent West could do nothing about it, for who would have the means to attack more than two hundred million human beings, soon to be ruled by sharia law? This seizure of power would be the starting point for a larger-scale operation, which would finally restore dignity to the victims of terrorism and Western slavery. The end of a humiliation that had lasted far too long. Soon they would have absolute deterrence ...

Darwis didn't know any more, but the little he had learned was enough to terrify him. As for the Germans surrounding the sheikh, they had given the impression since Krueger's departure that they were getting ready to celebrate a victory, in accordance with plans they had been brewing for a long time.

-- Pack up your instruments!, Saragih's man ordered.

-- Which ones?, Darwis asked just to make it harder for him.

-- I don't know, I'm not a doctor. That thing you wear around the neck to listen to the heart. Things like that ...

Darwis sighed, filling the makeshift briefcase that accompanied him when he was called to the bedside of a suffering fighter, then followed the messenger whose name he did not know with Adhi on his heels. The guard led him not toward the headquarters, as Darwis was used to doing, but deeper into the rainforest, along a narrow path crudely hacked out by machetes and cluttered with vines and intertwined lianas.

The sky was weighed down with dark clouds heralding tropical rain, and the humidity was so high that clothes stuck to the skin. They arrived in an artificial clearing in front of a primitive dwelling the size of a military tent. The sloping roof consisted of palm leaves assembled at the top of walls just high enough to accommodate short men, which excluded the Germans. Branches of all kinds, connected by lianas, had been used in its construction. The entrance was protected by a simple blanket attached to the doorway. Unusual patterns, reminiscent of foreign calligraphy, had been embroidered into the fabric. Saragih's envoy stopped at a respectable distance from the hut. A respectful fear could be seen on his face. He invited Darwis in an unsteady voice to come closer.

-- The sheikh wants you to make sure they are healthy. And they want to see the other one behind you. The one who never speaks. I'll be waiting for you here.

The smell of sandalwood, agar and lotus wood escaping from the interior mixed with the damp scents of the jungle. Darwis lifted the blanket. The messenger stayed outside and took a step back, moving closer to Adhi, who was content to observe the hut with his mouth ajar, looking intrigued but in no way frightened.

In spite of the precarious nature of its construction, it was so watertight that no light could penetrate the roof or the walls. A deep, vibrant and steady sound of particularly low intensity passed over Darwis's eardrums as his eyes adjusted to the dim light. He first saw the glowing tips of a multitude of incense sticks burning all around the room on the floor covered with a bamboo mat. In a corner, there was a trunk, and behind that, a pile of blankets.

At the center of the hut, the two monks whose Tibetan origin Kusumo had told him about were seated in the lotus position. Their hands rested on their lap, the right hand overlapping the left, the tips of their thumbs touching. Their shoulders were slightly raised and bent forward, their chins tucked against their throats, their spines as straight as stacks of coins. Both had their eyes slightly open and seemed to be looking ahead towards the opening through which Darwis had just come.

The continuous vibrating sound came from their throats. The phenomenon was all the more surprising since neither of them seemed to be breathing. The doctor approached them cautiously, without causing any movement or change in their eyes. Tibetans were more immobile than statues. He put his bag on the floor and took out a stethoscope.

The examination he then performed astonished him. It took all his concentration to detect distant heartbeats, the only sign of life in the two monks. He looked at his watch and counted. Their heart rate was less than thirty beats per minute. It was impossible to detect their breathing. Darwis had vaguely heard of such a phenomenon during his medical studies. The monks had reached a state of deep meditation that allowed them to control even the functioning of their organs. They were somewhere else. Far away. Very far away.

The doctor came out of the hut and asked how long they had been in this condition. The messenger replied that they hadn't changed their posture in a whole week.

-- The sheikh ordered us to take turns making sure that the incense sticks didn't stop burning around them.

-- And no one brings them food or drink?

Saragih's messenger shrugged his shoulders.

-- They're the ones who demanded that. So, are they still alive?

-- As much as you can be when you get into this state. And at night, does someone watch over them?

-- Not at all. It's even forbidden to approach here after a certain time.

Darwis went from one astonishment to the next. The two monks must be prime prey for the dozens of categories of predators that stalked the rainforest, not to mention poisonous insects and snakes. The messenger seemed to read his thoughts.

-- They say that the smell of their incense keeps wild animals away. If that kills the mosquitoes too, I'd like them to give me a few sticks.

-- Why is it that Saragih only called on me now?, the doctor asked again.

-- No idea. Maybe he got worried.

-- And you don't know the reason for their presence in the camp either?

Saragih's emissary was carrying his Kalashnikov slung over his shoulder, the barrel pointing down, his right hand resting flat on the magazine. Darwis noted that he was missing two fingers.

-- They are monks, infidels, he grumbled before spitting on the ground. And, by Allah, I have no idea.

He resumed the direction of the path and motioned for Darwis to follow him. He felt a sudden change in the atmosphere of the place. The light was the same, the concert of cackling and growling from the thickness of the jungle had not changed in intensity. It was something else.

He turned his eyes back to the hut.

The blanket blocking the entrance had been raised. The Tibetans were standing in front of it like two ivory statues and watching him.

-- Is that the *magic child?*, the older one asked.

-- Adhi is my adopted son, Darwis clarified.

-- Can he come closer?

At Darwis' request, the young man took a few steps towards the monks. The one who had spoken invited him to join him with a soothing gesture that was accompanied by a smile. To the surprise of his adoptive father, Adhi obeyed.

The monk then stood up on his legs and, although he was at least a foot shorter, managed to put his hand on the top of the young man's head.

-- He's a child in an adult body, he commented.

Darwis nodded, astonished by the young man's docility and silence.

-- He has locked himself up to escape the immense darkness, the monk continued. His karma is heavy, but he has agreed to pay the price. We will need the pure heart of a child for the upcoming ceremony. Do you agree, Doctor?

The monks had therefore been informed of his function in the camp and did him the honor of using his title.

-- Do I have any choice?, he replied, wondering what ceremony it could be. Saragih had been careful not to mention the imminence of such an event.

-- Chapter 24 --

Kahla, region of Thuringia

Present time

-- Volunteers? To do what?

-- We're passing through Kahla, Melany replied to the *Earth and Sharing* switchboard operator. My companion and I are travelling around the world and we want to make ourselves useful.

-- We don't use volunteers.

-- Perhaps you could put us in touch with a manager.

-- For what purpose?

-- To make an appointment. There are many ways to be of service. My companion and I ...

-- You will find a link on our site that will allow you to send us donations, the switchboard operator said. Thank you for your interest in our organization. *Auf Wiedersehen*.

She hung up. Melany turned to Jeffrey.

-- Well, so much for our discreet infiltration of an NGO whose staff seems to be overflowing with charity.

Jeffrey scowled.

-- I'm beginning to think that that Israeli woman is right about one thing.

-- What?

-- We're just two amateurs trying to play spies.

-- You really think that?

-- Every time we try, we fail.

-- Let's wait until tonight before coming to any conclusion!

***

The GPS in the rental car had led them astray and they had lost more than twenty minutes driving around in circles near the Wapelsberg before finally arriving at the rendezvous point. The snowy mass of the high plateau that had made the region famous stood out darkly in the twilight from the entrance to the village where Hanussen was supposed to meet them. Everything was asleep. Not a light in the windows of the farms and huts. Only a few barks occasionally tore through the blanket of silence that seemed to have weighed on the scene from all eternity. But, above all, there was no trace of Hanussen.

With all lights out, they had left the engine idling to take advantage of the heater. Piles of hardened snow separated by patches of ice flanked the vehicle as witnesses to the intense cold that settled in here from nightfall until midday. After half an hour of waiting, Jeffrey and Melany began to think that the magus would not appear that night. The roar of an approaching motorbike raised their hopes. A large BMW Motorrad soon came to a stop a few paces away from their vehicle. A stocky silhouette, dressed in leather, approached the right door. The man removed his helmet as he leaned over Melany's window. It was Karl Hanussen.

The magus never ceased to surprise them.

-- Can I get in the back?, he asked in a voice strained with anxiety. I really have very little time.

Hanussen sighed deeply as he settled down. He showed them a path between two mounds that would allow them to stay out of sight. They set off there and stopped a hundred meters down the road.

-- How long?, Jeffrey asked.

-- Ten, fifteen minutes at the most. I'm used to riding a motorcycle in the evening to relax by pushing the gears up a bit. They're aware of that. But I never come home later than ten o'clock.

The number of questions that tormented Melany as well as Jeffrey couldn't have been answered in a single hour. Neither of them needed to ask the first: who were "they"? Hanussen enlightened them with a few clear and distinct sentences.

-- The Nazis are everywhere in Kahla. From the post office to the power company. The majority of police officers support their cause. My phone is tapped. My assistant's only task is to watch me. Do not ask me why I trust you, or why I am ready to reveal all of this to you. In order to believe me, you would have to be willing to grant me talents that for you are in the realm of fairy tales. Let's just say that my intuition rarely deceives me. I understood perfectly who I was dealing with as soon as I saw you. I've been waiting for your visit for a long time.

-- Our visit, Doctor?, Jeffrey wondered with a hint of suspicion. Who do you think we are?

-- I don't know exactly. I just know that you are on the right side. And since you're Americans, I assume that you didn't come to me by your own initiative. Tell me if I'm mistaken?

There was as much hope as pleading in his voice.

-- And for what purpose would we have come to you?, insisted Melany who, like Jeffrey, was fearing a trap.

-- To find out more about the projects of Gerhard Krueger and the NGO that serves as the cover for his activities!

Silence followed. Melany felt her heart racing. Beginner's luck, Anat had diagnosed. Could it be that they were so close to their goal?

-- Now, make up your mind!, Hanussen said, slapping the flat of his hand on the helmet he had placed on his lap. Either you tell me what you came to Kahla for, or I'll leave and you won't know anything more.

-- You're right about one thing, Jeffrey finally blurted out. We are indeed investigating *Earth and Sharing*, which we have only recently learned about, but we're doing so in a private capacity. It's quite complicated. In our professional lives, on the other hand, we are attached to the State Department, each in a different capacity. But governmental agencies tend to get in the way. It's not even sure we'll still have our jobs when we get back to Washington. Have I satisfied your curiosity sufficiently?

-- It's not about curiosity, it's about safety. You don't happen to have a mint candy or anything else I could swallow? Stress causes me unbearable heartburn.

Melany searched her bag. She thought she had kept a candy bar from the hotel minibar. She found it and offered it to Hanussen, who swallowed a mouthful with pleasure before going on:

-- Do you know where we are? Near the ruins of the factory for the Messerschmitt Me 262 which could have changed the course of the war, if the Third Reich had developed it a little earlier. The hill topped by a plateau that you can see less than a kilometer away is still crisscrossed by a network of galleries, some of which extend for tens of kilometers. The Russians thought that they destroyed everything, shelling the hill day and night for almost a week. That's where they were wrong. And this is also where my story interests you.

-- Why us?, Melany asked. If you have something important to disclose, why didn't you do it earlier?

Hanussen waved his helmet impatiently.

-- I told you: this area is infested with Nazis. Their numbers have only increased recently. I was forced to move to Kahla after making the mistake of agreeing to offer my talents to Krueger. I am under close surveillance. My office and my apartment are full of bugs. They barge into my house regularly, knock over furniture, empty out my drawers and search the toilet bowl. That's the price I agreed to pay for staying alive. And you are the first persons from the outside world to visit me under false pretenses. After you left, my "assistant" put me through a formal interrogation.

Whenever she heard Krueger's name, it conjured up something buried in Melany's memory, but she couldn't quite put her finger on it. Hanussen looked at his watch.

-- What I am about to reveal to you is of the greatest importance. You know what to do with it. I am risking my life by meeting you, and yours will not be much better if you stay in Thuringia for too long. As soon as I have told you everything, leave!

He took a deep breath.

-- Hitler wrote three wills before his death. Two, known all over the world, and one that has all the appearance of delusion, remained secret until a Russian agent discovered it in the archives of the KGB ...

-- All of this, which we already know, is the starting point of our investigation, Melany pointed out. But keep going.

-- Everything revolves around this will, the magus resumed. When Krueger's men brought their proposal to me, I thought it was a joke at first. They wanted me to help them find the *tulku* of a historical figure from a secret document. Do you know what a *tulku* is?

Jeffrey replied that he did.

-- The money they offered me was not insignificant, but it was the challenge that really attracted me. Until then, the past had been my only field of exploration. As I explained to you, karmic astrology helps to understand a being's blockages based on the experiences one has experienced in past lives. Regression under hypnosis allows certain episodes to be relived and this mechanism is a healing factor. You have the right to not believe it, but my success rate speaks in my favor. As if it were just myself ... Have you heard of Edgar Cayce's readings?

-- Please don't side-track!, Melany sighed.

-- Pardon me. You are right ... No one had ever asked me yet to use my knowledge to predict a future incarnation before. Which is not possible during the lifetime of the person consulting. The decision to come back is made later, in another dimension ...

Melany was about to interrupt him again, but Jeffrey called her to silence with a firm grip on her arm.

-- On the other hand, the subject that interested Krueger's men was already dead and had left information about important events in his life. It was feasible. When they told me the name of the monster they wanted me to find, it was too late. I had already accepted. Krueger then gave me the documents in his possession.

-- In what form?, Jeffrey asked.

-- Several handwritten pages. Most of the text was made up of excerpts from a missing Tibetan sacred book ... It was an instruction manual.

-- The ***Kalakarma*** *Tantra?,* Jeffrey asked.

Hanussen showed his surprise with raised eyebrows, but went on.

-- I asked them for two months, because it was not a simple case. Krueger set me up in my office, as you know. The document testified that Hitler had been initiated by the *Gelugpas,* the "virtuous men" in Tibetan, better known as the Yellow Caps, whose spiritual leader is the Dalai Lama. How had he managed to get hold of the original ***Kalakarma*** *Tantra*, the only text that gives the keys to reincarnation? I haven't the faintest idea. Still, the documents attached to the will contained an impressive amount of information on how to find his *tulku*. They made it possible to calculate the precise moment of the lunar nodes during which it is necessary to meditate in order to connect to the soul in transit. Hitler knew of the existence of the sacred Tibetan golden urn, which is used to confirm the identity of the candidate. He knew the three extreme meditations that allow one to get in touch with the source of everything. I am a medium by birth, but I had never had such a terrifying experience.

-- Doctor, Jeffrey interrupted this time. You speak as if we were convinced of the existence of this parallel world. You may be comfortable there, but let us have our doubts. In short, this man Krueger was convinced that Hitler had been reincarnated. So he got it into his head to find his ... his *tulku* and called on you, a psychic, a specialist in past lives, to help him. So far, we're in the realm of crazy ranting. What worries us is that other extremists believe in it and are joining forces to foment a dirty trick somewhere on this planet. Where, when, why? These are the only questions we are really asking ourselves.

-- Your point of view is correct, the magus said approvingly. Except the will contained other information. Encrypted pages that I have only seen but did not understand. How do you think Krueger obtained the financial means to develop his operations?

That was Professor Herskowitz's thesis. Hitler would have left behind coded indications allowing access to large sums of money. In what form? Hanussen wasn't certain.

-- For decades, treasure hunters from all over the world tried to find several tons of gold that the Nazis removed just before the end of the war.

-- And you think ...?

-- That man is immensely rich. How could he have done so if he hadn't been able to decrypt the pages attached to the will? But that's not the worst thing.

Hanussen pointed his finger at the Wapelsberg.

-- Have you ever seen someone affected by a very high level of radiation? Such as the unfortunate victims of Chernobyl or Fukushima for example? A few years ago, all you would have had to do was hang around in the quarantined building of the Saint Joseph Clinic, twenty kilometers from here, to witness the same horror. Krueger made sure that there was no media coverage and, more importantly, that the government health authorities didn't intervene. In Kahla, he is the master. Officially, all those burned were the victims of a fire. But you won't find any evidence of such damage around those dates in the local archives.

Melany took a deep breath and suppressed a shiver. What had Almog Herskowitz said? If Hitler had really believed that he would reincarnate to continue his diabolical mission, he must necessarily have made certain to empower his *tulku* to achieve his ambitions.

-- Krueger would therefore have had a treasure and radioactive elements at his disposal. Or worse. But let's stay within the logic. Who would they be intended for? Have you managed to track it down?

Again Hanussen looked at his watch. He had barely two minutes left.

-- Krueger was hoping that I would guide him to a head of state. A dictator, of course. But all my calculations, based on the methods taken from *Tantra*, pointed me in the same direction. Southeast Asia. I discovered a place, Banda Aceh. A date that would correspond to the birth of a candidate, less than thirty years ago. A profile. That of an orphan with no family. Unfortunately, that's all I know.

-- Do you really think that such information would have been enough for Krueger to find his protégé?, Melany asked. Unfortunately, the 2004 tsunami must have created thousands of orphans. How many would be thirty years old today? Don't you have any other indication?

-- Only three letters.

-- Letters?

-- Yes. I, H and A. The candidate's name should contain those three letters. I tried to find out more but my meditation was interrupted each time.

-- Assuming that Krueger has identified his ideal candidate, what would his plan be?

-- Haven't you figured it out yet? Hanussen, resting his hand on the handle of his door, was annoyed. Krueger wants to provoke a coup in a country where there are many extremists. Once he puts his protégé in charge of the country, he will put at his disposal the most radical deterrent there is. In what form? Uranium enriched in sufficient quantities to make a dirty bomb or an already assembled nuclear device? I don't know. But he's been working there for at least ten years ..., he concluded with a gulp as he got out of the vehicle.

-- Ten years I've been a prisoner in this city where half the population displays the number 88 somewhere and wakes up every morning screaming Heil Hitler.

***

Back at the hotel, they wondered about the urgency of communicating to Franckel or Anat the incredible and terrifying information they had gathered from Hanussen. Their attempt to infiltrate *Earth and Sharing*, in the only way they thought possible, had failed immediately. At their level, there was nothing else they could do. The mission they had set for themselves would have to end there. Melany was about to dial the number the Israeli had given her, but Jeffrey dissuaded her. Hanussen had insisted that they leave Kahla as soon as possible. They agreed to contact her as soon as they reached the airport, before jumping on the first plane back to the United States.

Jeffrey's cell phone vibrated just as they were finishing packing their bags. He picked it up, listened, turned pale and replied that he would do his best.

-- What's going on?, Melany asked.

-- That was the institute where my brother is. He just had a stroke. It's not the first time, but his condition is quite serious. They managed to resuscitate him and put him in intensive care.

-- I'm sorry, Melany whispered, taking his hand.

They hugged each other for a few moments. The hotel receptionist expressed astonishment when they returned the key in the middle of the night, but a substantial tip put an end to her curiosity.

Once Kahla had been left behind, the road stretched across a plain surrounded by low hills beyond a wooded landscape that couldn't be seen at night. The first Erfurt-Berlin flight that would allow them to catch a connection to Washington took off at dawn and they decided to spend the night near the airport. The car radio, hooked up to a local station, alternated between information and folk music. Both were so absorbed in their thoughts that they paid no attention to the words and music coming out of the speakers. Melany suddenly felt she had enough of being invaded by airs to the glory of the country loves of a shepherdess and a city dweller. She scanned the station until she came across a classical music station broadcasting from Bayreuth.

-- Wagner, and Wagner again!, Jeffrey rasped.

-- Do you want me to find another station?, Melany smiled, who was sometimes amused by his grumpy side.

-- We're being followed!

-- But no, I just stumbled across two programs at random. If you want, I'll find you a German rap station. Unless you would prefer ...

-- Melany, we really are being followed. Look behind you.

A dark gray four-wheel drive Mercedes was following the same route as them at a distance of about thirty meters.

-- Are you sure?, Melany asked anxiously.

-- I didn't pay attention at first, but he's driving with his corner lights on. I just slowed down to let him pass us and he did the same.

They were not far from an intersection of two national highways. To the right, there was a small forest covered with snow that stretched down to a river whose surface reflected short bursts of light. No sooner had Jeffrey finished speaking than the Mercedes turned on its headlights and accelerated with a roar of its powerful engine. Jeffrey had complained that he couldn't rent a bigger vehicle, but the little Toyota was all Hertz had had available the day before. The car overtook them in a fraction of a second and made a U-turn in a squeal of tires. The lights blinded them and Jeffrey had to brake sharply.

The four doors immediately flew open and just as many men waving handguns sprang out.

-- *Steig aus dem Auto aus!*, or 'Get out of the car', the driver shouted. Hands on your heads. Hurry up.

Melany instinctively touched the reminder icon on her cell phone before obeying. She heard Anat's distant voice exclaim: "Ms. Carson?" after only one ring.

-- We're being kidnapped!, she exclaimed.

The rest unfolded at breakneck speed.

Two men grabbed Jeffrey, searched him, and forced him to settle into the back of the Mercedes. Another one pulled Melany out of her seat, grabbed her cell phone, removed the battery and threw it into the snow towards the river.

-- Who are you? And by what right?, she cried in vain.

The man didn't even hide his face. He had the head of a weasel with a shaved head. Cauliflower ears. He subjected her to the same fate as Jeffrey, lingering with relish on her breasts, buttocks and inner thighs, before pushing her back into her seat. He then sat down behind the wheel while his sidekick sat in the back seat with the barrel of his pistol against the young woman's neck.

The doors of both vehicles slammed with nearly perfect synchronization. The Toyota made a U-turn and headed back to Kahla, followed by the all-terrain vehicle behind which Jeffrey, who was now leaning forward with his head between his thighs, had been forced to stop.

Melany was paralyzed with fear.

-- Chapter 25 --

The premises of *Earth and Sharing* were housed in a recently constructed, plain-looking building located near a small industrial area a few kilometers from Kahla. The interior was a maze of corridors opening onto deserted offices with the exception of a handful of guards whose role must have encompassed much more than a security function, given their armament.

The walls were covered with posters extolling the merits and achievements of the NGO. Photographs of hungry but smiling children that *Earth and Sharing* employees were distributing food and drinking water to. Panoramic views of refugee camps. Enlargements of press clippings. The entire layout of the ground floor was probably intended to allay any suspicions about the real business of the organization.

The four men framing Melany and Jeffrey pushed them down the stairs to the basement. The atmosphere here was very different here.

The walls were covered with posters in honor of the Third Reich, some originals protected by frames, others simple reproductions glued to the walls.

The portrait of Hitler as a leader, father of the nation, protector of women and children, and even as a military leader appeared everywhere. The floor was covered with worm-eaten parquet, and while the lighting was reminiscent of the bunkers of the 1940's, the network of light bulbs protected by wire mesh added a vintage feel to the interior architecture that wouldn't have been out of place in a movie studio.

Jeffrey and Melany were led to the end of the last corridor and into an emptied archive room. The room smelled of urine and detergent. The ground was plastered with unidentifiable splashes. In its center, a table and two metal chairs. Handcuffs connected by chains were attached to the steel.

-- You're completely out of your minds!, Jeffrey protested when the four men pushed them inside.

-- Muzzles!, barked the one who had driven the all-terrain vehicle. And now take off your clothes!

Two of their captors left the room and closed the door behind them. Those that remained had been cast in the same mold. Tall in stature, blue eyes, blond hair cut short, straight nose, greedy lips fringed with a cynical or vicious grin.

-- That's exactly what I'm saying, you people are sick!, Jeffrey cursed. Do you really think we're going to be impressed by your little game? We're American tourists. The consulate knows where to find us. Do you want to trigger a diplomatic incident between the United States and Germany?

The slap from the man in black knocked Jeffrey's head back. He caught himself on the corner of the metal table and swore. The sharp edge of the table had gashed open his palm, and blood was beginning to flow. He pulled himself together and stepped towards them with one fist clenched.

-- Jeffrey, stop!, Melany whispered. It's useless.

Then, to the two men responsible for their interrogation:

-- My companion doesn't speak German. Speak to me, I will answer as best I can.

His intervention made the interrogator who seemed to be in charge smile.

-- You've been told to get naked!, he spat out in heavily accented English.

Without another word, Melany undid the buttons on her coat, which fell to the ground and covered the chains and handcuffs intended for her. She lifted the sides of her sweater, under the indifferent gaze of the torturers who had undoubtedly maimed more than one body as beautiful as hers. Jeffrey also took off his peacoat, not taking his eyes off Melany. A moment later, her two tattoos appeared: the cross of Wotan on her stomach and the stylized swastika on her shoulder.

The Nazi jumped up and glanced at his sidekick in astonishment.

-- *Scheiße, was zum Teufel ist das?*, German for "Shit, what in Hell is that?".

-- First of all, you should tell us why you kidnapped us, and just who you are exactly!, Melany demanded in a firm voice and a disdainful tone. Then we might answer your questions.

There was a moment of hesitation. Then the man standing closest to her forced Melany to sit down and the other one motioned to Jeffrey to do the same. The temperature of the room was deliberately kept low and the young woman, now in panties and bra, began to shiver with cold. The Nazis seized her bag, her coat and Jeffrey's coat and left the room without a word.

Once left alone, Jeffrey pointed to the ceiling to indicate the presence of a surveillance camera equipped with a microphone.

-- I think you should put your sweater back on before we catch our death of cold, he said with false assurance.

-- Why do I always have to find myself half-naked in situations like this?, Melany swore while pulling on her clothes.

-- Under other circumstances, I wouldn't complain about it.

-- Seriously? Couldn't you find anything else to cheer me up?

-- Yes, maybe, but I don't think that now is the time.

-- Try again ...

-- If you really want me to. I think I'm a little bit in love with you.

Melany gave a nervous laugh. Jeffrey had chosen the right moment to declare his love.

-- You couldn't tell me anything worse, she quipped. That's the sort of thing you say when you think you don't have a chance of getting away. But since I'm as stupid as you are, you might as well know it ... I feel like I do too. Could you just take the "little bit" out of your sentence?

They remained for a few moments without exchanging a word or a glance, with the impression of living a moment of pure absurdity. Neither of them would ever have thought of exchanging those words in a torture chamber. Jeffrey wound up breaking the silence.

-- And now? What's next, in your opinion?

Melany shrugged her shoulders in resignation.

-- At least they figured out who we are. Now that they know we're in the same camp as they are, we have a chance of getting out ...

The possibility of pretending they didn't know they were under surveillance was minimal, but whatever the case, it was better to continue this comedy. Melany wasn't giving in to panic, which was the most important thing.

They were left to stew for several hours and were exhausted, cold and sleepy when the door finally opened on the two men, who ordered them to follow them. They took the elevator, which took them to the third and last floor of the building.

A dark brown stoneware pavement covered the floor and this time no paintings or posters cluttered the walls, which were painted in shades of green.

They walked past an interior window opening onto a room with electronic panels, where half a dozen individuals of both sexes were feverishly busy in front of double computer screens. The man escorting Jeffrey pushed him forward roughly.

-- Look in front of you!

The Nazis quickened their pace to a padded door with a videophone in front to which they presented themselves before pressing a button.

A click.

Jeffrey and Melany found themselves in a huge office, elegant despite the somewhat old-fashioned taste of its occupant, who had a fondness for shades of green. Their escort slipped away. Indirect lighting revealed furniture that would not have been out of place in a 1960's apartment. An antique world map stood on a rotating base in the middle of the room. On the main wall, facing the windows, a gigantic fresco depicted the planet and its political boundaries. Elsewhere, there was only leather and chrome. Nostalgia was definitely a constant in Kahla.

A man of about sixty was sitting behind a glass plate in the shape of a half-moon, facing two armchairs of the same design and covered in black leather. With a cigarette in his lips, in front of an ashtray overflowing with cigarette butts, he was totally absorbed by some documents that had been placed in front of him.

The man pointed to the chairs and didn't look up until they were seated.

-- There are a lot of things that you're going to have to explain to me!, he announced in English.

-- What if we just began at the beginning, as among civilized people!, Jeffrey hissed. On the other hand, we don't know who you are.

The man's gaze wandered from one to the other, his lips pursed, his features expressionless, except for his eyes, which were animated by a strange fever that approached madness.

-- Indeed!, he conceded suddenly. What would our world be without a minimum of civility? My name is Gerhard Krueger.

The memory came back to Melany in an instant. She saw herself again in the central office of the INR, playing on the keyboard of a computer the day after the dinner during which her mother had mentioned the existence of Hitler's will. A few minutes before running into Jeffrey by chance.

-- Well met!, she said appreciatively. If I remember correctly, Krueger was your mother's maiden name and Gerhard was your middle name. Am I wrong, *Mr. Soloviev?*

A veil passed surreptitiously through the eyes of the former KGB agent, confirming her assertion, if there were any need. At least three decades had passed since his last photograph had been archived by the CIA, but Melany never forgot a face, and the years hadn't affected him too much.

Jeffrey stared at her in astonishment and admiration.

-- This is Soloviev? Really? *Our* Alexei Soloviev?

-- Or his ghost, since he died in a helicopter crash on the Russian border.

-- You know a lot more than I had imagined!, the Russian said, getting up to walk around his desk.

He leaned on the glass plate, exactly between Melany and Jeffrey. A packet of Bulgarian cigarettes protruded from his shirt pocket. He had let his own burn in the ashtray, which gave off a foul odor and stank up the whole space. Once standing, he was impressive. He was almost 6'4" tall and had the physique of an athlete familiar with the most demanding sports. His features, which were a little bit baby-like, had been hollowed out by the years and his hair was beginning to thin out, which accentuated the intensity of his eyes, which were a crisp blue and cold as metal. The mixture of Russian and German blood had made him an Aryan-type specimen bordering on perfection, except for his misaligned, tobacco-yellowed teeth.

-- I have the feeling that we're going to have a long, fruitful conversation ...

-- Chapter 26 --

Moscow -- 1995

It had been more than three years since Alexei Soloviev had discovered the will. It had also been thirty months since he had unsuccessfully tried to trade his discovery for passage to the West, an initiative due to a moment of weakness he regretted today. How many times had he read and reread the front page of the message offered to posterity by Hitler. At first, he had classified the Führer's words as emanating from a diseased brain. The very idea of life after death was contrary to the dialectical materialism that guided his entire education.

All the more reason for this ridiculous assertion on reincarnation written by a man at the end of his life, defeated and on the brink of suicide. But the energy emanating from the document was unsettling, to say the least.

"My spiritual will.

This is the most important of my wills. I donate it to posterity as I have donated my person to Germany and I know that my successor, Grand Admiral Dönitz, will make good use of it, even though he has not been initiated".

The writing was fine and tight, with a tendency to lean towards the right. Consonants spread out like claw marks framed small vowels, some as simple as a single stroke. A graphologist would have concluded that the author of these lines was a megalomaniac in the midst of depression, whose sanity had deteriorated rapidly, as evidenced by the barely recognizable signature.

"Beneath my public personality, that of the leader whom you have blindly followed, lies a strong and self-sacrificing soul.

The fight we fought together has led to a great victory. Blood has bathed the sacred soil of Germany. The destruction that followed this necessary war was inscribed in the runes and it was a sacrifice that pleased the Masters of the Universe.

Today, I will join them, with an exalted heart, a joyful soul, a clear conscience, satisfied to have accomplished my duty and followed my path.

The German people have proved that they are the greatest of all and that this Aryan fluid flowing in our veins, far from drying up, will soon become an unstoppable flood because the victory I have promised you is inescapable.

We must be able to accept a minor defeat, cleansing to the soul, in order to return to combat, strengthened by certainties.

The great German philosopher Nietzsche wrote: "What doesn't kill me makes me stronger." But what Nietzsche had foreseen by evoking the cycles of eternal recommencement, I have discovered. Death is not an end, it is only a beginning.

In my capacity as Führer, chosen by the highest divine authorities who inspire my people, I set out to explore the reality of the chain of lives, because one existence is not enough to reshape the world according to its true nature, as stated in Indo-European texts. They forged our culture and united the diverse origins of the great Aryan people.

With the help of scholars, ascetics and monks, I was initiated into the secret of the wheel of life and it was given to me to understand and share the methods that will allow you to find me, alive and equal to what I was during this earthly passage, born of a father and a mother in a future generation.

No matter who they will be and no matter where they will be, for you will be a legion to greet my return. It doesn't matter in what year, because the coming battle will be the last, before entering an area of peace and prosperity that will last a thousand years, as I have promised you.

My people, my compatriots, fear not. Death is only a door that opens at the entrance to a corridor. I will soon knock on the next one. I will reincarnate for you, thus pursuing my destiny. Together, we will finally eliminate this sub-humanity that hinders us in our race to the divine.

In this life I was only a child of Germany; in the next, I will lead you in your final battles.

Prepare yourselves to celebrate the Father of Victory ..."

Adolph Hitler

The following pages contained the translation of excerpts from a Sanskrit grimoire that he had also found, without any interest. Unlike the will, which he had managed to sneak out of the archives, the three volumes of the ***Kalakarma*** *Tantra* were far too large to escape the scrutiny he was subjected to every day before leaving the building.

What really interested Soloviev were the pages attached to the will, typewritten, and without any apparent meaning. If this information was encrypted, it was of great value. But the Russian agent had no notion of cryptography. He would have needed access to powerful computers, or he would have had to surround himself with specialists, who were not lacking in the same building. What could the following sequence of letters, similar to seventeen other blocks, possibly mean?

yxxs bqwt nyry pxwe pxpt wwbo detb ykzt huha llsk fuhj fjxb ordy ogyq jpfy eojb ehly flfu ljca dbxh jkmu pppj etod ebqu evwo njmk ijud lvdf bdqi hqzt mnok focu bjgr mhaq rdkl xfcc

Soloviev put away the copy on which he spent long minutes every day, having practically nothing else to do from the moment he arrived in the archives until he left for home.

At around 1 p.m., he stopped to go to the canteen. Since this was inside a group of buildings and overlooked a central courtyard, it was the only time of the day when he could see natural light.

His former colleague, Fyodor Gurevich, was already devouring his portion of stew with a glass of tea. He slid out his tray, containing a plate of *shchi* and a few *pelmeni*, so that he was sitting facing him. Alexei was not the talkative type, but loneliness weighed on him after so many years spent surrounded by his colleagues in premises ten times larger than the one he had been assigned to.

-- Careful with the *shchi*, sneered Fyodor. Cabbage makes you fart.

-- And who would that bother?

-- I don't know ... Imagine that Ivana is suddenly seized by a desire to visit you. They say there's not even an air vent where you work.

-- If you can call it work ...

Ivana Hvostoff was a fairly recent recruit, a little bit plump but with a bewitching look, whom Alexei had never met but who was often the subject of salacious discussions among the older members of the team.

-- Your transfer request still hasn't been successful?, Fyodor asked while lifting a huge portion of the stew to his mouth.

-- No. And watch how you eat. You're going to choke yourself to death some day.

-- Don't worry, I have a big mouth. But, *pizdec*, what are you doing all day with Adolph and Eva? Who is still interested in what happened half a century ago?

-- You have no idea, Alexei said evasively, following his first *pelmini* with a sip of *kompot*, a drink made from a seasonal fruit marinated in boiling water.

A memory suddenly came to mind.

-- Remind me: Ivana was recruited into which section?

-- Why? Do you want to do her yourself? Be careful, it looks easy, but she's a hell of a piece. You risk breaking your teeth.

-- Just curious, but answer me.

-- She was trained as a cryptologist, that's all I know.

Soloviev concentrated on his plate. That was exactly what he remembered. But how to gain access to the young woman and, even more difficult, how to obtain her cooperation without betraying himself? This was in the realm of the impossible, and he quickly gave up on the idea.

Luck was on his side, however, because, three days later, Ivana Hvostoff, who usually contented herself with a snack swallowed quickly in front of her computer screen, appeared in the canteen. She was alone. The other tables were occupied. It was a godsend. He asked for permission to sit across from her, which she agreed to.

Soloviev was quite a handsome man, but too rugged in appearance to have the charm to which women are sensitive. Ivana had a pretty face, but a rather full figure. She was reading a women's magazine while eating a hotpot. She barely looked at him as he sat down. How should he approach it?

Once more luck smiled at him with the appearance of Fyodor who, seeing him sitting in front of the young woman, displayed a mocking and complicit smile.

-- Ivana, he roared. Have you finally met Alexei, a legend in the archives department?

She looked up from her magazine, intrigued.

Alexei Soloviev introduced himself, hoping that Fyodor would not insist on keeping them company.

-- Okay, well, I'll leave you to it, he grinned before joining a group of colleagues who were beckoning him from a nearby table.

-- Soloviev ..., Ivana repeated. Are you the one who was transferred to the SMERSH archives?

He nodded.

-- So you have access to all documents and items seized from Hitler's bunker?

-- As well as from the Eagle's Nest and the Reichstag. Yes. The room is not big and we have it filled up to the ceiling.

The young woman suddenly seemed very excited.

-- It must be exciting to have access to so many historical documents. Evidence of a great victory. I would love to visit your department.

-- Unfortunately, access is restricted, Soloviev said regretfully. You know the rules. And then, what could be of interest to you?

-- I'm a cryptologist. I'm a beginner, but it has become my passion since I finished my studies. I've heard that you have several Enigma machines in the SMERSH archives? Our training at the center was mainly theoretical. We were shown the plans of the German encryption tool, but I've never seen one up close.

Soloviev felt the blood beating violently in his temples, which was his only way of expressing his emotions.

-- I do in fact have two, he confided, willingly appropriating the objects for himself. I don't even know if they work.

-- Oh, that's not difficult to verify, Ivana continued, now indifferent to her magazine and even her plate. You plug in the plug, type in a text, any text, after putting the machine in the encryption position, and then repeat the operation with the encrypted text to make sure it shows you the original. It's a fairly simple operation, as long as you know the code corresponding to the right cogs. That appears in the first three blocks of the message. I'll show you ...

She grabbed a pen from her bag and spread out a paper napkin on which she began to draw a schematic diagram of an Enigma machine, which she bristled with arrows associated with captions. Ivana was right to say that she was passionate.

-- It was a German engineer, Arthur Scherbius, who designed it on the basis of a Danish invention. Different versions of the device were used by the Nazis to transmit their military messages. They were unaware up until their defeat that the British had managed to reverse engineer their encryption system and had thus gained a colossal intelligence advantage.

Within a few minutes Soloviev found himself with the operating instructions for the most sophisticated electrical coding machines of the last war in his hands. A technology that had obviously become obsolete since then.

The two machines were stored on racks in a section of the archives he rarely went. He had taken the trouble to clean them two or three years before. The idea that an Enigma might have been used to encode Hitler's documents had crossed his mind, but since he didn't know how to use it, he quickly gave up on it.

After connecting the two machines, Soloviev precisely reproduced the procedure by Ivana had told him about. They worked perfectly.

When he composed the text transmitted by Hitler on the first Enigma, nothing happened. The machine didn't recognize any of the characters.

He attempted the same operation on the second one, which had a label that identified it as belonging to Luftwaffe headquarters.

This time, the miracle happened ...

Thus, after years of trying in vain to understand its meaning, Alexei Soloviev was finally able to decipher the most important pages of Hitler's will.

One month later, he resigned from the archives of the former KGB.

***

-- I'm going to save us some time!, Soloviev announced, his features frozen in an unfathomable expression. No need to pretend that you are tourists passing through Kahla to visit our porcelain factory. I know you came here to snoop around. I would now like to know how and why. And I don't have a great deal of patience.

Jeffrey had concocted a plan in his head. It was worth what it was worth, but he hadn't come up with anything else.

-- Ms. Carson and I have resigned from an agency under the State Department, he asserted, holding Soloviev's gaze. We have heard of some turmoil in the supremacist movements and this has led us to take a closer look, independently, at alliances between action groups of all kinds.

-- For what purpose?

-- We do not want America to become a cesspool invaded by the dregs of humanity. We guessed that a large-scale action was being prepared to counter this nauseating phenomenon ... And we want to be part of it.

Melany took a deep breath and confirmed it with a nod. Jeffrey continued, making it up as he went. He had to make an effort on himself because he hated having to pretend that he belonged to the Nazi camp. He explained that he and Melany had discovered the same ideal. The Western world was in full decadence and the situation in Europe was by far the worst since the Judeo-Masonic conspiracy had forced opened its doors, opening the old continent to massive immigration that benefited the supporters of globalization. America was not doing much better, either. The races mixed there shamelessly, and Wall Street was in the hands of the Jews. This was for the convictions part of it. As for the journey that had led them to Krueger, it had begun in Kurdistan when Melany, then an INR agent, had heard about the *Father of Victory* while on a mission. It turned out that her own mother ...

-- ... You may not have a very clear recollection of that episode, Jeffrey insisted.

He continued in the same vein, constructing a story parallel to the one they had really lived. Melany's mother had put her daughter on the trail of the *will*, as the result of which her daughter became close to the American Nazi movements, met the Mitchell family in Odyssey, sympathized with them and narrowly escaped from the FBI during a raid in which the local leader, Derek, was killed.

-- How did you recognize me?, Soloviev asked.

-- Your data sheet stops in 1998, a date that more or less corresponds to your departure from the FSB, explained Melany.

Alexei Soloviev nodded. For a fraction of a second, he looked confused.

-- Show me your tattoos, he said suddenly.

Melany gladly complied. Their strategy seemed to be working. She lifted her sweater, revealing the Wotan cross which was still visible enough. Soloviev leaned forward.

-- It's a nice job. As pretty as your story. There are, unfortunately, several points that do not fit.

A rush of anguish gripped Melany's chest.

-- If we can enlighten you ..., Jeffrey said.

-- Oh, that would take too long. For example, you would have to invent the reason for your presence in Kahla, without betraying Doctor Hanussen, whose name you are careful to never pronounce.

Soloviev turned to press the button on an intercom.

-- Bring him up!

The medium soon appeared, handcuffed, flanked by two guards who pushed him so hard towards the middle of the room that he lost his balance. His face was swollen and his right eyelid was completely closed. Blood stained the collar of his jacket, one sleeve of which was torn.

-- Doctor Hanussen, Soloviev said. Repeat in front of our guests what you have confessed to my men.

The medium looked up bleakly at Melany and Jeffrey. Fear and despair obscured any expression of regret.

-- They belong to the CIA, he said in a whisper.

-- But that's not true!, Melany protested.

Indifferent to her protests, Soloviev continued.

-- And what did they come to do in Kahla?

-- To question me, because they know that I have helped you. The US government is on your trail and these two have come looking for evidence.

Hanussen opened a desk drawer and pulled out a Makarov semi-automatic, the pistol that had never left him since his days as a field agent. He pointed the handgun at Jeffrey, moved it slowly towards Melany, and finally fixed Hanussen in his sight.

-- What did you tell them, Doctor?

-- Nothing, Gerhard, I assure you.

-- Ms. Carson, I am in a good position to know that the CIA invented a temporary ink for fake tattoos. I know this because the Soviet secret services had developed the same thing, long before you did. So it won't do you any good to keep on lying. What did Doctor Hanussen teach you?

-- Not much!, Melany protested, suppressing the trembling of all her limbs. We wanted to know his methods, he enlightened us in his theory ...

She took a deep breath and let it rush out.

-- And believe it or not, we do not belong to the CIA. Everything we've been discovering in the last few days makes us think we're delirious. What serious field agent could pass on to his superiors a report on ancient texts, a dubious will, all related to Buddhist beliefs, the Dalai Lama and Hitler? The INR has nothing to do with the CIA and anyway we have been excluded since we started this private investigation. What Jeffrey told you is true ...

The blast echoed against the walls of the vast room. A red flower appeared on Hanussen's chest and he lowered his head for a moment, looking astonished, before slowly collapsing, held back by the guards who let go of him and retreated a step.

Jeffrey wanted to leap to his rescue but Melany intervened. There was nothing more to do for the magus. She felt an intense grief, drenched in guilt and at the same time a choking hatred for Soloviev.

-- I will have more questions for you later, announced the former Soviet agent, as he stowed his gun in the drawer.

He immediately lit a new cigarette.

-- It remains to be seen which one of you I will eliminate first if your answers don't suit me.

-- Chapter 27 --

Soloviev

First decade of the new century.

The coded message contained geographic coordinates, along with the description of access to two underground passages just a few kilometers apart in the Thuringia region.

The first tunnel, which led to a cavity dug inside the Merkers mines, had already been discovered by the U.S. military, which Hitler could not have foreseen at the time he wrote his will. The United States had succeeded in depriving the Soviets of a colossal treasure by seizing the contents of the improvised vault, which was discovered due to the testimonies of the local population before the USSR took control of the region.

Soloviev had gone into a mad rage when he learned that 8,307 gold bars, 55 boxes of gold scrap, and dozens of bags filled with rings of the same metal, sometimes set with precious stones, all snatched from the victims of the Nazi death camps, had fallen into the hands of the capitalists at a time when the victorious Motherland was financially strapped and the Russian people were on the verge of starvation.

But, according to the deciphered documents, the second cache dug under the network of tunnels that crisscrossed the heart of the Wapelsberg contained a much greater quantity of the precious metal, in the form of ingots stamped by the Deutsche Reichsbank and marked with the Nazi eagle. A second tunnel, which started from the underground cache, led to an artificial cellar protected by a lead-coated armored door. Access was only possible if you were equipped with radiation-resistant clothing.

The document did not give a precise indication of the contents of the second cache, but Soloviev had a good idea of what he would find there. The archives of SMERSH contained some files about the uranium reserves of Nazi Germany, several tons having escaped the Russians as well as the Americans and the British, as well as about the capacity to enrich the same uranium with the primitive centrifuges of the laboratories of the Third Reich.

It was astounding that neither the Americans nor the Soviets had taken German research in this area seriously towards the end of the war, since the Allies had been convinced by their respective spies that Hitler had abandoned his nuclear program as early as 1942.

The Third Reich had in fact been only six months away from completing its own atom bomb on the day of Hitler's suicide. The Germans had the necessary know-how and technology. Surrounded by the Allies, they lacked only the time to carry out the first decisive tests. This had not prevented the Uranverein from exploding a "dirty" bomb in 1945. Dirty, in other words radioactive, and more powerful than the sum of its explosives.

But an unpleasant surprise awaited Soloviev during his first exploration of the Wapelsberg. The Red Army had pounded the hill so thoroughly that almost nothing remained of the REIMAGH and its tens of kilometers of underground galleries. The Nazi treasure was buried under thousands of tons of rocks. Only the main entrance to the factory from which the Messerschmitt 262's, the first German jet planes, had emerged, had been symbolically preserved, adjoined by a plaque in memory of the martyred prisoners who had died of malnutrition and ill-treatment during their forced labor.

However, Soloviev was not a man to abandon the project that had germinated in his brain forged in the greatest discipline. To survive, he had to set up his own security agency, providing bodyguards and intelligence to the oligarchs, whose recent fortunes had been chronicled in the Western and Russian media.

His frustration at the collapse of the Soviet Empire had reconciled him to his German heritage. From being a fervent communist, he had slipped into a similar ideology while being convinced that he held the key to a radiant future for humanity. A future predicted and manufactured by the two men he admired most: Stalin and Hitler.

If they were to be attacked by a sufficiently powerful external threat, would not the great Germany and eternal Russia have every reason to unite? The idea of a Europe built on a common ideal from which sub-humanity would be excluded had made its way into the brain of the former KGB agent. Like the Roman Empire in its time, the West was already facing repeated assaults from religious extremists and barbarians. They were dreaming of a *khalifate*? He would build them a Reich! These useful idiots were easily manipulated, since he would advocate the end of decadence in the name of a higher ideal symbolized by the return of a chosen man. It would be the end of the monopoly of finance and of cynical and sentimental traders. Make way for the warriors. For Wotan's men. Thuringia would be at the heart of the birth of the Fourth Reich, just as the Führer had intended.

A Reich of peace and harmony that would last at least a thousand years.

He spent the next ten years trying to find another opening in the granite rock, sometimes in the company of local geologists. The gallery from which the access to the underground cavern had been dug no longer existed. The most powerful detectors were not powerful enough to detect metal at such depths, even if there were large amounts of it.

These years of hope, failure, rage and frustration also saw him move closer to Russian neo-Nazi movements, such as Pamyat, where he found former KGB agents, police officers sacked for minor misconduct, dying Red Army soldiers and officers without pensions. He was able to form a sort of club with which he partly shared his secrets. Some took him for a madman, others followed him blindly. Many left behind by Soviet communism without even a religious belief to cling to in their misfortune, softened their despair by forcing themselves to believe in the return of a warrior Messiah who would restore their glory. The reincarnation of Hitler? Some would have preferred Stalin, but why not? The post-war period had failed to produce real leaders. Their hierarchical universe, reassuring because it was hostile to individual freedom, had collapsed and the Jews had regained power.

They were ripe for the advent of the *Father of Victory*.

Soloviev's many stays in the Thuringia region, especially in Kahla, brought him into contact with an underground world of Nazi sympathizers, ultra-nationalists, and ultra-violent radical communists advocating permanent revolution. This was, according to the latest information, led by organizations such as Hezbollah in Lebanon, the PFLP and Hamas in the Palestinian Territories, the Houtis of Yemen, or the GAM and Jemaah Islamiyah in Indonesia. Underground financial networks that everyone fed according to their means supported all these movements from Germany and other European countries.

It was a crack-addled skinhead tattooed with Nazi symbols from his ankles to his chin who finally directed Soloviev towards a natural opening hidden in the western facade of the Wapelsberg, some two hundred meters from the collapsed tunnel mentioned in the will.

The small cavity, isolated from view by abundant vegetation from spring to fall and by snow during the winter months, was used as a meeting place, an area for drug dealing and, on occasion, for orgies by a gang of degenerates. A crack opened into a seemingly inaccessible underground passage. Who among the skinhead's accomplices would have cared?

Their disappearance was the subject of features in local newspapers for several days, without ever being explained. Nobody cared very long about a bunch of punks whose only occupation was singing Nazi songs and injecting all kinds of drugs.

Among his clients among the oligarchs, Soloviev had gained the full confidence of a certain Olav Abramovsky, a former Red Army officer who had made a fortune in the supply of gas, the reprocessing of sewage and the recycling of industrial waste, over which he had a monopoly. His assets, after a few ups and downs on the stock market, were estimated at several billion dollars.

By ensuring his safety, accompanying him on his business trips and even spending time on board his yacht and his private jets, Soloviev had become his confidant. He had reached the end of his rope and it was time to ask for help.

Abramosvky had listened to him religiously and told him at the end of his talk that he now had a partner. All means would be placed at his disposal to find the secret cache. As for the application of Hitler's will ... *We will see about that ...*

Substantial funds were needed to overturn the municipal government of Kahla in the following elections. Once Soloviev and Abramovsky's pawns were in place at all levels of the local authorities, obtaining the necessary permits to excavate around the Wapelsberg was child's play.

A problem arose, which turned out to be insoluble until the dozen clandestine workers imported from Turkey finally crossed the last rocky barrier separating them from the cache.

In front of them were lined up more than a thousand boxes, each one containing fifty gold bars stamped by the Reich. Abramovsky, his eyes bulging and his forehead drenched in sweat, then revealed to Soloviev that he had had only one goal: to become the richest man on the planet. Thanks to this discovery, his goal had been achieved.

Soloviev said nothing. He just noted the information.

The workers, who couldn't believe their eyes, were directed to open the armored door and check the inside of the second cache, despite the warning "Danger -- Radiation" written in Gothic script. They couldn't read German any more than they had access to protective clothing.

Not one of them would survive.

Soloviev, for his part, felt obliged to honor Hitler's will.

It was on the basis of the same respect for a man whose last will he believed himself to be the repository that he would soon set out in search of a medium capable of following the indications of ***Kalakarma*** *Tantra* to the letter. Many of his actions would be inspired by the same sense of duty towards Hitler, such as the theft of the Golden Urn in the People's Republic of China, where lavish donations were made to a Tibetan Buddhist monastery in return for aid that would materialize in the presence at his side of two multilingual monks instructed in the rites of reincarnation.

But first it would be necessary to get rid of Abramovsky.

Soloviev was given the opportunity when the oligarch told him he had purchased an MI-26 Halo transport helicopter. The enormous machine, capable of lifting up to 56 tons, would allow them to repatriate the entire treasure of the Third Reich in a few back and forth trips. Soloviev would have his share, of course, on the order of ten percent, like any businessman, on the condition that he abandoned his foolish plans. The helicopter was carrying enough explosives to bury the second cache forever, the contents of which were dangerous and unsaleable as is, except to terrorist organizations. "Bad for business," Abramovsky said when Soloviev made one last attempt to convince him to hold on to the uranium.

The former KGB agent had already officially changed his identity by obtaining high-quality false papers in the name of Gerhard Krueger. Just as the helicopter was about to take off, he announced that he had just received an urgent message telling him that his daughter had been hospitalized and that he was being replaced by one of his men, a man named Petrov. Deliberately forgetting the small aluminum suitcase that contained his passport in the name of Soloviev inside the craft.

The explosives it was carrying made the victims of the accident unidentifiable.

Soloviev was dead. Krueger had just been born.

One week later, he met Karl Hanussen at a small cabaret in Berlin where the magus was showing off his skills.

-- Chapter 28 --

Kahla

Present time

The freezing cell contained nothing but a thankfully empty commode and a narrow mattress thrown onto the floor on which they huddled together in the vain hope of snatching a few hours of sleep.

Their interrogation had lasted a short time, with Soloviev evidently having other concerns. Convinced that they belonged to the CIA, he was content to conclude that he was deferring his decision on their fate until a later time. If the Western intelligence services were so close on his trail, there was much greater urgency.

They had been thrown a bottle of water. They were not entitled to any food.

In the first minutes of their incarceration, Melany had had the greatest difficulty in containing the shaking she had experienced since the cold-blooded execution of Karl Hanussen. Jeffrey tried to comfort her. Neither of them immediately dared to address the question of their future. Amateurs that they were, they had managed to track down Soloviev and to discover his plan. Some consolation!

Once she had calmed down, Melany whispered in Jeffrey's ear that they still had hope. Anat had received her call. She knew of their situation. But she didn't know where they were and had no way of locating them. Assuming she succeeded, how long would it take her to convince the German authorities to intervene? And in what way?

In order to calm their anguish and to keep their minds busy, they forced themselves to recapitulate in low voices what they had learned so far. Soloviev's attitude, his goals, his obvious megalomania and his ability to kill in cold blood revealed an implacable personality inhabited by a deranged brain. The former KGB agent had stumbled upon a windfall when he discovered Hitler's will and had devoted his life to carrying out the Führer's plans. Assuming that they were countered in time, even the slightest misdeed of which he was now nevertheless capable could lead to regional destabilization, local conflicts, an upsurge in attacks, and the death of innocent people. Probably in the thousands.

Soloviev had the financial means for his ambitions as well as a deterrent force. All that remained was to analyze and understand the esoteric aspects of his operation.

Hanussen had been content to carry out his orders by putting at his service what he considered to be a particular talent that nature had endowed him with. It was in good faith that he had carried out the calculations suggested by the will to find Hitler's *tulku*. He did not know that he was taking on such a heavy responsibility by directing the former agent converted to Nazism to an area as unstable as Indonesia. The worst possible scenario involved a terrorist leader being convinced that he was the reincarnation of the dictator of the Third Reich and taking up the torch on behalf of Alexei Soloviev.

-- I have to tell you something, Melany whispered in the dim light of the cell. During the hypnosis session, Hanussen made me remember a dream. Well, that's what I wanted to believe at the time. But I've been thinking about it ever since. I actually believe that he managed to make me relive something that doesn't necessarily belong to my memory.

-- What do you mean?

-- Not to the memory of my current life, Melany replied in a whisper.

This confession led Jeffrey to pull away from her for a moment. He swore as he roughly moved his elbow against the rough cement floor.

-- Of what?

-- Don't worry, Melany interrupted him. I'm not saying he made me relive a previous life. I've been thinking a lot since Herskowitz: you and finally Hanussen tried to shake my beliefs. Of course, I still don't believe in reincarnation. But nothing rules out the fact that we have inherited a memory associated with our genetic heritage. In this kind of memory of a dream, I saw myself holding the hand of a man who was supposedly my father walking into a barn where animals were being slaughtered. Cows or sheep. It was excruciating. But it didn't feel like a nightmare. I haven't told you about my family yet. Hardly anything about from my parents. But on my father's side, they owned a farm in Minnesota three generations ago. The architecture that I noticed in this second state was that of a typical regional building, with a double-pitched roof, red facades, grain silo, and a propeller vane. Do you think it's possible for regression by hypnosis to awaken some memory buried in our genes? After all, some people look just like their great-grandfathers. Why couldn't we also inherit some memories?

Jeffrey gave himself a few moments to think. The silence, when they were silent, was only broken by the sound of their breathing.

-- In your case, you may be right. But there is a problem. The thesis of genetic memory does not explain most accounts of past memories. I could give you other examples than that kid who remembered being a pilot shot down over the Pacific. I remember reading the story of a young English girl who, at the age of seven during the sixties, was writing songs in medieval French, a language she had no way of knowing. Her case was so intriguing that famous doctors studied her at length. The little girl had only received an elementary education. She was, however, able to describe, in detail, scenes that occurred in the twelfth century in the region of the Cathars. There was also the case of a young blind black slave who achieved worldwide fame as a virtuoso during the nineteenth century. He was able to play Beethoven, Mendelssohn, Bach and Chopin without ever having learned how to play the piano.

Melany looked for a cynical counterpoint to Jeffrey's illustrations, but another rush of anxiety squeezed her throat so tightly that she couldn't say a word. She huddled closer to him. The fact that Soloviev had not yet executed them was not necessarily reassuring. What would happen to them once he was convinced he knew enough?

This questioning was interrupted by the intrusion of Soloviev's guards. The two men in black uniforms ordered them to stand up and face the wall. They found themselves with their wrists bound behind their backs, then pushed out of the cell. Melany told herself that the interrogation would resume. No doubt in a muscular way.

It was with surprise that they found themselves outside the building. The industrial zone, frozen under the snow, was bathed in deathly silence. A distant glow announced the appearance of dawn. An all-terrain Mercedes was parked in front of the door, engine idling, with white smoke rising from the exhaust pipe.

A guard opened the rear door and pushed them inside.

***

The former military base with an airstrip was located about 30 kilometers from Kahla. It had belonged to the STASI, the East German secret police, until that was dismantled following the reunification of Germany. One of the organizations belonging to the Soloviev-Krueger conglomeration now owned it.

The Antonov AN-72 transport aircraft slowly pulled out of its hangar, lining up next to a Boeing 767-300 converted into a military transport at the foot of which half a dozen men were working.

The day had dawned. It had started snowing again. The runway and hangar looked as if they had come out of a black and white film.

As the Mercedes carrying Jeffrey and Melany stopped in front of the Antonov's access gangway, a convoy of eight armored vans joined the rear of the aircraft, whose loading ramp had been lowered. About twenty men riding motorized pallet trucks immediately tackled the cargo. Old crates, mixed with newer containers, began to pile up in the hold of the cargo plane.

A flatbed semi-trailer loaded with leaded barrels and driven by two men in radiation suits joined the convoy just as Jeffrey and Melany reached the top of the gangway. Jeffrey paused for a moment to observe the bustle of crowded trucks and coaches that had just joined them. The guard escorting him pushed him roughly forward.

The interior of the passenger cabin was fitted out as a troop carrier. Two rows of benches faced each other, separated by storage areas and weapon racks. A kind of cage had been built against the bulkhead separating the habitable part from the cargo hold. The guards closed the gate on Melany and Jeffrey. They had to sit on the floor with their hands tied behind their backs.

About twenty men in black uniforms silently settled down in the side rows, placing their helmets on their knees. There was a kind of commotion. All stood up and stretched out their right arms to shout in unison:

-- Heil Hitler!

Soloviev appeared, cigarette in his mouth, dressed in the same uniform as his men. He approached the gate separating the cell from the cockpit and crouched down to get down to the level of his hostages, while two soldiers, who remained three steps behind, pointed the barrels of their assault rifles at them.

-- The two of you are a big problem for me, he spat between the bars of the cage. I've had to rush an operation that wasn't scheduled to take place for another week, and I'm in the process of abandoning premises and infrastructure that cost me a fortune.

-- It's not as if you've worked hard to make that money!, Jeffrey challenged him.

Soloviev turned pale without noticing. A roaring sound made the craft vibrate, drowning out all noise. The door had just been raised. The roar of the engines gradually decreased to a tolerable level. A green light above the cockpit access indicated that the Antonov was ready to take off. The commander was only waiting for clearance from a distant tower.

-- I was tempted to subject you to the same fate as our mutual friend, Doctor Hanussen, Soloviev continued. Your presence is only a source of trouble. But some deaths are more valuable when viewed as sacrifices ...

-- Like that of a fawn on an altar erected to the glory of Odin?, Melany hissed in a voice trembling with rage and fear mixed together.

-- Or of Wotan!, Soloviev concluded without a smile. In the meantime, enjoy the trip and sorry for the discomfort.

-- What is our destination?, Jeffrey asked.

Krueger turned on his heels without answering.

***

Soloviev would have preferred to turn to the civic powers of his homeland, but after Gorbachev's betrayal, Russia was plunged into anarchy. The hopes of an entire people had been dashed and Marxism accused of infamy. The less-than-nothings, like Abramovsky, had become rich thanks to the corruption resulting from repugnant ways of thinking that the Soviet revolution had thought it had erased forever. Finance and therefore usury. Consumption at all costs. Individual freedom to the detriment of the greatest numbers.

By the time he had become Gerhard Krueger, he had convinced himself that the esoteric part of the will was nothing more than the final delirium of a sick brain deteriorated by drug abuse. But, in addition to his respect and recognition of the Führer, he was also aware of the symbol that his last ranting represented. How to rally those nostalgic for the Third Reich and convince them to use the inexhaustible forces of Jihad, without giving them a leader larger than life, an idol to worship, a *Father of Victory* as Hitler had conceived?

Like the Islamists, the neo-Nazis were evil idealists, arrogant and narrow-minded, fascinated by ultra-violence. All were waiting for their Messiah, who would put on the clothes of the Antichrist.

Thanks to Hanussen, who had been recruited after several failures in France and England, the research had led to the discovery of a man corresponding in all points to the idea that Soloviev's allies could have of a leader. A Eurasian gang leader, whose parents had been swept away by the 2004 tsunami. He and his gang were spreading terror in the slums of a city in Indonesia. They robbed tourists to buy weapons, beat up men they caught violating Quranic laws, threatened women with gang rape and sometimes whipped them in public, while preaching the violent application of sharia law on the island of Sumatra.

His father had been a well-to-do merchant and his mother a young Albanian girl. All family possessions having been swept away by the cataclysm, he had been left with the street, its natural violence, and the certainty that the death of his parents and hundreds of thousands of Indonesians was a divine punishment.

Soloviev's specialists had taken him in to train him for the task that would be his, while revealing his "karmic identity" to him. It had taken a long time and a great deal of money to convince him. But he was a natural warlord. An exalted one. They had fed him with anti-Western hatred, instilled in him a vengeful spirit, and had his spirituality forged by a Salafist Imam sympathetic to Nazism. He was ready ...

Ready to take care of more than two hundred million souls, including a small percentage of fanatics who, as everywhere, were the most active and the most conspicuous. In northwestern Sumatra, hardline Islamists who were in no way inferior to Daesh in substance or method were waiting for their hour of glory. All it took was a little help in the form of weapons and money and a breath on a few embers.

During the Third Reich, Hitler had been a living god for the majority of Germans. The Islamists were no different in their fanaticism. And it didn't matter who Soloviev's fellow fighters would be, as long as they enabled him to bring an end to corruption, to the rule of money and individualism.

The West had long been a lazy and bloated giant, which the Jihadists had finally awakened. Since then, the bourgeoisie has been in a panic. The laws had hardened, the masses were surviving in anguish, the system itself was being called into question.

U.S. imperialism had attempted to eradicate not only al-Qaida but even the thinking behind it. That had given birth to Daesh. Was Daesh finished? A more powerful organization would soon see the light of day where Western pigs least expected it. From chaos would arise a new world order that would put an end to this absurd and utterly meaningless concept of individual liberties that benefited only the wealthy and brought only tragedy to humanity.

Soloviev-Krueger proliferated in chaos.

The world was still unaware of the sleeping power represented by millions of Jihadists who were just waiting for a signal, a regrouping, a leader, an implacable leader of men to launch the great final battle.

Armageddon? Why not?

But that was only a legend and he knew better ones. For example, that of a man coming from the depths of the ages and from a mythical land called Shambhala, who would, a thousand incarnations later, dominate the world and lead it towards peace and harmony after a vast housecleaning. A man of whom, according to great occultists, Hitler had been and would be again the incarnation.

Wasn't that the most powerful of myths?

-- Chapter 29 --

Banda Aceh -- Indonesia

Present time

The streets were black with a hysterical crowd. Darwis had not returned to his hometown since the tragedy that took his wife and child. He recognized nothing except the Baitur Rahman Mosque, which had regained its magnificence, with its seven black domes, its seven minarets and its white arcades of Moghul architecture. Modern, European-style houses now replaced the swept and washed-away *panggungs*. Others, which had resisted the cataclysm, displayed their white facades behind brightly colored billboards in typically Asian disorder. Men and women were all dressed in black, the latter for the most part disappearing under the burkas that now replaced their traditional colored hijabs.

Darwis remembered nostalgically the cheerful atmosphere around the stalls, the tinkling of the bells on the delivery tricycles and the smoke from the exhaust fumes that had mixed with the swirls of the mobile restaurants before the tsunami. All of this had given way to an atmosphere of war, and most of the men who came to meet them were brandishing weapons, as did even the women, some of them holding a Kalashnikov in one hand and pushing a stroller in the other.

-- *There they are!,* the crowd suddenly yelled, without him realizing what it was about.

Saragih had done him and Adhi the honor of taking them aboard his own armored personnel carrier, an ATV armored personnel carrier of French origin seized from the regular army, which could hold up to twelve men with their equipment. Apart from the driver, an officer of the new GAM, Saragih was surrounded by four bodyguards and three Germans.

-- Stop, he ordered the driver as they reached a wide intersection at the center of which stood a colorful monument representing a five-petalled corolla engraved with golden characters and open to the sky.

The crowd here was denser and more excited. Suddenly, a small mobile crane made its way through the human tide. The cries became a clamor, and applause rang out. On the rear platform of the machine, AMG men were aiming their weapons at the two figures. It was difficult to make out their faces and silhouettes at this distance. Inside the vehicle, the Germans became animated and exchanged enthusiastic observations. Saragih turned to Darwis.

-- Looks like they didn't wait for me to celebrate my victory.

The doctor remained silent. Next to him, Adhi was starting to get restless. He took his adopted son's hand in his own to invite him to calm down, but he took it back sharply and began his usual rocking motion. Incomprehensible words came out of his mouth. There was nothing to be done at the moment. Adhi would calm down on his own. Darwis returned his gaze to the square, where the mobile crane was deploying its main boom. The bond that held the two victims together began to tighten.

-- Don't be moved, Saragih added in an icy tone. These are the mayor and the regional military governor. Men who waged a merciless war against me for a long time.

The variable motion of the crane had reached its peak. The line protruding from it became taut and the two men gradually suspended by their necks rose into the air. The victims began to writhe, while their torturers brandished the barrels of their Kalashnikovs towards the sky, inviting all the armed men to do the same. Dozens of machine guns fired at the same time. The staccato of the Kalashnikovs drowned out the howls of Saragih's supporters.

At a sign from the sheikh, one of his bodyguards grabbed the microphone hanging from the dashboard, and the vehicle's speakers spat out:

-- This is a message from your leader and new governor of Nanggroe Aceh Darussalam, Habib Saragih. Save your ammunition for later. Stop shooting. I repeat, save your ammunition!

An even greater clamor arose from the thousands of people who had spread through the streets of Banda Aceh like some sinister oil spill. The two victims stopped squirming at the end of the rope around their necks. A relative calm returned, punctuated by cheers as soon as one group saw the line of troop transports.

The convoy set off again, with Saragih's all-terrain vehicle in second position, heading for the Governor's Palace where he would formalize his power the following day, the first step in his irresistible conquest of all of Indonesia.

A succession of shocks distracted Darwis's attention. He looked back at Adhi and let out a cry.

He banged his head against the window of the armored vehicle with all his might.

***

The Antonov flew over Banda Aceh before pointing its nose towards the Sultan Iskandar Muda Airport, whose green and golden dome soon appeared through the low clouds. The landing was smooth, despite a strong crosswind that was bending the palm trees. Halfway through the flight Melany had fallen asleep with her head in Jeffrey's lap, but she was wide awake now and staring through the window with a fascinated gaze at the runway where a line of armored cars converged on the plane.

A feverish agitation seized the interior of the hull when they reached their stopping point. Soloviev was the first to exit it, surrounded by his close bodyguard. Melany and Jeffrey were pulled from their cell and taken to an armored car parked a few meters away from the gangway.

Sand-colored Humvees had formed a procession in front of the terminal entrance. The international airport had originally been a civilian building and had been renovated after the tsunami, which had allowed the transit of humanitarian aid for months and welcomed tens of thousands of tourists annually until the crisis erupted.

It had recently been transformed into a military zone.

Armored vehicles stolen from the regular army protected the surrounding area. Snipers had been posted at all four corners of the two terminals. The air traffic controllers carried out their activity under guard. Soldiers in black uniforms, mixed with local fighters, moved from one access to the other, while armed groups continued to form near the main runway.

Eight cars and a truck into which cases had been transferred from the hold of the plane set off towards the Governor's Palace. A second truck, protected by machine guns, took charge of the sealed barrels while a technician, equipped with a Geiger counter, checked their tightness to radiation.

The administration building had been under GAM control for a week, while the elected government in Jakarta regrouped its forces and prepared an offensive to retake the region. The civil war, an Indonesian Spring manipulated by Soloviev with the help of independence movements, was only at its beginning. The factions were only waiting for Saragih's appointment as supreme leader to move on to the next phase. It would be difficult to avoid a bloodbath.

Melany took Jeffrey's hand and squeezed it with all her strength. This time, no more pirouettes would be possible. They were at the heart of the cataclysm.

-- I don't believe it, she whispered. Jeff, tell me it's just a nightmare!

Jeffrey could only watch sadly through the bulletproof glass as the tide of people flowed in the same direction as them.

When they reached the heart of Banda Aceh, they were led through a maze of alleys to a small building with barred windows. Scarlet stains turning dirty brown stained the three steps leading to the main entrance. No one had bothered to clean up the blood of the police officers on duty who had been executed when the station was stormed.

***

Anat Galil hung up angrily after spending ten minutes trying to convince Franckel to get the *Bundespolizei*, the German Federal Police, to intervene in Kahla. The CIA director of operations had told her that such a request was not within his purview, that he would have to go much higher to obtain such a favor, and that the best he could do was to get in touch with the Landespolizei, the police forces of the various German states, which Anat strongly opposed.

-- Our teams are convinced that abnormal things are going on in this city. No one can guarantee the integrity of the local police. The German government has been far too lax in all regions of the former East Germany. Two of your nationals have been kidnapped and all you can do is call the local police? Anyone can dial emergency. We don't need the CIA for that.

-- Nationals belonging to the State Department and who disobeyed a direct order, Franckel said. The only thing missing would be a leak to the media. Officially, we have no agents in Germany. Especially agents working hand in hand with your government. The day the shit hits the fan, I want to be in the next room.

-- You're telling me you're abandoning Ms. Carson and Mr. Cartright ... because they didn't follow your orders?

-- You know as well as I do, Anat, that this kind of business is much more complicated than that.

After hanging up, the Israeli woman knew what she had to do. Unfortunately, Franckel had never shown any real enthusiasm for a mission he was following from a distance and even less so since the *Father of Victory* had been identified. His role was to report the results of his investigations directly to the Director of the CIA, who himself reported only to the President. As the terrorist nebula steadily subdivided to better extend over the entire planet, he refused to pass on information that neo-Nazis, motivated by an absurd myth, were threatening the security of the world by fomenting an alliance with the Jihadists.

He could easily imagine what the President of the United States would be like if his superior was called upon to inform him that the CIA was spending part of its budget on investigating the reincarnation of Adolph Hitler. It would be the end of his career. Not to mention the gibes that would follow him for the rest of his life.

Bob Franckel regularly closed similar files and was raging that the actions of two dangerous amateurs were forcing him to keep such an operation active.

But Franckel was also a man of integrity and the situation of Melany and Jeffrey worried him seriously, which he could not confess to a Mossad agent. Allies, certainly, but not to the point of washing their dirty laundry in the same tub.

As Anat called her base and waited for the green light to join the team of *kidonim* that had infiltrated Thuringia, Bob Franckel contacted his head of special operations in Berlin.

***

A skylight barely wide enough to hold three closed fists provided the only lighting in the jail. The dirt floor was soaked in urine. Feces formed small filthy piles in a corner opposite the entrance. The walls, with varying degrees of roughness, oozed with unspeakable fluids. The smell was unbearable, the heat appalling, and only distant screams punctuated the silence. They could scarcely breathe.

Melany and Jeffrey had lost all track of time. The dawn of daylight gave them the feeling that they had been locked in this sordid place for at least twenty-four hours. They hadn't eaten anything for two days and Melany came to regret the little chocolate bar she had given to Karl Hanussen. It was in vain that Jeffrey had drummed against the door, hoping to get even a crust of bread. They had to confine themselves to the obvious. The basement had been deserted by the guards. Only they and the other prisoners still remained.

They had come to wonder whether Soloviev was taking his revenge by letting them die slowly. Their presence in Kahla had forced him to abandon his headquarters and to prematurely rush a carefully planned operation into action. The former KGB agent was not a man to let those responsible for such a setback go unpunished. What could be more frightening than being buried alive?

Leaning against the rocky wall, Melany fell asleep again, her head on his shoulder. Jeffrey held her hand. They had not exchanged a word since the day before. Like him, she was sweating profusely. Thirst pushed them beyond the bearable. Without water, they would not survive very long.

Distant curses tore him from his torpor. They were immediately followed by the sound of hurried footsteps. A few moments later the heavy door with a peephole squeaked on its hinges. Three Indonesians in black uniforms burst into the jail, barking incomprehensible orders. Melany woke up with a start and huddled in his arms. Two guards separated them in order to grab Jeffrey, while the third one forced the young woman to stand up.

Pulled and pushed unceremoniously, they were brought to the surface amid the screams and hysterical laughter of the other prisoners. The sun was already high in the sky. Blinding. Despite their state of weakness due to dehydration, they were forced to speed up their pace in the alley, quickly leaving the police station behind. With eyelids wrinkled, Jeffrey scanned Melany's face. She was extremely pale. He struggled, forcing his two guards to tighten their hold.

-- At least give her a drink!

A blow of a rifle butt between his shoulder blades made him cry out. A burning pain shot down his spine. He turned around abruptly, ready to pounce on the guard, but the threat that he read in his gaze got the better of his first impulse. Despite the orders he had received, the Indonesian was only waiting for an opportunity to harm an infidel. Even more so, an American.

The Governor's Palace appeared as they left the alley. The building was in a state of siege, armored tanks forming a circle, barrels facing outwards. About a hundred heavily armed Indonesians, soldiers of a new army arising from the GAM, were stationed behind stacks of sandbags.

Jeffrey and Melany found themselves in a small room crowded with boxes of ammunition. A German they had never seen before came walking towards them.

-- I believe you speak my language, he said to Melany, handing them a bottle of water.

Without a word, the young woman grabbed the bottle and swallowed a long swig before handing it to Jeffrey. A surge of ineffable pleasure added to the relief at having been granted a reprieve. They staggered, as if drunk.

-- Follow me, the German ordered. Herr Krueger is waiting for us.

Soloviev was in the middle of a telephone conversation, standing in front of the window of an elegant room that must have been the office of the military governor. A tall Eurasian accompanied by two Germans was commenting on a map spread out on a table, pointing to certain places.

-- *Danke*, Günther, Soloviev said after hanging up.

With a nod of his head, he motioned the other occupants to leave the room, which they did with the exception of the Eurasian. That one, immense in his night-colored clothes, his fleshy lips framed with an implacable smile, exuded the magnetism that accompanies the powerful and the stars. His features expressed all the arrogance of a being eager for power and violence.

-- Sheikh, I present to you Mr. Cartright and Ms. Carson. The American agents I told you about. You will soon be leading the operations. It is therefore up to you to decide their fate.

Now rehydrated, Jeffrey was back to his former glory. This man, this Eurasian with an evil charm and an evil gaze, was therefore the one on whom Soloviev had made his choice. He was the puppet convinced that he had welcomed the Führer's *tulku*. He had all the makings of a little gang leader. Krueger had propelled him to the top of a terrorist organization that was preparing to overthrow the government of a country populated by more than two hundred million mostly peaceful and friendly Muslims. Their nightmare finally had a face.

-- And you are?

-- Habib Saragih. You must call me Sheikh when you address me.

The English of the leader of the GAM was barely understandable.

-- Sheikh, or *Mein Führer*, Jeffrey quipped.

Saragih's face closed in an expression of pure hatred. A dangerous glow lit up the pupils of his eyes.

-- These two snoops claim to have traced me on their own, Soloviev said. I couldn't get any further details from them.

The news brought a vague smile from Saragih.

-- We will find out more about that later. After the ceremony.

-- A ceremony?, Jeffrey said, persisting in the same tone. You mean a charade.

Melany had also regained some strength. With a slightly trembling hand, she mechanically smoothed out her wrinkled clothes stained with dried mud, a reminder of the hours spent in the unhealthy basement.

-- Herr Krueger has promised you a fictitious induction, she added. Either you are not fooled and are therefore quite an opportunist, or you have been brainwashed. In both cases, you'll soon discover that his plan doesn't make any sense. By the time you realize that you have been manipulated, it will be too late. I just hope that your cell will be as comfortable as the one we spent the night in.

-- Enough!

Soloviev leaped forward towards Melany to slap her but Jeffrey stepped up and grabbed his wrist. The Russian was endowed with phenomenal strength. For a split second, the two men took the measure of each other. Jeffrey didn't impress him in the least, but against all expectations, Soloviev pulled away and took a step back. Was it because of Saragih's acid look, in front of which he wanted to show his capacity to control, or was he reserving his anger and violence for a more opportune moment?

-- Do what you want with him, he told the Sheikh. Or, better yet, no. Send them back where they came from and let them stew for two or three days before questioning them.

The latter was scrutinizing the couple intensely. There was a black shadow of evil omen in his eyes and all the arrogance of a predator sure of his dominance but never satisfied.

-- Do you really think I'm a man who lets myself be manipulated? You have no idea who I really am. But I invite you to find out.

Saragih turned to Soloviev, who had returned to the window.

-- Your God is not mine, but both require sacrifices. There is nothing to prevent these two Americans from attending the ceremony. Isn't that so, Herr Krueger?

-- Chapter 30 --

Kahla, Germany

Present time

Anat and her team had been given permission to travel to Thuringia for twenty-four hours, but only on an observation mission. In other words, no action was possible and all contact with local authorities was prohibited, even on condition of anonymity. It was, however, a way of working that had proven its value. The security of several European countries owed a great deal to this intelligence with no detectable source, the origin of which was in fact well known to those responsible.

Anat kicked her foot into a muddy pile of snow that the sand trucks had formed around the building housing the premises of "*Earth and Sharing*". She, who had been born in Egypt and had spent most of her youth near the Dead Sea in a region where people take out their coats when the temperature drops below 70 degrees, was deeply affected in countries with harsh winters. What would be her next destination, once this mission was completed? Finland, Iceland or Sweden? The day the Agency needed to infiltrate the penguins at the pole, she was sure they would call on her.

In the meantime, she was forced to make several damning observations.

First observation: Melany and Jeffrey had indeed been kidnapped from the exact spot from which Anat had received the phone call. The snow covered the possible traces of an altercation or a meeting between several vehicles, but one of her *kidonim* had found a cell phone battery among the branches of a frozen bush near a river.

Second observation: The neo-Nazis no longer had a problem with displaying themselves in the region, judging by the number of motorcyclists with the number 88 on their jackets that they had come across and the signs for certain streets whose names had been covered and crudely replaced by those of officials of the Third Reich.

Third observation: No vehicles were parked in the parking lot adjacent to the NGO's premises.

Eytan, whom she had been teaming up with for several months, went to take a quick look inside the building. With the exception of a few pieces of furniture and posters still hanging on the walls, it was empty and deserted.

-- Looks like quite a mess in there, he said, coming back. Express moving. The door isn't even locked. You want to go and see?

Anat shook her head.

They were dealing with professionals and there were not enough of them to search for clues in buildings of such sizes. Some still-fresh tracks, barely covered with snow, suggested that many vehicles had been parked there between twenty-four and forty-eight hours earlier.

-- They got scared. The presence of our two free electrons must have triggered the panic. Is there an airfield or a military airport in the area?

-- I'll call and check.

Avi confirmed that there was a former military airport some twenty kilometers away. At her level, Anat could hardly find out if a plane had taken off recently. International flight plans were not made public. She called her embassy in Berlin. There had to be someone among the employees who was in contact with the German Air Ministry.

After five calls, which were made on the way to the terminal, it was confirmed that two jumbo jets, an Antonov and a Boeing, had taken off the day before, officially bound for Turkey. There was nothing to rule out the flight plan being changed in mid-flight. Either way, they were headed in the right direction.

-- There's no need to keep looking around for this couple, Anat sighed, genuinely worried about Melany and Jeffrey. Visiting the terminal won't tell us much either.

When they arrived in the vicinity of the hangars, as deserted as the "Earth and Sharing" building had been, a large black sedan with the mark 'Diplomatic Corps' on its license plate was parked nearby. Two men dressed in impeccable suits emerged from it. A bump, perceptible only by a professional, deformed their jackets at the height of their hearts. They signaled them to stop. They didn't need badges or dark glasses to give a whiff of intelligence services. Anat climbed out of her car, her arms raised.

-- Do you work for Bob Franckel?, she asked.

-- And you, who are you?, one of the two men barked, pulling his jacket aside to show he was armed. What are you doing here?

-- Don't they teach you to reason at the Farm[17]? If I know Bob, maybe we're on the same side.

-- That doesn't tell me what you are doing here.

-- Like you, we are looking for two of your nationals who must be having a tough time. It amazes me to find you around here. Bob gave me the impression that he didn't give a damn about this young couple.

Silence. The airstrip was disproportionately long in comparison to the size of the hangars. A colony of crows hovered above the woods that adjoined one end. The wind was blowing harder in the open countryside. Despite the thickness of her clothes, Anat was definitely frozen. She added sourly:

-- You won't find anyone. Neither the victims, nor their captors. I'm willing to bet the lining of my jacket and my hat that our friends are dead ... or already in Indonesia.

***

The ceremonial hall was not very large or luxurious, but it was of sufficient size to accommodate the limited number of guests. Black sheets covered the windows, and the indirect lights that lit up the hall gave it the atmosphere of a secret initiation ritual.

Only those closest to Soloviev, the masters of ceremonies and the main party involved, Habib Saragih, would be admitted.

In the center of the room was a long table covered with a white cloth embroidered with gold on which many artifacts of the Nazi era were displayed. Incense burned in large pots arranged along the walls. Black standards bearing inscriptions similar to the flag of Daesh alternated with swastika banners, among which hung a large painting depicting a stylized black sun. A banner hung above the platform bore the inscription *Ein Reich -- Ein Volk -- Ein Führer*. The phrase symbolizing the Third Reich had not been publicly displayed for decades.

Soloviev could have refrained from such a ceremony, but he was convinced of the importance of ritualization for the cohesion of his factions. He was going to offer pageantry to the fanatical, the insane, the narrow-minded ideologues who constituted his base, to the nostalgic fanatics of the Third Reich, to the Odinists and Wotanists who were ready to follow him blindly as long as he gave them a Führer, a goose step, and the hope of a chaos in which they could

[17] Familiar name given to the CIA Agent Training Center.

make their marks. It was the Thule Society rising from its ashes. The main hall of Wewelsburg Castle, SS headquarters under Himmler, transported to Southeast Asia. A Buddhist temple sponsored by representatives of the Nazi party, as had already happened eighty years earlier in Tibet. The number of witnesses would be small, but rumors would be allowed to circulate. You could deny it by laughing it off. And, in the meantime, the man chosen by Krueger would gradually take his place as leader, thus creating a new myth.

To those who would deny his authority, he could answer, in good faith, that he was the reincarnation of the Führer. An idol among convinced Islamists.

Until the day when so much blood will have been shed and the nuclear threat will have become intense that Europe and Russia would be ready to accept the obvious. The Savior had returned.

***

Before being taken under guard to the ceremonial room, Jeffrey and Melany were allowed to go to the upstairs public washrooms, a place almost as nasty as the basement where they had been locked up. Rubbish littered the ground and only one faucet was still in working order. The men of Saragih had taken a malicious pleasure in vandalizing everything.

-- Would you mind leaving me alone for a few minutes, she said to the soldier in front of the door who was devouring her with his eyes.

He was content to give a vicious little smile.

-- At least turn around, I'm not going to escape through the window!

Obviously he didn't speak English. She repeated her request in German. He did not flinch this time either. For a moment, Melany feared that he intended to rape her. But the man must have been ordered not to touch the American, because he simply tapped his wrist watch and barked an order. Melany's clothes were beginning to give off an unpleasant odor. That doesn't mean that she wanted to exhibit herself in front of him. So she just ran a little water over her face, washed her hands and straightened her hair.

When she rejoined him, Jeffrey was standing with his back pressed against a wall in the ceremonial hall, casually guarded by a disheveled Indonesian, a Kalashnikov slung over his shoulder and a cigarette at the corner of his mouth, with the barrel of his gun pointed at them. The soldier accompanying him pushed him roughly to the side and took up a position three feet from the couple, the barrel of his gun pointed at them.

-- I don't know what they're going to do to us, but I wish I could take taken a shower before I died!, Jeffrey joked.

-- *Utup mulut!*, the guard thundered in Indonesia.

-- I bet he's telling me to shut up!

A rifle butt to his ribs forced a grunt out of him.

It didn't take long for the room to fill up. Half a dozen armed Indonesians guarded the two entrances. On the gold embroidered tablecloth, three combat daggers were displayed in their leather cases stamped with the eagle and swastika, three belt buckles, one very simple and two beautifully carved, along with weapons from the Third Reich, three horn and boar-hair mustache brushes, three magnifying glasses and three Luger-Mausers including two P08-9 mm pistols, and one P07.65 parabellum with a mother-of-pearl stock, accompanied by their magazines containing eight bullets each.

One object in each category was believed to have belonged to Hitler.

Behind the display, an Indonesian with a strangely blank expression was holding a beautiful gold vase with chiseled patterns in his hands. Nearby, an older and smaller man kept observing a young man with a worried look on his face. Two Buddhist priests in orange robes and wearing yellow caps completed the scene like figurines, their eyes closed. Standing with their arms crossed over their chests, chins tucked into their necks, sleeves down, they seemed to have entered into a trance. In front of them, fourteen Europeans lined up in two rows, standing in a military posture.

Soloviev-Krueger arrived surrounded by his bodyguards, followed by Saragih, framed by his soldiers.

Krueger turned to his egregore. His face closed. His gaze cold. The words that came out of his mouth, though intended to move the audience, had the neutrality of a list. He spoke in German, and repeated every sentence in English.

-- Thank you for being here. Thanks to you, Dietrich, for the honor that you do us by representing the new NSU. Thanks to the Pamyat members for making the long trip to attend. Thanks to Bjorn and Sven for representing the Swedish Nordic Resistance Movement. Thanks to Leon, whose help in Switzerland has been invaluable to me. Thanks to Zoran and his associates, active members of the honorable Serbian Nacionalni Stroj and, above all, thanks to Wyatt who, through his position within the American government, made it possible to secretly assemble almost all the Nazi organizations active in the USA.

Melany met Jeffrey's frightened gaze.

Krueger clicked his heels and held up his right arm.

-- Sieg Heil!

All imitated him, except for the Indonesian guards. Saragih in turn faced them.

-- Sieg Heil!

-- Heil Hitler!, came out of every mouth like an exclamation of contained rage.

-- *Danke!*, Soloviev-Krueger thanked them, letting his arm drop. The Führer knew that one life would not be enough for him to fulfill his destiny. On his orders, teams of scientists left to explore Tibet to discover its mysteries and to trace the origin of the Aryan people. Several expeditions were carried out to Lhasa and to the temples on the highest peaks. Men came back invested with a great secret, that of the wheel of lives, of karma. What was once a myth, an illusion, has become a reality for new initiates. This secret, preserved in a book as old as civilization, was given to our master, Adolph Hitler. That is how he was able to promise his return. It took time, help, painstaking research, and the overcoming of many setbacks. When we discovered him, Habib Saragih was fatherless and motherless, like the Führer at his age. We awakened his warrior soul and taught him who he was, where he came from ... where he is to lead us. Thanks to him, thousands of fighters of all nationalities but linked by a common destiny have joined our cause. Millions more will rise up soon. In a few moments, once the ceremony is completed, Habib Saragih will only have one title: *Der Vater des Sieges -- The Father of Victory.*

New clamor.

-- Sieg Heil!

Melany experienced a chill, a mixture of disgust and dread as Jeffrey quietly looked around him. Krueger's bombastic speech interested him much less than the search for a means of escape. The attention on them had slackened, but the doors were closed and guarded by GAM soldiers. Any attempt at escape seemed impossible.

The older of the two monks whispered something in the ear of the young man carrying the gold urn, but he gave no reaction. The monk turned to the boy's protector. He repeated the request in a low voice, showing a patience and gentleness that revealed a long habit. Only then did the young man remove the lid of the golden vessel.

The two monks had put themselves in a meditative posture, hands clasped together, eyes half-closed, as straight as masts in their orange garments. A low, vibrating sound issued from their throats.

-- There are twenty-one sticks in that urn, Krueger explained. Seven with the word *Ha,* which means "yes" in Sanskrit, seven with *Nahi*, which means the opposite, and seven without inscription, indicating that no answer will be given to the question asked.

The vibration of the *Om* intensified. The lights dimmed further and someone took it upon himself to throw more incense into the jars, which crackled, emitting thick and fragrant billows of smoke. The room looked like the lair of some mythical animal.

-- There will be seven questions, Krueger concluded. At the end of this ritual, Habib Saragih will be called upon to find those among the objects presented in front of him those that belonged to him in his previous life. This will be the final test, and its confirmation.

Melany couldn't help but think that everything was rigged. Krueger would not risk failure during a ritual that would be the culmination of a decades-long battle.

Krueger designated the older of the two monks to act as the master of ceremonies. He took a step forward. His companion maintained his posture and continued to utter the mantra.

The words that came out of the monk's throat had a strangely delicate intonation.

-- Travelling soul, *tulku* whose return we call the return of our vows -- are you among us?

Melany widened her eyes. Under other circumstances she would have burst out laughing.

The young man carrying the golden urn half-opened his lips, frozen like a statue. The Indonesian touched him on the shoulder and with a nod of his head urged him to complete his task.

Adhi plunged his hand into the vase and took out a stick which Saragih seized before handing it to the monk.

-- *Ha!*, the latter announced, brandishing the answer above his head. The *tulku* has chosen to incarnate among us. He is here.

A murmur of approval.

"Is he a man made of flesh and blood?", he asked immediately.

A second stick appeared in Adhi's hand.

-- *Ha!*

"Is the *tulku* orphaned of father and mother?"

-- *Ha!*

"Has the *tulku* come to repair?".

No answer. The stick had no inscription.

"Does the *tulku* accept his mission?".

Again, no response.

-- Soul traveler, you who were a great leader, are you among us to guide us towards a higher form of spirituality, an understanding of the universe, and to participate in the union of men, leading them towards peace?

A murmur spread through the assembly of witnesses when it appeared that the answer was *Nahi.*

-- Silence!, Krueger thundered.

-- Has the traveling soul reached the age of first wisdom?

-- *Nahi.*

-- Soul traveler, whose presence among us we now know but whose goals and destiny we do not know, will the next divine message, in the form of a sacred rod, be touched by your present incarnation so that your identity may be confirmed?

Adhi looked disoriented. Melany exchanged another look with Jeffrey. They both realized that the young man wasn't quite normal. It was the expression of fearful children cut off from the rest of the world, insensitive to external reality, who have created their own universe and have taken refuge in it.

Saragih read the answer and handed the object to the monk in a triumphant gesture.

-- *Ha!* We have identified the carnal envelope chosen by the *tulku.* The *tulku* has become a man. The *tulku* is among us. Glory and welcome to the earthly vessel that welcomes the soul of this immense leader, may his name be ...

The monk stopped abruptly and stepped backwards. What happened next would remain forever etched in the memories of Jeffrey and Melany.

While all eyes had been on the monk, the young man had placed the golden urn among the objects spread out on the table. In the same movement, he had seized the most common of the three pistols, a 9 mm Luger Mauser with a black stock, known by Third Reich gun collectors as the Black Widow. With a confident gesture, he inserted the magazine lying next to it.

-- Adhi!, cried Darwis Haikal.

Saragih's guards raised their weapons. Krueger rushed at the young man in an attempt to snatch the Luger from him. Everything then happened at the speed of lightning.

-- *Es ist meine!*(18), Adhi said in a confident voice.

He aimed the barrel at Krueger and pulled the trigger. The ex-KGB agent's head snapped backwards, as if yanked by an invisible thread. A small hole in the middle of his forehead suddenly released a stream of blood. He stumbled,

[18] It's mine!

tried to catch himself at the table, dragging down the tablecloth and all the objects it contained.

A second shot.

The bullet, fired by a Saragih bodyguard, hit Adhi in the left shoulder, causing him to recoil briefly without further reaction. It was as if he didn't feel a thing.

With a slow gesture, Adhi pointed the Luger at Saragih. The sheikh was so stunned that he lost all his reflexes.

-- *Es ist meine!*, Adhi thundered again.

It was the voice of a man, but the intonation of a child who has found a lost toy and rebels against those who want to take it away from him.

The first bullet hit Saragih in the chest. The second one tore open his neck. A geyser of blood escaped from his jugular as Adhi emptied his magazine into him.

The Sheikh fell, his body falling across Krueger's.

Saragih's panicked guards didn't know who to shoot. A bullet hit Adhi in the abdomen as his adoptive father threw himself on him to protect him with his body. The two men rolled on the ground.

Faced with Saragih's men, Krueger's guards drew their weapons in turn. It was now impossible to define which camp everyone belonged to. Shots forced guards, soldiers and guests to scatter for cover behind the body of a companion who had fallen a moment earlier or behind an overturned table or an incense jar. One burst ripped one of the curtains from its support and bright light flooded the room. The monks rushed to the exits. Believing it to be an attack, the orderlies sprayed them with bullets. In a few seconds, the smoke from the shots added to that of the incense formed a haze, making it impossible to identify anyone beyond a few meters.

Melany let out a cry of pain and staggered.

A stray bullet had hit her in the calf. Jeffrey pulled her to the ground, cushioning their fall as best he could. Their guards rushed to the nearest incense jars for refuge. One was hit in the middle of his back and collapsed in the middle of the run. The second caught a bullet between his shoulders and staggered a few meters before falling in his turn. Everyone shot blindly at the figures that became less and less distinct as the cordite smoke thickened. The scene turned to carnage.

Jeffrey put one arm under Melany's, strengthened his grip and helped her crawl towards the jars. The trickle of blood from her wounds formed a straight line on the ground. The young woman grimaced in pain. They quickly found refuge behind the largest of the jars, a terracotta object filled with rubble on the surface of which granules of incense were burning as they emitted gauzy swirls.

A good half of the guests had managed to escape. Guards and soldiers continued to shoot at anything that moved.

-- Show me, Jeffrey said, bending over Melany's leg.

The bullet had passed right through the muscle, but the meager flow of blood from the two wounds was reassuring. No artery had been touched. Jeffrey took off his belt and turned it into a tourniquet.

-- Do you think you can walk?

Melany's look told him that she wasn't sure.

A few meters away, two forms were crawling on the ground in their direction. When they were close enough, Jeffrey recognized the Indonesian and the young man who had held the golden vessel and had started the carnage.

-- Don't move, he said to Melany.

Using his elbows and knees, he found himself within reach of the two men in a matter of a few seconds.

-- Let me help you!

-- *Thank you*, Darwis Haikal replied as Jeffrey grabbed a section of Adhi's clothing and pulled him towards him.

The jar was about ten meters from the door. Saragih's men and the Germans had positioned themselves on both sides of the room, separated by the overturned table. The firing had dropped from sustained to sporadic. From the outside of the building, a clamor rose, piercing through the thickness of the windows. It was the cry of rage of a hysterical crowd, dominated by the slogans of the leaders. They could hear the detonations from the street, but no one knew what was going on inside the hall. They had been promised the consecration of a leader, a coup d'état that would bring them to power, and now they wanted their bloodbath.

Jeffrey quickly checked Melany's calf. The bleeding had been contained. He slid his arm under her shoulders and squeezed it against him to make a bulwark of his body. The Indonesian removed the young man's shirt. A bullet had stuck between his clavicle and his scapula. A second one had passed through his abdomen. His eyes were open but he was unable to move.

-- You speak English?, Jeffrey asked.

-- A little, Darwis Haikal responded.

-- Is this is your son?

Darwis hesitated a moment, then answered in the affirmative.

-- What were you doing with the men your son shot?, Jeffrey continued suspiciously.

-- I am a doctor. Saragih gave me no choice.

Jeffrey unconsciously counted the successive miracles that had kept them alive until now and had brought them to the attention of the doctor. He looked closely at Darwis and concluded that he was telling the truth.

-- We have two solutions. Either we stay in hiding and sooner or later someone will end up pumping us full of bullets, or we try to escape. But we will have to run with all our might.

-- He won't be able, Darwis Haikal replied, looking at Adhi sadly.

Melany took Jeffrey's hand.

-- Me neither, she said. I can't stand up.

-- But, yes, I will help you. I'll carry you if I have to.

-- Go ahead, Darwis said. I'll stay with him.

At that moment, Adhi turned his face towards Melany. He no longer had that absence in his eyes that had set him apart. A mixture of sadness and relief filled his pupils. He opened his lips to speak.

-- Don't move, Darwis told him. Are you hurt?

The young man shook his head.

Two shots. Bellowing in German. The breaking of glass. The crash of a door torn from its hinges. Curses in Indonesian.

Darwis tore one sleeve of his shirt into a pad, which he pressed against Adhi's stomach wound.

-- You two -- go!

To his astonishment, Adhi squeezed his fingers and then, slowly, with obvious effort, he reached for Melany's leg. Without even looking at her, he put his hand on the wound in her calf.

-- What's this?, Jeffrey asked.

-- Let him do it, Darwis Haikal said softly.

Melany felt a shiver from the soles of her feet to the roots of her hair. An unknown warmth seemed to radiate from her wound. In a few seconds, the sharp pain gave way to a distant throb.

-- What's he doing to me?, she asked, stunned. I don't understand!

But the doctor was no longer paying attention to her. She turned her gaze to the young man whose hand had slipped and was now resting on the ground, his fingers brushing her leg. Adhi's features had frozen into an expression of extreme happiness, bordering on ecstasy. He looked as if he were startled.

-- *Ayha*?, he said in a last breath. *Air laut naik.*

-- No, no!, Darwis moaned. The sea is not coming.

A pinkish foam flowed from Adhi's lips. His eyelids closed. He couldn't hear him any more.

-- Doctor!, Jeffrey whispered after a few moments. We have to go. You can do nothing more for him.

Tears flooded the doctor's face.

-- Doctor?

-- I can't leave him.

Shooting had ceased in the room, but the staccatos of automatic weapons were bouncing everywhere else. On the street, as well as inside the palace.

-- We're going to have to, though, Melany said softly. Your life depends on it ... Ours, too.

-- We can't go anywhere without you, Jeffrey insisted. We don't speak your language and we don't know this city.

The doctor seemed to tear himself away from a sort of torpor. He leaned over to Adhi, placed a kiss on his forehead, then nodded.

-- I ... I think I'll will be able to walk!, Melany announced.

-- Of course you can, Darwis Haikal said.

-- On my signal, Jeffrey said, the three of us run to the exit ...

He left Melany behind to crawl towards the body of one of the guards, struggled to dislodge the submachine gun from the lanyard stuck under his arm, and returned to take refuge behind the jar. He fumbled for a few seconds for the safety which he triggered, activated it twice to put a bullet into the breech, and smiled at Melany.

-- Are you sure you can run?

-- I think it doesn't hurt so much anymore.

-- So ... pray that this works.

He crouched down, his head protruding from the top of the jar but protected by the smoke, and threw the weapon toward the other end of the room with all his might. It fell between two bodies and bounced off the elegant, tiled floor. The impact released the trigger of the firing pin. The machine gun fired a salvo, causing fire to return from the two opposing groups. Jeffrey pulled Melany by her arm, Darwis stood up, and the three of them rushed to the nearest door. The weapon thrown on the floor jammed, but both Germans and Indonesians continued to fire in its direction, while the three crossed the few meters that separated them from the exit.

In front of them, there was a large staircase that several men from the GAM were climbing four steps at a time. Two of them took up positions in front of the small group and called out to them, the barrels of their Kalashnikovs pointing at them.

-- *Apa yang terjadi?*, barked the smaller of the two, who had a beard and a keffiyeh around his neck. *Kemana kamu pergi?*

-- *Syekh telah dikhianati,* Darwis Haikal responded. *Jerman dan saya pergi mencari bala bantuan.*

The Indonesians glanced around in panic and resumed their run towards the ceremonial hall.

-- What did you say?, Jeffrey asked.

-- Later, the doctor said.

As he took the stairs, Jeffrey pointed to the long corridor that led to the other end of the building. In that direction, the path was clear. They came upon an ageless woman, dressed entirely in black and with her head covered with a hijab, who seemed to be lost. She began to scream. Melany rushed towards her and had no trouble controlling her.

-- Sorry, she said, tearing off her hijab, but I'm going to need this!

The unfortunate woman began to groan, hiding her head with both her hands. Jeffrey was tempted to knock her out, but they were no longer close to committing acts of violence and, seeing an empty office with the door ajar, he pushed her inside.

-- Shh!, Melany said, putting a finger to her lips. Shh!

As she backed up, she stumbled on the body of a man lying in a pool of blood. She cried out loudly. There wasn't a moment to be lost. The dead man had blond hair and was not wearing a uniform. Probably a guest of Krueger who had tried to escape the carnage but had been cut down. Perhaps even by the men on his own side. Jeffrey bent down to search him.

-- What are you looking for?, Melany asked as Darwis tried to calm the Indonesian woman down.

-- I've found it!, Jeffrey said triumphantly, holding up a cell phone and sunglasses.

Against all expectations, the woman fell silent as soon as the door was closed on her. With her gray hair falling on her shoulders but finally out of sight, she regained her modesty.

-- Doctor, I really need to know, how did you manage to divert the soldiers?

-- I told them that Saragih had been betrayed, that you were Germans and that we were going to get reinforcements.

Outside, more shots could be heard. Who was shooting who? The panic was contagious. The staccato of a machine gun echoed the bangs drowning out the roar of the crowd. Screams added to the confusion.

-- *Saragih sudah mati! Saragih sudah mati!* The news of Saragih's death spread like wildfire. With her head wrapped in a hijab, her leg bleeding, and her glasses masking the color of her eyes, Melany could pass for an injured Indonesian woman.

The Governor's Palace was located on a wide and long avenue crowded with hundreds of scooters zigzagging and backfiring in the midst of an agitated crowd, which was insanely advancing in waves.

Large billboards had been torn from their supports and smiling half-faces of women with lips blacked out with markers were used as doormats by hordes of men in black shouting slogans. Most traders had closed their stalls or lowered the gates of their stores. Many posters bore inscriptions in English, with Indonesian subtitles. *Masa Jaya. Sharp. Modena. Sahara. LG* ... But most of the names were barely recognizable after being smeared by sprays of rotting or by jars of sauce or paint, when the panel hadn't simply been ripped apart.

A woman in a burka stood in front of the group and shouted something, pointing her finger at Melany's face. A few strands of her blonde hair had escaped her hijab. She immediately corrected herself, which didn't stop the woman from spitting at her feet before running off to join a small group screaming Saragih's name.

-- *Saragih sudah mati!*, Darwis Haikal then shouted.

The women froze.

-- *Saragih sudah mati?*, one of them repeated.

The doctor nodded.

The women began to gesticulate, screaming hysterically, some striking their breasts, others slapping themselves on the top of the head. The three took the opportunity to walk away quickly. Above all, it was important not to run, but to move forward at the disordered rhythm of the populace, who had come to attend a coronation but who now feared an apocalypse.

They turned into the alley they had taken after being removed from the police station. Unlike the main arteries, this one was empty. Shutters closed above their heads. They stepped inside a small, deserted courtyard, and Melany collapsed onto the steps of an indoor building with green and pink walls.

-- How's your leg?, Jeffrey asked.

-- I don't understand it, but it's okay.

It was time to regroup their forces and to take stock. Everyone had had their share of miracles, but it was not clear whether they had any more left.

-- I'm very sorry for your son, Melany said. But I would like to understand: how is it that my leg doesn't hurt anymore?

The mask of sadness that had fallen over Darwis Haikal's face grew stronger.

-- I loved him like a son, but he wasn't mine. I adopted him ... and he had this gift.

-- Do you mean to say he was a healer?

-- Allah willed it that way, the doctor agreed.

Jeffrey had a strange look in his eyes.

-- How old was he?

-- I don't exactly know. Maybe thirty years old. Or a little less. His name was Adhi.

-- And he was an orphan?

-- His real parents disappeared in 2004, in the tsunami ... I also lost my whole family that year.

The doctor's voice broke.

-- Did Adhi speak German?, Jeffrey insisted.

-- Not a bit. He even had difficulty expressing himself in our own language.

-- But then, how did he ...?

-- A phrase he had probably heard. I have a vague memory of a German shouting at him for touching his gun.

-- And, why do you think he shot those two ... monsters?

-- Jeffrey, Melany cut in. What's the matter with you? Will you stop bothering this poor man and hand me the cell phone?

Although disturbed, Jeffrey complied. She immediately dialed Anat's number. The Israeli took a while to answer. She finally picked up after the fifth ring.

-- Melany! Thank God you're alive!

The young woman explained the situation they were in as quickly as she could.

-- We are following events in Indonesia very closely, Anat replied. Thanks to you, I finally managed to get Franckel involved up to his neck. The Federal Police eventually intervened in Kahla and the German intelligence services joined the CIA. Are you sure the leader of the insurgents is dead?

-- Certain. A crazy story, which I still can't manage to believe. But it's turning into hell. Can you get us out of here?

A silence. Then:

-- Don't go to the airport. Jakarta has regrouped its troops and the official government is preparing to launch a counteroffensive against the dissidents. That's the first place they will attack. Head towards the port and call me back as soon as you reach the coast. In the meantime, we will try to find you a boat.

-- Anat ... Do you know who Krueger was?

-- Of course. He was the same as Soloviev. His disappearance and resurrection were major points in our investigation. But I can't tell you any more.

-- ... And that he had discovered radioactive materials that belonged to the Third Reich? Did you know that?

Anat didn't answer.

-- The stocks were transported on the same plane as us. They're now somewhere here in this region.

-- Thank you for the information!, the Israeli replied in a strained voice.

Hanging up, Melany thought to herself that, barring some Act of God, this information would probably never be shared with the Indonesian government. The question of where the cargo of the Antonov had disappeared to still remained.

-- Do you know what direction the port is?, she asked Darwis.

After the tsunami and thanks to international aid, Banda Aceh had acquired a reputation as a modern, clean, and organized city. A paradise on earth, apart from the monsoon periods. The application of sharia law, which had worried the media and human rights organizations for several years, had not slowed down tourism, however. Only Muslims were concerned with the rigor of the Islamic texts. As long as the foreigners were spending their money, the morality police, who would go after the women for the slightest deviation in their clothing, left them in relative peace.

But a few months of harsh protest and violent revolts were enough to change the look of the jewel of Sumatra. Garbage was piling up everywhere. Gutted cars or burnt-out truck wrecks lay about here and there. Some walls, recently repainted, were riddled with bullet holes. The Indonesian "Spring" fomented by Krueger had taken its toll and, failing a return to calm, the pretty little town would soon look like a Middle Eastern combat zone.

At the intersection of two streets, men in black uniforms controlled the intersection with a BTR-152. The wheeled armored vehicle had belonged to the regular army, but the official insignias and the Indonesian flag had been painted over in black over the khaki paint. The gunner had left his post, letting the barrel of his weapon aim at the ground, in order to join his fellow revolutionaries, who were just as shocked. Rumors were spreading quickly among Saragih's forces.

For a moment, Jeffrey feared that they would take too much interest in his little group. He slowed the pace, making certain at a glance that Melany's scarf hadn't come undone again. The soldiers let them pass.

A family crossed the street in front of them. Local people not yet committed to the extremists' cause, judging from the color of their clothes, including the mother's golden hijab and the three daughters' multicolored scarves.

A convoy of black-flagged Humvees, followed by pick-ups with oversized wheels and each one carrying half a dozen men, emerged from a side lane and cut them off. The fighters seemed on edge, their machine guns pointed in a defensive posture. They barely glanced at them.

Explosions sounded in the distance.

Melany at first thought it was a thunderstorm, but the sky had only sparse high, white clouds. New explosions were heard, closer and more violent.

-- The fighting is starting, Jeffrey pointed out. Without Saragih and Soloviev's resources, I wouldn't bet on the bastards in black.

They walked for another half hour, meeting other panicked crowds and sometimes crossing deserted neighborhoods before seeing the sea at a bend in the slope.

The port of Ulee Lheue had been rebuilt from scratch after the tsunami. Its name was written in gigantic letters. It pointed to a landing stage flanked by a long terminal topped with brick-red roofs in front of which two white ferries lazily swayed. A sign in several languages announced the closure of the port until further notice.

Melany called Anat back.

-- We've arrived, but access is prohibited and all the boats are in the harbor.

-- I know. We're trying to find a solution.

-- We? Who's we?, Melany asked impatiently.

-- Me. The CIA. Our contacts in the Indonesian government and military ... Just give us a little more time.

-- I'm not sure I have much. The Islamists have so far lost their leader, but not their will to aggression, as far as I can tell. As for the Nazis ...

Melany paused. A decapitated snake can no longer bite. Better to stay away from its fangs, though.

-- Try to take shelter somewhere, Anat recommended. I'll call you back as soon as I hear anything.

A large chain blocked the opening of the double gate, which was protected by a roof that allowed trucks to access the terminal. The door for passengers was also padlocked. On the other side of the steel slats that made up the fence, two men stood guard in a Jeep.

Since the port was inactive, there was no point in trying to force entry. Darwis pointed his finger to the left where, some five hundred meters away, a shed with colorful walls stood. Jeffrey nodded. They walked in that direction, until a few dozen multicolored fishing boats moored to pontoons appeared.

A natural palm grove and white houses completed the peaceful picture, miles away from the confusion that had taken over the city. Here, life went on. The only concern of the fishermen was how many fish they could catch and resell in order to continue feeding their families. A blue and orange trawler, with an elongated bow, was heading out to sea.

Some children saw them and ran out to meet them.

-- *Selamat pagi!*, said the oldest member of the group, a cheerful-looking teenager dressed in a fluorescent blue T-shirt and a pair of jeans too large for him.

-- *Selamat pagi!*, Melany repeated, joining both hands in front of her.

-- *Selamat pagi!*, the children cried with all their hearts, their hands resting on their chests.

Far in the distance, a new explosion. A veil of anxiety passed over the eyes of the children. The teen motioned for them to follow them. The Indonesian sense of hospitality was no myth, as long as no political situation impeded it. The youngest of the children, who must have been barely seven, pointed at Darwis' shirt, one sleeve of which was half torn off. The doctor said something that made the kids laugh. Then they dispersed and ran away at full speed.

-- I told them a ghost did that to me!, the doctor explained in response to Melany's questioning look.

They came to an open-air market next to the pier, most of the stalls of which were empty. Fishermen bustling around an overturned boat looked up at them with surprised but kind eyes. A young Indonesian girl, her head covered with a bottle-green hijab matching her darker tunic, made a welcoming gesture from her stall, on which a few poor fish were displayed. Sea trips must have been infrequent recently. Melany joined her, called out *selamat pagi*, and mimed the gesture of drinking. She was about to die of thirst and hunger. The young Asian girl gave her a charming smile and took a bottle of mineral water out from under her stall, as well as a home-made bread.

-- *Dua ribu rupee!*, she said, stretching out her hand.

Whatever the price was, Melany realized that she didn't have any money on her. The Nazis had taken everything from them in Kahla. Jeffrey was no better off and Darwis shrugged his shoulders, signifying that he was just as helpless.

-- *Dua ribu rupee?*, The Indonesian said again, this time questioningly.

Melany shook her head in sorrow. She didn't even have a piece of jewelry on her that she could have traded. But the Indonesian was a good woman. She understood that these strangers needed her help. She offered the bottle and the bread and stammered a few words.

-- I don't even know how to say thank you in her language, Melany despaired.

-- *Thank you!*, the Indonesian repeated, upon hearing the word of English. You, thank you?

-- You understand English?

-- A little. Americans helped after the tsunami.

-- I promise to find a way to get it back to you. You understand?

The Indonesian woman replied with a smile that could mean yes as much as no. Melany took a big sip before handing the bottle to Darwis, who then passed it on to Jeffrey. They cut the bread into three pieces and devoured it in an instant. Further on, a few fishermen were busy untangling the meshes of a net. A boat with two men on board moved away in its turn. The phone vibrated in Melany's hand.

At first, she hesitated to answer. The cell phone had belonged to a guest of Soloviev. It could be anyone. Jeffrey encouraged him to accept the call.

It was Anat.

-- Are you near the port yet?

-- Something like that, Melany replied. We playing tourists in a small fishing village.

-- So listen to me carefully. I've managed to convince Bob Franckel to help you. It hasn't been easy, and expect an argument if you make it out ...

-- Anat!, Melany squeaked. Seriously?

-- Yes, I can imagine that for the moment you don't care about his rants ... You're lucky that the U.S. Navy has deployed several ships to the South China Sea. The USS Antietam is currently sailing less than fifty miles from where you are. It is a guided missile cruiser that is part of the Pentagon's strategic force. It is diverting from its course to get closer to Indonesian territorial waters. But it has not received permission to enter, and this is not the time to trigger a diplomatic incident. Can you find a way to reach it in the open sea? I'll send you the coordinates.

-- Right here, right now, immediately?

-- You have a two hour time window ahead of you.

-- Unless you steal a trawler ...

-- That's all I can do for you, Anat said. May Heaven protect you.

She hung up. Melany turned to the young Indonesian woman again.

-- Do you know someone who could take us on a boat?

-- Boat?, the woman repeated, pointing her finger at the docking area.

-- Yes. We need a boat. Can you help us?

-- I know. But he will ask for rupees.

Melany sighed. In the middle of the night, they could have tried to steal a boat, although they wouldn't be able to navigate. But the village was lively enough for now that they weren't taking any chances.

-- Wait, Jeffrey said, rolling up his left sleeve.

Luckily, Krueger's men had left him his watch.

-- This should be enough to rent a motor boat.

He undid the bracelet and held the watch in front of the Indonesian woman.

-- Doctor, tell her it's worth a lot of money. It's for her and the owner of the boat if she finds anyone willing to take us on board.

The young woman smiled and called behind her:

-- *Bintang!*

She explained to the fisherman what was expected of him, pointing to the watch on the one hand and the sea on the other. The man eyed the group suspiciously. Jeffrey handed him the item. He weighed it, eyed it from both sides and then bit into it before asking a question.

-- Is it gold?, Darwis translated.

-- Better than that. It belonged to my father. I could buy his trawler with it. But our lives are well worth it.

They agreed. The boat would be ready quickly, in enough time for the sailors to retrieve the nets and pour a few buckets of water on the deck.

-- There, Darwis said, our paths separate here.

-- Aren't you coming with us?, Jeffrey wondered.

-- Where? To America? I don't even know who you are. And I am a doctor. They will need me here.

-- Yet I feel like we still have a lot to say to each other.

-- Certainly. But sometimes it's better not to know everything. If one day the situation calms down and you return to Banda Aceh, ask for Doctor Darwis Haikal. You will find me eventually and I will be happy to see you again.

-- Thanks for your help, Melany said.

-- It is Adhi you should thank. But if he spontaneously healed you, you probably deserve it.

Darwis Haikal shook hands with them, smiled sadly, turned on his heels, and disappeared from view. As she followed him with her gaze, Melany discovered a multilingual sign partly obscured by brush.

"Here at 8:40 a.m. on December 24, 2004, a 35-meter wave broke, devastating everything in its path. The precise number of victims in Banda Aceh is still unknown but numbers in the tens of thousands. With international help, we have rebuilt ".

An explosion closer than the previous ones made her twitch.

***

The coast was rapidly falling back. The small green and white tuna vessel was equipped with a good engine, in addition to its three sails filled by the wind. In the distance, black smoke was visible. Large, equally dark clouds were gathering over the mountains of Aceh. One might think that nature didn't want to be outdone as the shooting continued.

Bintang, the owner of the tuna boat, was accompanied by his son, a talkative young man who experienced the presence of foreigners on his father's boat as an exciting adventure. Unfortunately, neither of them spoke a word of English. The sea was rough, but the boat was on course.

Before boarding, Melany had called Anat one last time to inform her of their departure. The Israeli had expressed her relief. She knew, she said, that they would find a way out. Since the cell phone was no longer useful, Melany offered it to the Indonesian woman in the market. She had never owned one and saw no use for such an object. However, she accepted it with joy. Once resold it would more than make up for the losses of the week. Maybe even of the month.

Bintang had suggested that they sit inside the cabin, sheltered from the spray and wind, but they preferred to sit next to each other near the bow, with their backs against the railing.

Melany's wound was no longer bleeding. The pain had returned, but the swollen edges signaled the onset of healing that shouldn't have occurred for several days. Neither she nor Jeffrey understood what might have happened. But they were alive. And soon, maybe, in safety. Nothing else mattered now.

-- Something's been puzzling me, Melany said after she finished devouring a piece of the onion and chili omelet Bintang had given them. Your attitude towards that poor doctor. Why did you insist on asking him so many questions about his son?

-- Because I'll never have an answer to the ones I ask myself.

-- How could he have helped you?

Jeffrey took a deep breath.

-- I know you're going to think I'm crazy, and don't think that my questions form a theory. But a set of coincidences troubles me.

-- I'm having trouble following you.

-- Let's go back to Karl Hanussen, who was in charge of discovering Hitler's *tulku* on behalf of Soloviev. Assuming that reincarnation exists, what would its profile have been? An orphan in his thirties, born in this region, not necessarily a warlord or even a leader. Remember the questions asked of the golden vessel. Has he reached the age of first wisdom? No. Is he holding the stick in his hand? Yes. Saragih didn't have the opportunity to declare his so-called identity by "recognizing" the objects that supposedly belonged to him in his previous life. Obviously, he knew the answers and Soloviev's staging could have worked ... But someone else beat him to it.

Melany widened her eyes and turned pale.

-- You mean to say that ...

-- ... That our new friend's adopted son changed the course of history after he claimed in German that the gun on the table was his. Did you remember his first name?

-- Adhi, Melany whispered, shaking her head. A, H and I, just like Saragih. Well, the coincidence is disturbing, but it's a very common name in Indonesia.

-- You're right. A series of coincidences. But still ... What are the first two letters of the Führer's first and last name?

-- Ad-Hee, Melany said in low voice.

A wave bigger than the others lifted the small tuna boat by forty-five degrees. They held onto the ropes, and Jeffrey suggested that they finally take shelter in the cabin.

-- Coincidences, Melany retorted, shaking her head slowly. Coincidences, nothing more.

They sailed until the coast disappeared, and for a good hour more, while the sea became more and more agitated.

Suddenly, as one wave fell, the long silhouette of the cruiser appeared.

The tuna boat signaled its presence with a siren call.

The American warship responded with an extended roar.

-- EPILOGUE --

Three months later

Article from the Jakarta Post

Failure of the Islamist coup in Sumatra

After three months of conflict, the Indonesian government has managed to restore calm in Banda Aceh and has regained control of Sumatra. The insurrection organized by the GAM under the command of its charismatic leader, Habib Saragih, has been totally brought under control and there have been some fifty thousand arrests to date, in addition to the number of deaths that confidential sources estimate at more than twenty thousand.

The secondary elements of the GAM movement, brought together under the leadership of Saragih's successor, Andi Rijadi, reached an agreement with the government whose terms are similar to the 2002 Cessation of Hostilities Agreement (COHA). This poorly implemented agreement led to bloody conflict until 2004. This time, the GAM agreed to the total disarmament of its combatants in exchange for a comprehensive amnesty that will allow them to reintegrate into civil society.

Little information has surfaced regarding the involvement of foreign individuals, particularly Germans and Russians, in the attempted coup d'état which, according to anonymous government sources, could have led to the outbreak of a major regional conflict. Several local observers testify that it would not have been long until Malaysia in turn caught fire under the impetus of Islamist organizations belonging to the same grouping as the GAM. This was obviously the objective of Saragih and his sponsors.

Assuming that the terrorist organization had taken power in Sumatra and then Jakarta, followed by an uprising by Malaysian Islamist movements, the chain reaction could have extended as far as Afghanistan and Pakistan.

But who was behind Habib Saragih's rise to power and what some call "the Indonesian Spring", in reference to the Arab Spring? The Jakarta government promised to shed light on these events of unprecedented gravity. But at the time that this newspaper is going to press, we have to make do with rumors and unconfirmed information that could indicate that several neo-Nazi organizations had come together to finance the GAM and Saragih.

Neo-Nazis and Islamists -- an unnatural alliance? Not so much, according to the analysis of our expert on page 7.

Washington D.C.

The CIA expert had guaranteed that the ink would fade within a fortnight, but there were still traces in the shape of a cross eight weeks later. Somewhat irritated, Melany closed her bathrobe. Of course, no discerning eye could have guessed the original shape of the tattoos. That at least was a relief. The fact remained that Franckel, and behind him the CIA, did not have full mastery over their products which, in retrospect, was cause for concern.

She found Jeffrey slumped on the living room sofa in front of a hearty breakfast. On the side wall, a TV screen silently displayed the latest financial information released by Bloomberg. As usual, Jeffrey was immersed in reading the daily newspapers. A cheerful spring light bathed the terrace and the living room through the large bay window.

-- You've been doing your daily inspection? he teased her.

Melany picked a croissant from the basket and bit into it before flopping down next to him.

-- You! These horrors have never bothered you. I wonder why not?

-- Because no tattoo will ever mar your beauty, he replied, putting a kiss on her lips.

-- That's right, make fun of me. Do you have any other platitudes in store?

-- If that's how you take my compliments, I'll keep them to myself. Did you read the headlines this morning?

He grabbed a copy of The New York Times from the coffee table and held it up in front of her. The front page headline of the newspaper read: "Mysterious Radioactive Shipment Disappears in Sumatra".

-- Our friends in the Mossad and perhaps those in the CIA must not have been idle, Melany concluded with a shrug.

Since their extraction from Indonesia, events had followed one another in a predictable but accelerated fashion. The cruiser USS Antietam dropped them off in Singapore, where a specially chartered launch picked them up. From there, they were taken to the airport under an escort provided by the local authorities in coordination with the U.S. and boarded the first plane to Washington.

Half a dozen FBI agents, accompanied by Franckel and four of his men, had been waiting for them at the gateway of the terminal. They were arrested for insubordination and obstructing a counter-espionage operation on foreign territory, and were both facing up to twenty years in prison. A convoy of three armored cars drove them to Langley where they were debriefed and interrogated for nearly a week. The conclusion of the meticulous investigation to which they were subjected could have been summed up in a sentence by Franckel.

-- And now, I don't know what in the hell to do with the two of you!

-- You mean you don't know how we should be rewarded for preventing a global conflict without any details leaking out to the media?, Jeffrey retorted, half serious and half joking.

The CIA Director of Operations couldn't help but smile. Instead of responding to Jeffrey's insolence, he stared at Melany.

-- You've made quite a mess of things.

-- We found the "Father of Victory". Wasn't that the primary objective of my mission?

The young woman held her own.

-- At the Agency, we've known for a long time that beginners have all the luck, Franckel grunted. Don't push your luck.

Since their *affaire* was a matter for the secret services and foreign policy, no civilian or military judge had jurisdiction to conduct their hearing. If they had disobeyed, it had been for a good cause and not for treason. Their fate could therefore only be settled by administrative decision. The verdict came quickly. Both were expelled from the INR and removed from the State Department's advancement lists.

Their careers in the diplomatic world ended there.

Jeffrey greeted the decision with a shrug of his shoulders. He undoubtedly had other plans, but he would tell Melany about them later. His inheritance would in any case keep him safe for at least a few generations.

Melany, for her part, took the verdict as an injustice and rebelled against it. She grumbled for weeks, disgusted at having run so many risks and having almost died several times, only to be disowned by her agency and the entire system. But "the system" had other surprises in store for her. Her anger vanished instantly when her mother told her about an "under the radar" interview she had just had with Franckel.

-- Contrary to what you might think, he admires the way you conducted the investigation. The Agency doesn't like loose cannons, but it must in this case recognize that your intervention prevented the worst. Franckel will never admit it, but he is grateful to you. That is also why ...

As discreetly as possible, using her mother as an intermediary, the Director of Operations invited her to retake her CIA entrance exam. This time, she wouldn't have to answer questions designed to determine her psychological profile. On this particular point, her file was marked "defense secret" and marked with an approval signed at the highest level.

A way for Franckel to thank her without doing so officially.

Once the investigation had been completed and the two had been released, their first initiative was to visit Professor Herskowitz again, this time at his second home in Truro, a small summer town in the middle of the forest on the west end of Cape Cod, where they were invited to spend a long weekend.

There, as red and gray squirrels shared nuts thrown from the porch by the professor's wife while a family of deer half-camouflaged by the foliage at the edge of the wood watched them curiously, they had the impression that their lives were returning to normal for the first time in a long time.

Fascinated by their story, Herskowitz allowed them to dispute a number of facts on which Melany and Jeffrey were at odds in interpreting.

But nothing would ever succeed in convincing the young woman that they had participated in events involving the slightest form of esotericism in the framework of their interpretation.

-- And yet, Melany, you must face the facts, Herskowitz concluded after spending so many delightful moments exploring their discoveries and their consequences. There is no rational explanation for what really happened during the Saragih enthronement ceremony. Like Dr. Stevenson, to whom our friend Jeffrey often refers at the risk of annoying you, I consider the phenomenon of reincarnation to be an interesting hypothesis rather than a certainty. But you will admit that the facts remain troubling. That mentally handicapped young Indonesian with the exceptional curative magnetism corresponded perfectly to Hanussen's description of Hitler's *tulku*. You continue to believe in a series of coincidences. Notably concerning his first name, composed of the first syllables of the Führer's name. You are probably right. But, as Einstein supposedly said: "Coincidences are God's way of remaining anonymous".

-- During my few days of imprisonment, I thought about everything that had happened without Jeffrey trying to influence me.

Jeffrey nodded with a disillusioned pout.

-- And what do you conclude from this?

-- It's all very simple. The will was drawn up by a sick brain. We all agree on that point. Not even Soloviev believed in it. He only used it to rally various groups of extremists by creating a common myth. Hanussen directed him towards Indonesia, which suited him perfectly if you know about the virulence of the Islamist movements in that region. The young Adhi did have healing skills, that's for sure. I've been studying the issue ever since, and natural healing magnetism is recognized by the medical world. Some hospitals even use hypnotists. Adhi was particularly gifted and I will be eternally grateful to him ...

-- What was spectacular was that the scars completely disappeared from Melany's leg.

-- ... We have no doubt, Jeffrey and I, that the ceremony was a staging rigged by Soloviev, after which Saragih, who knew the results in advance, would have been enthroned. Adhi and his adoptive father lived long enough in the insurgents' camp for him to soak up its atmosphere and to learn the few words of German he spoke. That didn't make him a disciple of Goethe. He had the mental age of an eight-year-old boy and must have thought he was playing a game when he grabbed Hitler's pistol. I'm certain that he was the first to be surprised when the shots went off, but he didn't have time to pull himself together and understand what he was doing. As for his first name, Einstein or not, it's even more a coincidence that about ten million Indonesians are named Adhi.

-- But, you will agree that events could have turned into a tragedy without a little help from destiny?

-- I have the weakness of believing, Professor, that we make our own destiny.

***

Ever since the stroke he suffered when Jeffrey was trying to escape from Kahla, his brother Benjamin had fallen into a near-vegetative state that worried the medical staff at the facility.

Jeffrey had already visited him twice since their return from Indonesia, but this was the first time that Melany had accompanied him since then. He warned her that Benjamin's condition was serious and that she would have trouble even recognizing him.

The large room with the view of the lake smelled of urine and aseptic products. The young man was lying unconscious and inert between the safety bars of his medical bed and was connected by sensors to a monitor for vital signs. On the screen, the horizontal line was regularly intersected by the appearance of a luminous point accompanied by its characteristic beep.

-- According to his doctors, he lost up to 95% of his brain capacity as the result of the stroke. He now only functions through reflexes. He was on a ventilator until last week and they've had to resuscitate him three times.

Benjamin was appallingly thin, and the grayish tint of his face gave him a corpse-like appearance that was only contradicted by the electrocardiogram.

-- I'm so sorry, Melany whispered as she took the hand of Jeffrey, who was holding his brother's.

-- There's not much to be done and it's not your fault at all.

A chickadee landed on the window sill that Melany had opened halfway when they arrived. The bird's song brought a semblance of cheerfulness to the oppressive atmosphere in the room. Jeffrey's eyes were moist and his face was closed off.

Melany moved her hand towards Benjamin's and, in order to imitate her companion, took it between her fingers, carefully avoiding the sensor that pinched his index finger.

The comatose young man shivered upon her contact.

-- What did you do?, Jeffrey asked, intrigued by his unexpected reaction.

Melany withdrew her hand.

-- Would you like to touch him again?

-- Why are you asking me that?

-- Just curious. Remove the sensor for a few seconds and take his hands in yours. Both at the same time.

Intrigued, Melany did so.

Nothing happened at first. In spite of the blanket pulled up to Benjamin's neck and the pleasant temperature of the room, the young man's fingers were frozen. But, little by little, Melany felt his skin getting warmer. Raising her eyes to his face, she noted with astonishment that he had regained some color.

-- I ... I don't understand, she said.

At that very moment, Benjamin opened his eyes.

Made in the USA
Coppell, TX
18 August 2021